PUTTING OUT
FOR A
HERO

C. ROCHELLE

CONTENTS

ISBN: 9798850651633

Cover design by divineconception
Character art by @biggsboi_

TYPOS & LANGUAGES

While many people have gone over this book to find typos and other mistakes, we are only human. **If you spot an error, please do NOT report it to Amazon.**

I *want* to hear from you if there's an issue, so I can fix it. Send me an email at **crochelle.author@gmail.com** or **use the form** found pinned in my FB group or in my link in bio on TT & IG.

GLOSSARY NOTE: Because our favorite Mafia Queen makes some cameos, I have included a short glossary in the back for Simon's infamous French swearing.

SLANG NOTE: There is always a bit of slang peppered into my writing. When in doubt, use Google, or contact me using the methods above if you truly believe it's a typo.

WARNING, CONTENT & TRIGGERS

Putting Out for a Hero is an MM romance between a villain and a hero. Our men find other men in tight supersuits incredibly attractive. **This is not your kid's superhero book.** This is *Sin City* and *The Boys* having a love child with extra spicy Spideypool and is **meant for 18+ adults** who can handle such things.

The **Villainous Things** series contains standalone books (each with HEAs) that feature interconnected characters and an overarching plot. You should read them in order (starting with **Not All Himbos Wear Capes**).

Please do not hesitate to email the author directly with any questions or suggestions for adding to the TWs.

NOW THE GOOD STUFF

Content, Tropes & Kinks:

- Superheroes/villains (and the "normies" who love them)
- MM romance (love is love)

- Dual POV
- Two households both alike in villainy
- *Knives Out*, old money vibes
- Single dad + his badass little queen
- Forced proximity + fated mates
- Hurt/comfort + found family
- Deathball (a made up sport that is more discussed than actually played on page because we're here for the smut, thank you very much)
- Former sports rivals-to-lovers who talk a lot of shit as a love language
- A very confused bi- (possibly Pan-) awakening meets "I've always been bi for you"/"I even pretended the woman I was with before was you" (it's complicated)
- Absolutely filthy dirty talk
- A himbo "I'm baby" golden retriever villain who must be protected at all costs
- A psychotic Godzilla hero who acts even more animalistic than usual
- An actual monster peen with fun ridges (like a "rocket popsicle") and a knot (HELLO, BREEDING KINK)
- Giant lizard man fetish (Baltasar)
- Jockstrap fetish (the author, let's be real)
- Lubricating lizard saliva (we made it easy this time)
- Purposeful size difference with preferred top & bottom roles (they like what they like)
- Consensual moments of predator and prey, along with a primal chase scene through the woods where *someone* acts like they're John James Rambo just to get the upper hand (and that lizard dick)
- Biting for mating purposes (plus, Balty enjoys pain from fangs and claws)
- Territorial cum play & lizards licking their mates clean

- A sexy but unwise use of grip tape
- Major praise kink with a smidge of humiliation
- Light feminization (mostly involving a grown-ass man in a "pretty princess" tutu, along with the use of the "c" word that isn't "cock")
- One MC getting big mad that he smells like cookies (if this was an OV, Balty would be an omega)
- A dude-oir photoshoot, eggplant parm, and a butt plug used as bait to coax out some full-sized lizard dick (in the bonus epilogue)
- All the stretching, blow jobs, rim jobs, frotting, and dicks in asses because this is an MM romance

Possible triggers (please also check above list):

- Sweary dialogue
- Naughty, medium-dark humor
- Cutesy pet names (with light feminization - see above)
- Excessive gift giving as a love language (it's a Suarez thing, I'm afraid)
- Bad puns on T-shirts
- Single dad with important child character (9-years-old and sassy AF)
- Questionable parenting (the guys are trying their best)
- Using religious phrases in an overtly sexual and/or casual context (oh, my God/Jesus Christ)
- Morally gray characters
- Angst, miscommunication, and a fist fight between the MCs, because these are two idiots in love
- Grief over the loss of a partner from cancer (no on-page details)
- Family betrayal (from Zion's parents) and trauma/loss of body autonomy through physical

abuse (for both) - mostly in the past with only vague, on-page details

- Self-worth issues related to intelligence and "usefulness" within one's family
- Neurodiverse MC (undiagnosed ADHD with high anxiety)
- Public humiliation (not between the MCs)
- Truly meddling siblings and a group chat that thrives on ball busting and a complete lack of boundaries or filter
- A mouthy opinionated brother who prefers cock and is very vocal about how much he personally prefers cock as his personal preference
- Potentially triggering misogynistic behavior/language, including men who enjoy going to strip clubs and casually use the words "titty bar," "tatas" (also used in reference to Zion's impressive pecs), "chick," "bitch" (reserved for meddling family members), and "whore/slut/pretty princess" (these are reserved for Baltasar)
- One MC checking out the other while they're unconscious and naked without explicit consent
- Cheating? (NOT between the MCs). Baltasar is engaged to Dahlia—Zion's sister—when the book begins. It's a business contract and neither wants it. There's never any contact between them, but Balty IS technically engaged when he starts things up with Zion.
- Brief threat of OW (other woman) drama. There's a single scene in a strip club where Zion teams up with one of the dancers to make Balty mad. Nothing major happens, but a hetero-presenting finger momentarily touches a bisexual cock (brace yourselves)
- So much jealousy and possessiveness (related to above, and then some, and usually not logical)

- Gunfire with a child nearby (she does NOT get hit)
- A loved one trapped inside a burning building (all's well in the end, I promise)
- Classist themes (between powerful supes and "lesser" supes)
- A very tense scene between two alphahole clan heirs where our sweet bb himbo is (temporarily) used as leverage
- In general, clan heirs acting like invincible assholes who believe they are above all the rules (I see you, Zion and Wolfgang)
- Mentions, not details, of gore (on par with the rest of the series), including the aftermath of torture on a deserving enemy where they lost their spying eyeballs.
- A cutthroat, dubious moral code for supes that isn't meant to be understood by normies. "It's how the game is played."

(Please also see the following page for a note on supe identities)

A NOTE ON SUPERHERO & VILLAIN IDENTITIES

A SUPE'S IDENTITY IS SACRED!

In this world I've created, superheroes and villains are supposed to guard ALL secret identities from normies— including their own, that of their family / clan, and even their enemies.

And when one supe addresses another as their supe name, that is a not-so-subtle way of making it clear they are considered the enemy at that moment. (Siblings may also do this to show the battle has begun—especially during notoriously cutthroat, annual White Elephant gift exchanges.)

To further clarify:
Captain Masculine = Supe name
Butch Hawthorne = Civilian name (for use around normies)
Butch Holt = Secret identity

Doctor Antihero = Supe name
Xander Marin = Civilian name (for use around normies)
Xander Suarez = Secret identity

STALK C. ROCHELLE

Stalk me in all the places!
(by joining my Clubhouse of Smut on Patreon, my Little
Sinners FB Group, and subscribing to my newsletter)

In memory of Mikki, who put up a fight.

And for my dad, who introduced me to the Dark Knight.

CHAPTER 1
BALTASAR

"Guys, I can't feel my nuts. I think my suit might have shrunk in the wash or something."

Although every inch of Wolfy was hidden beneath his matte-black supersuit, I could *feel* big bro rolling his eyes at me like a judgy shadow.

It was Simon who replied, no surprise. "Perhaps your body is going into fight mode, Baby Hulk, in response to the threat of adulting. Except, in your case, that means all available blood has rushed to the only head of yours that continues operating under duress."

It was my turn to roll my eyes, although I did it where Simon couldn't see.

Since he's fucking terrifying.

Tugging my supersuit out from where it was strangling my balls, I dared to grumble. "Why couldn't Wolfy and I just wear regular suits with our headgear? I'm gonna be dressed like a penguin soon enough with this wedding business happening next month…"

I swallowed hard as the reality of my situation—*a situation I'd offered myself up for*—washed over me.

It sounded like a good idea at the time.

Ever since Simon revealed just how much Wolfy did for our family behind the scenes, I'd been determined to pull my own weight.

Sharing juicy gossip, kicking ass at the Supremacy Games, and beating rival supes into a bloody pulp had been enough for my parents to consider me useful. But I wanted to offer more than that.

Something only I can offer.

There was stiff competition in our family. Wolfy terrified our enemies, Xanny was nerd-level smart, and the twins could get inside any opponent's head. But they were all super gay, and mostly off the market. Vi may have had the oven for baking a super-baby, but she was too batshit crazy for anyone to consider reproducing with.

Plus, she's a better enforcer than I could ever be.

When I'd first suggested marrying myself off to another clan with the promise of superior genes, Wolfy had been weirdly opposed to the idea. As soon as I mentioned I could *also* be a fly on the wall around whatever family I shacked up with, he said he'd consider it. As soon as he made his choice, he was suddenly all in.

I was too. Then, about halfway through our flight east to Sunrise City, I got cold feet.

It might have been before that…

Either way, it was too late for second thoughts. We'd just landed at the private jetport of one of the most powerful supe families in the country, and an army of rabid reporters were waiting for us on the tarmac.

Along with my future wife.

Again, I could *feel* Wolfy watching me through his ninja-of-death getup. "That's correct, Balty," he replied, and it took me a minute to even remember what we were talking about. "This *is* business. A business *deal.* One you and I discussed at great length, so it should come as no surprise that we are dressed in full gear because of what our supersuits represent…"

His words abruptly cut off, as if he were overcome with actual *feels,* for some reason.

What's his problem?

Simon laid a tiny hand on Wolfy's enormous forearm. "It won't be for long, *mon chou.* Would it help if I told you your arse looks like a Lycra-wrapped treat for me to devour as soon as we're back on the plane? *Délicieux.* Absolutely edible."

I awkwardly rejoined the conversation, even though my brain was still stuck on figuring out what got Wolfy all choked up a moment ago.

"Yeah, I get it. We need to show those khaki-wearing prepsters who's boss by looking uber menacing. But hey! Simon likes how your ass looks—*OH MY GOD…* Are you saying you're actually going to *eat* his ass later? Like, with your *mouth?!* I mean, cool. That's cool… I'm just gonna…"

Stumbling over the blanket I'd haphazardly tossed into the aisle, I hastily sped toward the exit, only to screech to a halt when I reached the door.

My vision was hazy, and I was breathing like Coach had made me run the field for days. And my chest *ached*. In fact, it ached worse the closer we got to Sunrise City.

What is my fucking problem?

Now I'm *the one feeling weird feels.*

It wasn't like my fiancé was gross. Dahlia Salah—Atmosphera —was a total babe and one of the most powerful supes of our generation. Any man in his right mind would be pumped to wife her up and start popping out supercharged babies together. But my nervous system was acting like I was about to fight for my life.

I didn't *think* it had anything to do with the Salah family being heroes. I'd never cared what another supe identified as. The whole point of this match was to show the world the Suarez clan didn't care about stuff like that—which was the truth.

Even if we're not sharing the whole truth about what we know.

Wolfy and Simon's trip to Argentina revealed heroes and villains had the same ancestors—who looked like something out of a B-movie horror flick. Xander had shown me the high res photos of the cave paintings—sent to us by the normie anthropologist, Doc, for our archives—and it was some freaky shit.

Like Godzilla on crack.

Kind of badass, though…

Thinking about one of my favorite monster movie franchises brought my already chaotic thoughts to another member of the Salah family. A fellow shapeshifting supe who was my only true competition at the Games. And the only one who could get under my skin on the field.

A man who I last saw at Wolfy and Simon's surprise wedding, of all places—since our **Mafia Queen** liked him, for some weird reason. Someone I really hoped wouldn't be standing there when I got off the plane.

Zion.

I sighed angrily. The realization that it was my asshole sports rival who was psyching me out pissed me off more than my shrinking supersuit.

Don't let him get in your head, Balty.

"Ready for the gallows?" Simon snickered as he appeared at my side. He was securing the jewel-encrusted skull mask that hid his identity whenever he appeared in public as Wolfy's 'assistant.'

Even though he's actually the boss around here.

"Totally," I scoffed, cracking my neck and doing a few hops in place to get my blood flowing. "I'm going to fucking *own* the gallows. The gallows are about to be my bitch. Just watch me, dude."

Simon was staring at me as if I'd suddenly shifted into my true form with my dick flapping in the breeze. There was no risk of that happening, of course—since my supersuit expanded with me. But now I could add *that* nightmare scenario to the list of things to potentially go horribly wrong today.

Please don't let my dick flap in the breeze in front of the cameras.

And Dahlia.

Or… Zion.

"Are you *nervous,* Balty?" Wolfgang was suddenly standing so close to me, I instinctively flinched, which then made me feel like a jerk.

I now understood our parents had used the threat of Wolfy to keep us all in line while we were kids. Despite their mind games, our oldest brother actually cared about his siblings —*loved* us, even. But even with all he'd done behind the scenes to keep us safe, he was still kind of scary.

Really scary, to be honest.

He sighed before stepping closer, invading my personal space like a test. "You are better than this, Baltasar. You are a fucking *Suarez*. The Salah clan may have *heroic* political influence, but only the oldest two siblings can hold a weak candle to what the six of us can do with actual power. You are not just a piece of meat. You are here with a purpose—to marry Dahlia, help her bypass Zion to take the throne, and then absorb their house into ours."

My heart was galloping in my chest, but I nodded and stood my ground, knowing it was what he wanted to see. "Yeah, I know, but…"

How the hell am I supposed to do all that?

*I'm only… **The Dumb One**.*

As if I'd voiced my doubts aloud, Wolfy turned to face Simon. Something unspoken passed between them as my brother absently plucked at his supersuit. Not like it was throttling his nuts, but more as if just feeling it on his skin was the problem.

Maybe that's why I never see him wearing it.

He must be allergic to being 80% more terrifying.

"Balty," Simon's voice was gentler than usual—the tone he usually reserved for Wolfy. "If you truly don't want to go through with this marriage, we won't make you, but you absolutely *must* play the part for today's press conference. Go through the motions before returning with the Salah family to their estate. Spend a couple of weeks gathering intel, while we come up with a reason you couldn't lower your standards with Dahlia. Ooh! Maybe we could concoct a *scandal!*"

The evil glee flashing in his green eyes made some of my tension disappear—even if my nerves were still humming.

My clan leaders have my back.

Unless I fuck this up…

"Nah, don't worry about it, Simon," I chuckled. "I just get a little nervous before I face off with this family."

Which isn't completely a lie.

One family member in particular.

Wolfy was watching me closely, and I wished I could see his eyes through his supersuit. Even if he was frightening as fuck, he was still my brother—a supe I'd always looked up to—and it would have helped to know what he was thinking at the moment.

I just want to make him proud.

Simon waved a dismissive hand. "Oh, don't fret, Baby Hulk. Wolfy and I will take care of the sound bites. If anyone speaks to you directly, just make up some *conneries* reply—say you're thrilled to align your prestigious clan with one as impressive as the Salahs."

I'm thrilled to align my prestig… get my clan all lined up with Dahlia's.

Got it.

I smiled so wide, Captain Masculine probably felt my dimples pound his dimples into submission from across the country. If there was one thing I knew how to do, it was to make the ladies swoon while smiling for the cameras.

Let's fucking do this!

Wolfy nodded at Simon, who took the lead and struck a pose that reminded me of an Old Hollywood starlet as our pilot prepared to open the door.

"Showtime, boys," Simon whispered from behind his glittering mask, sounding way more excited about this whole thing than I was. "Let's give these so-called *heroes* something to talk about."

CHAPTER 2
BALTASAR

"Major Obscurity and I were overjoyed by the news our daughter had fallen in love."

Jacqueline Salah—known as Lady Tempest—crooned into the microphone with one elegant hand placed over her Lycra-covered heart.

"That it was to a so-called *villain* was of no consequence to us. This Suarez clan has more than proven themselves heroic over the past year. First, they exposed the injustices Biggs Enterprises committed against famous heroes like Captain Masculine. Then they rallied again by ensuring society remained safe from the evil schemes of the odious Glacial Girl..."

Jesus, she's really chewing up the scenery with this speech.

I snuck a sidelong glance at Wolfgang, trying—and failing—to gauge his reaction to this steaming pile of horseshit. It must have been an agreed-upon narrative, as he and Simon were calmly letting her drone on instead of murdering my future mother-in-law.

Her words were bothering *me*, though. Sure, I could see why it looked better for everyone to think Dahlia and I were in love, especially since arranged marriages were frowned upon among normies. But ol' Jackie was really pushing how *superior* heroes supposedly were—as if the non-hero her daughter was marrying wasn't standing two feet away.

By now, even normies knew the only difference between her family and mine was that villains refused to work for humans, just so they could be painted as 'the good guys.' So I assumed she was only saying this to piss off my brother.

And they call me *dumb.*

Lady Tempest was probably acting out because we had her, and the Major backed into a corner. Dahlia had threatened Simon at a council event a few months back, and Wolfy capitalized on the social faux pas to pressure the Salah clan into aligning with us. I had no idea what deals they worked out before this marriage contract was piled on, because I wasn't super involved in that part of the family business.

Or any part, to be honest.

My cluelessness might have been why Wolfy was so hesitant to accept my offer to sell myself out for marriage. One of the many things he was a pro at was covering his bases, so there was probably no need for him to agree to my foolish plan.

So why did he humor me?

I'd left it up to him and Simon to figure out which family to target, but was still surprised when they suggested *Dahlia Salah,* of all people. We'd barely spoken a dozen words to each other, even with all the times we'd crossed paths over the years during my Deathball matches against her brother.

And just how Wolfy thinks I'm going to take over the clan from her…

Like a predator sensing weakness, *Zion* chose that moment to appear in my line of sight. He squeezed in among the reporters at the front of the makeshift stage before casually crossing his enormous arms over his colossal chest.

He looked like he always did. Aggravatingly self-assured, with a shit-eating grin that highlighted how perfectly white his teeth were.

His endorsement deals must be dentistry and being a jerk.

True to form, he was wearing jeans to this important press conference, along with one of the ironic, graphic T-shirts he seemed to have an endless supply of.

Today's choice was a gray-washed vintage tee with fabric so thin, his muscles were threatening to rip the fabric. It also said 'I'm With Stupid,' and I couldn't help wondering if he'd purposefully chosen it for this occasion.

Why even bother showing up at all?

Since I couldn't make a comment to his face, I narrowed my eyes as judgmentally as possible instead. Zion smirked in amusement, holding my gaze for so long, I had to look away before the press noticed.

Stupid long-shot playing son of a b—

"Blunt Force!" Hearing my supe name shouted by the famous Lady Tempest almost had me fully shifting—ready to battle the formidable hero.

That would have been embarrassing.

By the time I returned my attention to the stage, I realized everyone was watching me expectantly.

Fuck.

What did I miss?

"Please join my daughter at the microphone," Lady Tempest slowly spoke, over-enunciating each word, as if it wasn't the first time she'd said it.

Whoops.

I glanced at Simon, noticing him glare at Lady Tempest beneath his mask before he smoothed out his expression and nodded encouragingly.

Taking a deep breath, I approached the front of the stage, where Dahlia was waiting at the mic. Even from behind her iridescent Lycra, there was no disguising the impatience in her rich brown eyes. When the breeze picked up, I assumed that was her way of telling me to move my ass.

Yes, dear.

Reaching my fiancé, I took her outstretched hand in my sweaty one and dared to give her a squeeze of solidarity. I had no delusions we were going to fall in love or anything, but Dahlia always seemed like someone I could hang out with.

And now I don't have to worry about her trying to kill me.

I hope.

It wasn't like we were total strangers. Zion and I had gone head-to-head in the Games every two years since I'd graduated Junior Supremacy. So I'd seen enough of the Salahs to be familiar with the heavy hitters in the clan.

Dahlia always reminded me of a slightly less-frightening version of my mother, but I'd never dared ask her anything about her powers. Even in the neutral zone of the Games and related press conferences, the dividing line between heroes and villains was deep. There'd never been a chance to cross to the other side.

Until now.

It didn't change the fact I was standing there like an idiot while my future wife spoke to the reporters, like royalty addressing her subjects. She seemed so confident—with her clear voice and perfect posture—talking about how love conquers all obstacles and brings peace on earth.

Or something…

My focus on her speech lasted all of two seconds before it drifted to Zion again. His cocky smile had been replaced with an uncharacteristic frown that was squarely aimed at his younger sister.

That's weird.

That the Salah heir had stopped showing interest in ruling his clan was probably one reason Wolfy targeted this family with a marriage contract. Being fourth in line myself, I was lucky to be matched with second-born Dahlia—who was primed for greatness, with no one to challenge her path.

Has Zion suddenly changed his mind?

Familiar competitiveness washed over me. *This* I could handle. If there was one thing I was good at—besides charming the press—it was kicking Zion Salah's ass on the playing field. Any nerves I'd been battling evaporated as I smirked at my opponent, more than ready to crush him beneath my boot on the way to the throne.

"Do you have anything to add, snookums?"

Snookums?

To my horror, I realized Dahlia was handing off the spotlight, expecting *me* to actually use my mouth to form words and string those words together in a way that made sense.

Uhhh…

I couldn't even look to Simon for guidance, as he and Wolfy were now standing behind me. While I could effortlessly recite soundbites about my talents on the field, I didn't know *what* to say about this arranged marriage secret stealth takeover situation.

"Um," I began, before awkwardly clearing my throat. "I just want to say I'm thrilled to align my…"

My gaze accidentally drifted to Zion, and I found his frown had turned upside down. He was hiding his broad smile behind his fist in a way that suggested he wasn't trying to hide it at all.

"… align myself with a babe as hot as Dahlia Salah…" I trailed off as Zion dropped his head into his hand and snorted, which only made me more flustered. "So we can make babies and—*FU… DGE!*"

My words ended on a yelp as a blast of fucking *lightning* jolted through my veins. It was all I could do to channel our **Token Hero** so I wouldn't drop an actual F-bomb on the livestream.

Although the non-swear might be more embarrassing.

Having successfully cut me off at the knees, Dahlia smoothly took over. "Well, I sure appreciate the enthusiasm," she tittered. "But let's save that for the honeymoon."

This earned her some laughs from the crowd, although they were definitely more the *'laughing with'* than *'laughing at'* variety I usually got.

Sigh.

I don't know what possessed me to look at Zion again, but by some miracle, he wasn't even watching me anymore. Instead, he hastily abandoned his post to go check out something happening to the side of the stage, leaving me to continue making a fool out of myself in peace.

A small mercy.

Polite applause signaled that my public humiliation was at an end. After posing for a few photos with my pissed off fiancé, we all escaped to the makeshift backstage area.

"What the *hell* was that?" Simon hissed the instant we were all inside the hopefully soundproof tent. He ripped off his skull mask so Dahlia and her parents could better behold his fury. "At no time did we discuss giving Baltasar the mic. Who is to blame for this gross oversight?"

Mafia Queen in the house.

"That would be me." A diminutive lesser supe holding a clipboard and wearing what looked like a linen muumuu bravely faced off against our fearless leader. "As the Salah family's publicity director and master of ceremonies, it was *my* decision to make. I strongly felt hearing from the groom would add something special to the day." His beady eyes flickered to my face. "It sure added something, all right."

What an asshole.

Simon seemed seconds away from stabbing someone, but Wolfy calmly placed a hand on his *inventus'* shoulder.

"Well, *we* strongly dislike surprises." Wolfy spoke in a tone so icy, my nuts shriveled—which blessedly gave me some much-needed room in my supersuit. "However, as we are new business partners, we will forgive the misstep. This once. Are we understood, Mr...."

"Preek. Joshual Preek," the impressively unbothered PR man sniffed, as if he didn't know—or didn't care—that he was talking to a legendary supe who could explode his head like a watermelon. "And I will be sure to discuss future programs with you. In excruciating detail. Although..." Again, his greasy gaze slid to me, and I caught a hint of smug satisfaction beneath his words. "It could have been worse. Perhaps."

Okay, I officially hate this guy.

"I don't know," Dahlia chuckled. "Baltasar stopped just short of describing our imaginary sex life to an audience full of thirsty reporters." She gave me a once-over that made me feel as small as her minion. "But I said what I said out there. Save the baby-making attempts for the honeymoon, *Blunt Force.*"

Ouch.

And with that stone-cold use of my supe name, she swept out of the backstage area, followed by her mother and Preek the Prick.

The Major stayed behind to talk business with Wolfy and Simon. Since I had absolutely nothing to add to the conversation, I just stood awkwardly on the sidelines.

As usual.

"Psst... hey, Blunty! I've got a surprise for you." An unexpected stage whisper had me searching everywhere for the source—and probably looking like a fool while I did it.

Finding nothing nearby, I peered into a shadowy corner of the backstage tent, only to look down and find myself face to face with a demon.

A terrifyingly familiar one.

CHAPTER 3
BALTASAR

My blood ran cold as the Supay mask of Apocalypto Man leered up at me from the inky shadows.

WHAT THE FUCK?!

It took my racing heart a good ten seconds to return to baseline, but not before I'd almost fully shifted, awkwardly crowding the others in the confined space.

"Casse toi!" Simon shouted, attempting to shove me away with his tiny hands. "What exactly is your problem today, Balty?"

Everything.

Wolfy had gracefully sidestepped my overgrown form to confront the mysterious—although tiny—intruder. "Take off that mask this instant," he growled, his threatening tone making my hair stand on end.

"Behave, Sir." Simon smirked in Wolfy's direction before snapping his fingers toward the corner to hurry things along. "You heard the man. Remove the mask and hand it over so we can burn it. Chop chop."

Apparently, the wannabe demon was immune to the legendary Suarez intimidation, as the death god mask remained in place.

"Make me," came the defiant reply.

Wolfy took a menacing step forward before I finally registered what he was up against. "Whoa, whoa, whoa!" I returned to my normal size and desperately waved my hands, placing myself between The Hand of Death and mini-Supay. "It's a fucking *kid*, bro. Chill."

"Watch your language, Blunty." The muffled voice cackled. "I'm a lady."

My lips twisted as I turned and crouched in front of the little prankster—removing my mask so she could see my face. "Blunty, huh? So you know who I am?"

The mask was removed to reveal a girl who couldn't have been older than nine or ten. She was definitely a Salah, with the same mahogany skin tone and rich brown eyes as the rest of her clan, but her tightly curled hair was closer to Simon's honey color.

And she was looking down her nose at me like I was nothing but a raggedy peasant invading her kingdom.

A little queen.

"Yeah, I know who you are," she muttered, haphazardly tossing the mask at Wolfy's feet. "Everyone's been in such a bad mood all week, getting ready for *you* to show up and make things weird."

I huffed a laugh. "It's weird for me too, trust."

Wolfy toed the mask with his leather boot, weirdly hesitant to touch it. Simon sighed heavily and picked it up. Then they both returned to their conversation with Major Obscurity, as if the interruption had never happened.

Dismissed, as usual…

"So… where'd you get the mask?" I asked, resigned to my permanent designation as one of the kids.

Her mini-majesty narrowed her eyes, clearly debating whether I was worthy of an answer.

"My dad gave it to me," she finally replied. "He told me to sneak into your room when you were sleeping later, so I could give you a heart attack in the middle of the night. But I got bored of waiting."

I laughed again, more self-consciously this time. Our dead father may have focused most of his sadistic attention on Wolfy, but all of us had been at the receiving end of his wrath at one point or another. If I'd woken up to his Supay mask looming over me in the dark, I would have not only had a heart attack, but probably pissed the bed.

And I never would have heard the end of that.

It didn't matter that we'd all *watched* Butch burn our parents' corpses into ash once and for all. Apocalypto Man and Glacial Girl had been larger-than-life terrors that stuck with you long after death.

"Which one's your dad?" I continued conversationally, since this kid was the only person here who seemed to *want* to talk to me.

The Salah clan was even bigger than ours, and I assumed even the siblings who'd moved out of the family's estate had shown up today to watch me make a fool of myself.

And I didn't disappoint.

The little queen opened her mouth to reply when Wolfy interrupted, "Simon and I are heading home now, Baltasar. Did you leave anything on the plane?"

I rose to stand and met Wolfy's gaze, realizing he was giving me the chance to talk to him in private, if I needed to.

Or hightail it out of here.

I resolutely shook my head, determined to not show any weakness. "Nope. I'm going to go get settled in. I've got everything I need."

I've got this, bro.

"Daisy," my future father-in-law drawled in the bored, preppy tone most of this clan was known for. "Show Mr. *Suarez* to his quarters. Then you may change and go play with your cousins."

"Thank gawd," Daisy muttered under her breath as she stood and picked a wedgie under her floofy dress. Giving me another once-over, she spun on her heel and impatiently snapped her fingers. "C'mon, Bluntycups. I'll show you to the horse barn. The groomsman put down a fresh bed of hay for you to sleep on tonight."

Horse barn?

Bluntycups?!

With an awkward wave to Wolfy and Simon, I hurriedly yanked my head-covering mask back on and followed Daisy out of the backstage tent. It wasn't until the car waiting for us headed *away* from the barns, and toward the main house of the estate, that I finally breathed again.

I stifled a snort as we pulled up alongside one of those ridiculous circular fountains that seemed to grace the driveway of every rich asshole. Then, an actual butler opened the towering wooden door to usher us inside, and my jaw *dropped.*

It wasn't like I was a stranger to wealth, but this was *old money* on top of *hero money.* This was the kind of money that wanted you to know exactly how expensive everything was.

Where our family compound was modern—more like a luxury hotel now that Wolfy and Simon had rebuilt it—this looked like a Gothic mansion from an old horror movie. I honestly thought Dracula was going to fly out of the shadows at any moment and drink my blood. The endless line of family portraits framed in hideous gold didn't help. I could *feel* their eyes watching me as I followed my tiny tour guide deeper into the murder mansion.

She could be leading me to the dungeon...

For a moment, I panicked, worried this had all been an elaborate plan by the Salahs to hold me hostage for whatever Wolfgang would give to get me back. But I forced myself to breathe. Knowing my brother, he had promised a slow death for anyone in this family who dared defy us, and everyone knew he followed through on his threats.

Even if they don't know what a 'sweet murder baby' he actually is.

Simon's words, not mine.

"Here we are!" Daisy chirped, flinging open a door to reveal a room that was a lot smaller than I'd expected. It was still super lush—with deep, forest green walls, a matching velvet bedspread, and dark wood furniture—but it was clearly a room for throwaway guests.

Not someone joining the clan.

"We didn't go upstairs..." I mumbled absently, side-stepping the pile of my already delivered luggage to peek into the bathroom. Black and white octagonal tiles covered the floor, with a claw-foot tub dominating the space.

I feel like I'm at grandma's house.

Daisy scoffed behind me, and I realized this kid was behaving exactly as entitled as Dahlia did.

Which is how our shitty kids will no doubt behave…

"*Our* rooms are upstairs," she slowly explained—as if *I* were the child here. "Along with the wing reserved for important guests."

"Ouch," I chuckled, needing to laugh at how ridiculous this whole situation was. "Could your family make it any more obvious that I *don't* belong here? Jesus." When she looked taken aback by my bluntness, I quickly backpedaled. "It's fine. This will be fine, Daisy, thank you."

I grimaced. My sour tone made it clear how *not* fine it was, but I assumed a nine-year-old wouldn't pick up on it.

To my surprise, her snooty mask faltered as her gaze dropped to the floor. "I don't fit in with this family either," she mumbled, and I could only gape in response.

What?!

Almost immediately, Daisy lifted her chin once again, burying her emotion. "Dinner's at seven. Cook will ring the bell and you'd better not be late." She squinted at my too-tight supersuit. "And you'll definitely want to change."

Before I could ask what kind of dress code these psychopaths followed for dinner on a random weekday, she'd flounced away, slamming the door and leaving me to unpack.

And get the fuck out of this supersuit.

Even though I wanted to start by uncaging my nuts, I dutifully started peeling it off the correct way—starting with the hidden zipper at the nape of my neck that always took me five tries to find.

"Need a hand, Blunt Force?"

Not even bothering to hide my reaction, I groaned as the absolute *last* voice I wanted to hear rumbled through the stuffy room. Emphasizing my eye roll, I turned to face my old Deathball rival—the famous shapeshifting *hero* known as Scaled Justice.

"I know how to take off my own fucking supersuit, Zion," I grumbled, huffily working it partway down my chest to demonstrate. "And haven't you ever heard of knocking? Do I need to lock my door to keep out the creeps?"

Zion's gaze lazily dragged over my body in a very different way from how the rest of his family—including my fiancé—had looked at me so far. I froze, unsure if I should pull my suit back on or act as if nothing had happened.

Or, pull it off the rest of the way to really give him a show.

Where the fuck did that *come from?*

Luckily, Zion brought his wandering eyes back to my face, flashing one of his usual cocky grins. "I don't think there *is* a lock on this door. It's the room used by mistresses when they visit, so there needs to be easy access."

I scoffed, deciding to at least finish removing my arms from the tight sleeves so I could cross them over my bare chest. "I'm nobody's *mistress*. Or whatever the dude version is. I'm not..." My voice caught as Zion took another lecherous look. "I'm not just some piece of meat—"

"You're not?" he asked with faux confusion as he met my gaze again. "Last I heard, you were here because you were ready to get to baby-making with my sister."

I'm never going to live that down, am I?

"Ugh." I dropped my head back with another groan. "I didn't know I was gonna speak, dude! Usually they give me a script or something. But that *Preek* fucker decided last-minute that I should say something..." I trailed off. Warily eyeing my opponent, I realized I probably shouldn't insult the Salah family press secretary so early into my sentence.

Lord knows what rumors he'll start about me.

Zion chuckled in that easy way of his—like he was born without a care in the world. "It's cool. Preek *is* a fucker and I assure you, that decision was strategic and probably planned for weeks with Dahlia."

Seeing me deflate, his expression changed to one that suspiciously looked like pity. "If it makes you feel better, your official statement to the press was everything I'd hoped it would be."

"Fuck off, Z," I snapped, too annoyed to care that I'd accidentally shortened his name, as if we were *friends* instead of barely civil colleagues.

I have no friends here.

"So, I heard you met Daisy," he continued, apparently having no interest in fucking off.

Typical Zion.

I huffed a laugh, since thinking of the tiny terror made me smile. "I sure did. She made sure I knew my place before telling me I better not be late to eat—or else. Oh! What the fuck do you prepsters wear for dinner?"

A smirk twisted his full lips as he gestured at his 'I'm With Stupid' T-shirt. "I just dress like this." When I nodded, he cocked his head at me. "Daisy seemed to like you, though. That's rare."

That intel warmed me down to my bones. "Yeah, probably because she doesn't see me as a threat to her eventual world domination. You should tell whichever of your siblings she belongs to that they should watch out for that little queen."

Zion's smile grew, blinding me in the otherwise darkening room. "I'll be sure to do that." We stared at each other in awkward silence for a minute before he cleared his throat. "Well, I'll let you get back to struggling with your tight little supersuit—"

Little?

"Nothing about me is *little*, Z," I scoffed, annoyed when the nickname easily rolled off my tongue yet again.

His gaze dragged over my exposed chest and arms before settling on my face. "Me neither, *B*," he replied, unexpectedly dropping a nickname of his own. "See you at dinner."

CHAPTER 4
ZION

Baltasar. Fucking. Suarez.

If you'd given me twenty guesses—*fifty* guesses—I would never in a million years have picked *Blunt Force* as the man to lock down my sister.

Dahlia was the epitome of regal. She was statuesque, with sculpted muscles and a fuck around and find out vibe that made her intelligence even more lethal. That she'd been paired with a himbo I'd wrestled with in the mud for a crowd of fifty thousand was almost impossible to comprehend. But she could thank her legendary temper for that.

It's how the game is played.

What didn't surprise me in the least was that Wolfgang Suarez had used her misstep to strong-arm my parents into making an alliance with his clan.

Seeing his younger brother on Dahlia's arm for the rest of my life wouldn't be easy. But I was secretly pleased that my snobby family was being forced to welcome an outsider they saw as beneath them.

Too bad they couldn't manage it years ago...

Just like every time I thought of Mikki, my throat became raw and tears pricked my eyelids. I didn't know if I'd ever stop feeling this shattered about the situation, but at least I had the greatest gift to remember her by.

And now I have the perfect distraction.

As if on cue, Baltasar strolled into the grand dining room—two minutes early, and dressed in a T-shirt and jeans, just like me.

Oops.

There was nothing more satisfying than witnessing him take in the sea of cocktail attire. And my grin only grew as the slow—*so very slow*—realization that he'd made a fashion faux pas washed over his ugly mug.

Okay, not ugly at all, but whatever.

The Suarez family had always been blessed in life, including how unfairly attractive they all were. And in my totally unbiased opinion, Baltasar was the prettiest of them all.

His skin was a slightly lighter shade of golden brown than his older siblings, but he still had their signature unearthly amber eyes. Supes were naturally fit, but Deathball had sculpted Baltasar's body into a stacked work of art. The dips and ridges of his muscles were the epitome of temptation—inviting me to explore every inch of him with my hands and tongue.

He's what wet dreams are made of.

This unexpected beauty was why I first started questioning the validity of the hero and villain narrative. There was a strange—and clearly incorrect—emphasis in our textbooks that all villains were evil and *hideous*. All it took was one long, hard, bi-awakening look at my opponents during Junior League Deathball to realize that was a load of bullshit.

Especially when I spotted a certain opponent…

The one currently murdering me with his pretty eyeballs.

"I saved you a seat, B!" I sang out, patting the rock-hard straight-back wooden chair to my left, waiting with bated breath as Baltasar struggled to decide what to do.

"Um…" His gaze slid past all eight of my siblings and various significant others, to the head of the table, where my father was glaring at him in blatant disapproval.

Pops was so angry about the clothes, his camouflage power was kicking in, making him flicker like the lighting in a horror movie.

This is everything.

Baltasar visibly paled at the display. "I can just go change really quick—"

I sharply inhaled, bringing his focus back to me. "Mmm… I wouldn't do that if I were you. Nope. Cook will have your skull on a fence post outside her witch's hut if your ass isn't parked in this seat when she comes through those doors."

Baltasar's panicked gaze landed on the massive double doors at the far end of the room. I could practically smell the smoke burning as he gauged whether he had enough time to speed to his room down the hall and back before his fate was sealed.

Decisions, decisions…

His ridiculously broad shoulders slumped in such obvious defeat, I almost felt sorry for the big guy. But then I remembered how he *had* 'wiped the field' with me during our last match—my last Games before retirement. Exactly like Wolfgang had thrown in my face in Villefranche a few months ago.

And my beast doesn't like to lose.

Blowing out a breath, Baltasar lifted his head and met my father's frightening gaze with so much courage, I couldn't help but be impressed. "I'm sorry for the misunderstanding, sir. My family doesn't really dress up unless it's for a special occasion. Even then, it's usually just Wolfgang, because... well, he wears a suit every day anyway, so it's probably like changing socks for him—"

"Sit, Baltasar. Just... sit down and stop talking." Dahlia's annoyed voice cut through his babbling, sending her future husband scurrying to obey. "For the love of God," she added, with a dramatic eye roll to the rest of us.

I frowned at my sister across the table. First of all, *I'd* been enjoying the fresh entertainment. But there was also no need to be so openly rude to our new token villain.

It's like kicking a goddamn puppy, Dahlia.

That was why Baltasar Suarez had been the object of my obsession ever since I'd first encountered him in person— when I was 21 and he was 18. While the rest of his siblings ranged from threatening to downright terrifying, Baltasar had a naiveté to him. An unexpected sweetness.

When he wasn't viciously wiping the field with his opponents, that is.

I wish I could get a rematch...

"Why would you tell me this was okay to wear?" he hissed through his teeth as he took the seat beside me.

Not a moment too soon, either, as Cook suddenly used her cart like a battering ram to burst into the room. The usual dinner conversation started up around us as the food was dished out—our special guest already forgotten. Therefore, I didn't feel bad teasing the big guy a *bit* more for my private amusement.

He's just so cute when he's flustered.

"Sounds like *you* misunderstood." I smiled sweetly, enjoying his growing agitation. "I told you this was how *I* dressed. It was in no way meant to be fashion advice, since very few people can look as good as me in casual wear."

To my surprise, Baltasar's mesmerizing gaze raked over me—seeming to linger on my denim-clad crotch before hastily returning to my face to glare.

Interesting…

Despite all his hottie brothers being gay—*what were the odds?*—I'd never thought *Baltasar* swung any way other than straight. Women could like whatever the hell they wanted. But if a girl had bleached blonde hair, drank pumpkin chai, and wore those weird suede boot slippers with fashion flannel, Blunt Force would end up in her bed.

But now you're telling me I had a chance all these years?

That I might still have one…

I frowned and immediately banished the thought. Business deal or not, Baltasar belonged to my sister, and the last thing I needed was to give this family one more reason to hate me.

"How come *you* get away with dressing like this?" The man beside me continued to adorably stage-whisper, as if anyone was paying attention to us anymore.

The answer to *that* question was the elephant in the room, so I staunchly focused on accepting the platter of honeyed-ham my youngest brother's latest girlfriend was passing me.

"Because I'm already the greatest disappointment this family has ever known, so what's one more nail in my coffin?" I muttered, piling meat on both our plates before realizing I hadn't meant to say that out loud.

Jesus, I need to get laid or something.

It was Baltasar's turn to frown as he took the platter of ham and traded it for the scalloped potatoes coming from the other direction. "Why would *you* be a disappointment? Just because you're not hustling to take over the clan?"

A bitter laugh escaped me, but I lowered my voice to reply, "Oh, there's plenty more to the story than that, B, trust me."

I didn't dare say more in present company. The last thing I needed was to lay it all out on the table to my greatest professional rival.

Who's this fool gonna tell, Zion?

Thankfully, Baltasar didn't pry. Instead, he focused on filling *both* our plates with every main and side that traveled down the line. The sheer concentration on his face while he worked was priceless, and I didn't have it in me to explain that serving me wasn't actually a requirement of my clan.

He's trying so hard to fit in.

Good luck.

I'd only served *him* because I'd gone into dad-mode on autopilot as we were chatting—so conditioned to filling my daughter's plate before mine. In fact, I was used to eating most of my meals with my little girl, since *she* wasn't welcome in the formal dining room, especially not for special occasions.

Why include actual *family when we have arranged engagements to celebrate?*

"Where's Daisy?" Baltasar innocently asked the same moment I caught Dahlia snickering with our sister Rose while pointing at my shirt.

Ah, shit.

"Hey, B, switch seats with me real quick," I said before hurriedly standing and practically shoving his enormous body into my vacant chair.

Yes, I'd absolutely worn my 'I'm With Stupid' T-shirt for Baltasar's arrival today, and planned our seats so the arrow would point his way. It had seemed like a hilarious prank at the time, but now I wished I could somehow remove the shirt and burn it without making myself into even more of a family pariah.

"Uh, okay…" he mumbled, dutifully obeying in a way that made my dick twitch. "So yeah, where are the kids? I assume Daisy's not the only one running around with this big of a family."

I shot Dahlia a triumphant smile before digging into my meal, wanting to give myself a moment to decide how to answer. Baltasar would find out soon enough what the supposed issue was with Daisy—with *me,* mostly—but I wanted to delay the inevitable for as long as possible.

Because I don't want his fucking pity.

"She's at the kid's table in the kitchen," I finally replied, deciding that sounded normal. "Usually the children eat with us, but as you can see, our very grand dining room only holds so many self-important grownups at one time."

He chuckled before warily stealing a glance at both my mother and father at opposite ends of the long table.

"Well, maybe I should sit at the kid's table," he murmured, cheeks pinking ever so slightly—torturing me further. "Since Daisy was the only one who seemed to want to talk to me today. And it's gonna sound dumb but… the way she roasted me kind of reminded me of home…"

Goddamnit, Baltasar.

So much emotion welled up inside me—not only because of his warm tone while talking about Daisy, but because of how *she'd* taken to the big guy as well. I wasn't kidding when I said her approval was rare. From what my daughter had told me, Baltasar Suarez passed her test simply because he'd shown her kindness.

Which she doesn't get much of around here...

"Yeah." I cleared my throat and kept my gaze fixed on my lemon herb asparagus. "Busting your balls is how Daisy shows she cares, so consider yourself one of the queen's chosen."

"I'll take it," he muttered with another wary glance around the table. "Whatever keeps me from being beheaded."

I snorted, but kept my opinions to myself. Part of me knew I should warn Baltasar away from my daughter—if only to better assimilate with this pack of wolves. But I couldn't handle the thought of one more supe acting like she wasn't good enough for them.

This is dangerous territory, Zion...

It was absolutely ridiculous for me to covet this *villain* as an oversized playmate for Daisy. And it was even more insane that I kind of wanted to keep him for myself as well. But here we were.

What's one more nail in my coffin, after all?

CHAPTER 5
ZION

Hours later, I rolled over in bed to check the time. It wasn't unusual for me to have trouble sleeping—especially lately. But I was self-aware enough to realize my current restlessness was because of the man occupying the guest room downstairs.

Finding 3 am staring back at me in neon green, I sighed and grabbed the remote before sitting up and turning on the TV.

Late-night infomercials it is, then…

Unfortunately, what came on instead was SupeSports, since that's the channel I'd left it on. Even more unfortunate was that they were showing highlights from the last Supremacy Games in anticipation of this summer's events.

Where I won't *be playing.*

I hadn't planned on retiring yet—even though I was considered past my prime by some—but then life kicked my ass more than usual. Combined with my team's devastating loss in the finals two years ago, I hadn't even bothered joining them for spring training a few months ago.

It was only once the press hounded me I officially announced my retirement. I made up some bullshit about work-life balance, but the *real* reason was that I didn't trust my beast not to kill someone on the field.

While the sport I played was Deathball, actual deaths were fairly rare and definitely frowned upon. Yes, gameplay was violent and bloody as hell, but the supes who stepped onto the field were born for it.

Built to last and mean as rattlesnakes.

The council created the Supremacy Games so heroes and villains could battle in a controlled environment that catered to their strengths. Deathball was a suped-up mash-up of rugby, American football, and MMA, and was created specifically for those whose powers leaned toward the brute force variety.

Baltasar and I were fairly matched opponents in our supe forms—although I took great pleasure in being bigger than him as civilians. I relished when our teams met on the field. There was nothing I loved more than taunting him as he chased me, since I played offense as a long-shot while he led the defensive line as a grabber.

Positions affectionately referred to in certain fandoms as cum-shot and ass-grabber.

Those new to the sport were always surprised by how fast a giant lizard-man could run. I had to be quick to avoid being crushed by the tree trunks Baltasar called arms. He was the only grabber in the league who'd consistently sacked me. In return, I was the reason the big guy needed to stay on top of his game.

It was thanks to the two of us being so otherwise untouchable that the SupeSports talking heads focused so intensely on our rivalry. But while they might have created the drama in the first place, our respective publicity teams—and psychotic fan bases—fanned the flames.

Little did they know, all I ever wanted was to stick my dick in my rival's tight end.

My stupid crush on the *supposedly* straight Baltasar Suarez fueled my professional aggression against him. Every time I came across a paparazzi shot of him partying in Big City with yet another chick—or five—hanging off of him, I vowed to make him suffer on the field. That he refused to play dirty only made me angrier.

And getting engaged to my goddamn sister *was the shit icing on the crap cake.*

There was no doubt Dahlia was a target decided on by Wolfgang—since I'd never seen Baltasar look at her twice—but knowing it could have been *me* if only B liked cock...

I could make him like it.

I could make it so he never thinks of pussy again.

Fuuuck.

I dropped my head back against the headboard as one hand slid down my bare abs toward my hardening cock. The other fumbled for the remote, so I could change the channel and find some porn.

But then SupeSports started a Deathball segment.

"Perhaps the biggest news for the Games this year is how grabber Blunt Force will no longer be facing off against his favorite longshot, Scaled Justice."

Fucking hell.

"That's right! And even more mysterious than Justice's sudden retirement is the breaking news that Blunt Force is marrying his sister, Atmosphera. Do you think the two factors are related?"

With a growl that sounded more animal than human, I pointed the remote at the TV, completely uninterested in hearing the answer to that question.

Especially since it's a big-ass yes.

Then the highlights came on, with a montage of famous clips involving the two of us—most of which I'd seen before.

And jacked off to, let's be honest.

There was just something about watching footage of Baltasar facing off against me that drove my beast insane. And it oddly didn't seem to matter who won the play.

Although I prefer when I come out on top.

As if in answer to my fucked up prayers, a brand new clip filled the screen. This one showed Baltasar face down in the mud while I caged him in with my fully shifted body from above. I chuckled at how obviously I was rubbing my lizard dick against his Lycra-clad ass, but then froze as I watched myself scrape my fangs over his exposed neck.

When the fuck did that happen?!

While it wasn't against the rules to bite and scratch, the way I was teasing his skin suggested something far beyond sports-related aggression.

It looks like I'm trying to MATE with him...

The thought of that happening in real life sent such a bolt of searing lust through my veins, I had to forcibly restrain my beast from rising to the surface.

I was also harder than I'd been in a long time.

Quickly hitting pause on the livestream, I reached inside my shorts to give my aching dick a slow stroke.

On-screen, Baltasar had turned his mud-spattered face toward the camera. His eyes were half-closed while his mouth hung open—creating a slack and submissive expression on his pretty face. It almost looked like he was enjoying the experience.

I wonder if I could get him beneath me again…

A groan escaped me as I imagined us in this position, only naked—my ridged cock stuffing his virgin ass full until he was *begging* me to breed him.

Fuck, I want to hear him beg.

And I definitely want to breed him.

In the dark of my room—with only the light from the TV to illuminate my sins—I allowed myself to fully accept just how badly I wanted this man. How I'd wanted him since the first time I laid eyes on him.

Never mind that I would feel like absolute shit about this sordid jerk-off session tomorrow. Right now, I simply wanted to pretend there was a reality—a multiverse—where I could actually have what *I* fucking wanted for once.

Knowing my hand wouldn't satisfy me tonight, I quickly slid to the floor and pulled out my cock sleeve mount from under the bed. I practically shifted in my crazed haste to lube the opening with my precum and get the fuck inside.

I bit back a moan as I sunk to the hilt. The juxtaposition of the silky channel wrapped around my cock and the unforgiving hardwood of the floor beneath my knees was heady. Combined with the knowledge Baltasar's room was directly below mine, I knew I wouldn't last long.

If only he knew what I was doing over his sleepy little head.

"You love this, don't you, beautiful?" I growled, withdrawing partway so I could slam home again. "You've wanted my cock inside this tight ass of yours for so fucking long." Another thrust. "That's why you agreed to this marriage deal —so you could have *me* buried inside you every night. Breeding you. Owning you. Making you *mine.*"

All mine.

Thinking of Baltasar as *mine* made me go absolutely feral. My claws lengthened, scratching deep furrows into the leather mount—digging in for purchase as I violently pummeled into the sleeve. All human logic disappeared, replaced by raw animal need, and the sounds coming out of me matched my mental state.

Need to fuck him.

Need to breed him.

Mine, mine, mine.

With a groan that was almost painful, I came so hard, my vision whited out. Collapsing over the mount, I pumped it full of everything I had, imagining Baltasar making a puddle of his own on the floor as he tightened around me.

Imagining *my* name on his forbidden lips.

It took a solid minute for my brain to rewire itself into something that felt remotely human. Then it took another 20 seconds to realize I'd completely shredded the mount beneath me.

Well, fuck.

This was a problem for several reasons. Even in the throes of passion with other supes, I'd never let that part of me take over completely, and it was sobering to see what happened when I did.

Most concerning was now that I'd opened the Pandora's box of my deeply buried Baltasar Suarez fantasies, I didn't know how I could shut it again. Because I knew from experience that once my beast saw something he wanted...

There's little that will stop him from claiming it.

CHAPTER 6
BALTASAR

"Wakey wakey, eggs and bakey!"

With a groan, I attempted to roll onto my side and burrow beneath the covers, only to realize someone had dropped a 90-pound weight on my chest.

"C'mon, Bluntycups—up and at 'em. I wanna eat breakfast with you*uuuAAAH!*"

I jerked, then sat bolt upright as something hit the floor with a thud that echoed throughout the room.

What the fuck was that?!

Peering over the side of the bed, I was startled to find Daisy glaring up at me. Scrambling out from my nest, I quickly helped her stand, hoping she wasn't hurt too badly.

Kids don't break that easily, right?

"I'm fine, you big galoot!" She cackled, slapping my hands away and straightening her rumpled clothing. "But I'm staaaahving, so you need to get dressed so I can eat."

My blood ran cold. "Oh, shiiii… ugar." I corrected my language. "Does your family eat *breakfast* together in the dining room, too? Jesus, I need someone to make me a schedule that I can carry around in my pocket. No way in he… ck do I want to f… up again."

Shit, I swear a lot.

Daisy was staring at me like I had three heads. "I know about bad words, Blunty, even if I'm not supposed to say them. And no, we don't all eat breakfast together…"

Her face fell, and I remembered how she'd been noticeably absent from dinner last night. Before I could ask if she was *ever* included, she brightened. "But my dad said you wanted to eat at the kid's table with *me*, so move it!"

Dad?

I racked my brain to remember which Salah siblings I'd been seated near last night—trying to place who might have overheard the random comment I made to Zion.

Unfortunately, my memory was still doused in leftover trauma from fucking up on the dress code. Everyone had blended into one shapeless lump of disapproval that looked suspiciously like Lady Tempest.

The judgiest one of all.

"Yeah, hang on. Lemme just grab some clothes." I began opening and closing drawers, wondering if I'd brought anything that screamed 'uptight New Englander with blood bluer than my balls.'

Since Dahlia made it clear that there will be no pre-marital fucking.

Daisy saluted before leaving me to my own devices. I quickly decided on black pants and a button-up shirt I'd normally only wear to the club.

Knowing this family, I'll still be underdressed.

It didn't help that I was exhausted, since *something* had woken me up around 4 am. I'd leaped off the bed and assumed a fighting stance—convinced that a Salah had arrived to assassinate me on my first night in their murder mansion.

But then… nothing happened. The creepy-ass house had been deadly silent, except for a rhythmic creaking that sounded like someone was getting lucky on the floor above me.

Gotta keep popping out those self-righteous heroes, I suppose.

The strangest part—and what kept me awake for a while afterward—wasn't the faint noise, or concerns about being attacked. I'd felt unsettled, as if I were forgetting something important, and my chest *ached* the same way it did after certain Deathball matches.

I'd felt… *empty.*

Maybe this house is haunted.

Or I'm getting possessed by a heroic demon.

That last thought freaked me out enough to yank on the rest of my clothing at double-time before joining Daisy in the hall.

She was standing with her back to me—her pretty curls reflecting the glow from the Dracula-style torch lights—while staring up at one of her family portraits.

"Okay, little queen. Let's go get some grub…"

I trailed off as I realized she was *crying.* She quickly wiped away her tears and turned to smile at me like nothing was wrong.

Oh, no you don't.

"What happened?!" I demanded, feeling an immediate protectiveness flare up inside me. "Who do I need to pound into the ground?"

That made her laugh, although I didn't see what was so funny. "No one," she huffed. "Everyone. I dunno." She glanced at the nearest portrait again. "It's just... I'm never gonna be on this wall, y'know?"

No, I did *not* know, but I also didn't want to sound dumb. What I understood with absolute certainty was that I was not okay with this little girl being upset about anything.

Not while I'm around.

"I think we need to show these stuffy dead relatives who the *real* queen is around here," I drawled in my snootiest tone. Not waiting for Daisy to reply, I lifted her up to deposit on my shoulders. "There. Now you can look down on *them* and their Judgy McJudgerson faces."

She squealed with delight. "Not all of them are *dead*, Blunty. Not *yet*, anyway—ha!"

A true villain.

"Well, I assume the dead ones died of judgment," I dramatically huffed, making her laugh again. "So maybe those who are still alive should watch—"

"Oh, hi, Daddy!"

I spun to face whatever hero had crept up on me, only to come face-to-face with *Zion*, of all people. He was looking at me with such unreadable intensity, I momentarily considered dropping Daisy and running for the hills.

Is he about to murder me for touching his kid?

Hey, wait a minute...

"You have a *kid,* dude?" I sputtered—my brain finally catching up with the situation. "When did *that* happen?"

"Mine," he replied, still staring at me like he wanted to eat me alive. "I mean… *she's* mine, yes. Daisy is." He blinked rapidly before his gaze shifted to where his daughter sat on my shoulders. "For almost ten years now."

How the fuck did I not know this?!

It wasn't like I kept track of all the teammates or opponents who'd settled down. But families usually came to the Games, and I definitely would have remembered *Zion Salah* getting married.

But where was his wife at dinner?

"Yeah, my double-digit birthday is in August," Daisy proudly announced from her throne. "I'm a Leo."

Whatever that means.

Zion seemed to have snapped out of whatever weird mood he'd been in a moment ago as he flashed a more recognizable smirk. "Are you headed to the kid's table for breakfast, B? I warned Cook that you might join us."

A sudden vision of being chased through this horror house by the machete-wielding Salah family chef flashed through my mind. I briefly wondered if I should go eat with the grown-ups after all.

But I don't know if that would be any better.

I swallowed hard. "Is that… going to be okay with… Cook?"

Zion winked and spun on his heel before heading down a side hallway, and I obediently followed—since Daisy was hungry. It didn't take long to realize our undecorated route was reserved for the lesser supes who worked here.

And the heir to the Salah throne, apparently.

I lowered Daisy to the floor once we reached our destination. *Her dad* swung open the battered door, and I was greeted with a sight that was way more welcoming than the grand dining room.

The Salah's kitchen was enormous and state-of-the-art— although I didn't see the army of staff I would have expected with so many mouths to feed. Cook was blessedly busy at the far end, muttering in an unfamiliar language as she violently tossed ingredients into a frying pan.

Like that muppet chef… but less funny and more frightening.

Despite not knowing if I was still at risk of catching a butcher knife, I felt my anxiety evaporate as soon as I entered the space. The comforting heat from the stove, the aroma of cooking vegetables, and the sound of food preparation reminded me of my favorite place back home.

I wonder what Betsy's cooking right now.

Without my help…

"Hey, Bluntycups! Sit next to me."

The embarrassing lump that was forming in my throat dissolved as I obeyed Daisy's command. She was seated at a table that was well-worn and small—made to fit only six people comfortably. There was evidence that other messy eaters had already blown through this morning.

Forever at the kid's table.

"*Bluntycups*, hmm?" Zion hummed, unbothered as Cook suddenly slammed down a platter, making me flinch. Calmly scooping some of the mouthwatering omelet onto his daughter's plate, he warmly addressed her, "Is that a new type of flower, D?"

"Yup!" Daisy chirped. "I wanted Blunty to get a family name, too."

Wait…

"But…" I sputtered, too shocked to form words for a second. "It's the *girls* in your family who are named after flowers!"

Like princesses!

Zion's gaze locked on me—his expression so assessing, I squirmed in my seat. A slow smile crept over his face as he served me some omelet next, and both actions made my stomach do a weird flippy thing.

I probably just need to eat something.

"The name suits you," he chuckled evilly. "Perfect for when Daisy dresses you up in one of her tutus later."

Oh, hell no.

I rolled my eyes but focused on my breakfast instead of giving him the reaction he probably wanted. My fake-out became real as the first bite hit my tastebuds. The eggs were fluffy, and the vegetables were fresh—although the omelet could have used more crushed red pepper, in my opinion.

Not that I'd dare suggest it.

Now that I had some food in me, my annoyance returned at how unnecessarily out of place I felt here. We all knew heroes and villains were the same at this point. Even though this was a marriage of convenience, it wasn't like the Salahs were taking me in out of *charity.*

I was a goddamn Suarez—just like Wolfy had said—and I had no plans to bend over for this family.

Especially not Zion.

"Queen *Daisy* can call me whatever she wants," I sneered, leaning back and crossing my arms over my chest, trying my best to imitate Wolfy's death stare. "But *nobody* is putting me in a tutu."

I instinctively sat up straighter when Zion's gaze dragged over me again. "We'll see about that. For now, Daisy needs to get dropped off with her tutor, so I can give *you* the grand tour of enemy territory." He paused with a smirk. "Including the dungeon where we keep our villains..."

CHAPTER 7
BALTASAR

Zion had just finished showing me the underground gym when my phone started buzzing with notifications from **The Rabble** group chat.

I'm surprised it took them this long.

The Mouthy One: *In honor of my 24-hour ban on roasting Balty being lifted…*

Welp. That explains it.

The Mouthy One: *I need to know if Atmosphera has cut off your balls for safekeeping yet.*

The Mafia Queen: *Behave, brat. Surely Baltasar knew what he was getting into, volunteering as tribute to a woman famous for icing out every man who's ever pursued her. An uninspiring sex life simply goes along with the hetero breeding stud territory, I'm afraid.*

Fucking Simon.

Xander's burns were easy enough to deal with—since he was usually just looking for a laugh—but Simon had a natural talent for making it sting.

It didn't help that he was absolutely right. I'd *thought* I knew what I was getting into by offering myself up for this plan, but now realized I was even more of an idiot than everyone thought.

How am I going to survive an entire month with no pussy?!

Thing Two: *You'll survive, Balty.*

I cringed at the thought of Gabriel—and therefore, Andre—knowing what I was freaking out about. Luckily, I was almost positive they picked up on *vibes* more than anything with their mind-reading abilities. It wasn't like they were actually hearing my loser thoughts.

At least, I hope they're not…

Before I could even think of a reply to hide my growing panic —from everyone *but* the family psychics—the roasting continued without me.

The Mouthy One: *I'm not a brat, Simon.*

The Token Hero: *You kind of are.*

OooOOOoo…

There was nothing I loved more than Butch giving Xander a hard time, mostly because it was the ultimate karma. And I especially appreciated it at the moment, since it took the heat off me.

I owe you one, Cappy.

"Who the fuck is blowing up your messages?"

Zion's voice snapped me back to attention. I hastily silenced my phone before shoving it back into my pocket. "No one," I quickly replied, instinctively protective of my family. "Just some cape chasers looking for a good time."

I don't know what I expected. Maybe an eye roll or for him to call me on my bullshit. What I did *not* see coming was for Zion to advance on me so fast, I almost shifted into fight mode.

"Yeah, well, you can tell your fucking *cape chasers* that you're no longer available," he hissed. His dark brown eyes flickered to their yellow reptilian state as the pupils narrowed to vertical slits.

That is freaky as fuck.

And kind of hot…

Wait, what?

"Jesus, Zion," I huffed, not at all appreciating how his proximity was doing weird things to me. "I *know* I'm engaged to your ice-queen sister, okay? Chill, dude."

He slow-blinked as his eyes returned to their human state. "My sister…" he mumbled, as if that *wasn't* what his whole tantrum was about. "That's right. I won't have you disrespecting *Dahlia* by bringing your playboy Suarez shit to my house. And don't even think about sneaking groupies into your room when everyone's asleep, either. My room is right above yours, so I'll know."

"Oh, yeah?" I blurted out, remembering what I'd heard in the middle of the night and irrationally annoyed by it. "Won't you be too busy banging your *wife* to notice what I'm up to?"

Zion's jaw dropped, his expression uncharacteristically scandalized. "My *wife?*"

I threw my hands into the air, not even sure what we were arguing about anymore. "Yes! I'm assuming *you* didn't give birth to Daisy by yourself…" I trailed off. Giving him a once-over, I realized I didn't actually know much about giant lizard-man anatomy. "I mean… unless you did?"

Gross.

He gaped at me for another moment before barking a laugh. "No, Baltasar, I didn't lay the egg that hatched Daisy."

When I failed to hide my horrified reaction, he chuckled heartily. "She didn't hatch from an egg, B. Fuck, you're too easy."

Even though his laughter had been at my expense, it seemed to have broken the weird tension happening between us.

Which makes me weirdly happy.

Ugh.

As much as I would never admit it, I didn't actually think of Zion as the enemy. Out of everyone in this family, he was the one I knew best. Even if we weren't exactly friends, I definitely didn't want to piss him off so badly that he stopped me from seeing Daisy.

The one ally I have around here.

"She's no longer around," Zion replied. It took me a second to realize he was answering my original—*probably inappropriate, now that I thought about it*—question. "And she was never my wife."

I caught something like *sadness* in his normally serene expression before he spun on his heel and stomped from the room, forcing me to jog to catch up.

Shit.

I messed up.

While my name in **The Rabble** group chat was mostly accurate, I had enough sense in my empty head to shut the fuck up about this obviously sore subject.

Even though I'm dying to know more.

For... reasons...

My use for the family had always centered on gathering gossip. People *loved* to tell me shit they shouldn't. When you added alcohol to the mix—and half-naked bodies as distractions—it was child's play to get them to spill intel.

Fuck, what if I'm not allowed to drink anymore?

Or go to the club?

Or get a lap dance from a chick with amazing tatas?

I CAN'T LIVE LIKE THIS!

"What is there to do for fun around here?" I hurriedly asked, grimacing at the desperation in my voice. "Cuz I better not be expected to do nothing but sit around in my room and jerk off in my spare time."

Zion spun to face me so abruptly I almost plowed into him. His gaze raked down my body again with obvious interest, making my breath catch. I was suddenly hit with a vivid memory of the time I caught him making out with a Bat Blast player in the men's locker room during semi-finals.

Why the hell am I thinking about this right now?

"You're not a *prisoner* here, Baltasar," he scoffed. "I was kidding about the dungeon thing. We don't actually have one."

I huffed and rolled my eyes, pretending I hadn't been worrying about exactly that this entire time. "Yeah, I knew that." *I didn't.* "But I need an outlet to let off some steam—especially with the Games coming up next month..."

His eyes flickered yellow again, and I realized I'd hit yet another touchy subject. For the first time since I'd started playing at a professional level, I wouldn't be facing off against Scaled Justice on the field.

Since he abruptly retired, for some reason.

Which was… disappointing.

"What do *you* do for fun?" I blurted out, desperate to find common ground and not become lizard food on my first full day.

And super confused about the chub I'm sprouting.

Zion shrugged, as if he wasn't one misstep away from eating me. "I go out in Sunrise City, if I can get someone on staff to put Daisy to bed for me. But if you meant *here* at the estate—I work out, I swim, and I jerk off in my room. Right above your head."

I sighed, assuming he was fucking with me. Again. "Awesome. I'll keep that in mind when *I'm* jerking off below you."

He licked his lips. "Please do." Then his expression turned oddly serious. "Would you… like to see where I swim?"

His question caught me off guard. I'd actually thought he'd been about to proposition me into a circle jerk for two.

And we're going to ignore how I wasn't *immediately opposed to the idea.*

What surprised me the most was that Zion seemed almost *nervous* about sharing his little swimming hole with me. I'd never seen Zion be nervous about anything.

"Yes," I blurted out. "Show me."

Show me your weakness.

I might have been dumb, but I knew the value of identifying where an opponent's soft spots were located.

And that's what I was sent here to do, after all.

Zion smiled so openly at my reply, I felt like a jerk for looking for intel. But I still followed him down a long hallway that looked hand-carved out of the very mountain this whole creepy estate was perched on.

Another service area?

For mole people?

It was dark, damp, and smelled like fresh earth and standing water, which wasn't totally unpleasant. Ignoring how my body was reacting to this scent, I focused on not tripping over my own feet in the low light, since my supe vision only went so far.

Zion didn't seem bothered by the darkness at all. All this discovery did was piss me off more, as it was just one more thing he was better at than me.

He could chase me down this tunnel like it was nothing.

Why is that idea turning me on?!

Now I was irrationally horny and big mad about it. Zion may have openly swung both ways, but I was definitely straight.

Definitely, totally straight.

I had no problem with people fucking whoever the hell they wanted—as long as everyone was having a good time. I'd just never felt the urge to stick my dick in a dude, or vice versa, but now I was looking at my future brother-in-law like he was a better option than my babe of a fiancé.

I'm straight, but I'm just not thinking straight.

Oh, no.

What if my supersuit was so tight it cut off my air supply...

Through my nuts?!

My spiraling thoughts were interrupted when we arrived at what could only be described as a creepy grotto. There were rough-cut walls, flickering torchlight, and absolute silence except for the echoing sound of dripping water. An enormous pool dominated the space, with smooth stones gradually tapering down on the far side until it was so deep at the center, the water appeared to be black.

Fuck.

Who needs a dungeon when you have a death pond?

"How, um… how far down does it go?" I stuttered. Suddenly, I felt like the one showing weakness—being the land mammal alone with an aquatic, possibly egg-laying, lizard-man in his element.

"About 800 feet." Zion's gaze was riveted to the water. "It's peaceful down there. Quiet. Somewhere I can just be alone with my thoughts for a while when shit hits the fan."

"I can't think of anything worse than being alone with my thoughts," I muttered before snapping my mouth shut—embarrassed I'd said that out loud.

Keep your issues to yourself, Balty.

Of course, the predator in the room immediately zeroed in on my confession. "Oh, yeah?" His eyes were now on me—in full reptilian state. "What thoughts does a big, handsome guy who's been handed everything on a silver platter his entire life have?"

Handsome?

With every word, Zion had moved closer, herding me back-ward until I was pressed against the damp stone wall.

I swallowed thickly. "Too many," I answered hoarsely, over-whelmed by how goddamn *good* he smelled. Earthy like this cave, but muskier—like the air in a closed bedroom after an epic fuck-sesh.

Jesus. Christ.

What the hell is going on with me?

I'd never even *looked* at another dude before, except if I was sizing them up on the field. Of course, I'd seen plenty of naked and half-naked men—being a shapeshifting supe who went through clothing like it was my job *and* an athlete. But they were always just bodies taking up space.

Not this time. Right now, I was uber aware of the extremely good-looking supe *with a dick* invading my personal space—and of exactly how much I didn't mind.

Fuckfuckfuck.

I was actually shuddering, and it had nothing to do with the moisture seeping through the fabric of my shirt. I was also so hard, I legitimately worried Zion might get stabbed if he got too close.

He'd probably punch me in the face if that happened.

To my horror, he stepped closer, tilting his head to whisper in my ear—his breath cool against my sweaty skin. "Anything you want to share, B? You can tell me. I'll keep your secrets."

I want you to sink your fangs into my throat.

OHMYFUCKINGGAWWWD!

"I need some air," I choked out, not trusting myself to say anything else.

Zion immediately stepped back to give me space, blinking rapidly as if coming out of one of his lizard trances.

"Yeah, same," he mumbled before clearing his throat. "There's an exit this way that will drop us off near the gardens."

I should have noped the fuck out and gone back the way I came—parted ways and locked myself in my room until it was time for dinner torture again. But fresh air sounded amazing and I didn't *want* to stop hanging out with Zion for reasons I wasn't ready to psychoanalyze.

So I simply nodded and followed him out. Besides watching my step, I focused all my energy on getting my inappropriate boner to simmer the fuck down—at least until I could make a date with my hand later.

And I will absolutely not be thinking about Zion Salah while I'm at it.

Because I'm totally straight.

CHAPTER 8
ZION

I don't think Baltasar is straight...

This is trouble.

My beast had now fully imprinted on the villain—something that had only marginally happened once before. And human me was realizing there was more to my former Deathball rival than a pretty face and excellent game.

And stacks upon stacks of hot muscle.

This was now the second gauntlet he'd passed, with the first being how quickly Daisy had warmed to him. My daughter was extremely perceptive and did not suffer fools. While a big teddy bear of a man was the perfect playmate, she preferred the company of those intelligent enough to string a sentence together.

We both do, to be honest.

It might have been because I'd always talked to her like a little adult—since you had to grow up fast in our world—but Daisy could hold her own among my contemporaries.

I figured out that bringing an adorable little girl into a room full of deadly supes caused them to let down their guard—

enough for my mini-spy to do her work. I trusted Daisy's impressions of others implicitly, and she had a knack for gathering intel, which she reported back to me with startling detail.

It's almost like a superpower.

Of course, it wasn't *actually* a superpower, since Daisy had none. But this supposed flaw didn't seem to matter to the surprisingly *not* dumb supervillain who'd apparently taken a liking to her as well.

Damn, he looked good holding my kid.

Something had clicked into place when I stumbled upon Daisy perched on Baltasar's shoulders like a queen. Something that not only made her smile but threatened to fill the jagged hole left behind in Mikki's wake.

Which I didn't think was possible.

Now that I'd spent the morning with this man—enjoying his awkwardly endearing company while inhaling his heady pheromones—I knew in my bones I didn't want him marrying my sister.

Because he was mine *first.*

I'm in so much trouble.

Lusting after Baltasar Suarez was a problem for multiple reasons. The biggest—at least to my parents—was the recent press conference publicly announcing his engagement to Dahlia. Everyone in both families knew the match was only business, but the last thing *my* family would want was a scandal.

Case in point: My daughter being swept under the rug for close to a decade.

A familiar fury coursed through my veins at the way Daisy was constantly dismissed and disrespected by my parents and siblings. Unfortunately, she was old enough now to pick up on it. I tried to shield her from the passive-aggressive comments, but seeing how hurt she was at the end of most days was enough to have me permanently spiraling.

Usually at the bottom of my pond.

All because my family thought I'd reproduced with the wrong person. Someone different than us. Someone they could never accept.

And to add insult to injury, here we were suddenly aligning our house with the goddamn *Suarez* clan. As if villains hadn't been our sworn enemies for generations.

The irony was that the only member of my family who didn't immediately hold Baltasar's heritage against him was me. Even more annoying was the fact I would have gladly aligned the two of us years ago—figuratively and literally—if he liked men. Which he supposedly didn't.

Although the pheromones he's been putting off are telling a different story…

But what if I'm wrong?

I couldn't be sure if Baltasar was just revved up because of nerves—understandable considering his current circumstances—or if *I* was having the same effect on him as he did on me. I'd noticed a similar reaction when we faced each other on the field, but that was another high-stakes situation, so it wasn't the best comparison.

Maybe I should take the big guy offsite.

Loosen him up a bit.

See if he wants to mate with me.

Chill the fuck out, Zion!

I sighed. Now that I'd decided this villain was *mine*, I knew my beast wouldn't be satisfied until we'd at least attempted to claim him.

Which could go either way.

Since I'm still not sure if he goes both ways.

Awkward family dinners, here we come.

"Ohhh! Is this Cook's kitchen garden?"

Baltasar's adorably excited voice wrenched me from my thoughts. He had his fingers hooked through the elaborate fencing surrounding what was, indeed, Cook's precious kitchen garden—looking like a kid on Christmas morning as he peered through the gaps.

Why is he so excited about a vegetable patch?

Aaaand now he's trying to climb the fence…

"Whoa, whoa, whoa!" I shouted as Baltasar hooked his foot through a gap halfway up before attempting to swing his other leg over the top. "What the hell are you—"

"Relax," he chuckled in that cocksure way of his that made my cock sure as shit about him. "It's not like I've never scaled a fence before."

Not like this one.

But you do you, boo.

I shrugged and let him continue, morbidly curious to see Cook's custom-made security measures in action.

While the Suarez family had Xander as their mad scientist, we had my brother, Micah—known as Exo-Tech. He'd used his ability to manipulate non-organic matter to create a foolproof barrier to keep our household's herbs and veggies safe from deer.

And foolish supes who don't know any better...

"WHAT THE ACTUAL FUCK?!" Baltasar bellowed. I smirked as he suddenly found himself on the ground, with strips of neon orange nano-material swiftly coiling around him like boa constrictors. "What kind of Goonies booby trap shit is this? Get it off me, dude—*GET IT OFFFF!*"

"Mmm... I dunno, B," I murmured, crouching next to the hapless villain rolling around in the dirt. "Cook *really* doesn't like people messing with her ingredients. I might need to leave you here until you've learned a lesson about not touching things that don't belong to you."

Yeah, yeah... pot calling the kettle black.

I didn't care how much of a hypocrite I was being. Baltasar's muscles flexed deliciously beneath his button-up shirt, and I couldn't take my covetous eyes off the man wrapped up like a yummy treat.

He's probably wondering if shifting into his supe form will help the situation.

It might.

It would definitely help get him naked.

"Please, Z..." His voice unexpectedly cracked, snapping me out of my fantasy. "I-I really don't like being tied up."

Immediately realizing he wasn't playing, the protective instincts I reserved for Daisy went haywire. My vision tunneled as I unsheathed my claws and began mindlessly shredding his restraints.

Must. Protect. My mate.

"Ow! Jesus! Oh, fuck… *fuckfuckfuck."*

I froze. Baltasar had stopped thrashing and was now staring up at me—his eyes wide and filled with horror.

My human brain finally came back online, just in time to register that I'd not only thought of this man as my *mate,* but had accidentally cut him deeply enough to bleed.

Shit.

"Sorry, B. It was an accident," I muttered before quickly—and carefully—finishing my work on his upper half and moving lower. "You can stop looking at me like I was trying to—"

My words died on my lips as my gaze dropped to his crotch —and the extremely noticeable bulge that strained against his zipper.

Oh, hello.

"Did something catch your attention, Suarez?" I teased, enjoying this turn of events far too much.

"Jesus *fuck,* Zion, it's just a thing… that happens." Baltasar was blushing adorably as he wiggled under my scrutiny. "Stop looking at my—"

"Your *boner?"* I interrupted, pointedly staring as I slowly ran a claw through the material still tangled around his legs. "Don't be shy. It looks like you were telling the truth—*nothing* about you is little…"

"Oh, my fucking *GAWD!"* he groaned, dropping his head back and exposing his throat to me in a way that was unwise, given the circumstances. "Just… just get me out of this mess."

I'd rather help you make a mess.

"And *do not* cut me again, okay? Please…"

Oh.

Ohhhhh.

Blowing out the slowest breath known to man, I refocused on my work, accessing every ounce of willpower to *not* accidentally-on-purpose make him bleed again.

So, Shibari's off the table, but he likes pain.

I wonder if I could make him come from that alone?

Stop it, Zion.

Stopitstopitstopit…

I sliced through the final restraint at the same moment I inadvertently blurted out, "Why are you marrying my sister?"

It was his turn to freeze. "Um… I… Because… well… I dunno."

Oh, for fuck's sake.

He doesn't even want to do this.

"Okay!" he exclaimed—a bit too loudly—leaping to his feet before I could say more. "Thanks for the tour, and for cutting me… cutting me *FREE*, I mean. And for showing me your hole. *YOUR SWIMMING HOLE!* Jesus *Christ*, I'm done. I'm fucking done. I'm just gonna go to my room now. Alone. So I can… be alone for… alone time. *Jesus.*"

My beast was *clawing* to get out. I watched as this ridiculously stacked, awkward bundle of villainous sweetness adjusted his hard-on before spinning on his heel and fleeing the scene of his bi-awakening.

I must have him.

This was no longer about me simply disapproving of Baltasar marrying Dahlia. I was now officially scheming on how to steal him away and make him mine instead.

And why shouldn't I?

An evil smile worthy of the Suarez family stretched across my face. Thanks to this tasty prize falling in my lap, I'd reignited my will to rule this clan—to take back my birthright. Claiming Baltasar would be the perfect revenge against those who'd disrespected my daughter and the mother of my child. Plus, I'd finally get the chance to sink my claws into the man I'd wanted since I first laid eyes on him.

My beast purred with satisfaction.

Baltasar wants it too.

And zeroed in on my retreating prey.

He just doesn't know it yet.

CHAPTER 9
BALTASAR

The phone rang for way longer than it should have, considering it was the goddamn emergency line.

"Suarez family cat wrangler! How may I direct your bullshit?"

I inwardly groaned as Simon answered Wolfy's phone for him. Not that my brother would have been any better, since I had no idea what I was planning to say.

Or what the fuck is wrong with me.

"I think my dick is broken," I blurted out, putting the phone on speaker so I could toss it on the bed while I pulled my sweat-soaked shirt over my head.

"Pardon?" Simon choked out. "And your erectile dysfunction is our problem because…"

Erectile dysfunction!

Okay, maybe that's kind of accurate…

"Because it doesn't want Dahlia!" I yelped, resigning myself to the fate of hearing about this in every group chat conversation until the day I died.

And maybe even after that.

What I *wasn't* saying—what I had no intention of ever saying out loud—was that my dick knew exactly what it wanted. It was aimed like a torpedo at the *brother* of my fiancé—not only in his human form, but in his scaly, fanged, clawed, and oddly hot, lizard form.

Ohmyfuckinggod, those claws…

I didn't understand what had happened back there. Well, I kind of did, but the only other times I'd gotten turned on like *that* were during Deathball, which totally didn't count. I usually wasn't the only dude swinging wood out on the field because the pain had our testosterone raging. It was just a thing… that happened…

That mostly happened when I was facing off against Zion Salah.

Oh, fuck, oh fuck, oh—

"Balty?" Wolfy's calm voice was suddenly on the line. "Tell me what's going on."

I could still hear Simon in the background—ranting about a pay raise and threatening to quit if he had to 'hold Baby Hulk's hand through his hetero shit show.'

Dude, same.

"I-I don't think I should be here," I stuttered, sitting heavily on the bed as my entire soul slumped in defeat.

I'd barely been with the Salahs for twenty-four hours, and I was already fucking up the most important assignment I'd been given since Wolfy took over. All I wanted to do was pull my weight, but now I was proving to be nothing but dead weight.

It wasn't like I was worried about being eliminated or shunned. Our family didn't operate like that anymore. But the idea of facing the supes who regularly put their lives on the line for our clan made me want to sink to the bottom of Zion's death pond and never come up.

Stupid tears stung my stupider eyes as I glared down at my stupidest dick.

Every part of me is fucking useless.

"Can I just come home until it's time for the wedding?" I rasped, feeling like a little kid, crying to big bro. "Just until I'm locked down by Dahlia? That should be enough to stop... this... whatever this is..."

This not-so-hetero shit show.

Wolfy was quiet for so long, I picked up the phone again to make sure I hadn't accidentally hung up on him. Then I heard him take a deep breath and slowly let it out.

"No," he said, and my heart plummeted into my stomach. "You need to stay there and see this through."

Nonononononoooo...

Apparently, Simon shared my sentiment. He was now shrieking about being denied the opportunity to frame Dahlia for a scandal so sordid her ancestors would roll in their graves.

"Dahlia!" I shouted, rallying as an idea popped into my head. "Maybe I just need to get Dahlia to like me? I mean, we're not that different. We could be friends—*frenemies*—who fuck. Maybe I could even get her to lift this weird no-sex-before-marriage ban. That would solve things, right?"

Again, Wolfy was silent, and I cringed, remembering we didn't have the type of brotherly relationship that included swapping sex stories.

I should've called Xanny...

"Baltasar." Wolfy was using his stern Clan Daddy voice. "We talked about this. Supe marriages are about forming powerful alliances and producing even more powerful heirs. Most married supes—whether arranged or otherwise—don't care about being friends. Some don't even *like* each other, never mind *love*."

That strange ache I'd felt in the middle of the night flared up in my chest again. "Cappy and Xander are in love," I muttered, not even knowing what my point was, but plowing ahead anyway. "You and Simon are, too."

Then, as if I wasn't behaving like enough of a loser, I had to go ahead and *sniffle*.

Jesus... just give everyone a pay raise for dealing with me.

"I didn't think you cared about that, Balty." His tone had softened, making me wonder if this was the *real* him—the part our parents had trained Wolfy to hide from us—showing through.

That thought made me sniffle some more. "I didn't think I did. It's just... I think I'm just confused about a lot of shit right now."

Wolfy hummed thoughtfully, and I wished I had the balls to just tell him what was going on.

There was no reason for me *not* to tell my gay brother and his gay mafia queen that I might like dick. Hell, the whole gay family would probably throw me a big gay party to celebrate me joining the rest of them on the apparently more exciting side of the playing field.

Like the field where I met Zion...

"Why did you pick *Dahlia* as my match?" I abruptly asked, echoing Zion's question from earlier. "You already had them by the balls without a marriage contract..."

There was another pause before Wolfy spoke again, and when he did, he was back to business. "The Salah clan is the best fit for you. Trust me on that. Just keep doing exactly what you're doing and it will be fine."

I almost scoffed. There was *no way* Wolfy wanted me to continue popping boners every time Zion accidentally scratched me with one of his sexy lizard claws.

Since I doubt that's written into the contract.

But I needed to buck up—to show my family I could do this. I'd fucked chicks I wasn't super interested in before, and I could do it again. All it would take was enough alcohol to get me over my issues, but not so much that I couldn't get it up.

A perfect plan!

"Okay, bro, I can do that," I replied, forcing as much cheer as possible without sounding deranged. "Sorry to bother you. Oh! And did you know Zion has a *kid?* Anyway… I'll check back in soon. Later!"

I hung up—and turned off my phone completely—before I could continue babbling like an idiot. Grabbing a fresh dress shirt, I focused on buttoning it up with shaking hands as I debated what to do next.

Luckily, the mental state I'd reached to call the emergency line had deflated my boner, but I still felt unsettled. No way in hell was I going to jerk off after what happened earlier, so I decided on the next best thing.

I'm gonna go flirt.

With MY fiancé, of course…

I strode from my room with purpose. Dahlia had arrived at the gym with her personal trainer just as Zion finished that part of the tour, so it seemed safe to assume she was still down there, kicking ass.

I wonder if I could take her in the ring?

Challenging my future wife to a duel seemed as good a mating strategy as any—and one where I was fairly confident I wouldn't embarrass myself too badly. It was always a little awkward when two supes with vastly different powers met in battle, but it made things interesting.

Maybe it will even be fun!

And it's not like she'll try to actually kill me.

Right?

By the time I reached the lower levels, I was sweaty again, worrying Dahlia was going to take me down with a single bolt of lightning to the head.

When she was nowhere to be found, I breathed a sigh of relief, more than happy to not have to follow through on my lame plan. Then I heard her voice—along with Zion's—coming from the direction of his death pond.

And it sounded like they were arguing.

Ooh, gossip!

This I could do. If I was going to suck at the arranged marriage thing, at least I could bring Wolfy some juicy intel until I got my shit straight.

Or not straight...

"You don't have to be such a *bitch* to him, Dahlia," Zion huffed.

I heard a splash as I crept down the tunnel, and my cock gave an enthusiastic kick at the thought of seeing him in lizard form.

Down, boy!

"How dare you call me that! What happened to respecting women?" Dahlia spoke in a haughty tone that made my balls shrivel.

Problem solved.

"Yeah, you got me there," Zion laughed bitterly. "I hate women so much I fell for one, raised a kid together, and tried everything in my power to get this family to welcome her in. Guess I should have just waited for Mom and Pops to randomly become more open-minded about our potential spouses, hmm?"

My fists clenched as I fought the urge to shift and smash the tunnel down around us.

I don't even understand what I'm mad about!

Dahlia barked a laugh. "I doubt it would've helped in your case. Shit, I still can't believe you were stupid enough to fall in love with one of *them!*"

Love.

Zion was in love.

With… one of who?

Another villain?!

"Nothing about my relationship with Mikki was *stupid.*" Zion's voice had gone dangerously low.

As the eldest, he was the equivalent of Wolfy in this family, and if my brother ever spoke to me in that tone, I would probably faint like one of those weird goats.

But Dahlia was a different breed. She scoffed instead. "Yeah, well, I guess anything's better than the dumbass I'm stuck with now."

Okay, fuck this.

My plans to charm Dahlia into a friends-with-benefits situation shriveled faster than my nuts. I knew I wasn't the sharpest tool in the shed, but if she thought I was putting my prize-winning dick anywhere near her bitchy vagina with *that* attitude...

"Don't *ever* fucking call him that again."

Zion's voice was so threatening on my behalf, my cock gave a standing ovation. Shockingly, even Dahlia seemed to understand that now was *not* the time to press her luck. She muttered a half-assed apology and stomped away—thankfully, via the garden exit—to go be a jerk somewhere else.

Good riddance.

That left me standing in the tunnel, debating whether I should go back the way I came or try to hang out with an angry lizard-man.

My whiplashed dick decided it liked the second option best, and even though it was the *opposite* of what Wolfy wanted me to do, I followed the 'only head that worked under duress.'

Straight into the lizard's den.

CHAPTER 10
ZION

I was about to slip underwater to properly stew at the bottom when Baltasar unexpectedly walked into my cave.

Well, shit.

How much did he overhear?

He didn't look particularly upset, so I assumed he'd missed Dahlia being... well, Dahlia. As usual, his open gaze was adorably curious as it roamed over me, and I realized he'd probably never encountered me half-shifted like this before.

"Do you like what you see?" I drawled, pushing off from the edge of the pool to backstroke in lazy circles—giving him the full view.

The full *view.*

As I'd hoped, his amber eyes dropped to my cock, which, in this form, looked human enough—except for the iridescent scales, knot, and super fun ridges along the shaft.

The ladies love it.

The men love it even more.

"Your dick has scales," he stated, his signature candor one of the many things I liked about this villain in our duplicitous world of smoke and mirrors.

"Sure does," I chuckled. "I've been told they feel fucking fantastic hammering over your prostate."

He swallowed and took a step backward. "I don't... I wouldn't know anything about that."

Not yet.

I probably should've cooled it down until he was more comfortable with this obvious attraction between us. Unfortunately for him, Baltasar Suarez was impossible to resist.

And so fun to toy with.

Drifting back to the edge of the pond, I smoothly hauled myself out before completely shifting back to human form. To my absolute delight, Baltasar seemed disappointed by my transformation. There weren't many whose opinions I cared about—and that included my family. But having this man look at my scales in *admiration* made me feel like less of a freak of nature than usual.

Since there aren't any other supes like me.

Not that I've found, anyway.

Taking a step toward my prey, I cocked my head. "Are you just out for a stroll, B? Or was there something I could help you find?"

Your prostate, perhaps?

"I was hoping to find Dahlia—to get to know her a little better..."

My stomach sank, but I nodded. Even if Dahlia mistakenly thought Baltasar was a 'dumbass,' if he *wanted* to marry her, she would follow through with her end of the bargain, too.

Anything to get more power for herself.

As I backed into my pond, I canted my chin toward the garden exit and kept my tone unbothered. "Well, she went that way. If you hurry, you can probably catch—"

"… but I'm actually not very interested in hanging out with someone like her."

Fuck. Yes.

My beast roared to the surface again, and I saw Baltasar's eyes widen as proof flickered over my skin. "What *are* you interested in?"

He swallowed again, looking so deliciously innocent, I wanted to pull him closer and hoard him forever. "I don't know anymore. But I was thinking… Maybe you could…" The big guy sighed as if frustrated with himself. "I just need to get the fuck out of my own head tonight."

I smirked and grabbed a towel—deciding to give my man a break by covering up. "Well, I know just the thing. Let's survive dinner first and get Daisy into bed. Then I'll show you one of my favorite ways to relax."

———

"Holy shit! Is that a Ducati Panigale V4R and a Kawasaki Ninja H2R?"

I couldn't stop myself from smiling. As much as Baltasar was surprising me at every turn, there were a few things I could guarantee he enjoyed.

Speed, sports, and sex.

The perfect man for me.

Dinner had been rough, but it usually was the nights I sat with my family. I would have preferred to eat with Daisy in the kitchen, but it was clear the villain was expected in the dining room. No way in hell was I leaving him alone in that lion's den. Not after my sister's disrespectful comments.

She doesn't deserve him.

None of them do.

Dahlia tried glaring at me across the table at one point, but all that accomplished was me possessively throwing my arm across the back of Baltasar's chair. Her eyes had narrowed in challenge, but I held her gaze long enough to display my dominance.

Stand down, sis.

This family had become far too comfortable with my complacency over the past few years. It was time to remind them who I was.

Scaled Justice.

The goddamn heir to the Salah throne.

Putting Daisy to bed had been far more pleasant, even if she was pissed at me for not eating with her. I didn't mind being ignored. She focused her affection on Baltasar instead— insisting *he* read her a bedtime story while sitting in his over-sized lap.

I couldn't remember the last time my daughter cuddled with *me* like that. The sight of them already so comfortable with each other affected me so deeply, I had to briefly leave the room before I got too sentimental.

A high-stakes gentleman's wager ought to erase these mushy feelings.

"You know your bikes, Suarez," I chuckled, gazing at them—and him—adoringly. "So I expect you not to crash."

"You're gonna let me drive one?" Baltasar's eyes were as big as dinner plates before they narrowed in suspicion. "You didn't like, rig them to explode, did you? I don't think Wolfy would appreciate pieces of me being sent home for him to sort through."

I threw my head back and laughed. "You think I'd willingly endanger any of my babies like that? Pshh…"

Never mind that I'm not only talking about the bikes.

He nodded, satisfied with my answer. "Okay, so where's the track?"

Spreading my arms wide, I grandly gestured to the tarmac on either side of us. "Who needs a track when you have a runway?"

"Rules?" He assessed the stretch of asphalt before us with the same sexy focus he gave the Deathball field.

I shrugged, already half-hard just thinking about leaving him in the dust. "First man to the end wins."

His dimpled grin made my heart skip a beat. "And what will I win?"

Mighty sure of yourself, hmm?

This time, I gestured toward myself. "Winner gets whatever he wants from the loser."

Again, his gaze trailed over me in a way that was definitely *not* 100% straight, but he simply nodded and walked to one of my bikes.

The faster one, of course.

I cracked my neck and mounted the other, eager for the challenge. Sometimes I got my brother Isaiah out here to race, but he was currently involved in a torrid affair with the head groundskeeper. So he'd been busy riding *that* instead.

"All right." I pointed at his bike. "Now just be sure to—"

Baltasar shot me a wink and went full throttle before taking off like a bat out of hell.

You bratty motherfucker!

With a growl, I sped after him, leaning forward and ignoring my now fully hard erection pressing against the tank.

The Kawasaki he chose may have been faster, but my Ducati handled like a dream. Veering into his imaginary lane, I expertly grazed his back wheel, causing him to wobble and glare at me over his shoulder.

I took advantage of the hiccup to move beside him. "What's the matter, B?" I shouted over the roar of engines and wind. "You don't like how I look behind you?"

He rolled his eyes and aimed his gaze forward, imitating my earlier position until he was almost flattened against the tank.

That ass though…

I was so distracted by the idea of fucking Baltasar over either of my bikes, I didn't notice the incoming aircraft. Not until the change in air pressure caught my attention.

Shit.

Wildly gesturing for Baltasar to get the hell off the tarmac, I slowed down.

Then he sped up.

I gunned it again, determined to *make* him stop, but every time I started to catch up, he cut me off.

What the fuck is he doing?

Supes were fairly tough, but we weren't completely unbreakable. Extreme road rash would heal in a day or so, but I didn't know anyone who could recover from being beheaded by a business jet.

Does he have a fucking death wish or something?!

The Embraer Phenom 300 my parents used for quick business trips was descending at an alarming rate. To my horror, I realized Baltasar was counting on being able to squeeze under without getting clipped.

Not on my watch.

My bikes were going to be toast, but no way in hell was I allowing this man to get hurt—or worse—because of a stupid bet.

He's mine to protect.

The dust being kicked up was practically blinding me. I released the handlebars and flung myself at Baltasar's broad back, snatching him from his seat. Quickly shifting into lizard form, I protectively curled my much larger body around the villain before impact.

This is gonna hurt.

The underside of the plane actually grazed my dorsal crest. But I didn't have time to consider how close of a call it was before the tarmac was shaving off a few more layers. By the time we stopped rolling, I vaguely wondered if I had any scales left at all, but I stayed conscious long enough to check that Baltasar had survived.

For that, I'll sacrifice anything…

CHAPTER 11
BALTASAR

Why did he sacrifice himself like that?

I totally could have made it!

That asshole just didn't want me to win.

Fuck, this is all my fault…

For hours, I sat by Zion's bed, staring at his scaled chest, convinced that if I looked away, he'd stop breathing. I barely remembered shifting and carrying his unconscious, bloodied body back to the main house, but I'd been operating on instinct alone. The concerned, yet unsurprised, look the butler gave us told me it wasn't the first time something like this had happened.

Supes aren't known for playing it safe.

The rest of the staff also seemed well-versed in caring for the clan heir. Besides hauling the big lizard into his oversized bed, all I did was uselessly watch as a couple of lesser supes carefully cleaned his injuries. Though I *was* grateful nobody made me go sleep in my room as they left the hero to recuperate in his.

I wouldn't have listened, anyway.

At one point, Zion's parents stopped by, and the Major gave me a dressing down that rivaled my dead mother's. I happily took the blame for the accident—since they didn't like me anyway—but internally, I couldn't *wait* to yell at Zion as soon as he woke up.

Please wake up, Z.

Interestingly, his mother had stayed silent during my scolding. Instead of her usual resting judgy face, her shrewd gaze flitted between her son and me—assessing the situation.

Assessing *me.*

Nothing to see here, ma'am.

At least, I didn't *think* there was anything to see. After the dust had settled on the tarmac, I'd found myself miraculously unharmed. I *was* plastered to the chest of a giant lizard-man while I sported a raging hard-on, but the adrenaline was probably to blame for that.

I'm sure it was the near-death experience.

Being careless with my existence was nothing new. But my actions endangering Zion—resulting in him being laid up like he was—made my guts twist.

How am I going to explain this to Daisy?

Zion abruptly tossed his head from side to side, murmuring something unintelligible while frantically patting the bed next to him.

Searching for something.

"… my mate? I need my…"

Fuck.

That Zion was instinctively looking for the mother of his kid —Mikki—made me weirdly annoyed. But then I reminded myself the relationship clearly hadn't ended well, and my annoyance was replaced with sympathy.

I can pretend to be his mate... just to be nice.

It's the least I can do.

After double-checking that the door was locked, I lifted the covers and slipped into bed beside him. It probably would have made more sense to shift into a comparable size. But I'd already helped myself to a pair of Zion's sweatpants and didn't want to take them off again.

Plus, I kind of like being smaller than him...

The instant our bodies made contact, Zion pulled me closer. My presence seemed to settle him, even if my confused boner reared its ugly head again. I didn't even care, because his scales felt *amazing* on my skin. They were cool to the touch but smooth—like a sleek fish. Before I knew it, I was brushing a hand over his chest in wonder.

Okay, please don't *wake up now.*

At least not until I'm done being a creep.

Zion's reptilian coloring had mesmerized me since the first time I saw him on the field, and it was even more incredible up close. He was a blue so dark it was almost black, with iridescent purple scales peppered throughout—like a night-time sky full of distant galaxies.

Which makes sense, knowing what I do about our origins.

I chewed my lip, tempted to tell him the truth once he woke up. Zion seemed so confused about his unique powers and lizard form. Learning he was actually closer to what we'd all been once upon a time might be reassuring to the hero. Unfortunately, I was sworn to secrecy with the cave paintings and our supe origins, because it was *my* family who owned that information now.

And blood is thicker than murder.

Either way, I wasn't about to pass up the opportunity to see more of this lizard-man, up close and personal.

For… research purposes.

Since Zion had openly waved his dick around in the grotto, I reasoned he wouldn't be *too* mad if I checked him out a little more.

And if he is, I'll let him punch me.

That should get rid of my boner.

Maybe…

I glanced at his face to confirm he was still knocked out before tentatively trailing a finger lower, tracing his killer abs.

Dude has a fucking twelve-pack!

Then—before I could think better of it—I carefully lifted the sheet for a better look at his lizard dick.

Holy. Shit.

Obviously, it was enormous in this form—covered in scales that looked more like a flexible part of his skin than a protective layer. But the special features I'd glimpsed earlier, when he was half-shifted, were what really caught my eye. The shaft had four scaled ridges, like you'd find on one of those patriotic rocket popsicles.

So that's *what the ladies—and men—were raving about.*

I was telling the truth when I said nothing had ever touched my prostate. There'd been one cape chaser who tried sticking a finger up my ass while giving me a blowie, but I freaked out the instant she circled the rim, and told her to focus on the main attraction instead.

Even though it felt awesome.

Maybe because *it felt awesome.*

Returning my attention to Zion, I continued to look him over, frowning when I noticed the large, knot-shaped bulge at the base of his cock—separate from his balls.

What the hell is that *for?*

I can't imagine it fits inside anyone…

Swallowing hard, I stared at Zion's cock, racking my brain to imagine what it would feel like… 'hammering over my prostate'… filling me…

While he totally fucking owned me.

"Is this your prize, B?"

Oh, gawd!

"OH, GAWD!" I yelped, dropping the sheet like a criminal caught in the act. "I'm sorry! I was just… checking that every-thing… that your…"

"That nothing *important* got scraped off on the tarmac?" Zion chuckled, the deeper-than-usual timbre of his voice doing all sorts of things to me.

Things that cannot *happen.*

"Don't make it weird, Salah," I huffed, attempting to wiggle out of his hold and escape the scene of the crime.

Unfortunately, he only tightened his death grip, the slight sting of his claws digging into my biceps, making my cock give an enthusiastic kick.

Against his leg.

Just kill me now.

"What would you prefer to claim as your prize, then?" he purred, rubbing my erection against him, and coaxing a goddamn *whimper* from my throat.

"Claim?" I rasped, feeling something rearrange inside my chest at the thought of claiming this man.

Of being claimed by him, mostly.

"I didn't *win*, dude," I quickly added, clearing my throat before glancing up at him. "Nobody did. I'm only here because I wanted to make sure you were okay."

Because I'm really not okay with you being hurt for some ridiculous reason.

Zion was staring down at me, his unblinking reptilian face making it difficult to gauge his expression. I watched, mesmerized, as he slowly morphed into his half-shifted state —not quite human or animal. His gaze still locked on mine with a more easily recognizable heat.

He swallowed hard before barely whispering, "I'm not okay, B."

Me neither.

I spoke before I could stop myself. "What can I do to help?"

Anything.

Zion rolled onto his side to face me before hovering a clawed finger over my heart. "Touching you would help," he said, and I enthusiastically nodded in agreement.

Yes, please.

We both groaned as he lightly dragged a claw down my chest, although just what *he* was getting out of the experience was a mystery. *I'd* never been harder in my life. The more blood that bubbled to the surface of my skin, the more I feared I was about to blow all over the inside of my rival's sweatpants.

"Fuck, you look good in my clothes," he growled, pulling the sheet down to reveal my glaringly obvious hard-on tenting *his* sweats. "And just look at that big cock trying to come out and play."

His voice had taken on an even more growly tone, with a possessive edge that had me swallowing another whimper. I felt almost dizzy with the need to get on my hands and knees for him.

I'm in danger.

"Z, I can't..." I choked out as he traced my hip bones and teased the waistband, making precum dribble out of me.

Zion froze, his gaze snapping back to mine. "Do you want me to stop?"

"I-I don't know," I stuttered, beyond confused. What I *wanted* would change everything, but I was having a hard time giving a shit about that at the moment.

Just fucking touch me.

"Then this stops," he calmly replied, snatching back his hand and resting it on his abs.

Nooooo....

This time, the most pathetic whimper of all time escaped me —making him chuckle. "You're just dying for release, huh?"

"Yes," I whispered, practically delirious. "I n-need to come."

"Then pull out that gorgeous cock and get yourself off," he casually suggested, leaning forward until his breath was tickling my lips. "I want you to soak me in it. Just close your eyes and pretend I'm one of your cape chasers—"

"I don't wanna pretend," I mumbled as I quickly wrestled myself free, totally game for this fucked up plan. "I like looking at you..."

Why the fuck would I say that?!

For a moment I panicked, thinking Zion would kick me out of his bed after such a creepy confession. Instead, his warm brown eyes widened in surprise. "You do? Like... *this?*" He glanced down at his half-shifted form as if it wasn't the reason my cock had its own heartbeat.

"Fuck, yes," I whispered, starting to stroke and wishing he'd get his goddamn lips close to mine again. "I like this. I like all of it."

I just like you.

Unfortunately, it didn't change the facts. I was engaged to Zion's *sister.* If you ignored certain aspects of her personality, she was exactly my type. Or... what *used* to be my type, because—right now—the only supe in this house my dick seemed to be interested in was the big lizard telling me to come all over him.

Fuck, I wanna mark him as mine.

"That's it, beautiful," Zion coached, his gaze riveted on where I was fucking into my fist like an obedient little jackrabbit. "Show me that big load you've been saving just for me. Give me what's mine."

Yours.

The idea of being *his* only spurred me on. *"Fuck, fuck, fuck,"* I chanted, shuttling my hand over my aching cock with nothing but the sweat from my palm for lube. "Keep talking, Z. Please..."

Please don't stop.

He wrapped his hand around the back of my neck, resting our foreheads together and smirking when I gasped at the brush of his lips on mine. "You're the prettiest fucking thing I've ever seen, Suarez. From the moment I first saw you, I wanted this. Wanted *you.*"

Zion was obviously talking out of his ass—spouting random bullshit to get me to explode—but I still moaned like a whore to hear it.

Tell me I'm pretty.

As if he were a goddamn sex voodoo mind reader, he briefly slid his tongue—*his ridged lizard tongue*—over my bottom lip before sealing my fate.

"And I can't wait to see how *pretty* you are when you come for me."

"*Fuuuuck...*" I groaned as cum began spraying out of me—absolutely *coating* the man in front of me while I shuddered in ecstasy.

Yours, yours, yours.

My brain officially short-circuited. The next thing I knew, Zion's clawed hand was fisted in my hair while I sucked on his tongue like a clit.

Nope.

Like a cock.

Because I'm totally into cock now.

I continued to shoot until I wondered if I'd ever be able to come again—panting and mumbling nonsense that sounded a hell of a lot like begging.

I need it, I need it, I need...

"Fucking hell," I gasped, ripping my mouth away from his and staring at the mess I'd made.

My cum was dripping down Zion Salah's chest and abs, running in obscene rivulets between the scales—as if to remind me of exactly what I found sexy now.

What have I done?

"I... gotta go," I stuttered, launching myself off the bed so fast I got tangled in the sheets. "To my room... before..."

Before my fiancé finds out that I jerked off for her brother.

On *her brother.*

Fuck, that was hot...

"It *was* hot, wasn't it?" Zion chuckled.

Did I say that out loud?!

He didn't look at all concerned about what had just happened, even as I freaked the fuck out. That big lizard lazily rubbed his hand over his chest—spreading my cum around like he wanted every hot inch of himself to be covered in *me.*

Maybe I have a few drops left...

GET ME THE FUCK OUT OF HERE!!!

Jamming my spent cock back in my pants—*Zion's pants*—I spun on my heel and raced from his room.

And straight into a pissed-off Dahlia.

CHAPTER 12
BALTASAR

"What the hell were you doing in Zion's room?" Dahlia hissed. "It's three in the fucking morning."

Before I could ask what *she* was doing up, her gaze dropped to my crotch. I glanced down, grimacing when I saw the damning wet spot visible against the light-colored cotton.

Of course, all Zion owns is hottie gray sweatpants!

Okay, Balty, think fast…

"I had to piss," I blurted out. "And I guess I didn't shake my dick enough when I was done…" Her eyes narrowed and I realized I needed to explain *why* I'd be shaking my dick anywhere near her brother. "But I decided to check on Zion and make sure he's all right after the accident… Since I was up anyway."

Way up.

Dahlia scoffed. "Yeah, I heard you two idiots were out racing bikes on the goddamn runway."

I bristled—mostly because of how she was insulting Zion. Everyone knew *I* was dumb, but I refused to stand here and let her insult my man.

Wait, what?

WHAT?!

Oblivious to my internal meltdown, she continued, almost to herself. "I was told Zion was knocked unconscious…"

Something dangerous flared up inside me, and my focus narrowed on the perceived threat. Crossing my arms over my bare chest, I instinctively stepped in front of Zion's door— weirdly protective.

"What were *you* planning on doing if he was unconscious, Dahlia? Breathe on him? I've already checked in and now he's awake, so you can go f—"

"Find somewhere else to be," Zion's voice directly behind me sent a fresh jolt of lust shooting down my spine.

Please don't get a boner in front of your fiancé…

He darkly chuckled. "Can't you see I was busy?"

Oh, no…

He didn't…

It was like a horror movie in slo-mo. I turned and came face to face with a very smug-looking Zion.

Wearing nothing but hottie gray sweatpants of his own.

And still *covered* in my cum.

Oh, gawd.

"*OH, GAWD!*" Dahlia choked out. "What the fuck is the matter with you? No wonder you're not taking over the clan—"

"Who says I'm not?" Zion's growl had me readying for battle.

To protect my man!

Ugh, stop.

"I-I thought..." his sister stuttered, looking unsure for possibly the first time in her life before she shook it off. "You know what? Never mind. I just wanted to see how you were feeling. But obviously, you've recovered enough to be an asshole, so... bye."

Dahlia spun on her heel and headed down the hideously red-carpeted hallway. "C'mon, Baltasar!" she haughtily called over her shoulder. "I've changed my mind. I could use an outlet for my rage right now. Let's fuck."

Excuse me?!

My cock stirred to life again, but only because Zion growled so loudly it rattled the gold-framed portraits lining the walls.

They must have run out of room for being judgy downstairs.

Dahlia turned to face us with an evil grin, and I realized she was just using me to bait her brother.

"No. I mean, no thanks," I quickly spoke up—hoping to stop a brawl. But then I faltered as the full force of both heroes' gazes fell on me.

Talk about feeling like a piece of meat!

"I uh... I need to take a shit," I blurted out the first thing I could think of. "It's a matter of life or death. So..."

Without waiting for a reply, I turned and raced down the stairs, hearing Zion's howl of laughter echo behind me.

That ought to convince them both to leave me alone for a while.

Or forever.

Ignoring the nagging feeling that I didn't want *Zion* to leave me alone—for any amount of time—I arrived at my bedroom and locked myself inside.

There IS a lock—ha!

A sick feeling settled in my stomach. Crawling under the covers, I grabbed my phone—deciding that doom scrolling on social media was just what I needed to forget I'd directly defied my brother.

By coming all over my not-fiancé.

Gratification was delayed as I remembered I'd turned off my phone after my awkward conversation with Wolfy. Fidgeting on the bed, I anxiously waited for it to power on again.

Only to find multiple missed calls and texts.

From an obviously pissed-off Wolfy.

The One With Magic Fingers: *If you don't call me back immediately, I will channel my powers through the twins to drain your ass from here.*

Can he... do that?!

Not wanting to risk it, I quickly hit call—too scared to even giggle over the name I'd secretly programmed for him in my phone.

He'd probably drain me for that, too.

"Balty? Oh, thank fuck." Wolfy's extra-growly voice came on the line and I winced, realizing I'd either interrupted sleep or creepy sex with Simon.

"Tell Baby Hulk his timing is incredibly inconvenient, but I'm more than happy to continue gobbling your cock while he grovels on speaker."

Creepy sex it is.

A chilling thought occurred to me. "Did something happen?" I asked—suddenly terrified for the well-being of my other siblings.

Who do I need to pound into the ground?

"What? No," Wolfy muttered. *"You* dropped a bombshell and then disappeared for hours."

I did?

"What bombshell?" I scratched my head, trying to remember what I'd said before ten million other crazy things went down.

There was a long enough pause that I could *feel* Wolfy's stare from here. "That Zion Salah has a child," he deadpanned.

"Oh, that!" I laughed. "Yeah, her name's Daisy, and she's pretty much the coolest kid I've ever met. And my only friend here, besides… Zion…"

Sharing jizz is a bonding experience, right?

"Do you not understand what this means, Baltasar?!" Simon's mouth must have switched gears as his voice was suddenly close enough to blow out my eardrum. "Now you have *two* heirs standing between you and Dahlia taking the throne. Count them on your brain cells. One, two."

"Daisy's not a fucking obstacle!" I roared—the first time I'd ever dared raise my voice to Simon or my brother—and I was unsurprisingly met with deadly silence in reply.

Gulp.

The next thing I heard was a door being closed and what sounded like Simon's muffled ranting on the other side.

Double gulp.

"Tell me what's going on, Balty," Wolfy commanded, alone and as impressively calm as ever.

He won't be if I answer that truthfully.

"Nothing!" I yelped, a bit too loudly in the quiet room. "Everything's going exactly to plan, dude, I promise."

To my surprise, he laughed. The sound was so foreign that I tensed. "I'm sure it is," he murmured. "So you've made a new friend, hmm?"

I sighed, assuming he was making fun of me. "Yeah, but Daisy's like, really mature for an almost-ten-year-old. A little queen. Although, she's shunned by the rest of the family, for some reason…"

"What?!" Wolfy's raised voice sent me back under the covers like a dog in a lightning storm. When I fumbled the phone to my ear again, I heard him relaying the message to Simon in what sounded like an excited tone.

That's a good sign…

I think.

"Balty?" My brother was back on the line. "Slight change of plans. Find out everything you can about Zion's kid—who her mother is and where we can find her. Anything we can use as leverage. I want to know what dirt this family has swept under the rug."

I swallowed hard as he abruptly ended the call. It was one thing to gather random intel during my arranged marriage proceedings with Dahlia, but this request made me hesitate.

Daisy was just a kid—one without enough powers to be considered a threat—and her family didn't even treat her as one of their own. I could see why her unregistered existence would interest Wolfy and Simon. But she didn't deserve to get dragged into the politics and backstabbing of our world.

Not when I can shield her from it.

And this situation with Zion was even more complicated. The two of us had a shared history through Deathball, and this unexpected *pull* I was experiencing around him went well beyond an old rivalry.

At least, it feels that way to me…

Tossing my phone onto the bedside table, I turned off the light and flopped onto my back with a noise of despair.

What am I supposed to do?

I stared at the ceiling until my eyes burned, sporting a semi, and wishing I was still a floor above me—wrapped around smooth scales and hard muscles. Besides being confused about what I wanted, I felt guilty as fuck about who I wanted it with.

For the first time in my life, my allegiance was splintered and unclear. All supes had a deep loyalty to their clan—an instinct to defend their flesh and blood that was usually unbreakable. I couldn't imagine what it had cost Wolfy to betray our parents, but knew he'd gladly endure anything to protect the rest of us.

He could always be counted on for his family.

Unlike me, apparently.

This marriage to Dahlia was *business,* and scandalous side pieces were pretty common in these arrangements. Still, I couldn't bring myself to tell my brother what was going on between me and Zion. In the end, Wolfy was the Suarez clan leader. He'd use the affair as leverage for our family's benefit, no matter who he crushed along the way.

And I can't let that happen.

I didn't care about Dahlia or her parents, or the seven other Salah siblings who I couldn't keep straight for the life of me.

But I care about Daisy.

And… Zion…

Exhaustion slowly pulled me under, even though my guts felt so twisted up, I thought I might be sick. Mostly, I was terrified to realize I had absolutely no idea which side I would find myself on in the end.

What the fuck am I supposed to do?

CHAPTER 13
ZION

After Dahlia's failed attempt to lure *my* mate into her bed, I jerked off to the sweet scent of Baltasar on my skin.

Then I did it again. And again.

The need to claim the villain was all-consuming. And now that I was covered in him—in *us*—I feared for my sanity, but I also couldn't bring myself to wash it off.

He looked so pretty when he came for me.

He'll look even prettier when he does it again.

Waking up with Baltasar next to me had been unexpected. What surprised me more was finding him staring at my cock, with 'please, fuck me' pheromones pouring off him.

All supes were more highly evolved than normies, but I seemed to possess more acute senses than most. It might have had something to do with being part animal. Either way, if you gave Baltasar a head start in the deep woods surrounding my family's estate, I knew I'd be able to track him down.

We should totally play that game.

I still couldn't believe I'd persuaded him to not only get himself off next to me, but on me—not that it took much convincing. The man had even sucked on my tongue as he came, all the while moaning like other parts of me were buried inside him.

Fuck, he was so into it.

I groaned as my cock rallied to life again, legitimately concerned I was going to go blind at this point.

Or race downstairs to nail Baltasar to the bed.

"Daddy! Get up!"

Too late for that.

The light of my life bounded into my room, making me hurriedly sit up and cover my lap with a pile of blankets.

That still smell like Baltasar...

It was unsurprising that my sweet villain smelled like freshly baked cookies, but my snickerdoodle cravings would have to wait.

"Have you seen Bluntycups?" Daisy asked, trotting in place at the foot of the bed like she was ready to break into a run at any moment. "He's not in his room."

I froze. "He's not?"

Where else would he be?

A vision of Baltasar creeping upstairs to take Dahlia up on her salacious offer annoyingly rose to the surface of my mind.

No, he didn't...

Did he?

I'd been so proud of how he'd turned her down, assuming it meant he was reconsidering their engagement. Now I wondered if he was trying to play on both sides of the field.

Not that I'm one to judge...

"Nope!" Daisy replied with an audible pop. "But all his stuff is still there, so he didn't like, run home or anything..." she trailed off as she looked me over, her adorable little nose wrinkling. "Why do you look like you were hit by a bus?"

"Because *Bluntycups* and I played a game of chicken on the runway last night," I sighed, telling her the truth, as usual— no matter how stupid it made me look.

She snorted. "Does this mean he won?"

Her question made me pause. I'd always thrived on competition, and Baltasar Suarez was the only one who could ever give me the challenge I craved. While our race on the tarmac had scratched an itch—until it went horribly wrong—I noticed the idea of him beating me no longer made me see red.

It's because you don't see him as an adversary anymore, Zion.

Dahlia, on the other hand...

"Go have Cook get you started on breakfast," I growled, flinching when she balked at my tone. "I'm going to see if I can find Blunty," I added, more gently.

"Good idea!" She beamed, already forgiving me. "We can cover more ground if we split up. And I definitely need food before I join the search."

"You need food so you can concentrate during your lessons," I pointedly corrected. "I'll take care of this, D."

She nodded once in that serious way of hers that made my heart hurt. "Because you take care of what's yours. Got it.

Okay, I'm gonna go get some grub! Tell Blunty about movie night when you find him. And croquet! Theeenks, byeeee..."

Then she danced from the room, leaving me to gape as her initial statement caught up with me.

"Because you take care of what's yours."

Daisy was simply parroting what I'd told her countless times —that no matter how anyone else in this family behaved, *I* would always take care of her.

And her mom.

Even though I failed Mikki in the end.

But I won't with Baltasar—because he's mine.

With a snarl, I flung off the blankets and yanked on a pair of sweatpants before stalking into the hallway. In no time, I'd reached Dahlia's door.

The urge to kick it in was strong, but I opted for stealth and spying instead—half-shifting so I could press my sensitive lizard ear to the door and eavesdrop.

Relief washed over me to hear *Preek* chatting with my sister instead of Baltasar's slutty moans. Although why our PR handler was in her room at this hour was a mystery.

They're not fucking, are they?!

This would be the bombshell of the century, not least of all because Dahlia wasn't known for dallying with the help. And as for Preek—the man had such an icy demeanor, if I didn't know better, I might have assumed he was part reptile, like me.

But then he'd be a more powerful supe.

Even though I didn't fully understand where the hell my odd powers had come from, my parents had always seemed abnormally proud of my abilities. It was the main reason they were so disappointed when I shacked up with a normie—and why they shunned Daisy the way they did.

She was proof of the dilution of my supposedly superior genes.

The Salahs had worked long and hard for their superiority, through generations of selective breeding. All supe families did this. It was the only way to ensure dominance over the competition.

Not every family had the connections needed to produce more powerful offspring—which was how lesser supes came to be. These not-quite-normies had *some* powers, but usually nothing more than parlor tricks. For example, Preek had an uncanny gift of persuasion, which made him perfect for a career in public relations.

Or damage control.

Lesser supes often sought employment in the big houses of more powerful supes. Some accused them of trying to increase their social standing by leaching from us, but I didn't see how that would even be possible.

At this point in my life, I preferred the company of our staff over my family. They were the real ones. Without a horse in the race, they couldn't afford an angle, so I assumed they weren't trying to stab me in the back at every turn.

At least… most of them aren't.

"… and thanks to the resident meatheads calling attention to my arrival, your father interrogated me for close to an hour about *why* I was using the family jet."

So that was Preek *coming in to land last night.*

Dahlia scoffed. I heard the delicate clink of metal, as if she were seated at the vanity picking out jewelry. "I'm sure you told him you'd come straight from the lab?" she murmured in a taunting tone.

The lab?

Preek was unusually quiet. When he spoke again, his voice had a threatening edge I'd never heard him use with my sister. "If you tell them what we know, *you'll* be in just as much trouble as me. Never forget that, *Atmosphera.*"

I braced for impact, but Dahlia lightly laughed, dredging up Preek's unfortunate supe name for added bite. "Oh no, *Minor Influence.* If anyone finds out, it will be my *parents* who are the ones in trouble."

What the fuck are they talking about?!

The conversation veered to their usual—less incriminating—catty gossip. I slinked away with a heavy feeling in my chest, and by the time I reached the kitchen, my thoughts were a jumbled mess.

Cook noticed me sulking over my French toast and took pity on me. She brusquely mentioned Baltasar had eaten breakfast earlier than usual because of some Supremacy Games-related reason. Knowing his whereabouts gave me instant relief, before the weight of his absence hit me all over again.

Get a goddamn grip, Zion.

You're not actually mated.

No matter what your beast thinks…

I was confused and agitated and somehow still horny despite my record number of orgasms. Something was crawling under my skin—an awareness I couldn't decipher.

Something's wrong.

I need…

Daisy was already with her tutor, so I had hours of unstructured time ahead of me before she was free. Hours I would have normally spent bulking up in the gym, or doing drills on the Deathball field at the far end of the property until I collapsed in exhaustion. Neither option appealed to me, because there were no Games in my future to look forward to.

And the one man who could distract me is out of reach.

For now.

CHAPTER 14
ZION

I ended up in the gym after all, but only so I could use the excuse of working out while actually watching SupeSports.

Watching *Baltasar* on SupeSports, to be exact.

Apparently, Sunrise City News 23 had sent a car to collect him before dawn—just like they'd done for me countless times in the past. Memories of this unique brand of torture made me want to roll back into bed and sleep until noon, but Baltasar looked as fresh as a daisy on the massive flatscreen.

And quite fuckable.

B always impressed me with how confidently he conducted himself in interviews. He may not have been dropping profound wisdom, but his observations on the game were thoughtful, and his natural charm was unmatched.

Even on little sleep, the villain looked ready to play. I couldn't take my eyes off him—especially as his grass-green supersuit kept glitching against the green screen stadium scene behind him.

I wouldn't complain if his Lycra disappeared entirely.

Turning up the speed on my treadmill, I frowned as the conversation took a turn from gameplay to *me*. It was veteran commentator Doug Douglas—wearing his signature plaid suit with sneakers to look younger than he was—who segued.

"So, *Blunt Force*." He beamed at the villain so broadly, his veneers outshone his face-lift. "Tell us how it's been living under the same roof as Scaled Justice. Any murder attempts yet?"

They are gonna milk this rivalry until the day we die.

"I don't know what you mean, Doug." Baltasar shrugged, firing off those fucking dimples that made my dick hard. "Justice and I are both professionals, on and off the field."

A younger commenter whose suit gave off a slightly reflective sheen piped in. "Yeah, but even you have to admit, this engagement to his sister will make strange bedfellows out of you."

Baltasar froze in the way only supes could. "What do you mean?"

Oh, shit.

I suddenly realized that if B and I were going to continue fucking around—and I'd already decided we would be—he might need a little coaching on how to play it cool.

I'll coach him any day…

Luckily, the newbie commentator—*Kyle Something?*—didn't seem to notice how his comment had struck a nerve. "I mean, it's no secret how you two were always at each other's throats…"

Baltasar shifted on his feet—clearly getting antsy. One hand fiddled with where his supersuit ended at his throat while the other slid down to adjust his junk.

Fucking hell, B.

Now *I* was sporting an erection, which did *not* vibe with running as hard as I was. Stopping the treadmill completely, I hopped off and simply stood in front of the TV to continue watching.

There was something about this man getting all flustered that did things to me. I didn't care in the slightest if people found out Baltasar was mine, but I *was* curious to see how this awkward conversation would play out.

"... and I'm not sure I'm buying the whole 'heroes and villains are the same' story," the young buck commentator continued. "Not when I see how viciously y'all fight on the field—"

"Oh, we're definitely the same!" Baltasar interrupted with so much conviction, I stood up straighter and took notice. "It's a confirmed fact that the only difference between us is politics."

I narrowed my eyes. It wasn't as if the political coverup Captain Masculine and Doctor Antihero uncovered was news anymore. But I'd spent *years* studying every one of Blunt Force's tells, and this reply was more than a simple soundbite.

What do you know, Suarez?

"Since we're here to talk sports, not politics," Doug Douglas smoothly cut in—much to my annoyance. "Let's get into this year's Supremacy Games. Your team clinched the gold two years ago, Blunt Force, but Scaled Justice gave you a fight until the final buzzer. Are there any other... heroes"—he stumbled over the now disproved distinction—"who can handle you the way he can?"

Not likely.

Not the way he wants *to be handled.*

Again, Baltasar shifted uncomfortably, and I would have bet money he was blushing under his head-covering mask. "Well." He cleared his throat. "That rookie Star Hopper looks like he might give me a run for my—"

"Why *did* Scaled Justice retire?" Kyle Whoever cut in again, and from the look on Douglas' face, our boy was going off-script. "Surely you have insider knowledge, now that you're part of the family."

Motherfucker…

I braced for Baltasar's reply, but instead of making a joke or revealing Daisy's existence, he expanded in size as *Blunt Force* broke through. "For exactly the reason he told the press!" he barked. "To spend more time with his family. And anything other than that is no one else's business but his own."

Holy. Shit.

Fuck, that's hot.

"I hope I didn't make things worse for you…" Baltasar's voice suddenly echoed off the gym walls behind me. "I just… I didn't like how that Kyle fucker was being so nosey about personal shit. This is SupeSports not SNZ!"

That made me laugh. Supe Newz Zone was a tabloid journalism site that dug for juicy gossip by any means necessary —especially on high-profile supes. When the news broke about Masculine and Antihero last year, it was all they reported on for at least a month, which was fine by me.

Since I was as riveted as the rest of the public.

Besides the hero and villain pairing, what captured my attention the most about *that* scandal was the families involved. That the infamous Suarez clan allowed the only son of their parents' greatest enemies into their midst blew my mind.

Unsurprisingly, it also gave my late-night Baltasar fantasies an unhealthy boost.

And now I've finally got him within reach.

I muted the volume on the TV—noticing they'd abruptly cut to clips from the last Games after the failed attempt at mining for gossip—and turned to face the villain.

Baltasar must have brought a change of clothes to his interview, as he'd traded out his tight little supersuit for a T-shirt and jeans. I took my time looking him over, and couldn't stop the smile twitching my lips as he fidgeted under my gaze.

Deciding to put him out of his misery, I smiled and walked toward where he was hovering in the doorway. "You did good, B. You always handle interviews well."

The change that came over him was instantaneous. His cheeks pinked and his broad chest puffed out as he gave me a heartbreakingly hopeful smile. "You really think so? All I do is spew soundbites Wolfy preps me with. And if I don't know what to say, I usually just play dumb, which isn't hard since, you know, I'm the dumb jock and all."

My vision went red, and when it cleared, I found I'd pinned him against the doorframe. "Don't *ever* say that about yourself again," I hissed, my body expanding to tower over him as anger took over. "And if anyone else has something to say about it, I will fucking deal with them for you, understand?"

While Baltasar could have immediately matched my size and pushed me away, he didn't. Instead, he simply stared up at me with pretty eyes as big as dinner plates while he fucking *trembled.*

Like prey.

Jesus.

"I'm sorry, B." I grimaced and took a step back, realizing just how unnecessarily aggressive I was being. "I get kind of… protective when my beast… when *I* decide—"

His hand shot out to grab what was left of my shirt, stopping my retreat. "I don't mind," he whispered in a breathy voice that went straight to my cock. "And hey, I started to Hulk out on the news today, too, so…"

I purred in satisfaction and closed the distance between us again. "Oh, I *saw*," I growled in his ear. "You protected my salacious secrets and defended me—like a good little mate."

He sharply inhaled, and I quickly shifted back to my regular size and backed off for good. My shirt was a goner—falling from me in ribbons—but by some miracle, my sweats had enough stretch in them to mostly recover.

Good thing, since I already feel naked enough as it is.

"Mate?" he murmured, looking more dazed than scandalized.

"Yeah, who knows." I waved a dismissive hand, doing my best to play it off. "I can't always control what comes out of my mouth when my beast takes over…"

"Really?" Now Baltasar looked way more intrigued than I felt comfortable with—especially as I was lying through my teeth.

Mostly lying.

"What's all that?" I redirected, canting my chin at the shopping bags I'd only now noticed in the hallway behind him.

Again, he blushed and squirmed deliciously. "I, um… There was a mall across the street from the studio, so I bought Daisy some clothes. I mean, I know she has plenty of clothes, but these are *cool kid clothes*—not floofy dresses or dorky prepster shit. I thought she could use some graphic T-shirts… you know, like the ones *you* wear…"

He trailed off, and it took me a moment to realize he was nervously eyeing me—as if he thought I'd be angry. It took me another to realize my beast had started to rise to the surface again and zeroed in on him like a snack.

"You can look it over first—as her dad..." he stuttered. "That's why I wanted to find you first. Or I can return what I bought... Yeah, I'll just do that. Return everything. I probably shouldn't be buying stuff for someone else's kid, anyway."

"No," I blurted out. When he winced, I quickly clarified, "I mean, don't return it. She'll love it." When he brightened, I quickly glanced at the clock on the wall. "And her lessons are just about finishing up. Let's go find Queen D, so *you* can give her the clothes yourself."

The unbridled joy that swept over his face caused a wave of traitorous emotions to bubble up in my throat. Quickly turning toward the locker room, I mumbled, "I'm just... gonna go grab another shirt before—"

"I got you some shirts, too."

Fucking, fucking *hell, B.*

Clearing my throat, I rapidly blinked and faced the villain again. He'd pulled a tee out of a bag and was now proudly holding it over his chest—modeling it for me.

One that said, "I'm With Stupid."

With an arrow pointing straight down.

"Get it?" he excitedly asked. "The arrow's pointing at your dick, so—"

"I get it, B," I laughed, snatching it from him before pulling it on over my head. "It's perfect."

Absolutely perfect.

I couldn't remember the last time anyone had bought *me* anything—at least, something that wasn't meant to double as a passive-aggressive message. The same went for Daisy. I'd admittedly started dressing her like her preppy cousins in a pointless attempt to help her better fit in with my family.

But Baltasar just wants her to be herself.

"Lead the way, Suarez," I gestured for him to go ahead before grabbing a few of the bags to help.

Part of me wanted him in front so he could be the first face my daughter saw as he arrived in her lonely bedroom laden with gifts. Another part—the *stupid* part—just wanted to ogle his ass on the way. But mostly, I wanted to get myself back to baseline before he or Daisy noticed my raw emotions.

Because we can't have that.

This was dangerous territory, because Baltasar needed to remain a means to an end. Stealing him from Dahlia—and aligning with the Suarez clan for myself—would assert my dominance within my family. But here he was buying us T-shirts out of the goodness of his weirdly soft villainous heart, while my beast soaked it up as if our mate were providing food and shelter.

We really *can't have that.*

It was sad that someone being *nice* to Daisy—and me—was such a foreign concept, my immediate reaction was to shut it down, but this was my survival mode. I needed to maintain the stoic front I'd worked so hard to hone, to protect my daughter from seeing me as anything less than someone she could count on. No matter what.

Because I protect what's mine.

CHAPTER 15
BALTASAR

I didn't have much experience with little girls—since my only sister was older than me—so I wasn't prepared for the shrieking.

So much shrieking.

"Eeeeeeee! Bluntycups! I lurve it so mu-huh-huch. A *UNICORN?!* How did you *know* unicorns are my favoritest thing everrrrr…"

I could feel my cheeks heating as I snuck a glance at where Zion was lounging on the enormous beanbag chair in the corner. The 'goth unicorn' plushie had been an impulse buy near the register, but after one look at its big evil eyes and bloody fangs, I couldn't resist.

It has tattoos, for Chrissake.

To my relief, Zion shot me a wink before turning his attention back to where his daughter was tearing into the next bag on the canopy bed beside me.

Another joyful shriek blew out my eardrums as Daisy discovered her 'favoritest' set of shirts from today's haul.

Mine too, to be honest.

"DADDY—*LOOOOK!!!*" Her voice reached dog whistle territory as she held up a green ombré tee that said 'Lizard Queen' in silvery scaled letters. "And there's one for *you*, too!"

I cringed as she lobbed the larger shirt at her dad with impressive aim, bracing for his reaction. Zion was so damn hard to read sometimes, and I still wasn't sure if I'd overstepped by randomly dropping a couple grand on his kid.

And some notable change on him.

I hadn't intended to buy presents for my Deathball rival, but then I kept seeing things I knew he'd like. Thank fuck I'd had the sense to drop off a *certain bag* in my room before I tracked him down in the gym earlier. Otherwise, I would have been dying of embarrassment right now.

Even more than I already am…

"'Lizard King,' hmm?" Zion chuckled as he held the shirt open in front of him to read it. "Like Jim Morrison?"

"Who?" I frowned at the floor, trying to remember which supe went by that name while out of uniform.

His rumbling laugh washed over me like a drug. "It sounds like I need to teach you about classic rock, B. That's cool." Zion's voice turned sultry. "I'll teach you everything you need to know."

Oh, my goddd…

I swallowed hard as I dared to peek at him again. All traces of humor were gone. In its place was that confusingly hot, unblinking expression of his where he looked like he wanted to eat me alive.

Gulp.

When Zion stared me down like that, I felt about two feet tall and vulnerable as hell. Which, strangely, wasn't a bad thing.

My shapeshifting ability to bulk up had always been the pride of my parents—and a flex for my fans. But here I was, feeling some kind of way about the idea of *Zion Salah* overpowering me.

I'm baby…

"So, did Daddy tell you about movie night?" Daisy's voice snapped me out of my daze.

"I actually didn't get a chance yet, D," Zion replied, back to sweetly smiling, like he hadn't just threatened me with a woody. "Why don't *you* tell him?"

Daisy rolled her eyes at him in loving exasperation before grinning at me. "Okay, so Friday is movie night in this house. Well, at least with Dad and me. We used to do it with my mom, but… you know…"

Again, I did *not* know. But I also didn't want to show how desperate I was to learn everything about the woman Zion *loved* enough to risk his standing as heir to the throne.

I should just ask him.

Since Wolfy wants me to gather intel, anyway.

I tamped down the unease swirling in my guts and refocused on Daisy's excited babbling.

"… and since this is your first Salah movie night, *you* should pick what we watch!"

Uhhh…

I cleared my throat, suddenly flustered. "I'm, um, not sure if you would enjoy what I usually watch. Or if it would be… appropriate." When Zion's eyebrows shot up to his hairline, I hurriedly clarified, "I mean, *my* family watches a lot of bad action movies and musicals, and I like old… monster… flicks."

Zion's eyebrows stayed raised as his jaw dropped. "The infamous, villainous Suarez clan enjoys *musicals?!*" When I nodded, he grinned. "What are your favorites, B?"

I sighed, knowing I wasn't getting out of this. "*Young Frankenstein* and *The Toxic Avenger.*"

Please don't see a theme...

His lips curled wickedly. "And which *monster* is your favorite from the old B-movies?"

Just make something up, Baltasar.

"*Godzilla,*" I replied honestly, like the dummy I was.

You're just handing him ammunition.

Zion smiles so broadly, I swear, I heard his jaw crack. "You got a thing for big, handsome lizards, huh?"

I leaped to my feet so fast I knocked half the bags off the bed. "Yeah, none of those are probably okay for Daisy to watch, so—"

"Oh, we're watching *Godzilla,*" Zion chuckled low. "We're definitely watching that tonight."

I can't handle this right now.

It was bad enough that I'd abruptly ended my interview on SupeSports by Hulking out on their new commentator, Kyle Kyleson. While I didn't regret defending Zion to that asshole, I was dreading my next check-in with Wolfy and Simon.

Because I'm sure my on-air behavior was noted.

"Okay, then!" I replied, too cheerfully, and with a corny salute I had no business making. "I'm just gonna go get ready for dinner—"

"Are you eating with *us* tonight?" Daisy asked, her expression so hopeful my heart shattered.

I opened my mouth to reply when Zion answered for me. "No, D, he can't. Blunty is expected in the dining room, since Auntie Dahlia's in there."

Daisy scrunched her nose in distaste. "Why are you even marrying a meanie like Auntie Dahlia, Blunty? I'd rather you just be *my* second daddy instead."

OH, MY GODDD!!!

"I gotta go…" I mumbled, spinning on my heel and speed walking through the bedroom door.

This brought me into the living room, where I assumed movie night would happen later. Apparently, this was originally Zion's suite, but he'd given it to his daughter and moved into a smaller guest room further down the hall.

Probably to help her feel like she belonged.

"B, wait up." Zion was suddenly grabbing my arm before I reached the door to the main hallway—sending a jolt of *something* through me from the contact alone. "Don't worry about Daisy, seriously. It's fine if you need to eat in the dining room. I get it. It's tough when you're stuck between family loyalties…"

My breath caught as wave after wave of guilt washed over me. Not only was I expected to dig up dirt on the man currently comforting me, but I'd now fooled around with this man in his bed, while engaged to his sister.

And I'd do it again…

"I like pussy," I blurted out, for no reason other than making it weirder.

Zion blinked. "Yeah, I know. So do I. But I like cock more."

You do?

"But I... don't." I powered on, stubbornly determined to make whatever point I was trying to make. "I don't like cock at all."

The words tasted wrong on my tongue, but even worse was Zion's reaction. His expression shuttered, all friendliness replaced by cool detachment—leaving me feeling weirdly empty.

"Suit yourself." He shrugged as if he didn't care in the least. "I'm sure you're not at all interested in finding out how much I like cock."

You asshole.

Irrational anger washed over me. "You're just so fucking sure of yourself, huh, Salah?" I scowled, keeping my voice down so Daisy wouldn't hear us arguing from the other room. "You think you're such a cock wizard that you can land every straight guy you see? Is that it?"

Again, he blinked, his expression impassive. "Well, yeah. But I don't care about every straight guy—only the ones who aren't really straight. Like you."

I hissed through my teeth, recoiling from the hero as if he'd punched me. "Fuck you, Zion," I spat, turning away from him to wrench open the door.

"Mmm, I wish," he crooned behind me. "Whenever you're ready, beautiful."

With a growl, I stomped down the hall and grand staircase and didn't stop stomping until I reached my bedroom and slammed the door behind me. Every atom in my being was vibrating with rage—or something *close* to rage, but way closer to something I wasn't ready to examine. Not now, not ever.

Stupid Lizard King with his fucking lizard dick that's so stupid hot…

My internal rant fizzled out as my gaze fell on the obnoxiously bright yellow shopping bag I'd shoved beneath the bed before going to find Zion earlier.

While in the mall, I'd detoured into Tom, Dick & Harry's Sporting Goods. I needed to pick up a few pairs of gloves for practice, but on my way to the Deathball section, I passed through the Bat Blast aisle.

That's when I spotted the tape.

Bat Blast was like normie baseball, in the sense there was a bat and ball. The difference was that you were trying to hit the opposing players as they ran the zigzag line of bases with a ball that exploded on contact. Strength was a plus for playing this sport, but supes with deadly speed, accuracy, and precision were favored in the Games.

None of that was why I found myself standing in a Bat Blast aisle, staring at a display of Lizard Grip bat tape. Yes, it was the name that caught my eye at first, but what stopped me in my tracks was the *texture.* It looked and felt like smooth reptilian scales, and there was one with the exact same coloring as Zion's galaxy combo.

I hadn't allowed myself to think too hard about *why* I threw a roll of blue and purple Lizard Grip tape in my shopping basket before grabbing gloves. But now that I was back at the house—in the relative privacy of my throwaway guest room —I pulled the tape out of my bag and tentatively ran a finger over the Durasoft surface.

Fuuuuck.

What I *had* been thinking about nonstop was how incredible Zion's cock looked when I snuck a peek last night. While I mostly thanked my lucky stars he hadn't woken up to me touching him *there*, there was a not-so-small part of me that wished I'd at least gotten one good grope in.

I bet it feels just like this…

In 0.0001 seconds, I was as hard as a Bat Blast bat, which gave me an idea. A possibly dumb idea, but an idea nonetheless. An idea that—once it appeared in my head—refused to show itself out until I'd invited it to stay for a drink.

Imma wrap my dick in Lizard Grip.

And why shouldn't I? The packaging promised an 'even thinner grip' that felt as if 'nothing stood between you and your weapon.' The 'super slip-resistance in both wet and dry conditions' also caught my attention. Before I knew it, I'd cranked up my super speed to rip open the plastic and give myself a lizard dick.

Look. At. That.

For a few moments, I just stared at my creation. There were no rocket pop ridges, but the tape had gone on so smoothly that, from the base of my cock to the top of my foreskin, my skin looked exactly like Zion's.

The material was so thin, I could *see* my veins throbbing beneath the scaled pattern, inviting me to touch—to pretend this part of me belonged to someone else.

You know you want to, Baltasar…

Before I could think better of it, I wrapped my hand around my dick and gave myself a single stroke. And with a groan that sounded like I was in agony, I instantly came all over myself.

Holy fuckfuckfuuuuck.

My breath felt like it had been punched from my lungs. Hunched over my mess, I gulped in air to stop myself from passing out. I willed my head to stop spinning and my eyes to stop crossing, and for my shaking hand to unclench itself from my now oversensitive, scaly shaft.

I need to lie down.

Unfortunately, this house of psychos had other plans. Cook's dinner gong suddenly echoed through the halls—making me scramble to get myself cleaned up and changed before I was late.

I didn't have time to remove the tape, so simply tucked myself in and zipped up, deciding I'd deal with it after I ate.

Since I'll want to change into something comfy for movie night, anyway.

The realization that I had every intention of joining Zion and Daisy for their weekly family tradition made me feel all weird and warm inside. Never mind that Z had pissed me off by calling my bluff—I still wanted to cuddle with him on the couch.

With DAISY, I mean.

Zion can just sit at the other end.

With a sigh, I took one last look at my reflection in the mirror. I straightened my spine, preparing to spend the next hour with the people I *had* to be around before joining the people I *wanted* to be with.

CHAPTER 16
BALTASAR

My phone buzzed in my sweatpants pocket—uncomfortably vibrating against the Lizard Grip tape I'd been *unable* to remove after dinner.

Maybe I can steal some vegetable oil without Cook noticing...

Pulling out my phone, I grimaced to find a direct text from **The Mafia Queen** with nothing but a lizard emoji and a hand pointing to a watch.

Tick-tock, Baby Hulk.

I banished Simon's impatient voice from my mind and peered down to find Daisy had fallen asleep curled up against my ribs. Assuming Zion's eyes were still glued to *Godzilla Raids Again,* I quickly glanced toward the other end of the couch.

My breath caught in my throat to find him watching *me.* He didn't look away or attempt to hide the fact he was sizing me up. Except, instead of his usual emotionless predatory expression, a soft smile played on his full lips.

FULL lips?

"She fell asleep on me," I loudly whispered—not knowing what else to say.

Zion's smile morphed into an amused grin as he gracefully stood and walked closer. "Yup. She must really trust you... *second daddy.*"

I scoffed as he gently lifted his daughter and half-slung her sleeping form over his shoulder. "Gimme a break. I wouldn't know the first thing about being a dad."

He gave me an odd look. "I dunno, B. You figure it out as you go. That's what I did..."

I silently watched as he turned and carried Daisy into her bedroom, tamping down the overwhelming urge to follow him in and help.

He doesn't need your help, Baltasar.

While I no longer thought Zion was going to eat me for touching his kid, I still didn't understand why he was so cool with me hanging around for all this domestic shit.

Especially when she has a mother out there somewhere...

"Where's Daisy's mom?" I blurted out the instant Zion reappeared.

Real smooth, Baltasar.

He froze mid-step before quietly shutting the door behind him and joining me on the couch. Instead of taking his seat on the far end again, he sat right beside me—so close our thighs touched.

"Mikki died," he barely whispered, his dark brown eyes fixed on his hands, folded in his lap. "Cancer. There was nothing anyone could do."

Nothing he *could do.*

Tears filled *my* eyes, even though I had absolutely no frame of reference. Supes didn't get cancer or other normie illnesses.

While we died of old age eventually, the most common cause of death was murder—either on or off the battlefield.

When my mother, Glacial Girl, was defeated by Vortexio, and then finally killed for good, I only felt acceptance and relief. But now, I imagined Zion having to tell Daisy her mom was gone—while dealing with his own grief—and suddenly, my lips were on his.

This wasn't the out-of-body experience from earlier, where I was so lust-drunk I tried to suck his tongue down my throat. This time, I was licking, nibbling, and kissing Zion's *very full lips* with a startlingly aware, single-minded purpose that rivaled my focus on the field.

"What are you doing, B?" Zion murmured against my mouth, and for a moment, I worried I'd overstepped again.

The mixed signals I've been sending him probably don't help.

"I don't like you being sad," I replied, which—while not exactly answering his question—was also the truth.

My protective instincts had kicked in when that nosey SupeSports commentator tried to pry about Zion's business. And here it was, happening again. I had no idea if slobbering into his mouth was comforting or not, but I wanted to erase every ounce of pain this hero had ever felt.

And finding the right words is hard.

"How are you so sweet *and* so fucking sexy?" he growled. Effortlessly hauling me into his lap—he instantly erased my concern while demonstrating how much bigger than me he was in human form.

As if I wasn't already rock-hard...

Straddling his muscular thighs, I placed my hands on the back of the couch and began mindlessly thrusting my faux lizard dick against his real one. Some small part of me wondered if this changed things, but I decided it wasn't a big deal.

We have a few layers of clothing between us.

And the grip tape.

Zion hummed against my mouth as he returned my kiss, slowing my intensity by languidly stroking my tongue with his—lulling me into a trance.

Then he bit my lip so hard it drew blood.

"Fuck!" I gasped, although it came out sounding like a groan. I had to actually jam the heel of my hand against my cock to stop a repeat of the fastest O ever.

He chuckled as he pulled back to look at me, flashing the fangs responsible for the growing wet spot on my sweats. "I knew it. You like a little pain in the bedroom, huh?"

"I-I don't know," I admitted, unable to tear my eyes away from the smear of blood on his lower lip. I'd never dared ask for pain during sex before, but when I got hurt on the field, my cock noticed.

Especially when the pain was delivered by Scaled Justice.

I instinctively tilted my head to the side, not even sure what I was asking for, but knowing I needed it desperately.

Please...

Zion's gaze snapped to my neck, his eyes fully reptilian and a hunger in his expression that should have had me fearing for my life. With a rumbling purr, he curled over me, running his fangs over my jugular vein as my hips moved again of their own accord.

Please, please, please.

"You want it so bad, don't you, beautiful?" Zion's breath tickled my sweaty skin as his hands drifted down to cup my ass and grind me harder against him. "You want to ride my cock while I mate you…"

Yes.

"I don't know," I insisted, although the ragged tone of my voice told a different—more accurate—story.

Yes, I want to ride your cock while you mate me.

Whatever the fuck that means, I'm in.

Just like the last time I acted unsure, Zion immediately stopped and pulled away, holding up his hands so he was no longer touching me. His fangs disappeared, and he swallowed hard—his gaze flickering to my neck, looking *nervous* about what he'd almost done.

Is he not able to fully control his 'beast?'

WHY IS THAT SO HOT?!

"Please… don't stop. I want it." The whimper that followed was the most humiliating sound I'd ever made, but I no longer gave any fucks. "I need…"

I struggled to articulate *what* I needed, but I knew I trusted Zion to give it to me.

His lips curled in a cocky smile as his hands lowered to the waistband of my sweatpants. "I love how needy you are. Do you want my hands on you? Want me to play with that big cock of yours?"

"Yes!" I blurted out before immediately panicking. "Wait!" Again, he froze, and I wished I had the power to teleport myself under the nearest rock. "There's, um… there's a… problem."

Why am I such a mess?

Zion eased his palms to rest on the tops of my thighs—not in a sexual way, but as if to show me he was there.

Ready to witness my train wreck.

"Is it you being engaged to my sister or that you're not gay?" he deadpanned. "Because I'm already aware of those problems."

"Neither," I huffed, realizing those 'problems' hadn't even crossed my mind in the last twenty minutes. "It's more that I… accidentally… Well, it wasn't an accident, but I…" I hung my head. "There's a problem with my dick."

As expected, silence was Zion's only response.

I peeked up at him through my eyelashes to find the hero fighting a smile. "I disagree, Baltasar. Now that I've had the pleasure of seeing your dick, I can tell you it's perfect." His gaze fell to my crotch. "And right now, it still looks like it's ready to go."

"It is! I mean, I am," I stuttered, knowing I was beet red and getting redder. After more silence followed, I sighed, knowing I'd never hear the end of this. "I'll show you the problem, but only if… if you…"

If you promise not to laugh at me.

To my surprise, his finger was suddenly under my chin, forcing me to look at him. "I promise, I won't laugh at you," he solemnly spoke, as serious as I'd ever seen him. "Show me what's going on, beautiful, so I can help."

All my pent-up tension bled out of me. I took a deep breath and nodded rapidly, before reaching into my sweats and pulled out my throbbing, tape-covered cock.

Ta-daaa…

Zion's fist pressed to his mouth—more out of shock than to hide a smile. "What…" was all he said.

Sigh.

"It's Bat Blast Lizard Grip tape," I mumbled, not understanding why my artificially scaled dick was still hard in the face of humiliation. "I saw it when I stopped at Tom, Dick & Harry's, and then… after our fight earlier, I randomly decided to…"

I cringed, because I'd now made this nightmare situation worse by referencing 'our fight'—as if we were some sort of couple.

This would probably be easier if we were.

Then he'd be used to my shit.

"… you decided to make your dick look like mine," Zion seamlessly completed my sentence, which seemed like a very coupley thing to do.

He's already used to my shit, apparently.

"Yeah," I admitted, chewing my lip as I awaited the explosion of laughter. "And now I can't get it off." *Even though I definitely got off.* I sighed again. Defeated. "I just wanted to know what it felt like."

Might as well just overshare at this point.

Zion's gaze snapped to mine, and I noticed he was back to smirking—although it felt like a good thing. "You want to know how my lizard dick feels, huh?" Maintaining eye contact, he pulled himself out of his sweatpants. "Let me show you…"

Yessss….

I zeroed in on Zion's hand as it stroked his cock—which he'd shifted into galaxy-scale mode, just for me—and had to clench my fists to stop from taking over.

Taking over?!

Another pathetic whimper escaped me as I nudged my cock against his hand, like the needy slut I apparently was.

I'm just gonna own this dumpster fire.

Again, he chuckled. And again, it made me *more* comfortable instead of less. "Good idea. Let's compare." Zion moved his hand to my cock, giving me a firm pull that almost made me insta-blow.

Fuck, yessss…

At this moment, I absolutely did *not* care that I was engaged to someone else or that my dick was embarrassingly covered in an adhesive lizard finish. Right now, the only thing that mattered—that existed—was Zion Salah's enormous hand stroking my needy, possibly gay, cock.

Okay, my cock is definitely gay.

For him.

"Mmm… it's too close to call," he hummed as he removed his hand, much to my dismay. "Should we see how they feel together?"

Together?

"Together?" I mumbled absently, my gaze still longingly fixed on his hand.

"Yeah." His voice had gone low—soothing and inviting all at once. "I suggest you hold on to something, B, because I'm about to blow your mind."

I obeyed without question, moving my hands from the back of the couch to his broad shoulders.

It should have felt weird to be holding on to someone even more built than me—to be riding him while he jerked me off. But my body no longer saw any problem with what was happening.

My mind, however, was indeed blown when I watched Zion grab *both* our cocks and began stroking them as one.

"Holy *fuck,*" I gasped, practically dislocating his shoulders in my frantic attempt to not fall off the couch. "Holy fucking hell, *thatfeelssofuckinggood…*"

"Oh, you like that?" he purred, licking his lips as I began to thrust again. "Show me how much you like it."

I barely needed his encouragement. I dropped my forehead to the back of the couch and fucked Zion's fist like I was going for the gold at the Supremacy Games.

The texture of his smooth scales and hard ridges rubbing against my overly sensitive shaft made me see stars. It was all I could do not to think too hard about these same features inside me—'hammering over my prostate.'

Don't blow like a teenager… don't blow like a teenager.

The ache in my chest was back, and the sounds coming out of me were the neediest ones yet, but Zion praised me the entire time. He told me how beautiful I was… what a good job I was doing… how my cock felt so good against his, and how he couldn't wait to *fuck me* like the needy little cockslut I was…

OHMYFUCKINGGGGAWWWD!!!

My vision whited out as I came—until all I could see was a vision of me bent over for this man. Willingly. The *Godzilla* movie was roaring in the background, but the last thing I wanted to do was wake up Daisy—or the entire house—with my moans. So I did the only logical thing.

I sunk my teeth into Zion's neck.

"Fuuuuck," he choked out, arching beneath me—every delicious muscle straining with effort—as he joined me in release.

Luckily, my focus returned in time for me to watch him blow. And since *his* eyes were closed, I could openly stare as thick ropes of cum shot out of his gorgeous cock to cover us both.

I wonder what he tastes like…

I really want to know.

For a full minute afterward, we both simply panted and lazily thrust through our collective mess. Even with how sensitive I was, I wanted to keep this feeling going until it became too much—and maybe not stop even then.

This is what I want.

The clarity of that realization was immediately chased by a dose of reality—making me tense. I *had* to tell Wolfy about Zion now, as this was no longer just a one-time lapse of judgment.

I want to do this again.

With him.

"I'm…" I began, unsure where to even start with all the thoughts racing through my brain.

"Not gay. I know." Zion's voice was so shockingly cold it felt like whiplash. "But thank you for a most enjoyable evening, regardless."

What the actual fuck?

"Now." He smirked and brandished a claw. "Let me help you destroy the evidence."

I nodded, too stunned to do anything but mutely watch as he neatly sliced through the cum-covered tape surrounding my softening cock.

Part of me was actually sad to say goodbye to my makeshift lizard dick—even with how much trouble it had caused me. Mostly, I was annoyed that Zion seemed fine with pretending my entire existence hadn't just tilted on its axis. And that he'd somehow avoided drawing even the tiniest bit of blood with his claws.

Rude.

"Thanks," I muttered, peeling the tape off with a wince before hurriedly stuffing my dick back in my pants. "And yeah... thanks for the other stuff, too."

Thanks for making it weird.

Then I spun on my heel and strode from the room—too angry and confused to say anything else. The worst part was that I desperately *wanted* to stay. But I knew I'd just end up pathetically crawling back into Zion's lap, as if that was where I belonged.

And he made it crystal clear I don't.

I still wasn't entirely sure what this was for me, but it was obviously just a casual hookup for him. And if there was one thing I had plenty of experience with, it was how to behave like a fuckboy. Never mind that I wasn't feeling like I usually did after a hookup—satisfied and already forgetting their name—I was more than able to match Zion's energy.

If it's distance he wants, that's what I'll give him.

CHAPTER 17
ZION

Baltasar was acting weird.

More than usual, anyway.

It bummed me out since I enjoyed his signature sauce, but whatever was going on with the villain lately was confusing. He was still lavishing attention on Daisy—and eating meals with her when he could—but his interactions with *me* had been weirdly aloof.

Obviously, it had something to do with our hot as fuck play-time on movie night, but I couldn't figure out where something had gone wrong.

It couldn't have been his adorable grip tape situation.

Because that only made it hotter.

Sure, maybe I should have checked in with him more after-ward—since it *was* his first frotting. But the last thing I wanted to do was let a notorious playboy like Baltasar know just how into the situation I was by showering him in aftercare.

How into him *I am.*

Because the actual issue went deeper than him being engaged to Dahlia or fumbling his way through a bi-awakening. I didn't see either of those 'problems' as problems at all, or good enough reasons to stop.

Not unless he wants to.

The true line in the sand here was that Baltasar Suarez had been my number one crush since day one. Meanwhile, *he* was clearly just using me to get some shit out of his system before the wedding.

I still need to stop that wedding from happening.

It wasn't only that I wanted the villain for myself. There was clearly something shady going on in this family. Something that *needed* to be addressed before my younger—possibly scheming—sister married into a rival clan.

The conversation I'd overheard between Dahlia and Preek had been replaying in my mind for days. Normally, I would have gone straight to my parents—and let natural selection play itself out. But it sounded like *they* were the ones behind whatever was happening at this mysterious lab, so that wasn't an option.

It wasn't as if Major Obscurity and Lady Tempest had to tell me everything about the family business. Not at this stage, and not if they still believed I had no intention of claiming my birthright. But it was clear my sister had an ace up her sleeve, and a marriage to a Suarez would only give her more power.

If I was going to swoop in and steal Dahlia's fiancé—while taking over this clan—I needed to do it in the most *heroic* way possible.

Exposing a scandal ought to do it.

But who can I trust?

I used to be close with a couple of my brothers, but the way everyone sided with my parents against Mikki soured those relationships real quick.

I'd debated letting Baltasar in on what I knew. At the very least, it would add to his obvious dislike for my sister. The best-case scenario would be him immediately confessing his reciprocal feelings. He would agree to be my mate—Daisy's 'second daddy'—and join me in taking the throne in a scandal-soaked coup.

A guy can dream.

Unfortunately, I was currently stuck watching Baltasar pose for engagement photos on the great lawn with Dahlia. It was all I could do to keep my expression neutral, even as I imagined knocking the smug smile off my sister's face with my croquet mallet.

Because on Sundays, we play croquet.

Both wore head-covering masks to shield their identities, but instead of full uniforms, they were wearing their Sunday best.

Dahlia had chosen a tea-length dress that shone blindingly white against her skin—every inch of her flawless, as usual. Baltasar looked… nice, in a bland kind of way. Despite insisting on buying Daisy *non*-prepster gear, he must have picked up new clothes for himself during his recent shopping spree. I would have bet every penny I had he hadn't arrived at Chez Salah with a white polo shirt and white khakis in his luggage.

Dude looks like an orderly at an asylum.

Accurate, considering where he's currently living.

"I don't want Bluntycups to marry Auntie Dahlia." Daisy's voice snapped me out of my thoughts, reminding me she was watching this shit show along with me.

143

The rest of the family was barely paying attention—too busy gabbing and gossiping while we waited to play. Daisy alone was keeping me company while digging a hole in the perfect turf with her flamingo-shaped mallet.

Keep digging, sweetie.

Daddy might need to bury some bodies.

"You know how this family operates, D." I sighed, deciding it was probably best to keep my daughter ignorant of my murderous fantasies. "It's how all supe families operate—"

"Not Blunty's family," she interrupted, matter-of-factly. "This is the first arranged marriage the Suarez clan has done in the history of *ever*."

My brow furrowed. Arranged Supe marriages were a somewhat recent phenomenon, but if anyone understood the benefit of advantageous alliances, it was the scheming Suarez clan.

Then again, Apocalypto Man and Glacial Girl were already a match made in hell.

"How do you even know that?" I murmured in reply—distracted. The photographer had shooed my parents away, and jealousy simmered beneath the surface as I watched him focus on Dahlia and Baltasar alone.

Daisy scoffed, and I didn't have to look at her to know she was rolling her eyes. "It's public record on the USN's website, Daddy, along with basic birth registrations for powerful supes…"

Her voice trailed off, making my heart sink as I turned to face her. "Sweetie, I've told you—it's for the best if other supes don't know about you. Without powers, you're…"

You're vulnerable.

And I can't lose you, too.

She lifted her chin and nodded once, putting on her brave face for me, as always. I knew she wished she had powers—wanted to show this family what she was made of. I'd gently explained that if these abilities hadn't manifested by now, it was probably safe to say they weren't happening.

I'll protect you no matter what.

As my gaze drifted back to the action, my eyes narrowed. The photographer had maneuvered Baltasar until he was standing behind Dahlia with his hands placed on her lower belly—like a prom photo.

Or... a baby announcement.

The idea of Baltasar putting his cock anywhere near someone else—mating and reproducing with them—had me releasing a low growl before I could stop myself.

"You don't want Blunty marrying her either," Daisy stated the obvious, although how she'd figured it out was beyond me. "You want him for yourself. For *us.*"

Goddamnit, Daisy.

I quickly glanced around to make sure no one had heard her —shockingly accurate—observation. "That's not how it works, D. I can't just... take what I want."

"Why not?" She jutted out a hip as she continued relentlessly. "This is *your* house, isn't it, Daddy?"

I sharply inhaled, but stood a little straighter at her words. Daisy wasn't talking about the gloomy mansion behind us. She meant this clan—my birthright as heir to the throne. Like the little queen she was, she saw no reason everything in our sphere wasn't mine to claim.

For being powerless, she sure behaves like a purebred supe.

Now Dahlia was facing Baltasar, cupping his handsome face in her hands, playing the part of the adoring wife-to-be.

Another growl slipped through—louder this time—and Baltasar's gaze snapped to mine. While he'd been all smiles during these bullshit photos, he couldn't disguise the pure fury in his pretty eyes at my interruption.

That's interesting.

What's gotten your jockstrap in a bunch, beautiful?

"Eye on the prize, Suarez!" I called out. "And in case you need the reminder, that's my sister—not me!"

"Fuck you, *Justice*," Baltasar growled, his muscles rippling—polo seams straining—as his body fought to shift.

He's so cute when he's mad.

"You wish, *Blunt Force*," I cackled. Then I turned to the photographer, who was, unsurprisingly, watching this exchange with interest. "I bet the media would be way more interested in shots of infamous Deathball rivals together, don't you think? Especially with the Games coming up."

Especially SNZ.

"That's not…" The poor photographer's gaze darted to my scowling parents. "I was hired to—"

"I'll double whatever you're being paid," I interrupted. "Triple it."

"No thanks. I'm good," Baltasar stiffly replied—looking everywhere except at me—but I was determined.

"I just really want a memento of Blunt Force to remember him by." I paused long enough for the object of my obsession to make eye contact again. "Something to keep me warm at night after he marries Atmosphera."

Dahlia huffed and threw her hands in the air. "Ugh. I'm done. If those two idiots want photos together, God bless 'em." She then stomped over to join our parents before herding them and the others toward the wickets. "Let's play croquet. I have the sudden urge to violently crack some balls across the turf."

Girl, bye.

Pulling the mask I used while in human form out of my pocket, I slipped it on before joining Baltasar. The photographer had signed an NDA, but I still didn't want to risk anything leaking that could compromise my—or my daughter's—identity.

I just want to get some ridiculous photos with my unrequited crush.

Even though what I'd prefer is a butt-ass-naked dude-oir session.

"Okay." I positioned myself behind Baltasar, to mimic the cheesy prom pose he'd already done, before calling to the photographer. "So... I don't want to be too heavy-handed with the art direction, but if you could make these as sexy as possible, I'd appreciate it. I just need something to jerk off to later."

"What the *HELL*, Z?!" Baltasar roared, although when he twisted to glare at me over his shoulder, his expression was more alarmed than angry.

It's a start.

"What's the matter, beautiful?" I purred in his ear, too low for the photographer to hear. "Worried someone's gonna see how hot you are for me?"

I wheezed as he elbowed me in the ribs—way harder than was necessary—before spinning to face me. "I'm not *anything* for you. I don't know where you got the idea I'm here for you to fuck with..."

Wait a minute.

Is he… blaming me for making him do 'gay' shit?

"Fuck with or just *fuck?*" I growled as my beast began taking over. "Because I think I know which one you'd prefer."

The dreamy, deliciously submissive look Baltasar had shown as I half-shifted disappeared. His gaze snapped to focus with the same startling intensity I saw in the Games—like I was the enemy.

"The *fuck* did you just say to me?" he hissed. "You don't know shit, Zion."

So much big talk when we both know what you want.

I curled over him, loving how he *still* wasn't shifting to match me in size. "What I'm trying to say is..." I hovered my lips centimeters away from his. "Let's fuck."

With a wounded sound, Baltasar pulled back and punched me in the face.

WHAT THE FUCK?!

I was so shocked, I simply let him take me to the ground and start pummeling. "Stop treating me like a toy for your own fucking amusement, Zion!"

Excuse me?!

My rage exploded at how hypocritical this fool was—especially as *he* was the one who kept coming all over me and then insisting he didn't like cock. If Baltasar Suarez thought I enjoyed spending my time pining after closeted sad bi-bois while they got their rocks off, he didn't know me at all.

"You're one to talk, asshole," I hissed, flipping him onto his back and pinning his hands to the ground so he'd stop punching me. His accusations were laughable, especially when *he* was clearly the one using me...

Unless...

Despite his anger, Baltasar *still* wasn't shifting and throwing me off. Instead, he shuddered, staring up at me with a glazed expression as his hot muscles went limp and his body surrendered to me.

Just like he always did on the field when I got the upper hand.

"I'm not..." he choked out—way more upset than this trash-talk session should have made him. "I'm not just some dumb piece of meat for you to play with."

Oh, beautiful...

Before I could offer reassurances—or kiss him senseless, the current audience be damned—I was being yanked off of him by my father. I opened my mouth to argue, but then Dahlia was drowning me out with protests about damaging her fiancé's face before the wedding.

Priorities.

All I wanted was to be alone with Baltasar—to fix my mistake and cuddle the fuck out of him—so I stupidly fought against my dad's hold, even though I damn well knew better. To make things worse, *Lady Tempest* chose that moment to roughly haul the villain to his feet, and my beast did *not* like how she was handling my mate.

Must protect what's mine.

"GET YOUR HANDS OFF HIM!" I boomed, the sound of my fury echoing off the surrounding woods.

Both my parents froze. Dahlia stopped ranting. The photographer slunk away. And the rest of my siblings paused their gameplay long enough to gawk—as if croquet-related brawls were not a common occurrence in this family.

Isaiah has a wicket-shaped scar on his back to prove it.

Pops looked ready for nuclear detonation at this point. "I'm not sure what the *hell* is the issue between you boys, but we're going to my office to talk about it—now!"

"It's just old Deathball bullshit... sir." Baltasar tried to sweet talk my dad, even as he glared daggers at me.

Fuck, I'm sorry, B.

Let me make it up to you.

"Oh, I don't think this is Deathball-related at all," my mom snarled as she began dragging the much larger villain toward the main house. "But I have a fairly good idea what it's about."

I gulped as my dad followed suit, hauling me after them as I prayed my parents wouldn't immediately call off the wedding and send Baltasar away.

Not before I can make things right.

CHAPTER 18
ZION

Sitting in Pops' office always felt like being called to the principal, but with *my mate* sitting in the matching leather chair beside me, I was on extra high alert.

What if they separate us?

As usual, my dad was sitting behind his enormous black cherry desk, with Mom standing behind him. Baltasar was bravely maintaining eye contact with our patriarch, but I knew which supe was actually the one in charge here.

"I don't think it needs to be said that both of you behaved horribly in front of our guest." My mom spoke in a voice so ice-cold, my soul shivered.

Reputation was everything to this family. Even though the only outside witness to our tussle was some random photographer, that was enough to bring shame on our household for generations to come.

"And while I have my theories about what is truly behind this feud," she continued, making me tense, "it feels more pertinent to share a secret of my own."

That caught my attention. The Salah way was to play all cards close to the chest, so if my mom was sharing any intel, it was in *her* best interest to do so. Straightening my spine, I braced myself for whatever blow she was about to deliver.

Because it won't be kind.

"We didn't *have* to accept this marriage contract with the Suarez clan."

Baltasar gaped at her in astonishment. "You didn't?"

This is news to me too, B.

"No," she bluntly replied. "We'd already reached an… understanding with your brother, and signed off on the terms of our business partnership. Agreeing to *welcome you* into our clan was more a show of good faith than a strategic move. After all, Blunt Force…" She chuckled derisively, raising my hackles. "Let's not forget—you are fourth in line with only marginally impressive powers to speak of."

How dare she?!

I growled at the slight, and her attention snapped to me with a sickeningly smug expression. "That will be all," she coolly dismissed the visibly deflated villain. "Now I would like a word alone with my son."

Fuck.

Pops knew the drill. He stood and escorted Baltasar from the room, no doubt ready to deliver his famous post-dressing down pep talk. This included mild threats, empty platitudes, and the legitimately solid advice that *'sometimes, in life, you had to eat shit.'*

As soon as the door clicked shut behind me, the tension in the room ratcheted up to level eleven. And—true to form—the indomitable Lady Tempest calmly let the minutes tick by as we stared each other down.

The only saving grace was that my mate was out of immediate danger, which meant I only had the opponent across from me to worry about.

This I can handle.

My chest was *aching* with worry over whether Baltasar was about to be shipped back across the country. But I'd learned early on to never let another supe see you sweat.

Even your own family.

Especially your own family.

Once my mom was satisfied I wouldn't embarrass her by squirming in the hot seat, she spoke again. "Marrying Baltasar does not give Dahlia rights to the throne, you know."

Huh?

"What?" I blurted out, blindsided by her words. I'd been expecting her to call me out on my painfully obvious attraction to my sister's fiancé—possibly punished for it—so this was unexpected.

"I meant what I said, Zion," she continued—her expression giving nothing away. "Accepting the marriage contract from the Suarez clan was nothing more than an act of goodwill. Well, that and your father and I had hoped someone as even-keeled as Baltasar might… mellow out Dahlia a bit."

Good luck with that.

"Why are you reassuring me of my standing in this family?" I kept my expression unreadable as I tried to determine her angle. "I thought I'd already lost the throne when I *associated* with a normie."

My mother scoffed. "This isn't reassurance, Zion. It's a reminder. The throne is yours to lose, and lose it you will, if you don't start acting like a Salah."

That's it!

"And what does that mean, exactly?" I snapped. "Because the rules here seem to change by the day. Or does it simply depend on which powerful family waves a juicy marriage contract under your noses—no matter how *different* from us they are?"

Lady Tempest's deep brown eyes flashed electric blue, but I wasn't finished. "You act as if it were charity to accept Baltasar Suarez as Dahlia's husband, but she'd be *lucky* to have him. That man, that entire family, has superior genes—is superior to our clan in every way—and you and Pops *know* it."

To my surprise, she didn't explode, or slap me upside the head with a violent gust of wind. Instead, my mom's lips curled in a wicked smile before a raspy laugh bubbled up from her throat.

"Yes, the Suarez clan truly staked their claim as *superior* when all-powerful Wolfgang was born, followed by that puppet, Violentia." Her expression turned sly. "But our family knew something they didn't—something about our kind that could finally help us take back what's rightfully ours."

Um, what?

I would've already tuned her out—since dramatic monologuing was standard with my parents' generation—but, thanks to what I'd overheard between Dahlia and Preek, alarm bells were going off. The problem was, I didn't yet know how the secret lab fit into whatever scheme my parents were involved in.

So I'm gonna play my cards close.

"Okaaaay..." I shrugged, playing up my confusion. "Welp. Feel free to fill in the heir to your throne with whatever you know whenever you're ready."

Again, a sinister smile played on her lips. "Oh, we will. As soon as you show us that *you're* ready to fulfill your destiny."

Well, that's not ominous or anything...

I clapped my hands and stood, more than ready to get the fuck out of this suffocating room. "Assuming we're done here, I'm gonna go get cleaned up and then find Baltasar so I can apologize. You know... for the sake of goodwill and all."

That was the truth, even if my reasoning was less about saving face for my parents and more about sucking face with my mate.

Maybe I should grovel a bit too.

Give him a blowjob to apologize...

My mom nodded, although she tracked my movements like a predator as I backed out of the room.

"The throne is yours to lose, and lose it you will if you don't start acting like a Salah."

No pressure...

I cranked up my super speed to reach Baltasar's room in the farthest wing of the house, terrified I was going to get there and find him and his bags long gone.

Bursting through his door, I practically fell over in relief to find him pacing the room with his phone pressed to his ear.

"Jesus, Zion! Are you allergic to knocking?" His annoyed expression turned to concern as he looked me over—as if checking for injuries.

He totally has a crush on me.

I picked up Wolfgang's voice on the line, telling his brother to 'play nice' before Baltasar muttered his goodbyes and hung up.

You have no idea how nicely we play, Hand of Death.

Baltasar slid his phone into the pocket of his ridiculous—and now grass-stained—white pants before crossing his arms over his chest. "What do you—"

"I'm sorry," I blurted out, dying to touch him but trying to rein in my intensity. "I was a total dick earlier."

I hated seeing you with Dahlia.

And I want you to be mine instead.

His eyes widened in shock, clearly not expecting me to own up to my shit. "All right, um, apology accepted."

"Let me take you out tonight," I powered on, *needing* things to be okay between us. Needing to be close to him.

Baltasar grimaced, awkwardly shifting on his feet and dropping his gaze. "I don't think that's such a good idea."

Nononono…

"Since I'm already on thin ice with your parents and should be *thankful* for this opportunity…" he continued.

I growled, which snapped his gaze back to mine. It didn't take a rocket scientist to guess Wolfgang had just given him his third scolding of the past twenty minutes—reminding his brother why he was here.

Although…

Why would Wolfgang offer this marriage contract, if it supposedly wasn't necessary?

Baltasar lifted his chin in the cutest show of defiance. "And I don't want to do anything *stupid* that will risk fucking this up."

Okay, I deserved that.

I'm still not gonna back off, though.

Consent was important to me, but Baltasar clearly struggled with articulation. I'd started to suspect the villain was often saying no—or *I don't know*—when he really meant he needed extra time to process.

We need to get this man a safe word.

"Understood." I grinned, turning up the charm as an evil plan started brewing. "How 'bout we do some dude stuff—something a couple of bros would choose for a night out on the town?"

He chewed his tasty bottom lip. "That could work..."

Gotcha.

"Perfect!" My smile grew, only now it was genuine. "Get cleaned up and changed and I'll meet you in the kitchen for a quick bite before we head out." When he looked unsure, I added, "Trust me, no one is expecting you to show your face in the dining room after what happened. We've *all* been there in this house."

A small smile twitched his lips, making my heart go pitter-patter. "Okay, I'm in. But no tricks! After what a dick you were, I deserve to relax."

I snickered. "Well, we ain't going to the spa, but I guarantee—you'll like what I have in mind for you."

CHAPTER 19
ZION

"You brought me to a titty bar?" Baltasar asked, peering through the windshield of my limited edition Challenger at the hot pink neon sign flickering above us.

I snorted. "Yes, B, as a fellow Deathball champion, the strip club is like a second home to me."

He continued staring out the windshield with an unreadable expression. For a moment, I wondered if my sweet little villain had never been exposed to such a *scandalous* place.

I'll gladly debauch you, baby boy.

"Last I checked, the only Deathball champion in this car is me," he finally replied, casual as hell.

Oh, no you didn't!

"Watch your mouth, Suarez," I growled, even as a smile twitched my lips—more than happy to get back to our comfortable, cocky banter. "I could always come out of retirement and make you chase me on the field again next month."

"I wish you would," he spoke so quietly, I wondered if he meant to say it out loud. Then he cleared his throat and directly addressed me, "Why *did* you retire, Z? You're not *that* old."

Gee, thanks.

I considered how to reply. No one outside of the press had ever asked me why I retired—and no way in hell was I giving those vultures the truth—but this villain invited honesty.

And it might be time to let someone in again.

"Well, life kept kicking my ass these past few months and I just..." My gaze drifted away from him as our proximity in the front seat suddenly felt a bit too intimate. "I just couldn't take one more thing."

"What was the last straw?" Baltasar continued.

Okay, nope. Not going there.

"I can't remember," I lied, even though I knew exactly what finally broke me.

"Was it... Mikki dying?" he hesitantly asked, as dogged as he was on the field.

It was such a rarity for anyone else to even say her name that, for a moment, I was rendered speechless. A weight was lifted from my chest, even as everything I'd carried combined into one tangled, sticky mess of emotions. Overwhelming grief and fury at my family warred with the astonishment that someone cared enough to simply ask how I was handling Mikki's death.

Lock it down, Zion.

"Fuck... it's none of my business," Baltasar muttered, blushing profusely as he squirmed in his seat. "Just ignore me—"

"No, it's cool." I forced a smile, wanting to put him at ease. "It's definitely leverage my family wouldn't want you to have..." He flinched at the implication, so I doubled down on the reassurances. "But I *like* you knowing my dirty little secrets."

I want you to know me.

He gnawed on his bottom lip, his expression troubled. "I don't get what the big deal was with the whole thing. Did you really upset your parents so badly just by shacking up with a... *villain?*"

I smirked—not only because my actual villain was so off base, but because he sounded way more invested in my love life than he probably meant to.

"Nope." I laughed, deciding there was no harm in giving him more intel. "She was a *normie*, actually."

Oops, secrets out!

"Daisy is half-supe and half-normie?!" Baltasar exclaimed.

"Yes..." I replied, wondering why he was fixating on that aspect of the big reveal. "It wasn't planned. Hell, I didn't even know supes and normies *could* reproduce... since we're so different and all."

He was staring at me with a pinched expression—like he was dying to say something but just barely holding it in.

This man has no poker face.

"Just ask, B," I chuckled. "I know you want to—"

"Were you in love with her?"

Yet again, Baltasar Suarez caught me by surprise. I'd assumed he was going to have a question about lizard-dick mechanics, but here he was, curious about how committed I was to my last relationship.

He is nothing like I expected.

He's even better.

"I was," I thoughtfully replied. "It's hard not to care deeply about the person who carried—and co-parented—your child. Our first few years were rocky. We were both so young, and my family were absolute assholes about the whole thing, but we eventually found a groove that worked for us. I don't actually know much about supes like me..." I licked my lips, feeling suddenly vulnerable. "But I would describe my connection to Mikki as similar to a... mating bond."

Minus the bite, to seal the deal.

Baltasar sharply inhaled and looked away. "That makes sense. I mean, because you're... you must need that kind of thing. And she could make babies for you, so... I guess you were a good match."

He's so fucking cute, I can't stand it.

"Are you *jealous?*" I teased, chuckling when he swiveled to glare at me. "I promise, I would gladly knock you up if I could."

And that's a fact.

He rolled his eyes. "Whatever, Zion," he huffed, clearly not believing my back alley midnight confession. "I'm just shocked a *hero* like you didn't have the importance of using condoms hammered into your prude head since birth."

"Who are you calling a prude, boy?" I cackled, dramatically gesturing at the neon reflecting off my windshield. "I've been coming to Lycra and Lace since I sprouted my first nut hair.

Meanwhile, you're the one stalling out here in the parking lot—"

"Stalling!" Baltasar yelped indignantly—riled up, just as I'd hoped. "I have two pockets full of bills and am ready to make it rain. Stalling, my ass…" With one last huff, he clamored out of the car and slammed the door shut behind him, leaving me to shake my head in amusement.

He's too easy.

Hopefully, he gets even easier as the night goes on.

It was going to be a good one—not only because I was about to see my favorite ladies for the first time in forever—but because I'd brought the hottest supe along with me.

One who clearly has the hots for me.

If only he'd stop fighting it…

Plus, I'd successfully avoided his earlier question about what finally broke me.

It wasn't losing Mikki, even though watching her fade because of her illness was devastating. The real reason I retired from Deathball was that while at my lowest, I received the worst possible news a man could hear.

That the only supe I ever wanted was being given to my sister.

Luckily, I was alone—running drills out on my family's Deathball field—when word reached me about Baltasar and Dahlia's engagement. I'd immediately shifted into lizard form and torn through the woods to funnel my rage. In the end, I cut a path of destruction that looked like it was caused by a caravan of forestry equipment.

My parents had to come and find me and drag me back to the house, although I remembered nothing of that part of the ordeal. I woke up at the bottom of my subterranean pond and debated never surfacing again. The only thing that made me emerge was knowing there was *no one* outside of paid staff who would look after Daisy if I was gone.

I was all she had left.

Negotiations between my parents and Wolfgang had taken a while, so I had time to get back to baseline. By the time Baltasar stepped off his private plane, I'd quit my career and was ready to accept that my dream man was miraculously being welcomed into my family.

As a pretty prize for someone else.

But that was before Baltasar and I spent time together outside of an arena, before I got to know him better and realized he might not be so off-limits after all.

Before my daughter fell for him, too.

Wait. Too?

Easy, Zion.

The man doesn't even realize he likes cock yet.

…and you went and brought him to a 'titty bar.'

I snorted and exited the car, taking my sweet time strolling to where Baltasar was impatiently waiting for me. He was standing next to Axel, the club's bouncer—who was large for a normie, but still eyeing the enormous man beside him like a potential threat.

Admittedly, I was doing the same as I approached, for entirely different reasons. My mate looked fine as hell in dark denim and a sage green button-down shirt that offset his skin and eye color perfectly.

My ladies are gonna eat him up.

Well… they can try.

164

"Evenin', Axxx," I drawled, shooting the bouncer a salacious wink that made Baltasar frown.

More than accustomed to my bullshit, Axel simply rolled his eyes and made a show of unhooking the velvet rope to wave us through.

Such VIP treatment.

Lycra and Lace was *not* the sort of place that warranted a velvet rope, although it definitely needed security. The Sunrise City neighborhood wasn't the greatest, but the real danger was how the women who worked here—all smokin' hot to begin with—were toying with the taboo fantasies of every normie in this town.

And what's a man to do when his darkest dream is dangled right in front of him?

With a pointed look at my 'date,' I gestured for him to enter the club first, looking forward to sharing another part of myself that many didn't know.

I also might have been curious to see how many times I could make the villain blush before the night was through.

Since a flustered Baltasar is my favorite Baltasar.

CHAPTER 20
BALTASAR

It was just like Zion had said. Being a Deathball champion, I'd been to tons of strip clubs the world over, more times than I could count.

But never to one like this.

The interior so closely resembled a city street, it took my brain a moment to realize we'd stepped inside. Brightly colored graffiti glowed under the black lights, and a single streetlamp illuminated the concrete slab set up as the stage. A woman was deep into her set, down to nothing but clear heels and a bright blue thong. She gracefully performed for the salivating men in the front row, bouncing her ass for maximum jiggle.

Nice.

I was surprised Zion brought me *here,* but after everything that had gone down the past few days, it would be a welcome distraction from the mess in my head.

And the perfect place to remind me how much I love tatas.

Being told the Salah clan had only agreed to this engagement to be *nice* had stung like a bitch. It also made me mad as hell —at *both* families.

The first thing I did when Major Obscurity dropped me off at my room was call Wolfy. I'd used every ounce of willpower—and deeply ingrained fear—not to yell at my older brother as soon as he answered the phone.

He'd calmly confirmed what Jackie Salah had thrown in my face—our alliance did *not* hinge on me marrying into their clan. That only confused me more. Wolfy said the Salahs were the best fit for me, but he also didn't seem disappointed, or surprised, by me finally admitting Dahlia and I weren't a good match.

Weirder still was *my* reaction to his words. Although I was still angry at being left out of the loop, a tidal wave of relief washed over me to know I wasn't *required* to make it to the altar with someone I didn't love.

I guess I do care about stuff like that, after all.

Despite being weirdly understanding about the marriage thing, Wolfy insisted I stay where I was—to continue digging up dirt while he and Simon came up with an exit strategy.

It was a dangerous play. I would still need to behave like business as usual, but I was confident I could handle it. Staying was also a no-brainer since the idea of leaving Daisy behind made me want to throw up.

Even if the dirt I'm supposed to be digging up is on her...

And now, I was even more torn. Daisy's existence was a bigger scandal than Zion shacking up with a supe from the wrong side of the tracks. Mikki had been a *normie,* and Zion displaying original supe genes—which he knew nothing about—made Daisy the same subspecies as Simon.

This intel would be leverage gold for Wolfy.

And help Simon learn more about his ancestry.

But telling them will betray Daisy…

And Zion.

If I was going to be honest, I wasn't *only* staying for the little queen. As much as I wanted to deny whatever the fuck was happening between us, the thought of leaving *Zion* behind made me oddly anxious.

Because then I'll never see him again…

"There's my favorite guy!" a feminine voice shouted over the pulsing music, snapping me back to my surroundings.

Zion was hugging a woman dressed head-to-toe in yellow Lycra. My eyes narrowed at how tightly he was holding her but then widened when she turned to face me—revealing an outfit that was vaguely familiar.

Where have I seen that emblem before?

Lecherous catcalls from the front drew my attention back to the stage. The stripper had turned to face the howling crowd, showing off her blue eye mask, star-shaped pasties.

And the *very* recognizable M-shaped emblem decorating her glittery chest in red jewels.

Oh. My. Gawd.

"Is she… is that supposed to be…" I stuttered, too dumb-founded to speak.

Yellow Lycra proudly beamed at me. "Yup! Ginger's Captain Masculine act is always a big hit. It doesn't hurt that the Captain is one of the sexiest supes around, don't you think?"

I think I need to bleach my fucking eyeballs.

Yes, I could admit that Butch was good-looking. But he was my brother's *inventus,* and clearly the bottom in that relation-ship. He just didn't do it for me.

Because men *don't do it for me.*

Usually…

Zion slung his enormous arm over my shoulders—his touch and scent stirring up a weird combo of calm and horniness that rocketed from my chest to my cock.

I need a stiff… drink.

And a lap dance.

"*My man* is just a little overwhelmed, Shelly," Zion chuckled, rubbing the side of his face against my temple—the same way a cat would mark its territory. "But he's a certified cape chaser, so maybe Ari could resurrect Mikki's famous act for us… for old times' sake?"

His *man?*

CAPE CHASER?!

Wait…

"You got it, honey," Shelly cooed, giving me a once-over that had me squirming beneath her knowing gaze. "I'll spread the word that you're here and pass along your special request. I'm sure Ginger will want to bring you two boys some drinks when she's done on stage… for old times' sake."

With that, she sashayed away, just as my overstimulated brain recognized the emblem on her Lycra as a long-dead hero with bumblebee-related powers.

A hero who was defeated by my mother in a gruesome battle.

It wasn't until Zion led me through the crowd to a private box with tinted glass that my mouth finally caught up with the situation. "*Mikki* worked here? As a strip… dancer?"

Zion barked a laugh as he forcefully sat me down in a chair. "Yes. Mikki was the *star* of this fucking place. The crown jewel. You should have seen how the crowd went wild for her."

His voice was wistful as he took the seat beside me, but I also caught a hint of admiration as his focus drifted back to the stage. I warily followed his gaze. Horny man's Captain Masculine had blessedly finished her act and a new girl was taking her place in an outfit I didn't recognize.

Thank fuck.

I swear, no one better come out dressed like any of my brothers.

"Her being up there didn't... bother you?" I haltingly asked, still absorbing this latest bombshell. "Shaking her money-maker for all these thirsty dudes?"

Zion snorted and shot me an amused glance. "It would've been a little hypocritical of me to complain, especially since *I* was one of those thirsty dudes myself. Besides..." His gaze drifted to the stage again. "It's just a job. A performance. Like Deathball, or like being a supe in general. We're *all* pieces of meat, Baltasar, not just you."

"I'm not..." I began, but stopped and forced myself to *hear* what he was saying and then choose my next words carefully. "When I said that, I meant I didn't want you thinking I'm just your *fuckboy*." When his deep brown eyes widened, I quickly added, "It's all I've ever been to anyone, and it never bothered me before because that was all *I* wanted, too. But that's not what I want... with this."

I weakly trailed off as I gestured between us, suddenly realizing he might expect me to continue explaining myself.

And that was already a lot for one day.

Zion was observing me with the same unnervingly unreadable expression he had in lizard form. "And what *do* you want, B?" he quietly asked, the slight waver in his voice betraying his nerves.

"I don't know..." I replied, even though I had a pretty good idea.

I want you.

The door to our private box swung open and Ginger jiggled her way in with a tray of drinks. Thankfully, she was wearing a silky robe over whatever Captain Masculine getup she still had on underneath. "Zion! Baby, it's so good to see you!"

Baby?!

A growl escaped me as she set down the tray and slid onto Zion's lap, throwing her arms around his neck for an embrace. My outburst did not go unnoticed by either of them, and I could feel myself blush as my old rival smirked.

"Oh, hello, handsome." Ginger grinned as her gaze roamed over me suggestively. I nodded stiffly in return, realizing she probably flirted with everyone since that was usually part of the job description in these places. "You must be one of Zion's friends—"

"He's my *sister's* fiancé," Zion smoothly interrupted, making me flinch. "Right, B?"

That's bullshit, though!

"Right," I gritted out, glaring at him as he smugly maintained eye contact. I didn't know what the hero was trying to accomplish—besides pissing me off enough to crack him on the jaw again.

Ginger whistled low. "The tension in this room... woof." She chuckled and shook her head before her expression turned serious again. "How have you guys been holding up, Zion? How's Daisy?"

I picked up a Jack and Coke and tried to turn my attention back to the stage, but one eye was still firmly fixed on the pair beside me.

It's only because they're discussing Daisy.

"She's okay. As sassy as ever," Zion replied, allowing *this woman* to run her fingers through his hair. "She misses her mama."

"We all miss Mikki, baby," Ginger softly replied, sliding her hands down to cup his face, staring deeply into his eyes. "How are *you* doing?"

"Fine," he curtly replied, and I spun to face him as *something* yanked on my chest almost painfully.

What the fuck was that?

Zion was clearly *not* fine, but he obviously didn't want to talk about it—not with this chick, at least. This random piece of intel made me weirdly happy, and Ginger got the hint as she dropped the subject.

But then, she slyly glanced my way before leaning down to murmur in his ear, "Well, maybe I can help take your mind off things…"

The rest was lost as the crowd went nuts, bringing my attention back to the stage. It was currently empty, which implied that either the last girl ended her set like a rockstar or whoever was coming out next was about to bring the house down.

I didn't care either way. My gaze drifted back to Zion, annoyed to find he was now whispering in Ginger's ear. No matter how hard I strained my supe hearing, I couldn't catch what he was saying.

Rude.

The topic became painfully clear as Ginger slid down Zion's body, gracefully landing on her knees at his feet. He spread his legs to accommodate, and she began sliding her hands up his muscular thighs, headed straight for his cock.

Oh, hell no.

"Are you ready for a show, B?" Zion chuckled, his grin only spreading as I scowled. "I'm talking about *on the stage.* You're about to see my favorite Lycra and Lace act. The one that made me fall in love with this place."

"And a certain someone," Ginger unhelpfully added as she *unzipped his fucking pants* and reached inside.

"That's right," he softly smiled, his gaze going distant. "Mikki was everything I ever wanted."

My entire body was vibrating with anger and confusion and a bunch of other shit I didn't know how to name. If Zion wanted to get *serviced* right next to me—while dreaming of his perfect, dead not-wife—so fucking be it.

I don't give a shit.

With another growl, I stubbornly focused on the stage, determined to enjoy myself even if the next girl came out dressed as The Hand of Death.

Please don't come out dressed as The Hand of Death.

The emcee's voice suddenly blasted through the speakers, answering my prayers before crushing my soul to smithereens.

"We have a special request tonight! In memory of our beloved Mikki, Miss Ariana will perform as a supe you know and love. Your *favorite* sexy strongman in spandex. The one we can't help but wonder how big he gets—*everywhere.*"

Oh, no.

"The one, the only…"

Nonononono.

"BLUNT FORCE!"

Fuck. No.

CHAPTER 21
BALTASAR

The crowd was unhinged—their cheers deafening as they stomped their feet and pounded their drinks on the tables. With the way the club was vibrating, I thought the graffitied walls of Lycra and Lace were about to come down around us.

Since, apparently, I'm *the audience's 'favorite sexy strongman in spandex.'*

With really fantastic tatas...

My jaw was on the floor as the banging hot lady stripper version of *me* appeared to gyrate on stage in barely there green Lycra, causing massive boners left and right.

Including Zion's.

Although someone else *is handling that...*

Unable to stop myself, I took a peek at the action beside me. Ginger had Zion's cock out—which he'd left in human form —and was tracing one of her neon blue fingernails along its length while seductively gazing up at him.

I may have still been slightly confused about how I felt about Zion, but I knew I did *not* like Ginger looking at or touching him. Meanwhile, I was still processing the bombshells of

Mikki being a normie—and a stripper—and that her famous act was apparently impersonating me...

Oh, fuck...

Is that what drew Zion to her in the first place?

Even though I already felt like I'd been punched in the gut twenty times over, I forced myself to look at his face next.

To my surprise, Zion seemed to be completely ignoring the babe at his feet. He was obviously turned on—his cock hard and his broad chest rapidly rising and falling—but his hands were flat on his thighs and his focus was entirely on the fiasco happening on stage.

On his fantasy version of me.

Jesus, this is fucked up.

But also kind of hot.

Ugh.

Before I could look away, his eyes met mine. Instead of the smug satisfaction from earlier, they were filled with so much longing that I froze. The last thing I wanted to do was leave him alone with this woman, but the second to last thing I wanted was to watch someone else get him off.

I gritted my teeth, "I should probably go—"

Zion frantically shook his head. "Please don't," he choked, sounding as wrecked by this situation as I was.

He looks like he might die if I don't jump on his dick.

I should jump on his dick...

JESUS, WHAT?!

"Do you want my mouth on you, baby?" Ginger cooed up at Zion, not looking at all concerned that his gaze was locked on me instead of her.

Don't you fucking dare.

Zion replied, but not to her. "I *need* to get off, B…"

FINE THEN.

I leaped to my feet, and it must have seemed like I was about to storm out, as the look on Zion's face was close to panic.

No need to worry, since I've apparently lost my fucking mind.

"Stand up," I growled down at Ginger. "And get the fuck out of here."

Mine.

"Baltasar!" Zion scowled. "That's no way to talk to a lady."

I huffed, but softened my tone. *"Please,* get the fuck out."

Before he could scold me again, Ginger stood and warmly grinned at me. "No problem, handsome." Then she winked at Zion. "You owe me one, baby."

Did they just gang up on me?

I glared at Zion as Ginger glided from the room, but he was back to looking as unbothered as always.

"You can stand there and look mad if you want, beautiful. That works for me." He wrapped his hand around his cock and lazily stroked, keeping his eyes on mine. "But I'd prefer you on your knees."

Gulp.

As if the hero knew I was about to break, those gorgeous scales of his appeared on his skin and cock—like constellations guiding me—further testing my resolve.

He's just so fucking hot…

My vision grew hazy as my gaze dropped to his dick again—just in time to see the rocket pop ridges and bulge at the base appear.

I licked my lips.

Fuck it.

Let's go.

I dropped to the floor, and Zion sharply inhaled, as if he hadn't expected me to actually do it. He quickly recovered and shifted his weight to make room for me between his thighs. Otherwise, he remained frozen in place—as if he worried I might make a break for it.

Nope.

This is happening.

Now that I'd decided, I was all in. 110%. I was determined to not only blow this man, but blow his fucking mind, *and* blow all past, present, and future competition out of the water.

Somehow…

Unfortunately, this wasn't as simple as facing off on the field. There, I'd memorized my plays and my opponent's every move until defeating the enemy was second nature. This was way harder.

Pun intended.

This was ten million times more nerve-racking than when Preek put me on the spot in front of the press the day I arrived. Worse than every other time in my life when my brain wasn't fast enough to stop me from looking dumb as hell.

"Um…" I cleared my throat, feeling beyond vulnerable as my adrenaline plummeted.

This is the worst.

But then I lifted my gaze to Zion's, and the raw lust, hope, and understanding I found waiting there gave me the courage to admit to the problem. "I don't know what the fuck I'm doing."

Obviously.

Zion smiled in that magical way of his that instantly put me at ease. His hand drifted to my face, cupping my jaw so he could run his thumb over my bottom lip. Then he shuddered —as if just *touching* me gave him pleasure.

Fuck, I want to touch him back…

"Just show me how *you* like it," he murmured. "Then I'll know what to do when it's my turn."

When it's his turn?

He's gonna suck my cock?!

I was already half-hard just from being on my knees for him, but the thought of Zion's mouth on me instantly brought me to full attention. For reasons I was apparently no longer questioning, this man and his lizard dick did things to me no woman ever had before—no matter how fantastic her tatas were.

It looks like I'm kind of gay after all.

Gay for lizard dick.

The pounding music from naked lady Blunt Force's set was still rattling the walls, but Zion was no longer paying any attention to the stage. Instead, he was staring down at me with a heady mix of disbelief, awe, and a desire so intense, I felt it closing in around me. It was intoxicating and made my chest ache so badly, it would have freaked me out if I hadn't already experienced it in his presence before.

I think I'm just nervous…

"Go on, beautiful," he murmured, moving his hand to comb through my hair—petting me. "You're gonna do so good, I just know it."

I melted under his praise. Letting my eyes flutter closed, I leaned forward and ran my tongue up one of his ridges until I reached his dripping slit. Then I echoed his moan with mine as I tasted him for the first time.

Holyyyy fuuuuck!

It was a wonder I didn't immediately unload in my pants. I may have previously considered pussy to be my favorite snack, but Zion's dick was officially a five-course gourmet meal.

He tasted like how it felt to swim in the ocean on a perfect day back home—like pure sunshine mixed with skin and sweat. His salty flavor was my new favorite drug, and every drop only made me thirsty for more, as I greedily lapped up what I could.

I licked him as if he really was a goddamn rocket pop, almost coming every time my tongue hammered over those ridges.

Which probably would *feel amazing on my prostate.*

His earthy, musky scent was permeating my nostrils— invading my brain. Before I knew it, I'd dug my fingers into his thighs, wrapped my lips around his juicy head, and taken him all the way to the back of my throat.

"Jesus, *fuck,* B!" he shouted, his hand tightened in my hair, holding me still while he caught his breath. "I'm gonna fucking blow in two seconds if you go full porn star on me. Give a man a minute... *Jesus...*"

Pulling myself off with an audible pop, I smirked up at him, incredibly pleased with my rookie performance. "I can stop if you want—"

"Don't you dare," he laughed, pulling me toward him again. "I'm so revved up, I don't know what I'll do if you leave me hanging after all this time."

An unwanted vision of *Ginger* kneeling at his feet again made me growl. I snatched his cock with both hands, curling over it possessively, like a dog might protect its food.

All mine.

He smirked. "What's the matter, beautiful? Did you not enjoy seeing me with someone else?"

When I peeked up at him and shook my head, his gaze darkened. Digging both hands into my hair, he yanked my head back painfully before looming over me. "Well, now you know how I've felt for the last 10 fucking years."

Well, shit.

It was dizzying to realize how badly Zion wanted me—how long he'd *pined* for me in secret. I was also amazed I'd never noticed it before.

Maybe I was too busy pretending the feeling wasn't mutual...

No way in hell was I pausing the action to examine *that* train of thought—not when Zion was looking at me like he wanted to eat me alive.

And now I understand why.

This entire situation was going straight to my dick... and ego. "Well, it's a good thing I don't seem to have a gag reflex," I teased, letting a cocky smile curl my lip. "Because it sounds like you've been wanting to fuck my throat for a long time."

The instant the words left my mouth, I froze—but not because I didn't like the idea. To be honest, the thought of Zion taking control made me feel small and helpless and so turned on, my cock was trying to Hulk its way out of my pants.

Appropriate.

Apparently, Zion was having similar thoughts. His irises were bright yellow and his pupils had shifted into slits, which only made me dizzier.

And hornier.

"You sure about that, B?" he growled. "Because it *has* been a long time coming. And I won't be gentle."

"Yes," I breathed, softly tracing the vee under his crown with my tongue, needing him to know how much I wanted it. Wanted *him.* "I'm sure."

Make me yours.

With a snarl that didn't sound remotely human, he yanked me closer, sliding one hand to the back of my neck to hold me directly over his weeping cock. "If you need me to stop, pinch my thigh—hard. Otherwise, hold on for the ride."

The next thing I knew, he'd slammed me down on his cock so hard I *did* gag a little. That only seemed to spur him on, and all I could do was hold on—just like he'd said—as he treated my throat like his own personal cock sleeve.

Fuck, I fucking love it.

"Do you know how *long* I've wanted this?" he gasped, fucking up into my mouth, forcing me down on every thrust. "How long I've dreamed of making you mine? Of claiming every inch of you? Every. Fucking. Hole?"

My throat was raw, and I could barely see through the tears streaming down my face. But every atom in my body felt like it was being lit up like a firework on the Fourth of July.

If you'd told me a month ago I'd be on my knees for Zion Salah—submitting to him with his cock stuffed down my throat—I would have laughed. But at this moment, nothing felt more right.

This, this, this.

"Look at you," he praised, his thrusts growing more erratic as he neared the edge. "You are the most perfect fucking thing I've ever seen... and you suck cock like a goddamn champion."

I moaned like a whore at that, making Zion yank me off him with a grunt.

"Close your eyes, B," he gruffly commanded. "I'm gonna come all over this beautiful face."

Oh, my gawd, yes.

"Yes, please," I confirmed, sitting back on my heels and moving my hands to grip the base of his cock. "Mark me up."

Mark me as yours.

My eyes were shut tight, but I could feel the strange bulge on his shaft pulsing beneath my hands as he neared oblivion. Without thinking, I squeezed him there—*hard*—opening my mouth just in time for him to explode.

"Oh, *FUCK!*" Zion exclaimed, dropping his hand to cover mine. "That's right, beautiful—milk every drop. It's all for you. I can't wait to breed you. You're going to look so fucking hot with my cum dripping out of you..."

Give me all of it.

He absolutely *covered* me in cum, continuing to tell me all the filthy things he wanted to do to me. I found myself thrusting into the air in time with every pulse—desperate for any friction—but waited for him to be done before blinking open my eyes.

"Look. At. You." Zion murmured appreciatively, gently lifting my chin to better admire me.

"How do I look?" I huffed a laugh, feeling cum dripping down my neck, and not hating it at all.

"Like *mine*," he growled.

I shuddered under the combined weight of his stare and his words, but didn't look away.

His gaze softened. "How do you feel?"

There was only one right answer, and not because I knew what Zion wanted to hear. The truth was, I no longer cared if I was gay or straight or something in between. I wanted whatever *this* was—this unexpected thing that had been happening between us for however long.

Swallowing hard, I licked my lips, almost coming on the spot from the taste of him on my tongue. "I feel like *yours.*"

Like I was already yours.

He smiled, and I sat up a little straighter at the approval in his gaze. "Good," he replied before his eyes grew hooded again. "Now let me lick you clean."

CHAPTER 22
BALTASAR

Zion wasn't kidding about licking me clean.

To my horny delight, he pulled me up into his lap and languidly cleaned my face and neck, pausing every so often to feed me his cum with his lizard tongue. By the time he was done, I felt boneless, even though I still had a raging boner that needed to be dealt with.

Hopefully, by Zion.

With his mouth.

That I wasn't even second-guessing the direction of my thoughts anymore made it safe to say I was all in with this situation.

I am so super gay now.

"Should I take care of this needy cock for you, beautiful?" Zion cooed, palming my dick through my pants and squeezing hard.

"Fucking *please*," I gasped, dropping my head back and shamelessly thrusting against his hand. "I need to get off. In any way possible."

Zion hummed. "Hmm... is that right? I could get Ginger back in here to wrap her pretty lips around you. Or maybe even Ari in her Blunt Force outfit—"

Hilarious.

"No!" I growled, lifting my head again to glare at him. "I don't want any of those women touching me."

He smiled, slow and lazy, as if I wasn't about to explode. "Well, that makes two of us."

Irrational anger swept through me. "And I don't want to see them touching you ever again."

Zion's smile vanished, and I froze, wondering if I was being too demanding. Part of me—a big part—didn't care, because the thought of anyone else's hands on him made me want to go on goddamn a killing spree.

Jesus.

To my surprise, he didn't scold me or make a signature joke. "The ladies here are just friends, B. Well... more like family, but my point is—I've never been with any of them before, besides Mikki. When Ginger touched me, I was pretending it was you." My cock gave a kick at that intel, and he smirked before adding, "I've always pretended it's you."

The way he just tells me everything...

I knew I shouldn't ask, but I desperately needed to know how deep this fucked up rabbit hole went. "Even with Mikki?"

Zion's focus flickered to the stage behind me, where Ari was finishing up her Blunt Force tribute set to thunderous applause. "Most of the time." He met my gaze again. "Definitely when I was breeding her."

That is the hottest, most romantic thing anyone has ever said to me.

"Fuck… I need to come…" was all I could get out as I rubbed myself against his hand—delirious with need and harder to define emotions I'd never felt before.

"Well, then we'd better get going," he chuckled, sliding me off his lap and zipping himself up before rising to stand. "Because I need to snack on you where we won't be interrupted."

Yes.

That humiliating *whimper* reared its head again… making Zion growl… making me almost come…

We need to get the fuck out of here.

Now.

Zion clearly shared my opinion, as he hustled me out of the private box, and the club, with barely a goodbye to anyone. I'd expected him to speed back to his family's estate, so was surprised when he opened the back door of his Challenger instead.

"Get in, B." He smirked. "Let's pretend we're teenagers again."

Oh, fuck yes.

We were already sneaking around behind everyone's backs— which was both thrilling and terrifying—but the idea of actually behaving like a couple of horny teenagers sounded awesome to me.

I clamored onto the bench seat and pulled my shirt off before starting on my pants. By the time he climbed in after me and shut the door, I was down to wrestling with my shoes because I'd forgotten to take them off first. Once I was finally naked, I glanced up and stilled as I found Zion simply watching me with a strange look on his face.

Does he not like what he sees?

"Everything cool, Z?" I tentatively asked, trying to play it cool myself—even though my nerves were through the roof.

His gaze slowly lifted to mine, his expression raw and vulnerable. "I need you to understand just how *long* I've wanted this."

I swallowed hard, feeling a hell of a lot more naked than I already was. "How long?"

He huffed humorlessly. "Since the day you graduated Junior Supremacy."

Shit.

My last days at the training complex were seared into *my* memory as well. I'd been excited—and nervous, of course—but less about graduating and more about how I was finally getting to play with villains I'd been idolizing for years.

And against heroes I'd been keeping an eye on.

Supes didn't compete in the Games until they were 18, but the Junior crew had their own competitions that were televised and analyzed on SupeSports. Being raised to represent my family in the Games meant my free time was spent studying my competition instead of my schoolwork. By the time I began my training, I knew exactly how my powers would be used.

And everything about who I was up against.

I vividly remembered the day the hero known as Scaled Justice was officially announced as the Salah clan's representative. That he was also the heir apparent was notable, since a clan usually avoided casually endangering their first-born. But that wasn't what captured my attention.

His supe form did.

His hot as fuck supe form…

Zion mistook my silence for discomfort and immediately backpedaled. "I mean, I know you were barely legal back then." He grimaced. "But I think it started as more of a… fascination than anything else—"

"Why didn't you make a move?" I interrupted, not at all worried about a 21-year-old checking out my 18-year-old ass back in the day. "Or even just try to be friends with me?"

"B…" He sighed. "You know how it was—how it *still* is, despite whatever the USN is trying to accomplish. I'm a hero. You're a villain. Even if we'd only started a friendship, my parents would have murdered me, and then *your* parents would have swooped in to murder them and the rest of my clan."

He has a point.

"But we're not actually any different!" I cried, hating the anguish lining his face—wanting to do anything to take away his pain.

I wish I could tell him everything.

Oblivious to my growing agitation, Zion offered me a smile. "Yeah, I know that *now*. But even without the weird classist shit, *I'm*… different, y'know?"

This was torture. I had insider knowledge that would prove this man was the closest thing to what *all* supes used to be, but I couldn't share that intel without betraying my family.

But maybe I can tell him something *that will help.*

"I-I… remember the first time I saw you, too," I stammered, already feeling my cheeks heat. "Not in person, but… SupeS-

191

ports aired a clip of you during *your* time in Junior scrimmages, in your supe form. I got such a confused boner, I had to sneak off to my room and rub one out."

Zion barked a laugh. "A *confused* boner, huh? How flattering."

I rolled my eyes but reached for him, pulling him closer. "Z, I don't like men." When his expression started to shutter, I quickly elaborated. "Even now, I don't think another dude could turn my head. But I want *you* so bad, it *aches.*"

He released a shuddering breath before brushing his lips over mine. "Why do you think that is?"

"I don't know," I answered honestly. "But the… lizard thing sure doesn't hurt."

My mouth went dry as he sat back to pull his shirt off over his head. This revealed the gorgeous scales already dotting his chest and abs, and spreading outward as he half-shifted.

"But it's not like I jerk off to *Godzilla* or anything," I dumbly added. "I just like how *your* supe form makes me feel…"

Might as well go big with telling him how weird I am.

Zion cocked his head as he removed the rest of his clothes— way more gracefully than I had. "And how do I make you feel, B?"

Here we go.

I blew out a slow breath. "Like… prey."

His eyes flashed yellow as he pounced, pinning me flat against the leather seat with a growl that should have scared the shit out of me.

Instead, I'm hard as a fucking rock.

Big surprise.

"Foolish little villain," he hissed as his eyes turned fully reptilian. "You don't have the slightest idea what you're tempting me with." He dragged his nose along my neck, deeply inhaling and making me moan. "Want to know why I play long-shot on the field, instead of defense? Because my coach and I realized early on that I enjoyed the chase a little *too* much. That once I caught my *prey,* there was no guarantee I wouldn't rip them to shreds."

I groaned and rubbed myself against him, leaking all over his lizard dick as his body shifted more—filling the backseat with his bulk.

Yes, yes, yes.

"You won't hurt me, though," I croaked, even though *how* I knew that was unclear. The strange *pulling* sensation had returned to my chest, but it felt good now that I had his skin —and scales—on me.

It feels… right.

"No, I won't," he murmured into my neck before pulling back to hover his almost fully reptilian face over mine. "But I still want to devour you. I still want to tear you in half. Because you're my *mate.*"

Zion let the word hang in the air between us while staring at me unblinkingly, clearly wanting to see my reaction to his possessive, primal, crazy lizard-man talk.

I fucking love it.

At this point, I was so worked up, there was no hope of getting out a complete sentence. Instead, I did the only thing I could think of—the thing I couldn't stop thinking about.

I tilted my head to the side and offered my neck to him.

Please...

His gaze snapped to my neck, and I watched, enthralled, as his fangs lengthened before my eyes. Just as quickly, he shook his head and peered down at me with an assessing look. "That's a conversation for another time, beautiful. Right now, I want to taste you in another way."

The wave of disappointment I felt was magically erased when Zion slid down my body and positioned his mouth only inches away from my throbbing cock.

He glanced up at me with a broad grin. "Should I lose the fangs?"

I really was dumb, as I vehemently shook my head. "No. Leave 'em. I trust you won't bite my dick off."

Zion scoffed, turning his attention back to my sacrificial offering. "Not a chance. Not when I've been given such a treat to savor..."

My racing thoughts instantly turned to white noise as my cock was suddenly enveloped in hot, wet, oddly sticky heat.

Holy fucking fuckfuckfuck!

The only thing that stopped me from coming on the spot was Zion pulling off me again and gripping the base of my dick so hard I yelped.

"So needy," he snickered, lightly dragging his claws up my shaft, making my hips punch into the air. "So ready for me to take care of you."

"Fuck, yes," I sobbed, absolutely unhinged after a single lick. "Just get your mouth back on me, Z. Get that goddamn lizard tongue all up in my shit. Fucking *please!*"

I had no control over what was coming out of my mouth, but apparently, Zion was taking my words seriously. Before I could clarify—or try to interpret things myself—he was pushing my thighs onto my chest and swiping his tongue up my ass crack.

Over my hole.

"JESUS FUCKING CHRIST!" I howled, gripping my dick with both hands in a desperate attempt not to pressure wash the interior of his car.

He lifted his head and peered up at me with that infuriatingly attractive smug smile plastered across his face. "Do you want me to stop?"

Are you joking?!

This was, without a doubt, the gayest thing I'd ever done, but I couldn't care less. I was all in with the lizard dick—and tongue—and I needed to come like I needed air.

"Don't you *dare* fucking stop, Salah," I choked out. "Show me what a *champion* can do."

He chuckled and extended his *very long* lizard tongue to lap over my balls one by one—teasing me while I writhed. I was about to beg like my life depended on it when he not only licked my hole again, but pressed into it. I tightened around the intrusion at first—uber aware of the ridged texture—but his saliva had the same consistency as lube, so it slid right in.

Well, that's *convenient…*

The noise I made when he hit what must have been my prostate sounded like a dying animal, but I had to hope that would be a turn-on to a predator like him.

"Z… I-I'm so close…" I gasped, riding his tongue like I was being paid to do it. "I can't stop…"

Can't stop, won't stop.

In a move that had to be practiced, Zion seamlessly slid his tongue out of my ass and lowered his mouth onto my dick just as I detonated. I shouted obscenities into the dark of his car as he then prolonged my orgasm for what felt like years— slipping a finger into my ass and massaging my love button until it was game fucking over.

RIP me.

Zion calmly drank down what had to be a bucketload of cum before climbing back up my shuddering body to deliver a sweet kiss.

"How was that?" he murmured against my lips as I moaned at the taste of myself. "Was that okay, beautiful?"

I huffed a laugh, so wrecked, I debated just sleeping naked where I lay and dealing with the fallout come morning.

"Yes. Fuck, yes, it was better than okay." I adjusted my position so he could *see* how genuinely I meant that.

The way he was looking at me—like I hung the fucking moon —made my breath catch. "What are we gonna do?" I whispered as panic rose in my throat.

Because there's no way I can stay away from you now.

He deposited another kiss on my lips, instantly calming me. "I'll figure it out, B. We just need to keep this situation between us under wraps until I can look into some things…" When my face fell, he added, "Trust me. I protect what belongs to me."

He protects what belongs to him.

And I belong to him.

That thought soothed every atom of my usually chaotic being. Exhausted, I shut my eyes and allowed myself to drift off to sleep, trusting that Zion would take care of things.

That he'd take me home.

CHAPTER 23
ZION

"Daddy, can you *staaahp?* You're driving me nuts."

I stopped pacing and turned to face my daughter. She was sitting cross-legged on the bed, wearing a T-shirt showing elements from the periodic table that read, 'I Only Use S Ar Ca Sm Periodically.'

The tee was a blinding neon blue and, paired with the stone-washed jeans she had on, Daisy looked more like *my* kid than she ever had before.

All thanks to Baltasar…

"Why don't we go watch Blunty practice?" Daisy chirped, apparently knowing damn well why I was wearing a hole in her bedroom rug.

I miss my mate.

Like a fucking fool.

Her idea was doable. Sunrise City was hosting the Supremacy Games this year, so it wouldn't take us long to get to the college campus where everyone was practicing.

But what if I see my old team?

My abrupt retirement had *not* gone over well with either my teammates or my coach, and the last thing I wanted was to deal with any more drama.

Then it hit me. Heroes and villains still played against each other in the Games—probably to appease our deeply ingrained thirst for blood. Daisy and I would be at the field where Balty's team of *villains* was practicing, so the chance of running into another hero was minimal.

How scandalous.

"Okay, let's go." I clapped my hands together as she leaped off the bed with a delighted squeal.

"Yas!" Daisy pumped her tiny fist into the air. "And when he's done for the day, we can take him out for ice cream."

Like a little family.

The urge to simply whisk my daughter and Baltasar away to an undisclosed location had been strong since our fateful night together at Lycra and Lace. But I was determined to uncover the secrets my family was keeping before officially staking my claim on the villain.

And this clan.

My parents had flown somewhere on their private plane yesterday, so I'd taken the opportunity to rifle through Pops' office while they were gone. Unsurprisingly, there'd been no file named 'Top Secret Lab.' I *did* randomly discover a vintage photo of my mom outside a jungle cave with an unfamiliar man in a safari outfit.

Maybe she was into spelunking in her younger years?

I'd made a mental note to grill the pilot when they returned, since Preek had 'borrowed' the plane last week to sneak off to the lab. Even if the pilot didn't know *why* he was transporting the lesser supe, he'd at least know *where* they went.

But how did Preek know it even existed?

"Are we going or what?" Daisy snapped me out of my internal sleuthing. She'd thrown on a leather jacket and trendy boots and, all at once, I glimpsed my future with a teen girl.

Send wine.

Or whiskey.

"We're going, we're going," I laughed, almost as giddy as her as she hustled me out the door.

I was aching to be close to Baltasar, even if it was from the bleachers as he ran the field. I'd been sneaking into his bedroom the past few nights—for more tasty third-base action—but it was killing me to not fall asleep with him in my arms.

About half-an-hour later, we were driving through the local Superversity campus where practice was being held. Approaching the Deathball fields felt surreal and caused my beast to pace beneath my skin in anticipation of a non-existent match.

Taking a breath, I focused on our current logistics. "All right, sweetie, do you remember the drill?" I parked the car and slid on a pair of mirrored aviators followed by a SupeSports base-ball cap I'd been given after an interview.

Anything to keep my identity under wraps.

Daisy rolled her eyes behind her hot pink shades. "If anyone recognizes you and asks, I'm one of Auntie Rose's kids. I'll also share anything I overhear after we leave."

I blinked. "This isn't an intel job, D. We're just here to support Blunty."

She scoffed at my stupidity as she booted open her door. "It's *always* an intel job, Daddy. You taught me that. And aren't we going to be around a bunch of *villains* all day? Talk about juicy gossip!"

My heart soared at how unafraid—and excited—she sounded to be hanging out with supes who were historically deemed the 'bad guys.' In reality, it didn't matter that Baltasar and I were from different sides of the tracks. *He* was the one who'd fully accepted my daughter on sight, when an entire clan of heroes—her own family—had refused to.

A true hero among villains.

It also soothed something in me to know my girl didn't possess the old prejudices my generation was raised with. This open-mindedness, combined with being an unregistered half-supe, meant she could seamlessly fit in anywhere in the future, if need be.

Hopefully, there won't be a need.

Every supe had a contingency plan for when things went sideways, and I'd made Daisy memorize ours in case I wasn't there to guide her. If shit hit the fan, she knew where to go and next steps, but I realized I needed to fill in Baltasar as well.

Since there's no one I trust more with her safety.

But today wasn't about that. We were here so Daisy could watch Baltasar wipe the field with his teammates during scrimmage.

And so I can watch my mate get hot and sweaty.

No one questioned us as we claimed a spot behind the chain-link fence, only a few yards away from the players. All Supremacy Games-related activity had been officially declared neutral zones by the supe council. Security wasn't needed to keep the peace, and it was for the best. If anyone caught wind that Scaled Justice was here—lurking around the villains' practice area, no less—the SupeSports reporters would be on me like white on rice.

I immediately found Baltasar in the tangle of bodies currently wrestling for the ball. It looked like he'd just taken down his team's starting long-shot—a villain known as Nitro Dart—and was therefore Hulked out, violent, and covered in mud.

Just how I like him.

Play paused so their coach could lay into the long-shot for his poor performance, and Baltasar shifted back to his civilian size and jogged toward the bench. Smitten kitten that I was, I shamelessly ogled my man as he took a long drink of water before pouring the rest over his head to cool down.

It wasn't the first time I'd snuck a peek at him on the field. Only this time, it felt like an invisible tether connected us, confirming we belonged together, even if plenty of supes would disagree. Their opinions didn't matter, however, because I knew, without a doubt, that this one was *mine.*

And I haven't even mated with him yet...

Baltasar rubbed his chest—as if he were feeling something similar—before searching the stands. His gaze fell on where we were leaning against the fence, and I almost swooned like a Victorian broad when a smile stretched across his handsome face.

I've got it bad.

"What are you guys doing here?" he asked, looking so happy about it, my heart skipped several beats.

Terminal level bad.

"We missed you," Daisy replied in that no-bullshit way kids did. "Daddy was a mess until I suggested we come here to watch you practice."

Way to blow up my spot, D.

Baltasar grinned like he'd won the lottery. "Is that right? Well, I missed you both, too. Mostly you, little queen, but your dad's crossed my mind once or twice."

Brat.

"And what exactly were you thinking about, B?" I growled, although any heat in my tone was of the bedroom variety. "Was it about how *I* could get your ass in line? On the field, of course…"

He blushed—adorably flustered, as always. "Um, yeah, actually. I *could* use some help with my plays. Coach has been so busy ripping Dart a new one, he's not even bothering with the rest of us."

I smiled, amazed at how Baltasar was so oblivious to how elite he was. "He's not bothering with *you* because you're the fucking star of this team. But I'll gladly watch your performance and shower you with praise afterward."

"Easy, Z," he grumbled, adjusting his suit as he awkwardly shifted on his feet. "There are *kids* present."

"Oh, please," Daisy scoffed. "I'm not an idiot. I know you two are totally in *lurve* with each other."

JESUS!

Baltasar turned scarlet before muttering something and hustling back to his team. I glared down at Daisy, who was looking far too smug for my liking.

"You think you've got me figured out, huh?" I grumbled.

"I *know* I do," she shot back, sassy as ever. "Mom told me all about your crush on Blunty."

What?!

I was rescued from replying to *that* bombshell by a man suddenly materializing beside me. "Excuse me. Are you... Zion Salah? Scaled Justice?"

Ah, fuck.

Turning to face the newcomer, I found a supe who looked no older than 19 or 20, generically attractive, with a muscular build made for speed. The power pouring off of him was almost suffocating, but that was unsurprising, since I knew exactly who the hero was.

"Star Hopper." I nodded brusquely, referring to him by his supe name to assert my dominance. "What brings you to the villains' field?"

The new darling of SupeSports grinned. "I could ask you the same thing! *I'm* here to monitor my competition." His impressively sharp gaze drifted to where Baltasar was positioning himself for the next play. "Not that there's much to be found here... besides *him.*"

"Who?" I asked in faux innocence, instinctively compelled to mess with this asshole.

Especially if he's trying to mess with my mate.

His smile was friendly, but something warned me not to be fooled by his baby face. "You know who. Your new plaything out there."

"Excuse me?" I snapped, my beast rising to the surface as a threat was identified. "What exactly are you implying?"

Internally, I was sweating bullets. It had been dumb as hell to come here today. If other supes were lurking around the stands the way this one was, it wouldn't take much to pick up on the vibes between Baltasar and me.

Star Hopper—wisely—took a step back. "Isn't that why you're here?" he murmured, blessedly eyeing me in confusion. "I assumed you've been training Blunt Force, since he'll be joining your clan soon. Especially now that you're…"

Retired.

"You're a Blunty fan, too?" Daisy cut in, playing up the innocent child persona I'd taught her to convey around other supes. "Isn't he the bestest?"

The hero blinked down at her, as if he hadn't noticed she was there until this moment. "I wouldn't say a *fan*, but he's certainly talented… for a ball grabber." His eyes met mine again. "But the best in the league is standing right in front of you."

Smug asshole.

"Yeah, my uncle's a freakin' legend!" Daisy smoothly replied, leaning into my side—discreetly soothing my beast before it ripped this fucker's head off. "Did you want an autograph?"

That's my girl.

Star Hopper barked a laugh, genuinely smiling for the first time since he'd joined us. "Scaled Justice *is* a freakin' legend, and you got me, little lady. I couldn't pass up the opportunity to introduce myself. I'm Ziggy." He extended a hand, which I gladly shook, feeling electricity zip up my arm on contact. "Ziggy Andromeda."

I chuckled as he released me, glad to feel the tension from a few moments ago dissipate. "Your parents were David Bowie fans, huh?"

His gaze drifted skyward as a secretive smile twitched his lips. "Something like that." Then he cocked his head and smirked. "It's a shame you retired, Zion. Lord knows your future brother-in-law's team could use a long-shot who'd give my team a challenge. See you around!"

And with that, he disappeared. Not like he simply ramped up his super speed and hustled away. The hero literally vanished before my eyes.

That's... concerning.

In the end, I decided he wasn't a threat to me or my mate. Star Hopper was just another Deathball player sizing up the competition—like we all did—but he'd unwittingly given me an idea.

Daisy and I climbed the bleachers to watch Baltasar finish up practice for the day, but I found myself analyzing the performance of his entire team. Once they headed to the locker room to shower and change, I told my daughter to sit tight while I jogged out onto the field to chat with his coach.

Perhaps I'm not done with Deathball, after all.

CHAPTER 24
ZION

Understandably, the coach for the Championship-winning villains was caught off guard to see *me* on his field—and doubly shocked by my idea to help them clinch the gold once more.

I guarantee no one was more surprised than me.

But Star Hopper was correct. The current long-shot was doing nothing for the team. Since this position was the equivalent of a quarterback *and* a receiver in American football, it was kind of important for them to not be a total fucking mess.

While *I* could've done the job with my eyes closed and one hand tied behind my back, that wasn't what my offer entailed. Instead, I'd volunteered to make a long-shot out of Baltasar.

There was no doubt in my mind he could do it. Not only did that man have *my* moves memorized—which was why he tackled me more often than anyone else—but he was *fast*.

And if he half-shifted, he could be even faster…

But Baltasar had worked hard enough for the day, so I would wait for another time to share my evil plan with him. Right now, we had more important matters to discuss.

"Which one are you gonna get, Bluntycups?" Daisy was hanging off Baltasar's enormous arm, waving a hand toward the board of flavors at the unfortunately named Swirlies. "I'm getting Unicorn Sparkle. With *extra* sparkles."

She shot me a haughty look, wordlessly challenging me to defy her demands.

I wouldn't dream of it.

"Uh... I was actually looking at the... popsicles," Baltasar replied, enticingly *blushing* for no other goddamn reason than to turn me on. "I just need to cool down, since it was balls hot out on the field today—oh *shit!* I shouldn't have said *balls* in front of Daisy."

This. Man.

My daughter cackled. "I told you, I know about swears. Daddy says I just have to wait until I'm 18. Then I can cuss up a storm."

He smiled down at her with so much adoration, my knees went weak. "Oh, is that the official ruling from on high?"

When his gaze met mine, it was *my* turn to blush, while praying on all that was holy he didn't notice. "Yeah... like I said." I shrugged, playing it cool. "I'm just figuring out this dad thing as I go."

Baltasar's expression turned serious. "You're doing an awesome job, Z. I would have killed to have a father like you when I was a kid."

Jesus Christ.

I cleared my throat and quickly averted my gaze to the flavor board. "Okay, does everyone know what they want? We can go eat at the park before we figure out what's next on the agenda for the day."

Moving right along.

Daisy bounded to the counter to instruct the stoned normie employee on how best to make her Unicorn Sparkle. I put in my order and hid my smile as Baltasar slapped a rocket pop of all things down on the counter, along with his platinum card.

"My treat," he gruffly said. "Since you two made my day by coming to practice."

It took all my self-control to not tackle this fool to the grimy ice cream shop floor and kiss every hard inch of him.

Because I totally lurve him.

Goddamnit.

It wasn't news that I was head over heels for this man, but he'd previously only existed as an unattainable fantasy. Now that the dream was becoming reality, I was experiencing something I hadn't felt since learning about Mikki's diagnosis.

Helplessness.

I thrived on control—and my beast behaved best when I had something to direct my unwavering attention toward. Taking a deep breath, I focused on what I knew to be true. My daughter's existence was still a secret. Baltasar Suarez was already mine. I was determined to get to the bottom of this secret lab mystery before taking over my clan.

And I was about to go to town on three scoops of caramel crunch with sea salt.

"C'mon, Blunty! We have the absolute best spot in the park to chow down *and* watch the geese be jerks."

"Sounds awesome." Baltasar laughed as he let Daisy pull him out the door.

We were soon set up in 'our spot,' which was in the shade of a large oak on a hill overlooking the rest of the park.

With the best view to watch the Canada geese terrorize everyone.

Daisy was howling at the feathered carnage, and Baltasar was dramatizing it with play-by-play commentary. I couldn't take my eyes off of *them.*

Despite her magnetic stage presence, Mikki had actually been a fairly reserved person in real life. Sure, she had a wicked sense of humor once you got to know her, but she'd rarely joined in with Daisy's antics. That had always been *my* schtick, while she took care of our daughter's emotional and material needs.

When Mikki got sick, I got a crash course on the logistical side of parenting, and admittedly threw myself into *that* to cope with the entire fucked up situation. Daisy and I still maintained our traditions from when her mama was healthy—like movie night and Swirlies ice cream in the park. But it always felt a little... lifeless.

Not anymore.

Baltasar was the missing piece in our little family and I had never been more terrified.

I can't fucking lose him, too.

Entering survival mode, I took slow, even breaths—willing myself to not assume the worst was going to happen.

Everything is going to be okay.

Everything's okay...

"What did you just do, Z?" Baltasar's voice brought me back to the present. To *him*. "You felt agitated and then you felt calm. How?"

I blew out a breath, wanting to share this part of myself—with *him*—but struggling to do so. "Well... I quiet my mind and focus on my breathing until all the stress and worry fades into the background. I prefer to be at the bottom of my pond, where there are no distractions, but I've learned how to make it work most anywhere."

Baltasar was staring at me like I'd just told him I walked on water. "Could you teach me how to do it?" That goddamn *blush* again. "How to not... think so much?"

Just marry me already, Suarez.

"Sure I can, beautiful," I murmured, dreamily imagining just dragging him to the bottom of my pond to stay with me forever.

"Gawd, you two are so gross," Daisy grumbled—her face covered in glitter sprinkles. "It's cute."

The oddest sensation suddenly washed over me. It was as if everything I felt for Baltasar was hitting me all at once, but the usual clarity was missing. Instead, each layer was so intertwined and tangled, it was difficult to separate one emotion from another.

If these are even my *emotions at all.*

Who else would they belong to, Zion?

Wait a minute...

Just as I realized Baltasar had mentioned how *I* 'felt' agitated, a familiar figure briskly crossing the park caught my eye.

Is that… Preek?

Our publicity director was weaving through the blankets and barbecues—his floral patterned muumuu billowing behind him like a cape. It wasn't unusual for him to be in the city on our behalf, but the suspicious conversation I'd overheard had put the lesser supe at the top of my shit list.

Followed closely by my sister.

"Marrying Baltasar doesn't give Dahlia rights to the throne."

But what if something else does?

Something like intel about a secret lab.

Clamoring to my feet, I wrestled the car keys from my pocket and tossed them to Baltasar. "Can you drive Daisy home for me, B? I'll meet you there."

"What… where are you going?" he mumbled, sucking on his rocket pop and messing with my focus.

"I need to see a man about a lab," I replied, quickly bending to kiss Daisy on the head—keeping one eye on Preek the entire time. "I'll explain later."

Every instinct had me wanting to kiss him goodbye as well. But the last thing we needed was for a supe who knew either of us out of uniform to see it and blow this whole thing wide open.

Not yet.

"But what about your ice cream?" Daisy huffed. "And you also promised we'd do more fun stuff with Blunty!"

Preek was about to disappear into a cluster of cabanas. It was now or never. "I'll make it up to you, sweetie. Here," I tossed a hundred-dollar bill at Baltasar, causing his eyebrows to shoot up to his hairline. "Take our girl somewhere fun."

"Sure thing, Z," he replied as I turned and raced down the hill. "I'll take good care of her."

I know you will, B.

CHAPTER 25
BALTASAR

I'm totally awesome at this second daddy thing.

After Zion had randomly run off, the little queen finished her ice cream—and his—before asking me to take her somewhere *I* liked to go as a kid.

It took me a few minutes to come up with an idea. Fun had *not* existed in my parents' vocabulary—unless you counted murder—but there was one sibling who'd always been ready to get into mischief with me.

Violentia.

Even though there was a distinct age divide between both sets of Suarez kids, the twins and I were occasionally included in our older siblings' schemes. Wolfy loved to spoil Gabe and Dre—since they were all on the same creepy wavelength. But Vi knew *I* was the guy to corral when she had a bad, possibly illegal, definitely ill-advised idea.

And that's how little Balty learned about gambling!

"RUN YOU FREAKIN' HORSE, RUUUUN!!!" Daisy stomped her little feet on the rickety bleachers—waving the race

program over her head like she was a charioteer cracking a whip. "C'mon, Buttercup! Go, girl, GOOOOO!"

A smile stretched across my face as Buttercup—who was picked on the name alone—took the lead in the homestretch, leaving her competitors in the dust. Daisy whooped as the horse crossed the finish line because, of course, the little queen had shown no interest in place or show bets.

My girl came here to win.

It already blew my mind that Zion trusted me enough to be around his kid at all. But to leave her completely in my care—and then call her *ours*—made me warm and fuzzy.

I've got it bad.

I was so proud of Daisy's victory that I took about eight million photos of her cheesing it up while collecting her winnings at the window. I couldn't wait to tell Zion how much fun we were having with the money he'd left us, but before I could send him a text, the Queen of the Track took charge.

"Now I get to take *you* shopping, Blunty!"

What?

"Uhh… like for clothes?" I mumbled, blindsided that she'd want to spend her hard-earned dollars on me.

"No. Nothing boring like that." She laughed and carefully slid her money into her shiny Chococat purse. "I want to get you something special. Something that will make being with us feel more like home."

Arghh, my heart!

I dropped my gaze to the dusty floor, not wanting Daisy to see me tearing up right in front of her. That was when I spotted a discarded brochure for a local farmer's market and I had another—extremely risky—idea.

Violentia would be so proud.

And that was how I found myself sneaking through the service hallways of the Salah haunted mansion, carrying a dozen hippie hemp bags full of exotic fruits, vegetables, and spices that Daisy had insisted on buying me. My girl was resting in her room before dinner, and Zion hadn't returned from his top secret mission yet, so I was left to my own devices. And right now, I was determined to get in the good graces of the formidable lesser supe who cooked for this family.

Gathering my courage, I quietly entered Cook's lair, surprised —and relieved—when I found it empty. Various pots were simmering on the stove, so she couldn't have been far. The only thing I needed to do was leave my humble offering at her altar and scuttle away.

Except…

My curiosity about what was cooking got the better of me. Creeping closer to the stove, I peered inside the largest pot to find what looked like mushroom soup. Grabbing a spoon, I tasted the broth, and while it was *good,* it was missing… something.

With a grin, I dug around in one of my bags until I found the jar of saffron threads I'd purchased. Glancing at my watch, I estimated there was still plenty of time for the saffron to bloom before I quickly tossed in a pinch.

"And what exactly are you doing to my soup, villain?" Cook's heavily accented voice echoed off the meat cleavers swinging above my head. "Do you plan on *poisoning* this family?"

"What? No," I stuttered, brandishing my jar of saffron like an exorcist with the cross. "I saw you were cooking mushrooms and knew I'd just bought some saffron…"

My babbling tapered off as Cook snatched the jar from my sweaty hand before giving it a suspicious sniff. "Saffron?" Her gaze narrowed. "What are you… *fancy* or something?"

I glanced down at the worn tee and jeans I'd changed into after Deathball practice. Both were now covered in track dust, farmer's market clippings, and a red stain from my rocket pop.

Yeah, I'm fancy.

"Well, I don't need your *fancy* here," she sneered before pulling out a wooden spoon from *somewhere* and pointing it at the door.

"Wait!" I cried. "I… Well, you see, our chef—Betsy—taught me how to cook. I was always hanging out in the kitchen anyway, so it probably made me less annoying or something. Anyway… Daisy wanted to buy me something today that reminded me of home, so I thought, maybe…"

Jesus, I sound deranged.

Cook peered past my shoulder, her eyes widening when she saw the mountain of bags on the counter. Then her gaze narrowed on me once again. "You think you're going to take over my kitchen? Just like you plan to take over this clan?"

She's only half-wrong…

"No!" I was desperate, needing this almost as much as I needed Zion.

Where is *he, anyway?*

"It's just…" My shoulders slumped in defeat. "I really want to help you cook, because I miss Betsy and my siblings…

Plus, Zion's been who knows where for hours. I just need *something,* so I don't feel so fucking useless around here all the goddamn time." I sniffled. "Pardon my French."

Cook's judgmental expression softened exactly one iota before she turned to the pot, dipped in her spoon, and took a taste.

I held my breath.

When she turned to me again, her permanently scowling face was so grotesquely twisted, I recoiled.

Is that... is she... SMILING?!

"All right, villain," she chuckled, handing me *her* sacred spoon. "Let's see what you can do."

YESSSS...

Unable to hold back a—less terrifying—grin of my own, I ran to my bags before returning with a few items. Chanterelles, fresh parsley, and a bottle of dry sherry a local winery had imported from Spain. By the time Cook rang the dinner gong, we had our soup, a garlic-crusted roast rack of lamb, and some biscuits I made from scratch to soak up all that saffron-goodness.

I'm in the zone.

The work had *almost* distracted me from the weird ache that had settled in my chest since Zion left us in the park. It certainly made me forget I was supposed to be dressed to the nines and seated across from Dahlia in the dining room.

Whoops.

"Our villain is in the kitchen!" Cook bellowed from the other side of the swinging doors. "And it's where he will eat from now on, unless you need to parade the poor boy around for a special event. I've asked for help in the kitchen for *years,* so now that I've got it, I don't plan on giving it up."

Well, damn.

I braced myself for Major Obscurity or Lady Tempest's inevitable explosion. When nothing happened besides a low murmur of agreement, weeks of tension drained from my body. To add to my attitude of gratitude, the service entrance door swung open, and the youngest Salah kids came tumbling in.

Followed by Daisy and Zion.

Thank fuck.

I practically tripped in my haste to reach my man, but then stopped short, realizing I *couldn't* wrap my arms around his neck and kiss him like I wanted to.

This sucks.

Zion's expression had been troubled when he entered the kitchen, but it changed when he spotted me. The most gorgeous grin stretched across his insanely attractive face as he took in my apron and flour-covered hands.

"You *cook,* B?" he asked, licking his lips as if it wasn't just the food he was hungry for.

"I do…" I confirmed, suddenly shy. "I love cooking."

Zion looked past me to where Cook was banging back through the swinging doors, before nodding in approval. "It smells so good, beautiful," he murmured—low enough that only I could hear. "I can't wait to put it in my mouth."

Lord!

I could feel my cheeks heat, but I shook it off and shot him a smirk I knew showcased my dimples.

All's fair…

"Take a seat, Z," I sternly replied, before shooting him a wink. "And be sure to save room for dessert."

His warm brown eyes trailed over me with singular intent. "Always," he replied with a wink of his own.

CHAPTER 26
BALTASAR

By the time I finished helping Cook clean up from dinner and got into bed, I was beat. Even though Coach had been focused on verbally clobbering our long-shot today, he still worked the rest of us hard. Add in keeping up with Daisy this afternoon, and I felt like I could sleep for a week.

Of course, I had no trouble waking up a few hours later when a giant monster slithered through my balcony doors.

My instincts were on high alert. I knew what had arrived was dangerous—that it could eat me alive. However, my dick was so hard, I decided I'd just use it as a weapon if I needed to.

Ultimate sword crossing.

"Mmm… is my mate as starved for me as I am for him?" Zion's voice changed octaves as he morphed into the half-shifted form I couldn't get enough of.

"Fuck, yes," I gasped in a breathy voice that would have embarrassed me a week ago. "I missed you so much today my bones ached."

Along with my boner.

Zion's gorgeous scales caught the moonlight as he climbed onto the bed, pulling the sheet off my body so slowly, I whimpered in frustration. While I would have preferred to sleep naked, Daisy liked to barge in to wake me up in the mornings. So I was currently wearing boxer briefs that did nothing to hide how ready I was for *my mate.*

I still don't know what that means for him, but I am here for it.

"Fuck, I love you needy," he murmured, teasing my waistband with his claws while leaning down to force his tongue into my equally needy mouth.

I groaned, grasping his broad shoulders for leverage as I helped him shimmy me out of my underwear. I was already drunk on his taste—on the feel of his scales and skin under my fingertips.

On *him.*

"You looked so fucking hot on the field today," Zion growled into my mouth. "The way you made that rookie long-shot submit, all sweaty and jacked up in your tight little supersuit."

My cock was absolutely *obsessed* with this brand of dirty talk. Exhibit A: The precum I was smearing on Zion's rock-hard abs as I rubbed myself all over him from below.

More, more, more.

"It gets me so hot watching you dominate other players," he continued, apparently intent on making me blow without even touching me. "Especially because I know what you *really* want behind closed doors…"

Oh, is that right?

Zion was absolutely correct that I wanted him owning my ass in the bedroom, but old rivalries died hard.

Super hard.

Counting on the element of surprise, I flipped him onto his back and quickly straddled his hips. Doing my best to use my weight to hold down the larger man without shifting.

"What about when I used to dominate *you* on the field, Salah?" I growled, placing my hands on his enormous pecs as I leaned down to trash-talk—just like old times. "When I made *you* submit to me on the regular?"

Instead of clapping back, or flipping us over again, Zion gave me a slow, filthy smile. "I liked it. Just like I like this." His hands landed on my waist, coaxing my hips to rock forward, sliding our dicks together and making my eyes cross. "And I *really* like the idea of you riding my cock. Just. Like. This."

"*Fuck*, Z," I choked out, shamelessly rubbing myself on him like a cat in heat while feeling him up. "I really want to." *I really did.* "But I've just… I've never… you know…"

I'm a butt sex rookie.

Zion immediately stopped grinding me over him, his gaze softening. "I know, beautiful." He lightly trailed his fingers up my thighs—soothing me. "We're gonna go slow and we'll only go as far as *you* want to—"

"I want it," I blurted out. "It's just… the only thing that's ever been in my ass was this one chick's finger, and she kind of surprised me with it. Oh! And your fingers… and tongue. Which was also a surprise, but I *liked* that. Fuck. I babble a lot when I'm nervous. I'm not sure if you've noticed…"

He stifled an adoring smile. "I've noticed, B. I like that too." His expression turned serious. "I've also noticed you struggle to articulate your thoughts, but I *need* you to be clear about what you want and don't want. Let's start with a safe word."

Uhhh…

I chewed on my bottom lip, suddenly wishing Zion was back on top, making me feel small and safe again. While I'd had a ton of sex, it had all been fairly vanilla—especially compared to the freaky deaky shit my brothers seemed to be into.

"Mine is *tuxedo*," Zion offered with a soft smile. "Because I hate wearing them. Just pick a word that you would *never* say in the heat of the moment—something that turns you off just thinking about it."

That's easy.

"Dahlia," I replied, without hesitation.

Zion sharply inhaled, his dick twitching between us as he registered what I was telling him by choosing his sister's name.

I don't want her.

I will never want her.

I only want you.

"That'll do it," he whispered.

Then we simply stared at each other in the dark for a few minutes while he stroked my thighs and I toyed with his nipples.

I can't help it.

The man has fantastic tatas.

"I think Dahlia's up to something," he blurted out. "Her and Preek together."

As expected, hearing my fiancé's name immediately caused my dick to lose its enthusiasm. Sliding off Zion's lap, I stretched out beside him with my head propped up on my arm, giving whatever he was about to say my full attention. I had a million questions, but also knew I needed to tread carefully. Even with this strong connection the hero and I shared, *Dahlia* was his clan.

Blood is thicker than murder.

"What makes you say that?" I carefully asked, wondering if this had something to do with him disappearing today.

He took a slow breath, but didn't immediately reply. For a minute, I panicked, thinking he somehow knew Wolfy had tasked me with gathering intel on his family.

Even though it's the last thing I want to do.

Then he rolled over to face me and pulled me closer, instantly calming my anxious thoughts. "The day after the motorcycle accident, I overheard the two of them talking about a... lab somewhere," he murmured, his focus on my chest. "It's apparently my *parents'* secret, but I suspect Dahlia plans to use it as..."—Zion met my gaze—"leverage."

I flinched, because that was the same word Wolfy had used when ordering me to dig up dirt on Mikki.

This is an impossible choice.

Zion misinterpreted my reaction, rubbing slow circles on my back as if to reassure me. "I don't think it's anything we need to worry about, except..." The circles momentarily stopped. "After Pops escorted you out of the principal's office, my mom mentioned how marrying *you* won't give Dahlia the right to the throne."

I deflated and dropped my gaze. "Yeah, no shit. Like your dad said when he dropped me off at my room... I should be *grateful* for this opportunity, since I'm just a fourth-in-line nobody with lame powers—"

My words cut off as Zion roughly gripped my chin and forced me to look at him. "Are you kidding me, Suarez? Your powers are why you play Supremacy-level Deathball. And how you wield those powers is why you're a fucking champion."

I grinned like an idiot. "Thanks, Coach."

A secretive smile twisted his lips before he sobered and got us back on track. "My point is, my mom felt compelled to tell me the throne was 'mine to lose'—like I should step it up, and quick. I don't think she's aware Dahlia knows about the lab… but she must still think she's up to *something*, right?"

That backstabber!

"I don't know, but we need to figure it out before she makes a move," I huffed, only to have a wave of shame wash over me.

I'm such a hypocrite.

The entire reason I'd been sent to marry Dahlia in the first place was to help her take the throne from Zion and absorb the Salah clan into ours. But here I was, having the nerve to act like *she* was the only enemy around here.

It's how the game is played.

But I don't want to play anymore.

"Are you… all right?" Zion was eyeing me with concern.

Exactly *how* he knew I was spiraling sent my already spiking anxiety through the roof. "I just don't want anything bad to happen to you. Or Daisy."

And that's the truth.

He deposited a kiss so sweet and trusting I almost started confessing on the spot. "Don't worry, beautiful. We'll figure this out—*together*—and in the meantime, we'll keep our enemies close, you know?"

Ugh.

I nodded stiffly before cuddling even closer, relaxing at least a little as he squeezed me tight. "Yes," I whispered against his skin. "Together."

Even though I'm actually the enemy.

CHAPTER 27
ZION

"BUSTED!"

I jolted awake, sitting up and rapidly blinking the sleep out of my eyes as I took in my unfamiliar surroundings in the harsh morning light.

Oh, fuck...

I'd apparently fallen asleep in Baltasar's room—like an idiot —and now my daughter was standing at the end of the bed, looking smug as hell.

"Gimme five more minutes, your majesty..." Baltasar sleepily murmured, burrowing further beneath the blankets.

Not a morning person, I take it.

This silly piece of intel filled me with a stupid amount of pleasure, but my contentment was short-lived as Daisy cackled in triumph.

"Oooooh, Auntie Dahlia is gonna be so *maaad...*"

"Dahlia? Where?!" It was my mate's turn to shoot up in bed, his pretty amber eyes widening as he registered the situation.

"Ah, fuck. *Fudge,* I mean." He turned to me with a grimace. "I'm sorry, Z…"

I furrowed my brow. "What are *you* apologizing for? *I'm* the one who fell asleep in here because I couldn't stop spooning you."

Baltasar blushed while Daisy squealed, jumping up and down while clapping her hands. "Ahhh, this is the best day ever! Blunty's gonna be my second daddy and you're gonna get married and we'll be a family!"

She's not wrong.

Noticing that my mate looked overwhelmed by Daisy's bold declaration, I pointed toward the door. "Go play lookout, D. If anyone asks, you're waiting for Blunty to get dressed and you haven't seen me at all."

My mini partner-in-crime saluted and slipped into the hallway, firmly shutting the door behind her way louder than was necessary.

Baltasar was chewing his lower lip and staring down at his lap, as if he truly thought he'd done something wrong. "I'm sorry if you didn't want Daisy to find out yet… or at all…"

Oh, you ridiculous himbo.

"Come here," I huffed, dragging him closer in a tangle of blankets. "I don't give a shit if Daisy knows, B. She won't tell a soul and—let's be real—it's not like she didn't have our numbers, anyway."

Baltasar was quiet for long enough that I tilted his chin so he would look at me. "Is something else bothering you, beautiful?"

Besides the indirect marriage proposal…

He looked like a deer caught in the headlights. "I-I just…" he stuttered. "I need to think about some things."

Excuse me?!

"Okaaaay." I frowned, wishing I could get inside that head of his and help him figure out his shit. I'd meant what I said about taking things slow—and I didn't want to rush him into anything—but we still needed to operate like a united front.

Plus, we're kind of on a time crunch here.

Unless…

"Are you…" I didn't even want to say it out loud, but needed to know. "Have you changed your mind about… *this?*" I gestured between us, not wanting to freak him out more by attempting to define what *this* even was.

Besides my wildest dream.

"What? No!" he exclaimed. "It's just… Wolfy sent me here with certain instructions…"

Ohhh…

Of course.

Being the oldest, I'd never had to worry about the pecking order in my family. I answered to my parents—just like the rest of my siblings did. Other than that, I was untouchable.

Despite what Dahlia might think.

"Would you like me to speak to Wolfgang with you?" I offered, barking a laugh when his eyes practically bugged out of his head. "Your brother doesn't scare me, Baltasar. Neither does Simon."

Since we all know who's actually the boss in that clan.

"Really?" He was looking me over with a mix of astonishment and admiration before shaking his head. "No. No, thank you. I should talk to him alone. It'll be okay. I think..."

Baltasar looked terrified, and a protectiveness unlike anything I'd ever felt before flared up within me.

"If Wolfgang tries to hurt you, I will fucking end him," I hissed, feeling my beast roar beneath the surface at the promise of violence. "The only thing separating us in power is that my parents are still around, and I would amend that in a heartbeat if it meant protecting you."

He gaped at me. "Y-you'd do that?"

You have no idea what I'd do for you.

"Yes, beautiful." I took a slow breath, willing myself to calm down. "I've been waiting for this to happen for far too long to lose you now. If you'd rather talk to Wolfgang alone, that's fine. But please tell me if he says anything that upsets you— so I can make it better."

By threatening him with bodily harm.

My sweet villain looked like he was about to cry, which only served to turn me on. However, he quickly crawled into my lap and hid his face before any tears—or boners—could make appearances.

It's probably for the best.

"Wolfy would never hurt me," he mumbled against my chest. "He's actually really... *sweet* to the rest of us. Most of the time."

I froze. While I didn't think Wolfgang was *evil*, he was one of the most deadly villains of our generation, and known for being merciless with his enemies. I *had* noticed the Suarez siblings genuinely got along with each other—beyond the ingrained familial loyalty most supes possessed. But a *caring* clan leader was especially unusual in our cutthroat world.

And very good to know…

Baltasar didn't seem to realize he was giving me dangerous intel about the leader of his clan—insider information I could use against them. A sudden vision of not only ascending *my* throne but stealing Wolfgang's as well rose to the surface, but I quickly tamped it down.

No scheming when your mate needs you, Zion.

"Our *parents* were the ones who made sure we were afraid of Wolfy," he continued, unprompted, and I was more than happy to let him ramble. "It was their way of keeping us in line. I guess he went along with it because he had plans of his own—"

It was Baltasar's turn to freeze as he finally realized he was unloading fairly classified information to the heir of another clan.

I laughed. "If it makes you feel any better, I figured it out on my own that Wolfgang is the one who got both your parents taken out." When he glanced up at me in alarm, I smoothed my hand through his thick hair. "First, no one here's crying over the deaths of Apocalypto Man and Glacial Girl. More importantly, it showed the rest of us that the story we'd been sold—about not being able to kill our parents—was a load of crap. *That* was a game changer, and that Wolfgang brought it to light only made me respect the man more."

Even if I would still face him in battle for you.

Baltasar searched my face, as if gauging just how insane I was about him. "I don't think you'll need to worry about ending anyone. Wolfy and Simon already knew I was having second thoughts about this marriage thing, so it won't be a total shock to hear I'm out." His shoulders slumped in defeat. "I guess I'm just worried…"

Okay, that's a start.

"Worried that they'll immediately send the plane to take you back to Big City?" I offered, although I wasn't exactly sure if that was what was bothering him.

It is fairly high on my list of concerns.

Baltasar's gaze snapped to mine again—his expression oddly anguished. "No. They'll want me to stay here for as long as possible."

Why does it seem like that bothers him?

I wanted to get him to elaborate, but tiny fists banging impatiently on the door put an end to the conversation.

"C'mon, Bluntycups!" Daisy hollered from the hallway. "I wanna eat already!"

That's our cue.

"Oh, shit!" Baltasar swore, scrambling off my lap and the bed before stumbling toward the dresser. "I forgot our queen was waiting."

I lazily watched as he yanked on his clothes, covering all those delicious muscles in moisture-wicking, high-performance fabric.

A travesty.

"Do you… mind if I call Daisy that?" he hesitantly asked, tossing a pair of sweatpants my way. "*Ours?* Y-you said it yesterday, but I wasn't sure if you meant it…"

He's absolutely ridiculous.

Casting the sweatpants aside, I rose from the bed and stalked to where he stood, using my larger body to cage him in against the dresser.

"Daisy *is* ours, B," I growled, brushing my lips over his and loving how he shuddered—even though I was the one standing here naked. "Just like you are *mine*. And *this*"—I drew back to better look at him—"is *it* for me. If you want it, too."

Please say yes.

I held my breath until he solemnly nodded. "Yeah, I do." He paused, as if there was a 'but' in there he wasn't elaborating on. "Just let me... figure out some things."

With Wolfgang.

It took some effort, but I staunchly buried my frustrations. I had pined after this man for years. Of course, I knew what *I* wanted, but my mate had other obstacles. Baltasar was already dealing with the brand new experience of being attracted to a man. On top of that, he now had to break the news to his clan leader that he wanted to deviate from the plan.

A plan that involves a legally binding contract with another family.

Maybe we can just switch one contract out for another...

Deciding to give my boy a break, I backed off—physically and otherwise. "What's your plan for the day, beautiful?" I innocently asked. "More Deathball practice?"

Even though I already know the answer to that.

Baltasar dragged his gaze from my cock to my face, although he didn't look embarrassed to have been ogling me. "Uh, yeah. But Coach weirdly told me to stay here—that he'd arranged for a personal trainer or something."

I turned toward the bed to hide my grin. "That *is* weird," I murmured, grabbing the discarded sweatpants and stepping into them before facing him again. "Mind if I join?"

His breathtaking face brightened, erasing any doubts I'd had about how he felt about *this*. "That would be awesome! I mean, I know we don't play the same position, but I would love any pointers you could give me."

Oh, I've got plenty of pointers to give you.

"I'll see what I can do." I smirked as I walked to meet him again, delivering a quick kiss before pushing him toward the door. "Now run along to breakfast with *our* queen. I'll sneak out of here in a few and meet you guys in the kitchen after I grab some clothes from my room."

Baltasar adorably blushed at my use of 'our' before obediently leaving to join Daisy. I listened as my daughter's excited babble to her *second daddy* faded and counted down from 30 before placing my hand on the knob. Sneaking one more glance over my shoulder at the invitingly rumpled bed, I slipped through the door into the empty hall, and headed for the grand staircase.

Easy peasy.

I made it to my room when I heard a door opening farther down the hall. I noticed it was Dahlia's at the same moment I realized it was *Preek* who'd exited.

Perfect timing.

Because I'm choosing violence this morning.

CHAPTER 28
ZION

I stepped back into the hallway and slammed my door shut, snapping the publicity director's attention to me. For a moment we simply stared at each other, and I had to give the lesser supe credit for not immediately shitting himself.

Since I know I'm looking at him like he's my next meal.

"Morning, Preek!" I sang out, grinning broadly as I casually leaned against the wall. "Don't be shy. Come on down here so we can chat."

He swallowed before making his way down the hall—the only sign he was nervous, thanks to his otherwise bored expression. "Dahlia and I were having a breakfast meeting—"

"Did you find everything you needed in the city yesterday?" I interrupted, catching him off guard with the seemingly unrelated question, just as I'd hoped.

"Yes," he slowly replied, shrewdly narrowing his eyes. "Were you also running errands at the...?"

Oh, you wanna play a guessing game?

"The tailor," I offered, maintaining my smile but allowing a little fang to creep in—just for fun. "And the Asian food market... and the drugstore."

Preek's expression grew pinched as he no doubt tried to determine how much I'd seen of his day. But nothing was *hitting* like I wanted it to.

Let's try this.

"And the perfumery."

I let that one hang in the air—since it was the stop that had baffled me the most—and I was rewarded with the tiniest twitch of Preek's left eye.

There it is.

"Yes, well," he sniffed, smoothing his hands down his seer-sucker ensemble so he could avert his eyes. "I've been wanting a fresh scent for summer, and—"

I advanced so fast that he had no choice but to scramble backward until his body hit the mezzanine railing. Using my larger frame to loom over the lesser supe, I took a slow inhale, drawing it out. When I scented Baltasar like this, it was a show of ownership and affection—a way for me to breathe him deep enough into my lungs that he'd become a permanent part of me. That's not what this was.

This was pure intimidation.

"I dunno, Preek," I murmured, straightening to my full height. "You smell the same as you always do to me." I paused, allowing my beast to rise to the surface—to show him what awaited should he make a wrong move. "Like prey."

The man was shaking, but he still had spirit. "You're insane," he hissed. "And I doubt your parents would be thrilled to learn—"

"That you've been poking around their business?" I grinned as he paled, feasting on his fear.

"Why exactly are you bullying the help?" Dahlia's haughty voice rang out, and I immediately turned to face her— showing Preek he wasn't threatening enough to worry about me showing him my back.

"Oh, *the help* was just heading down to breakfast. Which is a good idea." I grinned innocently at her before glancing over my shoulder to the man still warily eyeing me. "Since he'll need his strength."

Being smart enough to recognize his opening, Preek raced down the stairs without another word.

Run, rabbit, run.

He was already forgotten as I stalked toward my sister. "A word, Dahlia?"

She rolled her eyes before dramatically gesturing into her room. "Come on in. I'd love to hear whatever the fuck *that* was about."

I'm sure you would.

I waited until she closed the door and gave me her full attention before I struck. "Do you know why Preek recently used our private plane?"

True to form, Dahlia didn't flinch or attempt to lie. Instead, she stood her ground and faced me head-on—like a true supe. "Do *you*, Zion?"

I laughed, appreciating her brass balls. The truth was, I had nothing. When I questioned our pilot, it turned out he wasn't working that night—and his alibi checked out. I planned to get my claws on the plane's black box for the flight data, but figured I'd go straight to the source in the meantime.

Because when people panic, they make mistakes.

"I'm working on it," I shrugged, content to let her wonder just how much I knew. "But now's your chance to come clean, before I go straight to Mom and Pops and blow this whole thing wide open."

She stilled in the way supes did when readying for a fight. "I would highly recommend you not go to them—"

Rage blasted through me—white-hot and all-consuming. "Are you *threatening* me, Atmosphera?" I boomed, half-shifting until my borrowed sweatpants strained at the seams.

Instead of matching my energy—as she'd unwisely done countless times before—Dahlia submitted by lowering her eyes and keeping her voice calm. "Just give me time, Zion. I didn't want to say anything to you until I was absolutely certain about what's going on here."

Oh.

To say I was shocked was an understatement. I'd expected denial, rage, redirection—even thinly veiled threats—but this almost sounded like Dahlia wasn't the enemy, after all.

So who is?

"Tell me what you know," I gritted out.

My only thoughts were of protecting my daughter and mate. If my sister knew something that could keep them out of harm's way, she needed to start talking.

Dahlia met my gaze again, with an almost pleading expression. "I don't *know* anything. Not yet. Just let me keep digging… and get through this stupid wedding first."

Nothing about Baltasar is stupid!

I scoffed, beyond done with the opinion that man was beneath her. Especially when *she* paled in comparison. "If you couldn't care less about marrying Baltasar Suarez, why the hell are you even doing it?"

Especially when I'd kill to make him mine.

"BECAUSE I HAVE TO YOU IDIOT!" she roared—eyes flashing electric blue as she involuntarily levitated a few inches off the floor. "Mom told me I needed to marry him to keep the almighty Wolfgang Suarez happy with our clan partnership. I'm not an heir like you, remember? I'm just a spare. So I don't have a choice."

Well, that's a different story than what I was told...

I still wasn't sure who was playing *who* here, but I also knew how this world operated, so wasn't about to let an opportunity for leverage pass me by.

"Hey, sis, it's gonna be okay," I soothed, pulling Dahlia back down to earth and crushing her in a hug that was perhaps a smidge too tight. "Maybe we can figure out a way for you to get out of this marriage contract, hmm?"

She stiffened in my arms. "What do you mean?"

Gotcha.

"How 'bout this?" I rubbed soothing circles on her back, pretending it was Daisy or Baltasar, so it would feel authentic. "*I'll* look into this marriage contract while you continue whatever super top secret research you're doing. When we each find out more, we'll reconvene and share. Sound good?"

She silently considered for a good minute while I did my best not to hold my breath. It wasn't like I needed Dahlia's blessing to steal Baltasar from her, since I was going to do *that* either way. But knowing my sister wasn't planning on pitching a fit about her broken engagement would give me one less thing to worry about.

Plus, it won't hurt for her to think she owes me one.

"Fine," she huffed, wiggling out of my hold so she could fix me with a haughty stare once again. "But in the meantime, I don't need you sniffing around and getting in my way. Let *me* handle this."

I hummed noncommittally in response, already focused on bringing up her photographer's contact info on my phone. I'd paid him a pretty penny to claim the engagement photos he'd taken were unusable, but now had a better idea of what he could do with them.

Something to get this scandal rolling.

"Yeah, yeah," I mumbled when I realized Dahlia was waiting for a verbal response. "If you're *sure* you don't want my help with whatever you and Preek are up to…"

Not that it's going to stop me from 'sniffing around.'

"I really don't, Zion," she murmured as I raised my phone to my ear and spun on my heel.

The rest of her reply was half-lost as I strode from the room, entirely focused on the call connecting and my next steps. It wasn't until after I'd finished speaking to the photographer that I fully registered what she'd said as the door shut behind me.

"Because I really don't think you want to know."

CHAPTER 29
BALTASAR

I awoke with a groan to the unmistakable chime of a missed video call on my phone.

Please let it be a twin butt-dialing me…

When I saw it was *Wolfy*, I scrambled to sit and tried to make myself presentable by desperately raking my fingers through my messy bed head.

Sex hair is probably more like it.

Ever since he and Daisy surprised me at Deathball practice, Zion had been sneaking into my bedroom every night through my balcony door. This was the best setup, because he could easily scale the house in lizard form, while I loved going to sleep knowing a big scary monster was coming for me.

Literally.

I no longer felt like a total newb at handling a cock that wasn't my own, and Zion's bottomless patience in bed never embarrassed me. I enjoyed being his student—not only because pleasing him lit me up like the praise ho I apparently was, but because we had a *big* goal we were working toward.

Me riding that lizard dick.

Even if I'm still a little nervous about it.

I definitely knew what I wanted—Zion topping me—but it was weird to be a virgin all over again. Despite my nerves, I knew he would take care of me, so for now, I was content to let him keep stretching me with his fingers and magical lizard tongue.

Working me as hard as he does on the field.

A few days ago, I'd been surprised as hell to arrive at the Salah's Deathball field only to find *Zion* waiting for me. He'd somehow convinced my coach to let *him* train me, and I was all for the arrangement. It got me extra attention from my man and didn't have to catch a ride into Sunrise City at the crack of dawn.

Win-win.

Part of me wondered if he'd offered to help to stay connected to Deathball, but it was obviously such a sore subject, I didn't want to ask. It was safe to assume that part of the reason was to keep me close to him—close to home.

Wait…

Do I really think of this place as home?

Or just him?

The sound of another incoming video call snapped me out of my thoughts. Not wanting to piss off Wolfy any more than I already had, I propped up my phone on the nightstand and turned to face it. When the screen showed *both* Wolfy and Simon seated in front of my brother's laptop, I knew something was up.

*Something bad, judging by our **Mafia Queen's** sour expression…*

"Why do you insist on leaving a trail of destruction in your wake, Baby Hulk?" Simon huffed, holding up a glossy photograph that made my stomach drop into my nuts. "Care to explain this?"

It was a shot from when the photographer came to take engagement photos of Dahlia and me. I'd been told those were unprintable.

But apparently, some had turned out just fine.

My mouth went dry as I stared at the grainy printout of Zion and me rolling around on the croquet field after he taunted me into throwing a punch. Only this didn't look like a fight. With the way he had me pinned—and the way we were staring into each other's souls—it looked like…

"It looks like you were about to *fuck* your fiancé's brother, Baltasar!" Simon barked. "Surely that can't be correct."

Welp. I guess this is my opening.

My gaze briefly flickered to Wolfy, who was sitting calmly beside his seething *inventus,* his expression as impassive as ever.

It's now or never, Baltasar.

"We were actually just brawling in that photo," I replied, marching past Simon's muttered 'thank fuck' to bravely soldier on. "But we are. About to, I mean." When they both just stared at me, I clarified, "About to fuck."

Might as well let it all hang out.

From three thousand miles away…

Simon's face was a symphony of emotions. Shock morphing into confusion then rage—his pale skin turning a shade of red I'd only seen on perfectly ripe tomatoes.

"We are currently strengthening our business alliance with a prominent clan through a very public engagement. And you've waited until this moment to decide you fancy some cock, hmm?" Simon's voice was deadly quiet, which was ten million times more terrifying than his yelling.

I fearfully glanced at Wolfy, expecting to see my funeral in his eyes, but caught what looked like a *smirk* before his attention was drawn off-screen.

When he looked at me again, his expression was unreadable once more. "We'll figure something out, Balty." Simon opened his mouth to protest, but my brother placed a gloved hand on his *inventus'* narrow shoulder to calm him. "It actually makes things easier if you marry straight to the top."

Easier?

Oh. Right.

Easier to take over the Salah clan…

"Have you dug up anything on the mother of Zion's kid?" Wolfy asked, and I tensed.

"Zion Salah has a *kid?!*" Xander suddenly appeared in the background, dressed in his wetsuit and carrying what looked like a lab specimen box. "When did *that* happen?"

Ten years ago this August.

"Never mind the child." Simon twisted in his chair to face Xander. "**The Dumb One** is apparently now **The Suddenly Gay One**—*for* Zion Salah."

"Sugar…" came Butch's voice from somewhere offscreen the same time I heard Vi snort in amusement.

Great.

The gang's all here.

We're just missing the twins.

As if on cue, my phone buzzed twice with two new texts, but I couldn't bear to see what Gabe and Dre had to say.

Not until I've had a drink.

"Well, Balty?" Wolfy smoothly brought us back on track. "Any new intel you want to share?"

Nope.

Absolutely not.

"The mother of his child is dead," I gritted out, feeling my supe form start to Hulk its way to the surface. "And you need to leave the kid out of this."

The silence that descended on the other end was so loud you could have heard it from space.

Even Xanny shut the fuck up.

For a full twenty seconds, I was stared into an early grave by both clan leaders, with the only sound being my phone blowing up from all the texts the twins were sending me.

"Butch." Wolfy's icy voice made me flinch. "May we have a word with you in private? You too, Vi."

Oh, no...

"You. Stay on the line," Wolfy growled at me before he and Simon rose and walked off screen.

My heart was racing—threatening to pound its way out of my chest—and I was *pouring* sweat as my vision went fuzzy around the edges.

What the fuck is happening?!

"Hey, hey, buddy." Xander's voice cut through my panic and I blinked to find him sitting in Wolfy's chair. "Talk to me."

"What?" I croaked, in desperate need of some water.

He grinned. "Soooo... you're into dick now, huh?"

I barked a laugh, thankful for his signature bluntness. Maybe it was because he wasn't raised as a supe, but Xanny always gave it to you straight.

Or... not so straight.

"No," I carefully replied. "Just his. Zion just... does it for me."

Xander chuckled. "That sounds familiar." Then he turned uncharacteristically serious. "Do you... have any questions? Since, you know, I'm a gay man who loves cock. A personal preference, but it's made me quite the expert."

Jesus.

"Um..." I stuttered, feeling my cheeks go up in flames, but realizing I should probably take him up on his offer. "Is it gonna hurt?"

His eyes widened. "Oh. Well, yes... but not that much if he properly preps you. And it's a *good* pain, if you know what I mean."

Yes. I do.

I didn't want to talk about my potential kinks with **The Mouthy One**, but I could tell he was bursting at the seams with questions of his own. "Just *ask*, Xanny—"

"What's his lizard dick like?" he blurted out—rolling his eyes when I glared and growled possessively. "I'm asking for *science*, Balty. It's not like the cave paintings show any nude scenes. Doc has yet to discover any pre-Colombian cave porn during his decades of research in the jungles of Argentina. So, help me out here."

Okay... for science.

"Well, it's covered in these purple scales that go from light to dark and shimmer like galaxies. And it has ridges, like a... rocket pop." I licked my lips, suddenly parched. "But the thing I can't figure out"—*and I'm way too embarrassed to ask*—"is the bulge at the base that's kind of shaped like a... knot. It, um, gets bigger right before he... you know... and he likes me to put pressure on it—really squeeze it. I dunno. It seems to make him go into primal lizard beast mode."

Aka, hot as fuck mode.

"Fascinating... Like the *bulbus glandis* of canid mammals, instead of the hemipenis found in most scaled reptiles." Xander had been tapping notes into his phone as I babbled, but he put down the device to give me his full attention. "Has he ever mentioned anything about *'breeding?'*"

I nodded slowly. "Yeah, he has, now that you mention it. I thought it was just... dirty talk. Right?"

Right?!

My brother snorted. "Unless you've magically grown a womb, yes, it *is* just dirty talk. But there's a biological reason behind it. Either way, it sounds like you're gonna have a good time once you get to the main event. Try not to worry about it too much." He sobered again. "That big lizard treats you well, right? I don't want to have to fly there and kick his ass."

"Yes!" I exclaimed, feeling a weight lift from finally being able to talk about this entire beautiful mess. "No one's ever treated me as well as he does. I'm listened to, and cared for, and he never makes me feel stupid." I cleared my throat as tears pricked my eyelids. "And whenever I'm near him, there's this *pull* in my chest—almost like I'm connected to him. It's worse when he's not around, though. Like, right now, my chest *aches.*"

Xander was grinning wildly. "Is that a fact? You know, that sounds exactly like..." His attention suddenly snapped off screen. "Shit. They're coming back. Listen, Balty, just hang up. I'll tell Wolfy we had a bad connection and try to talk Simon off his murderous ledge. Go enjoy your day, and your rocket pop lizard-dicked *inventus.*"

Say what?

I was about to make him repeat himself when the screen went dark. But I'd heard him perfectly.

Well, shit.

CHAPTER 30
BALTASAR

Finding out Zion was my *inventus* definitely cleared up a few things. Unfortunately, he'd gone into the city for some reason, so I didn't get the chance to share the news before an unexpected guest arrived.

Two unexpected guests.

Captain Masculine and his mother, Smoldering Siren.

Fuck.

Despite the scandalous leaked photos, Major Obscurity and Lady Tempest were more than happy to focus on fawning over the celebrity visitors. They offered to give their fellow heroes a tour, invited them to stay for lunch, and pretty much acted like a couple of cape-chasing simps.

Smoldering Siren graciously accepted, and I realized, too late, she'd been sent as a distraction—so her son could take care of family business.

A family member's *business, to be exact.*

"Hey, Baltasar." Butch gave me his million-dollar smile—the one that graced billboards across the land. "How's it going?"

Sigh.

He'd found me digging around in Cook's kitchen garden. Literally. Now that I was the unofficial sous chef, I'd gone back to the farmer's market and bought some plants, which I'd spent the morning finding homes for. Luckily, I'd been given a key to the garden this time, so I didn't have to deal with that possessed fencing again.

Or my repressed trauma.

"I assume Wolfy sent you here," I grumbled before freezing. "Or… Simon."

Cappy wouldn't… kill me, would he?

WOULD HE?!

"Wolfy, yes." Butch nodded, still smiling, but with the unmistakable focus of a predator. "Walk with me, Balty. Let's chat."

Gulp.

Along with The Hand of Death, Captain Masculine was on the short list of supes you wouldn't want to meet in a dark alley. The difference was that Butch had a kill list of *villains* that made his made-for-TV smile all the more terrifying to nobodies like me.

I locked the garden gate behind me and tried my best to casually stroll beside him like I wasn't internally fighting for my life.

That lasted all of two seconds.

"Is everyone pissed at me?" I blurted out, physically unable to play the game like these pros.

Butch froze and turned to face me. "What? No, Balty. No one is pissed at you." He grimaced. "Well, Simon was… displeased, but Wolfy calmed him down by promising a scandal." Another pause. "But you seem to be way ahead of us on that."

I ran a hand down my face, wondering if Zion knew about this publicity shitstorm yet. I could have easily texted him, but I'd been too mad at myself for getting us into this mess in the first place with my temper.

The paparazzi always catch me at my worst moments.

When I didn't reply, Butch continued. "So. You and Zion, huh?"

Here we go again.

"Yes, Cappy," I huffed, knowing full well this mess was already the talk of the group chat—which I'd also been avoiding like the plague. "Me and Zion. And no, I didn't see it coming any more than any of you did. I don't even *like* dudes, dude!"

Butch threw his head back and laughed, giving me a genuine smile. "Understood. Completely. But the heart wants what it wants, doesn't it?"

The dick wants what it wants, too.

Suddenly, I remembered Butch had only been with women before Xander. "How did you *know* Xanny was the one for you? Especially since all you wanted was pussy before him?"

The hero known as Captain Masculine blushed so deeply that I thought he might immediately take flight, never to be heard from again.

Is that what I look like when Zion makes me flustered?

Jesus, I hope not…

"Um, well." He cleared his throat and rallied. "I can't say I was that into… *pussy*," he whispered the word like the purity

257

police might hear him, "no matter who it was attached to. But as soon as I met Xan, I just *knew*. He was all I could think about or focus on, and that was without the whole *inventus* pull..."

He rubbed his chest before gently adding, "Not that you *need* to be an *inventus* to have a connection like that with someone. It sounds like you simply met the right supe for you."

I furrowed my brow, surprised **The Mouthy One** hadn't run his notorious mouth to his *inventus* about my business.

That's very unlike Xander...

Or anyone in my family.

Butch misinterpreted my expression and hurriedly kept talking. "But you shouldn't worry about anyone in the family being *angry* with you about Zion. To be honest, Wolfy didn't seem bothered by it at all."

This only added to my confusion—and dread. "Then... Why did he send you here?"

Before he could reply, a familiar voice hollered across the lawn. "BLUNTY! I wanna show you something!"

Butch's blue eyes zeroed in on Daisy's approach like a hawk watching a field mouse. "Is that the kid?" he asked, and my blood ran cold.

Oh, no...

"Oh, hi." Daisy reached us, eyeing the supe watching her like his next meal, while I instinctively pulled her against my side. "You're that guy on the sign by Waffle House—the one advertising spandex or something."

Butch smiled, but no light reached his eerily cold eyes. "That's me. Captain Masculine. But you can call me Butch. What's *your* name, little girl?"

"You don't have to answer him," I hissed, shifting my body so that Daisy had to peer around me to see the hero.

Back off, Cappy.

My future brother-in-law glanced at me for only a moment before turning his unwavering attention back to his prey. "Oh, but we're going to be *family* soon, from what I hear. Isn't that right?"

"Butch…" I warned, but Daisy was fearless.

"Maybe. Maybe not." Her voice was nonchalant, even as her tiny fingers tightened in the fabric of my shirt.

I've got you.

Blade Runner Butch laughed humorlessly. "Fair enough. I would love to speak to your parents, though. Are they around?"

"That's enough," I growled, even though I highly doubted I could take the famous hero in a fight.

But he's not getting near Daisy unless I'm dead.

"B-Blunty?" Daisy's voice was more unsure than I'd ever heard it, and I suddenly felt like maybe I *could* take The Captain, after all.

"What's the matter, kid?" Butch's voice had gone sinister— leaving no doubt in my mind that heroes and villains were exactly the same when push came to shove. "Are your powers not strong enough yet to fight your own battles? I wonder what sort of powers you have…"

"Ah!" Daisy's yelp brought my attention to her, finding *my* girl rubbing her chest with a tearful expression. "What are you doing to me?"

I'M GONNA POUND HIM INTO THE GROUND!!!

"I SAID THAT'S *ENOUGH!*" I bellowed, instantly shifting into my full-sized fighting mode and tackling a shocked Butch to the manicured lawn. "Run, D! Get back in the house, now!"

Daisy screamed, but took off running. Tensing, I braced myself for the inevitable anguish of Captain Masculine burning me alive with his firepower.

But then, nothing happened.

"*Cheez-its,* Balty," he huffed from somewhere beneath my bulk before pushing hard enough to shove me off. Neither of us stood. We just sat on the grass across from each other, catching our breath. "Where the heck did *that* come from?"

You touched what's mine.

I shifted back to civilian form, not even caring that my junk was now flapping in the breeze. If I was going to be honest, I got a sick satisfaction from knowing it would make Butch uncomfortable.

How a choir boy like him shacked up with a dirtbag like Xanny is beyond me.

"Is *that* why Wolfy sent you?" I snarled, still pissed despite the ceasefire. "Because you can tell him she's *mine,* and if he has something to say about it, he can say it to me and Zion."

Butch was gaping at me like he'd never seen me before—and maybe he never had.

Maybe none of them have.

Not like Zion has.

"Why are you so protective of someone else's kid?" he slowly asked, like he was doing his best to understand.

"Because Zion's my *inventus*," I gritted out, panting through the rage still simmering beneath the surface. "Any further questions, Cappy?"

Butch opened and closed his mouth a few times, and it was a good 60 seconds before he spoke. "Well... *fuck.*"

I couldn't help it. I laughed, and once I got going, I couldn't stop, and then *Butch* joined in until any tension that remained between us had evaporated.

Along with any chance of this staying out of the group chat.

"I've made a mess of things, haven't I?" I finally asked, shaking my head at my own stupidity.

Butch looked surprised by my question. "I wouldn't say that. Things have gotten more interesting, that's for sure, but it's already an unusual situation." His expression turned wary. "She's... half-normie, isn't she?"

Well, fuck is right.

Uninterested in handing over intel about those I cared about, I simply pressed my lips into a thin line and stared him down.

He nodded once. "Got it. I didn't hear it from you. Although you need to understand, I am obligated to share this discovery with Wolfy and Simon, along with the *inventus* thing." When I still didn't reply, he added, "But I will also let them know the girl is off limits."

My breath rushed out of me as my shoulders slumped. "Thank you."

I owe you one, Cappy.

Butch gracefully rose and smiled, back to the friendly supe I knew. "C'mon. Why don't you show me around, since it sounds like we're staying through lunch. That's plenty of time for me to gather more indirect intel to keep our Mafia Queen happy."

"Whatever keeps me off his radar," I chuckled before standing. Too late, I remembered I was completely naked, with nothing but shredded clothes littering the ground.

Well, this is awkward.

"Here." Butch threw me a pair of sweats he'd apparently flown across the county with. "Xan told me to always carry a pair for you."

I caught the pants and focused on pulling them on, not wanting the hero to see how choked up *that* indirect intel made me.

"Thanks," I said once I was decent, and my emotions were mostly back to baseline. "First, I need to go check on my girl before I give you the tour. Oh! And I also want to tell you all about this strip club Zion took me to…"

Blood may be thicker than murder…

But it doesn't mean we can't fuck with each other along the way.

CHAPTER 31
ZION

Murder was my only thought—my only endgame—as I stalked toward the dining room. Fury ignited my blood, breathing fire into my veins.

He's a fucking dead man.

My mood was already foul after my pointless trip into the city, and that only worsened when I saw the photos had been leaked two days *earlier* than I'd specified. To make things worse, I hadn't had the chance to fill in Baltasar on my plans to ignite a scandal.

He's probably freaking out.

And blaming himself…

But all my frustration, annoyance, and worry paled compared to the pure *rage* I was currently feeling—squarely aimed at one supe in particular.

Captain. Masculine.

The first thing I saw when I returned to the house was my daughter's tear-stained face as she threw herself into my arms. At first, I panicked, thinking Baltasar was hurt, but when she finally calmed down enough to tell me what happened, I saw red.

How dare Butch behave that way in my *house!*

Leaving Daisy in her bedroom with trusted staff, I headed downstairs, where our *special guests* from Big City were apparently enjoying lunch.

I'm going to kill him.

I'm going to kill…

Killkillkillkill.

My boot connected with the dining room door before I even registered I'd reached my destination. Maybe it was because the room was full of powerful supes—or that this house was far from drama free—but no one batted an eye at my violent entrance.

I stabbed a finger at the man sitting in *my* seat next to *my* mate. "You. Outside. Now."

"Is there a problem, Justice?" Captain Masculine calmly asked, setting down his fork and casually leaning back against his chair as if nothing were amiss.

Of course, Big City's greatest superhero remained as unruffled as ever when threatened by a bloodthirsty lizard-man. Meanwhile, Baltasar looked like he was going to faint.

"Zion!" my mom scolded. "Is that any way to address such a decorated hero gracing our home with his presence?"

Oh, spare me.

I ignored her completely, keeping my gaze locked on my opponent. "You fucked with what's *mine.*"

My rational brain was screaming at me to stand down—reminding me I personally *knew* the man behind the famous blue mask—but my beast only saw a threat to those we loved.

Masculine arched an eyebrow before slinging an arm over the back of Baltasar's chair, enraging me further. "Do you mean the mysterious little girl I spoke to earlier?" he mused—thoughtful and challenging at once. "I wasn't aware you had any children…"

Bullshit.

Based on Daisy's recounting of the confrontation, it was clear the hero had been sent here to snoop. And his singular focus suggested my *daughter* was the target.

But how would Wolfgang know to look for her in the first place?

My gaze drifted to Baltasar's stricken face just as my mom spoke up again.

"We only recently learned of the girl's existence ourselves." She daintily dabbed her lips with a paisley-patterned napkin, but I noticed her hands shook. "Zion was quite the Lothario in his younger years, and apparently he had a bit too much fun with a lesser supe a decade or so ago…"

"A lesser supe, huh?" Captain Masculine smirked and my blood ran cold.

He knows.

He knows she's half-normie.

Which means Wolfgang knows.

And there's only one man who could have told them.

My fury was replaced by an anguish so acute it was a wonder I didn't fall to my knees.

This time, when my gaze landed on Baltasar, I made sure he saw just how deeply his betrayal cut me. He frantically shook his head, but I was already stalking from the room. I needed to walk the fuck away—to block out the buzzing in my ears, the pull in my chest, and Pops' idiotic addition to the conversation.

"Naturally, we'll be registering her with the USN as soon as possible."

Like hell you will.

Daisy didn't even *belong* to this family. They'd never shown any interest in claiming her before, and this acknowledgment was simply to cover their own asses in front of Masculine and Smoldering Siren. She was mine—mine and Baltasar's until he acted like a goddamn Judas by selling us out to his older brother.

"Z, wait!" Baltasar grabbed my arm as I stomped down a service hallway—as if he had any right to touch me.

"You traitor!" I hissed, slamming him against the wall and pinning him there with my larger body. Yet again, he didn't shift to match me, and this continued submission only aroused—and enraged—me. "Why would you tell them what Daisy is?"

"I didn't!" he cried. "I swear, I didn't. Butch figured that out on his own today."

This tracked with what Daisy had told me. She'd felt the invasive pressure from a much more powerful supe—testing what she was made of.

An experience I'd hoped to shield her from.

"How did he know to look for her here, Baltasar?" I gritted out, *daring* him to lie to me about that pesky little detail.

The only reason I was humoring this conversation at all was because my daughter had gone on and on about how *Baltasar* had saved her. How he'd faced off against the famous Captain Masculine so she could run to safety, and checked on her afterwards to make sure she was okay.

You infuriating man.

Just let me hate you.

"Because I'm a fucking idiot who mentioned you had a kid during one of my first check-ins with Wolfy." Baltasar hung his head, and I could *feel* the shame and self-loathing radiating off of him. "That's all I'm good for in my family. Gathering gossip and opening my big, stupid mouth so they can use that intel however they please. I was already getting cold feet on the plane ride here—already knew I didn't want Dahlia—but Wolfy and Simon told me to suck it up for a while. They wanted to see what dirt I could find on your family while they came up with a scandal to end the engagement."

I released him and backed away, trying to process everything he was spouting off.

He... never wanted to marry Dahlia?

"I'm so fucking sorry, Zion," he continued, his pretty amber eyes filling up with tears. "I know it probably doesn't mean much, but I wasn't planning on telling Wolfy anything else about you—or Daisy. And I-I told them they needed to leave her out of this. That she's off limits."

I'm sure that went over well.

An annoying blast of *pride* swept through me as I envisioned sweet Baltasar going to bat for Daisy. If any of my siblings had the balls to try something like that—especially after I took the throne—it probably wouldn't end well for them.

267

And I don't instill the terror of Wolfy and Simon combined.

"I gave you access to my *kid*, B," I spat, determined to stay mad, even as my resolve was breaking. "How do I know I can trust you?"

He took a step toward me, as if testing the waters, and I had to admire his bravery. "Because the idea of betraying you or Daisy makes me feel like I took a knife to my gut. And the thought of losing either of you makes me want to drown myself in your death pond."

Well, shit.

Wait… death pond?!

Baltasar's words gave me an idea—something that might chill us both out. "C'mon." I grabbed his arm and pulled him further down the service hallway, toward a back staircase.

It's time you experienced my pond for yourself.

As much as I wanted to hate this man, I could also understand the impossible situation he'd been in. Loyalty to your clan was prized above all else. If Baltasar felt the way I did about him, he'd probably been struggling with where his loyalties lay since the day he arrived.

In the end, he'd challenged a powerful supe—a member of *his* clan—for my daughter. And in my book, that told me everything I needed to know.

Plus, the thought of losing him *also makes me want to die.*

"Are you going to drown me?" Baltasar asked as we reached my fortress of solitude—sounding heartbreakingly resigned to the idea.

I guess I should put the big guy out of his misery.

"No, B," I chuckled as I removed my clothes. "But if you don't want me murdering your future brother-in-law, then I need to get my ass in my pond, pronto."

"But why am *I* here?" He was eyeing the dark waters nervously, as if he had anything to fear while with me.

Truthfully, I could never hurt the villain—even if he sold me out to his entire clan—and there was nothing I could do to change that.

I've been a goner for him since we met.

Fully naked, I moved closer, fiddling with the bottom edge of his T-shirt. "Because the only other thing that soothes me, besides submerging myself in these waters, is being close to you. Even the few hours we were apart today felt like torture."

"There's a reason for that..." he murmured as I pulled his shirt over his head and got to work on his pants.

"Yeah, I know," I laughed. "You're my *mate,* that's why. And even though I don't always understand these weird animal urges I have, I *know* you're mine. Now get in the goddamn pond, Baltasar."

He looked like he wanted to say more, but wisely obeyed instead. To my amusement, he walked around the pond and entered at the sloped side—so he could tiptoe his way closer to the water's edge.

"Don't tell me you can't swim, Suarez!" I heckled before diving in so smoothly, I cut the water like a knife. When I resurfaced, I found him still easing his way in. "What were you thinking, shacking up with a water monster?"

"You're not a monster," he huffed as he *finally* got his ass in the water. "And I swim in the ocean back home all the time."

Hearing him call Big City 'home' stung, so I dipped back underwater to clear my head. Sinking lower, I allowed the silence, the juxtaposition of weightlessness and pressure, to remind me that—even if I didn't know what the fuck I was—I was *here*.

Movement far above caught my eye, and I watched as Baltasar paddled around with the confidence of someone who did, in fact, swim in the ocean all the time.

As if I needed further proof that he was made for me.

The longer I watched him from below, the more I felt my beast rising to the surface—zeroing in on the helpless 'prey' in our habitat.

No, I would never hurt Baltasar, but I still wanted to devour him—to claim him so thoroughly that he lived in my bloodstream. Having him close was soothing, but being inside him would make everything better.

Time to show him who he's playing with.

CHAPTER 32
ZION

I struck when Baltasar was too far from the rocky edge to grab onto anything substantial before swiftly dragging him down into the depths.

To my surprise—and my beast's disappointment—he didn't struggle, or attempt to fight me off. My mate simply wrapped his thick arms around my scaly neck and pressed his mouth to mine.

Ready to drown with me.

It wasn't a true kiss, since I didn't have lips in this form, but it wordlessly conveyed everything Baltasar had been struggling to say. Or that I'd been too stubborn to hear.

I'm here.

And I see you.

My human brain reminded me my mate couldn't breathe underwater, so I quickly shot to the surface again. Gently laying Baltasar down on the sloped shore, I let him catch his breath while I half-shifted to better match him in size. Then I simply stared at him like the coveted treasure he was.

All mine.

"Please, Zion," he breathlessly panted, looking like a literal wet dream with his glistening muscles and hard cock. "Please…"

Oh, I love him needy.

I had a fairly good idea what he was asking for—especially as he placed his feet flat on the damp stone and presented himself to me. But I needed him to use his words.

"What do you want, B?" I purred, retracting the claws on my right hand so I could trace a finger over his twitching hole. "Do you want me to fill you up? Stuff this needy hole tight so you know who it belongs to?"

"Fuck, yes." Baltasar's voice cracked as his cock kicked at the thought. "But I want *more*. Please, Z. Make me yours."

He already was mine—and he goddamn knew it—but my fangs were lengthening with the promise of sealing the deal in the only way my beast cared about.

In blood.

I tamped down *that* thought and refocused on my mate. Coating my fingers in lubricating saliva, I slowly pushed two inside him, hissing at how tight he still was despite my midnight visits.

"Let me in, beautiful," I crooned, tracing a claw from my other hand along his inner thigh, making him squirm. "Then we can really play."

Propping himself up on his elbows, Baltasar zeroed in on the claw teasing his skin. "What are you gonna do?"

Something you'll like.

His voice was breathy—with a slight waver that went straight to my dick—but his increased heart rate and rock-hard cock gave him away.

"Relax for me and I'll show you." I waited until he let me slide my fingers the rest of the way in before slicing a shallow cut on his thigh.

He immediately tensed up again, clamping around me as he dropped his head back with a groan. "Fuuuck, Z... I can't—"

"Use your safe word if you need to," I murmured before bringing my head down to lick his wound. I knew the ridges on my tongue added another bite of pain, but judging by how Baltasar was riding my fingers, he was on board with all of it.

Good boy.

"No, I-I like it," he confirmed, sharply inhaling when I sliced him open again. "It reminds me of when you would accidentally cut me with your claws during the Games."

Accidentally, hmm?

My gaze stayed locked on his face while I lapped up his blood. "Did you like it then, too?"

Baltasar's hand wrapped around his cock, loosely stroking as he tried to take me deeper. "Hell, yes. Each time you hurt me, I got so fucking hard, I could barely concentrate on my plays. And you tackled me during the last Championships, your *fangs* scraped my neck. I... oh, *fuck.*"

With a whimper, he stopped stroking—squeezing the base of his cock in the universal Hail Mary of staving off orgasms.

It would probably be smart to call a timeout...

This conversation was heading into dangerous territory. Before I could stick my tongue down his throat to silence him, Baltasar uttered the magic words.

"All I can think about is you sinking those fangs into my neck."

Jesus FUCK!

In one motion, I withdrew my fingers and propelled myself halfway across the pond. It was a good thing I did, as I was two seconds away from mounting him, burying myself knot-deep, and breeding him while I delivered a mating bite.

And he doesn't fully understand what that means.

"Zion?" Baltasar sat up and eyed me nervously. "Did I do something wrong?"

"No, beautiful," I reassured him, although I kept my distance. "You're just asking for some pretty heavy shit. I don't want you locking yourself into anything permanent with me until you've had time to clear your head."

Not when you're dick-drunk, in other words.

"What's the fucking difference, Z?" Baltasar huffed, uncharacteristically pissed as he rolled onto his knees. "You're already my *inventus.*"

Time ceased to exist. The world outside could have been burning—descending into the apocalypse—but my focus had tunneled one thing only.

My mate.

My... inventus?

"What makes you say that?" I croaked, even though I knew it was correct. I felt the truth of it in the deepest recesses of my soul.

His voice softened. "I talked to Xander about us. How my chest aches when you're not around. How there's this *pull* that's probably always been there—drawing me to you. I've just been too clueless to notice."

Well, fuck.

It *had* always been there, at least for me. I'd chalked it up to a painfully unrequited crush that turned into an unhealthy obsession, but for someone like *him* to experience this same torment...

Oh, no.

My heart sank as I realized how much Baltasar had endured without even realizing what was causing his suffering. The constant anxiety, racing thoughts, nervous energy, and sense of worthlessness were likely caused by this unfulfilled connection.

Although his terrible parents no doubt added to all the above.

"I'm sorry," I choked out, suddenly feeling less than worthless myself.

You would have thought I'd be ecstatic. *Inventus* bonds were the holy grail for supes. It was a way to join forces with another to annihilate your competition through nearly unstoppable, combined power. Historically, they hadn't always included deeper relationships, but it was understandably difficult to feel *that* intertwined and not take it to the next level.

There'd been so few reports of matched pairs over the past hundred years that many believed evolution had phased it out. Then the villainous Suarez clan rocked our world by matching an unregistered family member with one of the most powerful heroes of our generation.

Show-offs.

Not to be outdone, Wolfgang then somehow bonded with a *normie.* It was safe to assume the rest of the family also possessed whatever superior gene was necessary to continue the trend.

His brow furrowed. "Why are you apologizing? I *want* this—"

"You don't know that!" I barked, harsher than I meant to. *"Inventus* bonds aren't rational. They're nothing but a... glitch in our DNA."

Just like how my DNA is one big glitch.

"That's not true!" he shouted back with a surprising level of confidence, considering he didn't know what the fuck he was talking about. "There's a reason *inventus* bonds exist, Z..."

I laughed bitterly. "Yeah, they exist to lure unsuspecting baby bi's into signing their lives away."

It was one thing to have genuine compatibility with someone else, but a whole other thing to have no choice. And there was no reason for Baltasar to get stuck with someone as genetically flawed as me.

When he only glowered, I continued, "Because that's what you'd be doing. I'm already high key obsessed with you, B. If I sealed the deal with a *mating bite?* Fuck... I think I might actually kill you if you tried to leave me."

And I refuse to put you in danger.

Even though making you mine is everything I've ever wanted.

Baltasar rose to his feet and stared me down with the same impressive intensity he showed on the field. "Shut the fuck up, Zion," he growled. "For the first time, I actually feel *clear* about something. If *you* need time to think about it, fine, but my mind is made up. I want this, I want you, and I want that fucking mate bite."

Well, look who's found his words.

"Well, then you're a fool," I scoffed, still trying to push him away, even as every part of me wanted to close the distance between us. "Because I'm nothing but some *freak of nature."*

His face fell, and too late, I realized how deep my offhand comment would cut. Baltasar had been told he was stupid his entire life, and here I was adding to the pile.

But maybe it will show him what a mistake this would be.

"Yeah, I *am* a fool," he muttered as he stomped over to his pile of discarded clothing and started redressing. "A fool for thinking this thing between us was nothing but a sports rivalry, and a fool for not realizing the truth sooner. But there's one thing you're wrong about, Z. You are absolutely *not* a freak of nature, but I won't bother explaining why until you're in a better fucking mood."

"Fine," I fired back, *needing* to see him walk away before I sunk to the bottom of my pond to stew. "Consider this your last warning, B. The next time you beg for my bite, I won't hesitate."

And then you'll only have yourself to blame.

The man of my dreams huffed a laugh as he pulled on his shirt. Fully clothed, he turned to face me, and then maintained challenging eye contact as he walked back to the sloped side of the pond and took a seat.

"I'm not leaving," he bluntly stated, and the larger meaning was heard loud and clear.

I'm not going anywhere.

I accept you.

I love you.

That last one may have been wishful thinking, but our hearts sure felt like they were pumping to the same beat—inextricably tied to each other since the day we first crossed paths.

Until the day I die.

Not trusting myself to reply, and certainly not wanting him to see my traitorous tears, I quickly disappeared beneath the surface. It took longer than usual to find my calm buried deep within the darkest depths, but I eventually got my nervous system back under control.

And when I surfaced again—hours later—I found Baltasar Suarez still waiting there for me.

CHAPTER 33
BALTASAR

The next morning, I woke up with bright green scales covering the skin on my forearm.

Assuming I was still dreaming, I groggily brushed my fingers over the dimly lit mirage, but froze when I felt the familiar texture I'd become obsessed with.

WHAT THE FUCK?!

With an undignified yelp, I shot out of bed and stumbled into the bathroom. Flicking on the fluorescents, I found *yellow eyes with reptilian pupils* staring back at me from the mirror.

WHAT THE FUCKING FUCK?!!!

I sprang backward, knocking over some weird metal rack that had been left empty for me to fill with imaginary beauty products.

Too late, because I woke up like this.

By the time I'd picked up the rack and looked at myself in the mirror again, all traces of my ancient heritage were gone.

Did I... imagine it?

With a huff, I splashed some cold water on my face, determined to shake off my lingering bad dream. All this accomplished was to remind me of the scent of Zion's death pond grotto. Earthy and damp—a visceral reminder of the man I wanted more than anything.

My *inventus.*

It had taken my brain a few seconds—*okay, a few minutes*—to fully register Xander's bombshell, but as soon as his words landed, everything became crystal clear.

I'd always felt like something was *missing* from my life, and oddly, that feeling magnified after graduating from Junior Supremacy. You would have thought finally getting to where I was *supposed* to be would have been calming, but it only ramped up my agitation. The one thing that always brought me back to baseline was wiping the field with my Deathball opponents.

Mostly when I faced off against Zion.

My peace has been right there in front of me this entire time.

The fucked up part was, now that I'd accepted this connection, Zion seemed to want to push me away. He had every right to be mad that I'd told my family about Daisy's existence. I'd done what I could to make up for it—even sat my ass on the cold, hard shore of his death pond for hours—but he didn't seem to understand what I was trying to show him.

I'm not going anywhere, dude.

When he'd emerged from the pond to find me still waiting, all I got was a curt nod and a command to get changed for practice. I'd hoped 'practice' was code for something else, but nope. That stubborn lizard made me run so many laps around the field—*before* drills—I thought I was going to die.

I'd gone straight to bed afterward, although I woke up hours later to find that someone—probably Cook—had sent up a tray for dinner. After eating, I passed out again, and the next thing I knew, I was hallucinating about turning into a lizard-man.

Probably because the real deal didn't even bother to sneak into my room last night.

Is he... done with me?

Just as I started to spiral into second-guessing everything, the voice that started my days with sunshine echoed throughout my room.

"Oh, Bluuuuunty! Daddy says it's time for you to eat. Apparently, you're gonna need your strength before meeting him for practice."

My heart simultaneously soared and plummeted into my stomach at the news he had evil Deathball-related plans for me. In the end, I would run a million laps just to hang out with Zion Salah.

My inventus, whether or not he likes it.

"Oh, so *first* daddy isn't mad at me anymore?" I joked as I walked out of the bathroom to greet my girl—1000% shamelessly fishing for intel.

Daisy gave me an odd look. "Why would he be mad at *you?* You saved me! I think he just got a little scared."

Scared for her.

Because of me...

The memory made me grimace. "I'm sorry about yesterday, little queen. I don't think Cappy... Captain Masculine meant to be so scary. He's just intense as fu... dge when he's in *Blade Runner* mode."

She used the toe of her boot to nudge at a dirty sock I'd left on the floor. "Yeah, he was weird. Why was he so interested in me, anyway?"

Blowing out a slow breath, I sat on the edge of the bed, patting the mattress so she'd join me. "Because I made the mistake of telling my brother, Wolfgang, about you. I didn't understand why your existence was a secret, but now I get it. Your dad was trying to keep you safe, and *I* messed up." An idea popped into my head. "What if I told *you* a secret in return?"

Daisy laid a tiny hand on my now scale-free forearm and grinned up at me. "I love secrets! And I pinky swear not to tell anyone. Well, except for my dad."

I smiled back at her. "That's okay, because I want him to know this, anyway."

Taking a deep breath, I gazed down at the little girl who'd come to mean so much to me. A half-supe who didn't fit in with her own family—who would never have her portrait hung in the stuffy hallway alongside her judgy ancestors.

Who needs 'em?

She's my family now.

"I know another supe like you—a half-normie," I began, smiling as Daisy's entire face lit up. "Unlike you, he didn't even know he was part supe until recently. Now he shares powers with his *inventus* and is one of the scariest villains I know."

Although, he was probably born scary.

"You mean I'll have powers someday?" she gasped in awe. "And I'll be able to zap anyone who makes me mad?"

That's the spirit!

I laughed. "Yeah, I'm pretty sure you will. In the meantime, we need to continue to keep you safe, okay?"

Her grip on my arm tightened. "From other supes."

It was a statement, not a question, and my heart shattered as I thought about how terrified she must have been under the scrutiny of Butch's Blue Steel.

I still can't believe I took on Captain Masculine…

"Yeah, D, from other supes." There was no reason to lie to her —not when it was clear Zion told her what was what. "But I want you to know that you don't need to be afraid of *my* family. The Captain might have acted like a jerk, but he was just doing his job. I promise, none of them will actually hurt you."

Especially now that they know what you are.

And that I'll pound them into the ground.

Daisy was quiet, absorbing what I'd said. "Is your family… nicer than mine?"

Uhhh…

"I don't know if *nicer* is the right word." I smiled, wrapping my arm around her shoulders and squeezing her close. "But they would never reject you just because you have normie blood. They might tease you mercilessly, but it's how they show they care. In the end, I always know my siblings will have my back and we have a lot of fun together. We do movie nights, and the holidays are a pretty big deal in our house."

Since they give us themed reasons to be competitive.

A sudden vision of Daisy seamlessly existing among my clan made my breath catch. I barely had the right to claim this girl as my own—especially when Zion and I were on such shaky ground. But, regardless of what happened, I needed her to understand I had no intention of abandoning her.

"Your dad and I still need to talk about it," I stammered, suddenly overwhelmed by the magnitude of my own emotions. "But I-I hope you can *both* join my family someday."

Hopefully without Wolfgang forcefully taking over this one...

Daisy solemnly nodded. "As long as I'm with you and Daddy, I'll be happy."

That did it. I didn't even try to hide my tears, because if there was one thing I wished I'd experienced as a kid, it was proof that the adults in my life gave a shit.

I guess it's time for me to be that adult for someone else.

"Me too, your majesty," I murmured, daring to lean down and give her a sweet kiss on top of her curly little head. "Me too."

CHAPTER 34
BALTASAR

I ate breakfast faster than I should have—considering I was about to have my ass handed to me on the field—but the *need* to see Zion was making me restless. It was comforting to know this feeling stemmed from our *inventus* bond, but I was still eager for confirmation that he was all in with me.

After promising Cook I'd be back later to help with dinner prep, I hustled through the creaking hallways of the Salah haunted mansion, headed for the back door.

I wish Zion would head for my back door....

"Baltasar?"

I screeched to a halt as an unexpectedly *nervous* sounding voice called from behind me.

"Dahlia." I turned to face my faux fiancé, bracing myself for whatever the hell *she* wanted.

Considering she's barely said two words to me since inviting me to hate fuck.

She cleared her throat. "Have you... seen Preek anywhere? I haven't been able to find him since those photos of you and Zion showed up on SNZ."

Either she was telling the truth or was a fantastic actress, because she looked genuinely worried. This then made *me* worried—although about what exactly, I wasn't sure.

And I'm not about to show her any weakness.

I crossed my arms and gave her my best Blunt Force stare. "So you've misplaced your partner in crime? Boo fucking hoo, Dahlia. It's probably that asshole's fault the pictures were leaked, anyway."

Dahlia gave me a confused look. "Did Zion not tell you?"

My eyes narrowed. "Tell me what?"

She put up her hands and took a step backward. "Listen, this is between you and him, and I am not getting in the middle of it. Go ask that idiot yourself if you want to know who leaked the photos."

Oh, I will.

Not even bothering to reply, I spun and stomped my way down the hall and out the back door. I continued stomping until I reached the farthest field, where the 'big idiot' himself was waiting—tossing a deathball into the air, casual as could be.

"Did *you* have something to do with those photos landing on SNZ, Salah?" I growled, not stopping my trajectory until I was right up in his face.

Just like old times.

His nonchalance faltered for a split second before that sexy as fuck smirk spread across his annoyingly perfect face. "Maybe. Maybe I'm willing to play dirty to get what I want."

Is that right?

I scoffed and stepped back. "Oh, you *want* me now? Because you've been acting all hot and cold lately, like you could take it or leave it."

Zion caught the ball and stared me down so intensely, his eyes flashed yellow. "Stop getting your panties in a bunch, Suarez. You know I want you."

Of course, I knew in my soul that what Zion Salah felt for me was real, but I was still hurt by his sudden coldness. "First of all," I huffed. "You've been acting weird since yesterday, and second, I'm wearing a goddamn *jockstrap*, not panties."

So there.

"Mmm... good to know." His gaze flickered downward, and my scowl grew as I hardened under his scrutiny. When his eyes met mine again, all humor was gone from his expression. "And I'm sorry I've been distant. Finding out this is an *inventus* bond is fucking with me. It... it's almost like you didn't have a choice."

Is THAT what's been bothering him?

"Z..." All anger left me as I approached him and slung my arms around his neck. "I don't think that's how this works. The way my brothers look at their *inventuses... inventi?* Whatever. Let's just say I never gave a shit about love until I got a front-row seat."

When a tiny smile appeared on his face at my half-confession, I decided it was as good a time as any to drop the bombshell of his existence. "And it's not any different from your mating thing."

He rolled his eyes, but there wasn't any heat behind it. "You don't know that, B. Nobody knows about my *mating thing,* because there are no other supes like me to compare it to."

Here goes nothing.

"Actually…" I cleared my throat. "We do know about supes like you. At least, *my* family does."

Zion froze, and I carefully released him, slowly backing away as I eyed him warily. His lizard flickered over the surface a few times—like ripples on the water—but he got a hold of himself before replying.

"Is that a fact?" His voice was deadly quiet, but I stood my ground, determined to get this out in the open. "The almighty Suarez clan has some secrets, hmm? Secrets you get to lord over other supes—to buy and sell for more power. Get your greedy hands on more pieces of the pie?"

He's not wrong.

"Yeah, we have secrets, Zion," I snapped, refusing to let him dominate me until I'd said my piece. "Just like your family, and every powerful supe family, does. The difference is that I'm gonna tell you this secret, so here we fucking go. What you are"—I gestured at him—"is what *all* of us were at one point. What we still are, in some ways. When our ancestors first landed on this planet, they arrived as giant lizard alien badasses. It's only because of generations of cross-breeding that we look human today."

It was Zion's turn to back away and deliver some serious side eye. "Are you *high*, Suarez? You never struck me as the tinfoil hat type…"

Sigh.

"I know this sounds crazy," I admitted, running a hand down my face. "But it's the truth, and I can *show* you the proof my family keeps in our archives. There's a cave in Argentina, with ancient paintings that *show* our ancestors first arriving—"

"A *cave?*" Zion interrupted, his eyes going wide. "Like, in the jungle?"

I nodded enthusiastically, glad he was no longer thinking I was a conspiracy theorist. "Yes! Wolfy and Simon have seen it —and Xanny too, since he's working with the anthropologist in charge down there. This evidence is the entire reason normies were able to get so-called *heroes* to kneel for them with those contracts…"

My words trailed off as Zion clutched his chest, sending a jolt of pain shooting down our *inventus* bond as he doubled over and placed his hands on his knees.

Oh, fuck.

"Z?!" I ran to his side. "Shit. Are you okay? This was probably a lot to hear all at once, huh? Fuck. Once my mouth gets going, it's hard to stop it sometimes."

All the time, really.

I breathed a sigh of relief as he waved me off. "It's not that. Well, it *is,* but…" His gaze snapped to mine. "I think my parents know about this cave, B."

My blood turned to ice in my veins. "That's not possible," I choked out, knowing how hard my family had locked down this intel.

Wolfy's going to murder someone.

Zion looked more on edge than I'd ever seen him. "It might be nothing but…. when I was digging around Pops' office recently, I found an old photograph of my mom standing outside a jungle cave with some random guy."

Simon's going to murder everyone.

My thoughts were oddly clear as I zeroed in on the problem. "Do you have this photograph? Or did you take a picture of it?"

I needed to get this evidence to my family. If it was Doc in the photo, he'd remember meeting Lady Tempest—at least, in civilian mode. And if it wasn't, he might be able to identify who it was.

At least, I hope so...

Zion shook his head. "No. I thought it was just some random vacation photo, so I tucked it back where I found it. We need to get into my father's office again, and then talk to Dahlia—"

"Dahlia?!" I scoffed. "Why would we talk to *her*? Didn't you say she and Preek were up to some shady bullshit?"

He sighed. "Yeah, I thought they were, but then I had a come-to-Jesus with my sister recently." When I glared at him, he at least had the decency to look apologetic. "I'm sorry I didn't fill you in—on that conversation or the SNZ photos. I'm just... I'm used to taking care of things myself."

And of taking care of everyone else.

But who takes care of him?

"Well, you don't have to do everything alone anymore," I huffed. "Because now you have me."

He tried to turn away from me—as usual—but I was too quick. Before that big lizard could hide his big feels, I closed the distance between us. Planting my hands on either side of his face, I *forced* him to look at me and patiently waited for his response.

I'm not going anywhere, remember?

"Why did you tell me this?" he quietly asked, still attempting to keep his emotions under wraps. "I highly doubt you were given permission to spill classified information to a rival heir."

Still being stubborn, I see.

"I told you because you deserve to know," I quietly replied, letting him see everything that was in my heart. "And I also didn't want you to think I was choosing them over you." When his jaw dropped, I continued, ready to lay it all on the table for my former Deathball rival. "You need to understand, if I was forced to choose, I would choose *you,* Zion. Every fucking time."

"Jesus, Baltasar," he huffed, his breath tickling my lips as he dropped his forehead against mine. "Just when I think I can't fall in love with you more, you pull some smooth shit like this. Damn."

He loves me!

Grinning like an idiot, I kissed him, knowing we were too far away from the main house for anyone to see, and not giving a flying fuck either way. All I could focus on was Zion's soft lips on mine—his ridged tongue sliding into my mouth, lighting me up. The entire Salah clan could have been standing on the field with us, and I wouldn't have noticed.

I can't wait until everyone knows he's mine.

"Are you just trying to get out of drills, Suarez?" he murmured, although he didn't seem in a rush to put an end to our make-out session.

"Maybe." I smiled against his lips. "Maybe I'd rather go be secret spies together and solve this nefarious mystery."

He hummed, distracted, as I tugged on his bottom lip with my teeth. "Mmm… we would make a pretty good team."

My smile grew. "We'd be even more unstoppable if we were bonded, you know. *Mated.*"

Gotcha.

As expected, he pulled back and gave me a stern look that only egged me on. "Baltasar... I told you, the next time—"

"Yeah, yeah, I know," I interrupted, untangling myself from his arms so I could remove my shirt, tempting him further. "That the next time I *begged* for your bite, you wouldn't hesitate. But I told you. I. Want. That. Fucking. Mate. Bite."

Gimme.

Zion's eyes turned fully reptilian as he grinned broadly, his fangs lengthening before my eyes. "As you wish, beautiful. Strip down to your jock, and start running. I'll give you a five-minute head start."

He canted his chin toward the vast pine forest that stretched across his family's property, and my heart rate kicked up a few thousand notches.

Oh. My. God.

"You wanna play chase, huh?" I asked, feeling my mouth go dry even as my cock soaked the jock in question with precum.

He chuckled low—the sound telling me I needed to get undressed, stat. "That's right. And you'd better not *let* me catch you. Give me a challenge, Suarez. Run for your life."

CHAPTER 35
BALTASAR

There was nothing like running through the forest while only wearing a jockstrap to make you question your life choices.

Although, at least the jock is keeping my boner in line.

Because no matter how potentially dangerous my current situation was, I had never been hornier.

Come and get me, you crazy lizard.

Taking a deep breath of fresh pine and earthy decay, I put my head down and ramped up my super speed. While I was dying for Zion to catch me and finally make me *his,* I also wanted to give him the chase he'd asked for.

I wanted to make him proud.

Jesus, I really am a praise whore.

And a lizard whore.

My five-minute head start must have ended, as a bone-chilling roar echoed off the surrounding trees, bringing me back to the present.

HERE WE GOOOOO!!!

Knowing he was in hot pursuit kicked my flight instinct into high gear, but my body only *half*-shifted. Weirdly, despite my increased bulk, I was moving faster than ever. This made me absently wonder why Zion always chose full Godzilla mode when running from me on the Deathball field.

Another roar—much closer this time—forced me to stop thinking about my professional game and focus on *this* not at all professional game, instead. My legs pumped, twigs snapping beneath my bare feet as the trees became a blur of green, but I knew it was only a matter of time until he caught me.

Unless I play dirty as well.

Literally.

The squelch of muck between my toes gave me an idea, and I veered left, following my nose to find the source of moisture. I knew stopping was dangerous—especially with a primal lizard on my tail—but the only way I was going to gain an edge was to mess with what gave him his.

I smirked in triumph when I found a gully thick with mud. Knowing every second counted, I quickly slid into the ravine and crouched, slathering handfuls of mud over my chest, arms, and legs. The only time I paused was when I felt those imaginary *scales* on my forearms again, but when I looked closer, all I could see was mud caked over my skin.

Must be lizard envy.

I didn't go full *Rambo: First Blood Part II* with how thickly I spread the mud around. I also avoided my more… delicate areas—but I hoped I'd done enough to mask my scent from the predator pursuing me.

My senses went on high alert as something *big* crashed through the underbrush on the ridge above me before abruptly stopping with a chilling growl.

Shit.

I didn't know if it was because Zion could tell I was close by, or if he'd lost the trail altogether, but I held my breath—waiting to see what would happen.

He huffed a few times, as if scenting the air. I crouched lower into the mud when movement from above sent pebbles tumbling down to where I hid. But then he growled in frustration before miraculously continuing on his original path, deeper into the forest.

Sucker!

The competitive side of me did a little victory dance. Other parts were doing a much hornier dance, so instead of doing the *smart* thing and heading back the way I came, I decided to turn the tables.

Time to hunt the hunter.

Feeling as badass as John James Rambo himself, I crept back up the ravine and peered over the edge. Zion was nowhere to be seen, but it was pretty clear which direction he'd gone.

Deciding to test my theory, I half-shifted for speed again, while doing my best to keep my steps light. My survival instincts were *screaming* at me to turn and run in the opposite direction. But I doggedly followed the hero's trail of destruction—determined to get what was mine.

Despite the risks.

If the big lizard hadn't killed me when he thought I'd betrayed Daisy to my family, it was probably safe to assume he wouldn't now. Not when I was offering my ass on a primal chase platter.

And my ass is so ready.

Unfortunately, my daydreaming with a capital D distracted me from realizing Zion's trail had gone cold. I instantly returned to civilian size and slowly spun in a full 360—focusing all my powers on my super sight. My brow furrowed in confusion, as the only disturbance I saw in vegetation was from the direction I'd come.

That's… weird.

The snapping of a single twig was the only warning I got before I was hit from behind and taken to the ground so hard, my breath was punched out of me.

FUCK!!!

"Silly little prey," Zion chuckled in my ear. Caging me in, he rubbed his lizard dick along my exposed ass crack, making me whimper. "You thought you were going to hunt *me?* When you've been my obsession for years?"

"I had you for a minute, though, right?" I croaked, feeling like I'd won, either way.

He chuckled again, carefully dragging a claw down my arm to scrape off a chunk of caked mud, making me shiver. "You did," he admitted. "But now look at you. So dirty."

"Fuck…" I moaned, digging my fingers into the dirt and rubbing myself against him from below. Absolutely *feral* for it. "Please, just fucking *fuck* me already. *Jesus.*"

With an amused huff, Zion sat back before using one enormous scaled hand to flip me onto my back. I gasped as I came face to face with him in full lizard form, feeling my cock try to tear its way out of my jockstrap at the sight.

"Hey, handsome," I whispered, meaning it with my entire soul.

And every other part of me.

Especially my dick.

What looked like surprise passed over Zion's reptilian face before he morphed into his half-shifted state. When I whined in disappointment, he good-naturedly rolled his eyes. "It would be ambitious for you to take me in full form, B—especially for your first time. I'm not *that* much of a monster."

With a huff of my own, I gripped his face in my hands and tried to pull him down for a kiss. Before our lips could meet, he extended his tongue for me to suck on, and I moaned at the feel of its textured surface in my mouth.

"I don't think you're a monster at all," I murmured when he withdrew. "But I *do* think you're stalling when you should be ramming that thick cock inside me and going to town."

"So impatient," he growled before sitting back on his heels. "I'm not stalling, B. I'm *trying* to get my human brain back online first. The chase brought out my beast, and *he* shouldn't be the one in charge when we play."

Says who?

"But that's what I want!" I whined, trailing a hand down my filthy chest and abs to palm myself through my jock, noticing how his reptilian gaze tracked the movement. "I want you exactly how you are, and I want you to *fuck* me like that, too."

Someday…

Zion released a low rumble as more scales spread out over his skin. But he simply took a deep breath and wrapped a hand around his cock, giving himself a slow stroke—continuing to edge us both.

Knowing I almost had him, I bent my knees and placed my feet flat on the ground, showing him everything. "C'mon, Z," I growled, growing more impatient by the minute. "Give me that cock and that goddamn bite."

The snarl he released made my hair stand on end, but I simply spread myself wider, drawing his gaze down.

Right where I want him.

"This is a dangerous game you're playing, Baltasar," he muttered. Using his thumbs to open me up, he leaned down and swiped his tongue over my hole, making me buck into the air. "I try not to let out my beast during sex. He might tear you in half just so no one else can ever have you again."

I dropped my head back and moaned as his tongue made another pass—lighting up my sensitive nerve endings. "No one else ever will, Zion. I'm yours."

I've always been yours.

He made a purring sound as he breached me with his tongue, coating me inside and out with his magical lizard lube saliva while he stretched me. I tightened my grip on my dick—desperate to slow the inevitable—even as I rode his tongue like a needy little whore.

There's still one more card left to play.

"Please…" I begged, ramping up the whine in my tone and going in for the kill. "Please *breed* me."

Oops.

Zion froze for only a moment before he was suddenly face to face with me again, dominating me with his enormous bulk—enveloping me in his musky, earthy scent.

"Is that what you want, beautiful?" He tilted his head, lightly running his fangs along my neck as he nudged his dick against my opening. "You want me to fill you with my seed? You want it to be dripping out of you for days—until everyone knows you took my cock like the good little breeder you are?"

Oh, my fucking GAWD, yesss!

"Fuck, yes," I gasped as he slowly, mercilessly pushed the dripping head of his enormous—*holy hell, it was big*—cock into my ass. "Fill me up. I want everyone to know who I belong to. I want you to breed me... oh, *fuuu...*"

My words ended with a strangled sound as he slid home—as those ridges I'd fantasized about hammered over my prostate, exactly as advertised. I instantly exploded, seizing up as I coated the inside of my jock with cum.

...uuuuck!

"That's it." He scraped his fangs down my neck, only just starting to pump his hips lazily as I shuddered through my climax. "Open up so I can give you all of me."

There's more?

"Gimme..." I murmured anyway, feeling my body go limp as his fangs finally pierced my skin—like a gazelle frozen in fear while being devoured by lions.

What a way to go...

He latched onto my neck where it met my shoulder, firing off my synapses as searing pain radiated outward from his bite. I tensed before a wave of pure euphoria washed over me. All I felt was calm—a sense of *rightness* and certainty.

This.

Then a second wave hit, and I was suddenly experiencing the moment from *both* our perspectives—the giver and the receiver. Joined as one with one continuous, glorious loop of sensation and emotion.

Pleasure, anguish, desire, power...

Love.

Zion hummed against my skin as he increased his pace. Sliding his hands through the straps of my jock to cup my ass, he held me in place for every punishing thrust. Caring for me even as he wrecked me.

Pound me into the ground.

I was so full—I thought he might actually tear me in half. But another blissful orgasm was already building in my spine, so I dug my nails into his biceps and held on.

More, more, more.

The sounds I was making were some mangled combination of sobs and moans—with his name on my lips, chanted like a prayer. My safe word danced on the tip of my tongue, but I swallowed it down, more than happy to be dragged into the depths of delicious, dreamy surrender.

Give me all of it.

It was only when I felt the insistent pressure of his extra bulge against my already aching hole I realized what he—and my slutty subconscious—already knew.

My ass was about to get bred.

As if sensing the trajectory of my thoughts, Zion paused with his mouth still on my neck and his ridged rocket pop buried to the hilt. Waiting for confirmation that this was truly what I wanted.

"I said breed me, and I goddamn meant it," I choked out, hooking my heels around the back of his muscular thighs, bearing down for what I knew was coming.

For what I wanted more than life itself.

With a groan that sounded painful, Zion pushed his way deeper, stretching me beyond my limit as *all of him* popped into place. His cock immediately started pulsing, and I arched my back with a howl. I came so hard I momentarily blacked out, smearing my release on his abs as it overflowed from my jock.

Holy, FUUUUUUCK!!!

Zion was snarling like a wild animal—buried so deep, I could feel him in my guts—but he kept his mouth locked on my neck, penetrating me at both ends.

Claiming me completely.

I might have come *again* during the seemingly endless time it took for him to fully empty himself inside me. Or maybe my soul left my body entirely to orbit around the earth like a wayward satellite. Either way, the next thing I knew, I blinked open my eyes to find Zion gently lapping at the bite on my neck while I lay sprawled over his broad chest.

With his lizard dick still trapped inside me.

"Z…" I croaked, not even attempting to move a muscle, and not sure if I *could.* At the moment, I would have been content to simply live out here in the woods like a couple of wild sex beasts.

"Mine…" he growled, sounding like he was still firmly in lizard brain mode.

That's cool.

Imma sleep now, anyway.

"Yours," I replied, allowing my eyes to flutter closed again as exhaustion swept me under, feeling like I finally *belonged* somewhere, for once.

I'll always be yours.

CHAPTER 36
ZION

Mate marking Baltasar was a bad idea.

And breeding him was worse.

It wasn't because I hadn't wanted to. Lord knows, I did. But I could already feel my beast going *feral* beneath the surface—daring anyone take him away from me under penalty of slow and painful death.

So, it wasn't the best time for an unexpected visitor to be waiting for us back on the field.

"I didn't realize deep woods mud wrestling was a part of the Deathball champion regiment…"

With a vicious growl, I shoved Baltasar behind me, hiding his mostly naked, mud-covered, freshly fucked perfection from view.

Mine.

"Star Hopper," I gritted out, knowing he was missing nothing of this incriminating scene. "What are you doing here?"

He grinned. "I came to see *you*, Zion, although…" His gaze lowered to take in my *fully* naked, mud-flecked, and also freshly fucked appearance. "I wasn't expecting to see so *much* of you... Not that I'm complaining."

It was Baltasar's turn to growl, so I stepped aside to give him room. I knew allowing my mate to see his opponent would help settle him and assert our combined dominance.

Two against one, asshole.

A few tense moments passed until I realized the hero had casually addressed me by my first name instead of my supe name.

So he's not here to fight...

I forced my beast to stand down as I considered the implications. "Did my parents tell you to find me out here, *Ziggy?*"

See? I can play nice, too.

The Deathball star gave me an impassive stare worthy of the field, clearly debating how much truth to give me.

"They don't know I'm here," he finally replied, surprising me with way more honesty than I was expecting. "And I'd like to keep it that way."

Okay, I can work with that.

"Deal." I walked to our discarded clothing and tossed Baltasar his sweatpants before pulling on mine. "I'd also like to keep what you've seen out here between us. For now."

That last bit was for my mate, and I made sure to briefly meet his gaze when I said it.

I want the world to know about us.

Baltasar's expression softened, and I heard Ziggy chuckle, drawing my attention back to him.

"I hope you know SupeSports is gonna have a field day with this sordid affair once it gets out." He laughed and shook his head. "Not that it will be that big of a surprise to the other players, from what I've heard."

"What do you mean?" Baltasar looked slightly panicked, and my beast writhed beneath the surface in response to his emotions.

Which I can now distinctly feel…

Our visitor cocked his head at my mate. "You sacked Scaled Justice more often than all other grabbers combined. That sort of success rate suggests a deeper motivation than the desire to stop a goal. Unless…" He shot a sly smile my way. "The *Lacertus* was letting you catch him—"

"I didn't *let* him do shit!" I barked, in no mood to have this rookie question my game. "Even with Blunt Force sacking me now and then, I was still the highest scoring…" my rant trailed off as the full weight of his words sunk in. "What did you just call me?"

Lacertus?

Ziggy shot a look over his shoulder, toward the main house, before facing us again.

"It's what you are, Zion," he stated—his expression unreadable once again. "It's the same species many supes on your planet are descended from. Although, the DNA has become too diluted over time for the original, lizard-like form to emerge."

Until now…

"What do you know about our ancestors?" Baltasar carefully asked, but something else about Ziggy's bombshell caught my attention.

"Wait. What do you mean... *'your'* planet?" I snapped, wanting to get all the facts before deciding if this man was a threat or not. "Where the fuck are *you* from, then?"

I better not be dealing with an actual tinfoil hat nut job.

"A galaxy far, far away." Ziggy smiled faintly, with a glance to the sky above. "I was assigned to Earth to check up on things, but stuck around because, well..." He shrugged, looking embarrassed. "You know how to have a good time down here."

Playing Deathball, apparently.

"Whoa, whoa, whoa!" My mate excitedly waved his hands. "So you're, like, an *alien* from another planet who came here on a fucking spaceship?!"

Ziggy Andromeda threw back his head and laughed. "To be fair, *you* are the aliens to me. But yes, I'm from another planet —even if I didn't need a spaceship to get here." He winked at me. "Hence the name."

Star.

Hopper.

"Well, shit," I huffed, dragging a hand down my face, doing my best to absorb all of this. "So, you're familiar with these *Lacertus...* creatures...?"

Lizard alien badasses.

The hero—or whatever he was—gave me a hard look. "Yes. Nasty fuckers. Known for traveling through galaxies, conquering planets along the way to grow their empire... except *here.* For reasons my kind have yet to understand, the *Lacertus* arrived on Earth as conquerors, but crossbred instead. Any idea why that is, Zion?"

With a scoff, I crossed my arms over my chest. "It sounds like *you* know more about this shit than I do, Andromeda. There's never been a supe like me in my family. It's not like I can go ask my non-lizard parents about my mating habits, or why I look the way I do."

Plus, I don't want them knowing I'm sniffing around.

Yet.

Ziggy nodded, satisfied with my answer. "That's exactly why I came looking for *you*, Zion. Besides the strange science experiment that's been going on here for the past few thousand millennia, I want to understand why *you're* showing such dominant *Lacertus* traits. Meanwhile, other supes who carry the same DNA"—his gaze shifted to Baltasar in a coldly assessing way—"can't seem to make a single scale appear."

So he knows who has it and who doesn't.

I wonder if the entire Suarez clan does…

It was all related, from my DNA to the cave paintings and Baltasar's family cornering the market on *inventus* bonds. This long-shot playing alien was in on it… along with whatever top secret bullshit my sister insisted on investigating while I sat here like a fool.

To say I was frustrated would be an understatement. I still didn't know *who* piloted the plane for Preek the night of our tarmac bike race, and the *destination* remained a mystery.

Since the black box was conveniently wiped clean.

I also realized I hadn't even told Baltasar about the lab yet, because—as usual—I'd stubbornly tried to handle everything myself.

"You don't have to do it alone anymore… because now you have me."

"I think we need to have a little chat with Joshual Preek," I muttered to Baltasar, even though the last thing I wanted to do was put my mate in anyone's line of sight. "Maybe let our alien friend here deal with him."

"Your clan's publicity director?" Ziggy frowned, producing some high-tech blinking cube from his pocket and tapping on random lights.

"Yes…" I eyed the object warily, unsure if he was planning on leaving behind a futuristic grenade after he star hopped his ass out of here. "He borrowed one of our planes recently for unauthorized business, and knows something he shouldn't."

That was the extent of what I wanted to say in present company. Because of that pesky family loyalty I couldn't seem to shake, I didn't want Ziggy Andromeda going after Dahlia with his weird cube contraption.

But Preek-the-Prick is fair game.

"No worries," Ziggy replied, tucking the cube away, much to my relief. "Interrogating suspects is a specialty of mine— especially ones who don't freely talk."

I narrowed my eyes, reading the subtext of his statement loud and clear.

We should consider ourselves lucky Star Hopper believes what we're telling him.

Before I could straight up ask him if *I* was a suspect, Baltasar raised his hand, like a schoolboy waiting to be called on in class. "Um… guys? I don't think Preek's on the payroll anymore."

WHAT?!

"What makes you say that?" I calmly asked, determined to keep my cool, even with my beast rippling over my skin.

My Lacertus, *apparently.*

Hungry for prey.

Baltasar's concerned gaze roamed over my face, as if he could also feel my agitation. "I ran into Dahlia on my way out here today. She asked if I'd seen Preek—said he's been missing since those pictures went viral."

Fuck.

I groaned, annoyed that something I would have previously considered a happy accident was now majorly inconvenient. "My parents probably fired him. It's literally his one job to keep photos like that off SNZ."

Ziggy hummed, seemingly unconcerned by our little drama as he pulled out the cube again. "I'll find him. In the meantime, don't *you* go disappearing on me—lest I have to track you down as well."

This guy.

I rolled my eyes at his not-so-subtle threat. "I'll do my best not to turn into a bloodthirsty conqueror of the human race."

He huffed a laugh, his gaze on the cube. "If I truly thought you had plans for that, you'd be dead, Salah."

Baltasar growled again—drawing my attention to him—and I did a double-take as his pretty amber eyes appeared to turn *yellow* for a moment.

What the hell?!

I snuck a glance at Ziggy, breathing a sigh of relief to find he was too busy messing with his tech toy to notice Baltasar's lizard-like qualities.

It's probably just an inventus *side effect, anyway.*

"Is that all, *starman?*" I huffed, wanting to get back to my precious alone time with my mate.

Ziggy shot me a grin that would have been charming had I not been watching him like a hawk. "For now. Be good, Earthlings."

And then he disappeared.

Well, at least we know he's not just lurking around like an invisible man...

"Jesus!" Baltasar hissed, rubbing his eyes. "That was freaky as fuck."

I chuckled and pulled him close. "I'll protect you from the alien long-shot, beautiful. The good news is, as long as we don't step out of line, Ziggy won't shoot a laser beam up our asses."

Jokes.

He gave me an odd look. "I think he'd aim for our heads, Z. At least... I hope so. My ass still kind of hurts."

Fuck, I love you, you big himbo.

"Are you just trying to get out of running laps, B?" I teased, cackling when his eyes widened in horror. "I'm kidding! That was enough of a workout for one day. Let's go have a soak in my pond so I can take care of you."

As my mate.

Baltasar gave me a shy smile before pulling on the rest of his clothes. His fingers tangled with mine as we walked side-by-side back toward the main house. Once we neared our destination, however, he placed more distance between us.

A grumpy growl escaped me, and he laughed. "I'm not trying to blow up our spot! At least, not until we get the chance to grab that photo from your dad's office and talk to Dahlia or whatever..."

I could tell he still wasn't sold on the idea of trusting my sister. "Dahlia wants out of this engagement, B. I traded helping her for intel on whatever she discovered."

With Preek.

Frowning, I realized I needed to sort out this lab business before the lesser supe used what he knew against us.

And that requires not doing everything alone.

Once we were in the safety of my pond, I confessed, "I know more than what I told Star Hopper."

Even though it's still not enough.

Baltasar grinned and paddled closer before depositing a sweet kiss on my cheek. "I figured. We don't know what his deal is yet. But the more you tell *me*, the more I can help." He grimaced. "And I promise, I won't just go run and tell Wolfy."

"I know you won't, beautiful." I grabbed my villain and licked my way into his mouth. "Although, I'm not gonna lie... the idea of you *running* sounds good to me."

As long as I get to catch you.

CHAPTER 37
ZION

One benefit of my unusual supe form was the ability to breathe underwater.

Therefore, one benefit for my mate was the underwater blowies.

I smiled around Baltasar's cock as he did his best to thrust deeper into my mouth. But I was holding him immobile, pinned against the rocks like the pretty prey he was.

"Fuck, Z… *fuuuuck…*" he panted—the words muffled to my ears from above the water's surface.

His hands were palming my head, but more so he could hold on to something than to take over my rhythm. If there was one thing I'd figured out about Baltasar Suarez, it was that he preferred me being in control—even if he liked to pretend otherwise.

Good thing, because I own his ass now.

Cheating a little by unhinging my jaw, I slid his cock all the way down my throat, swallowing around him as my lips met his groin. Knowing he was close, I lightly pressed my fangs against his sensitive shaft—just barely breaking the skin—and smirked as Baltasar immediately shouted, blasting cum straight into my guts.

My perfect little pain slut.

Not waiting for him to recover, I resurfaced and pulled his still shuddering body into my arms. "You taste so sweet," I murmured in his ear, biting the lobe as I paddled us toward the shore. "You smell sweet, too."

"Fuck off, Z," he mumbled, although there was no heat in his words as he snuggled closer. "I'm not... *sweet.*"

I grinned, loving how much he pretended to hate what his body obviously wanted. "You are. Like cookies. *Snickerdoodles*, to be exact."

Like a tasty treat.

He stiffened before raising his head and gazing at me in horror. "What?! Why... why the fuck would I taste and smell like a snickerdoodle?"

I deposited him on the sloped rocks before climbing out to join him. "What's wrong with snickerdoodles?" I teased, greatly enjoying how riled up he was. "They're my favorite."

Baltasar huffed and stomped over to our collective pile of clothing. "It's just not very *manly*. Why can't I smell like *you* do? Like Old Spice and testosterone had a baby that immediately roundhouse kicked the nearest person the second they were born."

My laughter echoed around the cavern. "Is that so? Maybe we should bottle up these manly pheromones of mine and sell my sweat as cologne. We'll call it *Lacertus*, make a super pretentious commercial, and advertise on SupeSports during the Games."

That got him to smile, and I preened as I strolled over to join him. After a few minutes of comfortable silence while we redressed, he inhaled deeply. "It's not a bad idea, Z. We could probably just fill the bottles with your death pond water, since this entire grotto smells like you."

It does?

Our conversation reminded me of the one errand of Preek's I still couldn't figure out. But there were bigger picture things I needed to fill Baltasar in on first. "So... There's a mysterious lab my parents are involved with, although I don't know *how*. I only discovered it existed by eavesdropping on my sister and Preek. Those two somehow discovered it... and I'm fairly certain *that's* where Preek went when he borrowed the plane. Dahlia said she wanted to investigate more before involving me, but I don't want to wait any longer."

Too many loose ends for my liking.

Baltasar was as serious as I'd ever seen him, nodding attentively, and I marveled yet again at how the man *could* focus when it mattered.

He doesn't give himself enough credit.

"Yeah, Dahlia needs to tell us what the fuck she knows," he growled, giving me an instant boner. His determined expression faltered as he abruptly back-pedaled, looking almost panicked. "I mean... tell *you*, since you're the clan leader. Future clan leader. Not me..."

He's adorable.

Softly chuckling, I wrapped my arms around him from behind and pulled him close—breathing him in. I wanted to take full advantage of this private time before going back upstairs, where the rest of my family would be too close for comfort.

"I would never expect you to answer to me, B," I murmured against his messy hair. "As my mate—my *inventus*—you would rule this clan by my side."

Baltasar tensed. "I'm… I don't think I'm cut out for that. Nope. Definitely not."

I spun the villain and squinted at him. "You *do* understand we're mated for life, right?" When he nodded enthusiastically, I squinted harder. "So how else did you see this ending up?"

My parents will kick the bucket, eventually.

Hopefully, sooner than later.

He cleared his throat and averted his gaze. "I dunno… maybe you and Daisy could just, you know, join my clan instead?"

I almost laughed. But then I reminded myself that Baltasar was fourth in line. He had no clue how we heirs were *groomed* from birth to dominate, conquer, and rule. Sure, if two heirs married, they typically combined their powerful houses. But no way in hell would a firstborn simply fall in line to another leader without a fight.

Even to a supposedly benevolent ruler like Wolfgang.

And especially not to a tyrant like Simon.

Then I remembered how close the Suarez siblings were and my heart softened. "Are you worried about me taking you away from your brothers and sister?"

His gaze snapped to mine again. "What? No! I couldn't see you *forbidding* me from seeing them. And you already told me you don't actually have a dungeon for villains." When I laughed, he smiled, and my heart thumped from the raw emotion I saw on his gorgeous face. "Like Daisy told me earlier, as long as she's with the two of us, it will be home. I feel that way about you guys, too."

"Jesus," I hissed, pushing away from him, feeling my heart rate ratchet up. "She *said* that?"

This is it for her, too.

Baltasar grinned, apparently enjoying *me* being flustered as well. "She sure did! I'm officially her second daddy now, dude." His humor faded as he cleared his throat again, almost nervously. "It came up because I, um... I said she would be welcome in my family—even with what she is. *Especially* with what she is."

My heart almost punched its way out of my chest—for a different reason this time. "What does your family want with my daughter, B? And don't lie to me. You're *my* clan now, as much as theirs!"

Mine.

Thankfully, he didn't seem threatened or disturbed by my possessive outburst. Instead, he bravely stood his ground and, for a split second, I saw his eyes flash reptilian yellow again before returning to their pretty amber color.

You're a part of me.

"They don't want anything. Well, they might be interested in *protecting* her, now that they know what she is." When I growled impatiently, he boldly rolled his eyes—proving he knew he had nothing to fear with me. "Okay, so I told Daisy a secret about my family this morning. You know, to make up for spilling the tea about her existence."

That piqued my interest. Secrets and intel made the supe world go 'round. Therefore, I was more than happy to gather anything I could on the Suarez clan.

Knowledge is power, after all.

"What did you tell her?" I asked, curious what he'd shared with my little spy, knowing full well she'd turn around and tell me.

Baltasar smiled slyly, and I knew something big was coming. Taking a deep breath, I nodded, implying he should get on with it.

Just rip off the band-aid.

"Simon's only half normie," he replied, his grin growing wider when my jaw dropped open. "He's a normie whose supe side contains ancient DNA, just like Daisy's does, apparently." He gestured at me. "That's how he bonded with Wolfy —and why he can leech my brother's powers, even though he has none of his own." He paused thoughtfully as I continued to gape. "It also might explain why he's a raging psychopath."

He fits right in.

"You mean..." I could barely form a coherent thought, let alone words. "Daisy has a chance of finding an *inventus* someday and wielding *their* power?"

She'll be able to fight.

It was Baltasar's turn to pull me into his arms as I collapsed against him in relief.

She'll be safe.

From the moment Mikki told me she was pregnant, I'd been *terrified*. Not about becoming a father, but about the target this painted on my daughter's back, simply for being the heir to the throne after me. And when it became apparent Daisy hadn't inherited powers of her own, I knew it was only a matter of time before another clan saw her as leverage. As prey.

But now she can be a predator, too.

"I want you to tell me everything your family knows," I mumbled into his broad shoulder, inhaling that fresh baked cookie smell he didn't want to hear about. "Tell me about the cave paintings, the *Lacertus* creatures, and half-supes. Everything."

"Of course," he murmured, running his hands down my back —comfortingly. "Both you and Daisy deserve to know. And now that my family knows what Daisy is, they'll make sure nothing happens to her, I promise."

Because now she's valuable to them.

I sighed. Worse things could happen to my daughter than being watched over by the almighty Suarez clan. But first things first...

"Let's go find that photograph in Pops' office." I straightened and blew out a slow breath to prepare. "I want leverage before I try to make a deal with Wolfgang."

Baltasar furrowed his brow. "Why would you need leverage? I told you, he'll *want* to help if she's like Simon."

Oh, you sweet summer child.

I chuckled and slung an arm around his shoulder before leading him away from my pond. "Rule number one of ruling a clan: Always have leverage. Not just on your enemies, but on your friends as well."

Especially your friends.

"It's how the game is played," he sighed, clearly under-standing enough about how our world worked to know how things had to go.

"Goddamn right, Suarez," I snickered. "Stick with me, beautiful. I'll make a clan leader out of you yet."

CHAPTER 38
BALTASAR

My heart was racing as I followed Zion into Major Obscurity's office. The only other time I'd been inside was after our brawl on the croquet field, when Lady Tempest cut me off at the knees.

Just because my powers aren't as impressive as hers.

Or anyone's really...

"Are you all right, beautiful?" Zion asked, eyeing me warily as he quietly shut the door behind us.

I froze, praying he couldn't actually feel the insecurity pouring off of me in the same way I could now feel *his* stronger emotions. That Zion could completely quiet his mind when stressed out was goals. The last thing I wanted to do was drag him into *my* mess of a headspace.

"Yeah, I'm cool." I shrugged, blasting him with a dimpled smile to throw him off the trail. "I was just thinking about what time I have to get my ass to the kitchen to help Cook with—"

My bullshit ramble was cut short as Zion zeroed in on my forearm, and I followed his gaze to find a smattering of familiar bright green scales decorating my skin.

So this is really happening.

"Look at that…" he murmured, and when his hungry gaze met mine again, his pupils had turned to slits—zeroing in on his prey.

Chill, dude.

My ass can't handle another lizard mating dance just yet.

"Must be an *inventus* thing," I quickly replied—willing myself *not* to get a boner from him looking at me like I was a juicy steak.

I actually had no idea how our newfound connection worked. It didn't *feel* like I was siphoning power from Zion to turn into a lizard. If anything, the agitating pull I'd experienced since arriving at the Salah estate had finally settled—which I assumed meant we'd completed the bond.

During our deep woods, mud wrestling adventure.

I awkwardly shifted on my feet at the memory. My ass was sore, but it was a good pain—just like Xander had said. I flushed, realizing I'd essentially outed myself as a bottom to my blabbermouth big bro, but then remembered he hadn't even told his own *inventus* about me finding mine.

Maybe sex talks are the only thing that's sacred in this family?

Zion took a deep breath and chuckled knowingly, making me blush deeper, before blinking away his reptilian features like it was nothing. "As sexy as you look sporting scales, it might give us away before we're ready. Try to relax, B. Breathe in for a count of four, hold it for four, then exhale for four. Rinse, repeat."

I nodded and began my hippie-breathing exercises as Zion strolled to the bookshelf on the far wall and began removing dusty volumes, one-by-one. It didn't take long for me to lose count and stop breathing altogether, but my scales had already faded, so I must have done something right.

Just as I moved to join my *inventus* and help him search for the photo, my phone buzzed in my pocket. Pulling it out, I found my brother Gabriel was calling.

Which means Andre's on the line as well.

"What's up, losers?" I answered with the special greeting I reserved just for them. The twins may have been leagues more powerful than me, but I was still older, and I would lord that over them until the day I died.

"Get the fuck out of that room and start walking east," Gabe hissed in my ear, making my hair stand on end. "Leave the lizard behind to do his thing. You're playing the distraction."

What?!

"Do it, Balty," Dre piped in, ganging up on me, as usual. "Move your ass."

JESUS CHRIST, OKAY.

"Uh, I need to take this call," I muttered to a confused-looking Zion. "I'll play lookout."

He waved me off, and I hurriedly slipped into the hallway. It was empty in both directions, and there were no windows to give me directional clues.

"Which way's east, dudes?" I sighed, immediately admitting defeat.

"Fucking hell," Gabe groaned.

Heavy silence followed, and I patiently waited. I knew from experience the twins were combining their powers to do some witchy psychic thing, and if I interrupted them, there would be hell to pay.

I wonder if they're each other's inventus... inventi...

That would be weird.

"Walk toward the judgy bust at the end of the hall," Dre clarified, and I snorted, easily identifying the monstrosity he was referring to.

Now you're speaking my language, dudes.

"Okay, I'm headed toward the bust of Judge Judy Salah the Sixteenth." I chuckled, which earned me a sigh from one of them.

So grumpy.

"Stop walking," Gabe snapped, and I obeyed, feeling like we were playing Red Light, Green Light, with a side of impending doom. "All right, listen up, asshole. When she rounds the corner, pretend to hang up, but keep the call connected when you put the phone back in your pocket. Ask her about a trip she took to Argentina. Say you heard the staff talking about it or some shit."

"Who?" I mumbled, beyond confused. I didn't have to wonder for long, as the 'she' in question rounded the corner with signature murder in her stormy eyes.

Lady Tempest.

"Okay, talk to you later," I chirped, before sliding my still-connected phone into my pocket. I was already *pouring* sweat, but determined not to fuck this up—if only to buy Zion some time.

"Oh, hey, Jackie… Jacqueline. Miss Tempest, ma'am…" I stuttered, stepping into my future mother-in-law's path so suddenly, she almost plowed me over. "Do you have a minute to talk about a trip you took?"

I sound like a drunken bible salesman.

"What?" she snapped, looking me over like I was a filthy street urchin begging for change.

"When you went to Argentina," I clarified, and she noticeably stiffened. "Um… *Preek* mentioned you visited the country at one point."

Preek?!

"Preek?" Lady Tempest echoed my frantic thoughts, narrowing her eyes and making me sweat more. "You've seen Preek?"

"Not recently." I cleared my throat. "I, uh, assumed you fired him after those pictures got leaked. Sorry about that…"

She waved a dismissive hand. "The photographs are inconsequential, Baltasar. It's not as if anyone in this family—or beyond—is ever surprised by how you and my son behave around each other." When I simply stood there, catching flies, she added, "Like a pair of degenerate bar brawlers."

Got it, thank you.

Ma'am.

I filed away the intel that Preek was *missing*, not fired, before doggedly continuing the world's worst interrogation. "So, what was Argentina like? You know, my father was from there, but I've actually never been—"

"Neither have I," she brusquely interrupted. Her gaze wandered over my shoulder, toward Major Obscurity's office door, and I prayed she wasn't thinking of going after the photograph. "Regardless of what Preek was blathering about, he misunderstood. I would never waste my time in such an uncivilized place, especially with the sort of monsters who hail from there."

Ouch.

But… fair.

"Okay, well, thank you for your time!" I gave her my most camera-ready smile, even as I kicked myself for failing my assignment from the twins.

What else did they expect?

Lady Tempest moved to sidestep me, and I boldly grabbed her arm—desperate to appease the two psycho psychics breathing on the line

Please don't kill me.

"Wait! Do you know an anthropologist named Dr. Lorenzo Torres-Maldonado? He studies ancient civilizations in South America and I was hoping to… apply for an internship with him. Yeah. You know, after the Games are done."

The formidable hero's growing irritation had now given way to bewilderment. "An *internship?* What on earth would someone like *you* do for an anthropologist?"

Someone like me…

"Lift heavy things," I deadpanned, ignoring what sounded like a snort coming from the depths of my pocket.

Lady Tempest hummed absently in agreement. Her gaze drifted dangerously toward her husband's office again, and I realized I was running out of bullshit to distract her with.

Maybe I can fake an injury.

She'd probably just step over me...

Then, like the tiny miracle she was, Daisy came marching around the corner with a paper in one hand and a pencil in the other. "Oh, hi, Blunty! Excuse me, Gran? Can I interview you for my family tree project? Ms. Doyle says we need to pick someone that's not our parents."

Her *gran* looked surprised. "Oh, well... wouldn't you rather ask one of your aunts or uncles? I'm extremely busy, Daisy, and I—"

Enough of this.

"This is your *grandchild!*" I hissed, feeling my supe form bulging under my skin. "How about you find the time to treat her like a part of this family—which she *is.*"

Lady Tempest was looking at me like I had three heads, and for a moment, I feared maybe I'd sprouted some extras. Sneaking a glance down at my forearm, I sighed with relief to find no new scales had appeared.

That would have been awkward.

Although, not any more awkward than me yelling at Jacqueline Salah.

"Very well," the formidable supe breezily replied, bringing my shocked gaze back to her face. "I can assist with your assignment, Daisy, and then perhaps we can get some ice cream."

It was Daisy's turn to look shocked, but then a tentative smile stretched across her face. "That sounds awesome, Gran! I have the perfect questions to ask you..."

Her sweet babbling grew faint as they disappeared down the hall, and my heart shattered, knowing full well Lady Tempest had only agreed to save face in front of me. It wasn't until I heard Gabe calling my name from my pocket that I unclenched my fists and pulled out my phone.

"Yeah, yeah, I know, I fucked up," I snapped into the phone, sharper than I meant to. "The only thing I got out of Lady Tempest was her thinking I'm a bigger freak than she already did."

"What are you talking about, Balty? You kicked ass!" Dre laughed. "We got that shady lady on lock, thanks to you."

"What are you talking about?" I sputtered, cupping my hand over my mouth to muffle my voice. "I didn't get her to say anything about Argentina. She denied it all."

Gabe took over again. "Yeah, but the minute you mentioned Argentina, her mind went to Argentina—to the cave Doc's working on. She's *been* there, Balty. Tempest knows about the paintings and our history."

Well, shit.

"So, she knows Doc?" I excitedly whispered—thrilled we had a break in the case.

"No, she doesn't," Gabe replied, although he didn't sound upset about it. "*That* she was being truthful about, at least."

"Good idea to ask if she knew Doc, though," Dre added. "Genius."

Well, there's a word I don't hear every day.

Or ever.

I slipped back into the Major's office, smiling when Zion grinned at me from across the room while waving a photo triumphantly. I strode to meet him and snatched it from his hand for a closer look.

The photograph was sepia toned, worn with age and creased down the middle, but clearly displayed the same cave we had documented in our archives. A younger version of Lady Tempest stared back at me, but even back then, she already had the 'I will crush you into dust' quality that made her naturally terrifying.

And you just scolded her in front of her grandkid.

I blew out a breath to the count of four, determined not to get angry all over again on Daisy's behalf. Zion gave me a concerned look, but he lacked the psychic abilities needed to drag this baggage out of me.

"And dang, bro. Did your balls get bigger since you left home?" Gabe spoke loud enough to be heard by everyone in the room—apparently set on roasting me in front of my *inventus*. "You almost went full Hulk on Lady fucking Tempest."

I opened my mouth to reply when Zion pulled me close. "Yeah, you did. You defended my little girl. *Our* little girl."

Squee!

"Everybody's shacking up around here," Dre grumbled. "It's weird. Hi, Justice!" he added, just to be an annoying little shit. "Heard you're gonna join the family."

"Hello, Shock and Awe." Zion chuckled, although neither side seemed serious about the supe name dropping. "Thanks for being our wingmen."

"No problem at all," Gabe smoothly replied. "Thank *you* for delivering dirt on your family. Our bloodthirsty leader will be most pleased."

"Wolfgang?" Zion asked, although his grin told me he knew the answer to that.

With eerily similar cackles, the twins hung up, leaving me with nothing else to do but stare down at the photograph to avoid meeting Zion's gaze. I couldn't believe I'd talked back to his mother—had 'almost gone full Hulk' on the famous hero. I'd been ready to fight to the death over the same offhand dismissiveness Daisy probably dealt with every day.

But that's the problem, isn't it?

She shouldn't have to deal with it at all.

Zion must have taken pity on me as he left the subject alone. Instead, he gently took the photo from me and flipped it over. "It says, 'At the site with Richard and T.' It's not much, but it's something."

Taking a few quick photos of the evidence, I finally looked at Zion—silently asking for permission to share this with my family.

Please, trust us.

His mouth pressed into a thin line, but he nodded, and I texted shots of the front and back to the twins for confirmation.

Double Trouble: *Yeah, that's the guy she thought of when you mentioned Argentina.*

I gritted my teeth as Zion returned the photograph to its hiding place. We were hot on the trail of something big, and I was both eager and nervous to find out what it was.

Whatever it is could change everything.

It was also a big deal that my heir apparent *inventus* had just freely given up his 'leverage' to a rival clan. But I trusted our bloodthirsty leader would know what to do with the intel.

And Wolfy will too.

"Are you ready to do this?" Zion asked as we stealthily left his father's office behind.

I nodded, knowing he meant investigating the mystery, but all in for all the things, either way. "Are *you?*"

He looked surprised by the question, and took a good minute before resolutely replying, "I am. I *want* to know what's going on. No matter what."

CHAPTER 39
BALTASAR

It turned out the guy in the photograph with Lady Tempest was dead.

Richard Cabrera had been part of the original archeological dig at the cave, and Doc suspected he may have been the one to leak the evidence.

Which might be why he's no longer with us.

Unfortunately, that left us with one less person to question, which disappointed my family's interrogator, Xanny, the most. Even though he wasn't the kind of guy who went looking for a fight, I knew my brother took pride in his work.

Especially if it involves a scalpel.

"Maybe the 'T' stands for Tempest?" I absently mused as Zion slid his hand under my tutu.

Huffing, I batted it away. The only reason I was wearing the ridiculously floofy thing was because Daisy had insisted on it while we watched some princess ballerina movie.

And we all know I can't say no to her.

The little queen was currently passed out cold at the other end of the couch. So we'd turned off *Isabella Frou-Frou's Big Caper,* or whatever, to discuss what we knew so far.

"Nah, I don't think the 'T' is for her," he replied, boldly reaching beneath the floof again. "The way it's worded implies *three* people were present, and the others probably only knew my mom as her civilian name. Plus…" He gave my thickening cock a squeeze. "The note's in her handwriting."

"Z…" I stifled a moan, no longer caring about the case when he touched me like that.

When he touches me at all, really.

Knowing he'd successfully distracted me, Zion smirked and removed his hand. "Let me just get D into bed, and then I'll take care of you."

Yeah… take care of that D before you take care of mine.

By the time he emerged from Daisy's bedroom again, I was trying—and failing—to get myself out of the tutu.

Why are the buttons so goddamn tiny?!

"Don't you dare take that off," Zion growled, and I stiffened. In more ways than one. "My room. Now."

Wait, what?

"I can't… I can't just walk down the hall like this, Z," I hissed. "I'm already on thin ice with your parents—especially with how I freaked out on your mom earlier."

Zion released another growl, only this one sounded more like a purr as he stalked closer. "Yeah, you showed Lady Tempest that Blunt Force is not to be fucked with." He backed me against the door, looming over me. "I was so proud of you when I overheard you standing up to her. And I've been waiting to reward you all day."

"Reward me?" My voice had a breathy quality I would have cringed at under different circumstances.

He chuckled low before gently pulling me away from the door so he could open it. "That's right, beautiful. But you're not gonna find out what I mean until you get your tutu-covered ass into my bedroom."

You don't have to tell me twice!

Okay, so maybe twice.

I was out the door and halfway down the hall faster than Isabella FrouFrou, reclaiming her kingdom. Zion caught up with me a moment later, wrapping a hand around the back of my neck in a possessive way that quickly tented my sweats.

And my tutu.

The tiny part of my brain that was still operating decided everything was fine. If any Salahs stumbled upon us, I reasoned they'd just think it was more of the 'degenerate bar brawler' behavior we were apparently known for.

"You look so fucking pretty, Baltasar." My name on Zion's wicked tongue made me shudder as we continued our path. "My pretty princess."

"Fuck off," I croaked, even though I was so horny I could barely see straight. "I'm no one's *princess.*"

My grumbling turned into a startled yelp as he tightened his grip and dragged me down a service hallway. Once again, I could have matched him in size and put up a fight, but as he used his bulk to deliciously press me into an alcove from behind, I moaned instead.

Okay, maybe I'm a slutty *princess…*

"Shhh," he hissed in my ear, sliding his hands up under my ridiculous tutu to toy with the waistband of my sweatpants. "I doubt you'd want anyone discovering us like this."

Like… this?

"You're not fucking me in a tutu, Z," I huffed, although my cock seemed to be all aboard this Big Caper.

"I am," he replied as he dropped to his knees—taking my sweats and briefs with him to the floor. "And you're going to beg me for it."

"Oh, yeah?" I twisted around to glare down at him. "You really think I'm gonna—"

My words were lost as he spread me wide and shoved his goddamn lubed lizard tongue into my ass in one smooth motion.

Jesus!

"*Fuck!*" I choked out, planting my palms on the wall of the alcove and instinctively adjusting my stance so he could go deeper. "If I had a tongue like yours, I'd never leave my room."

Zion's laughter was muffled, and he concentrated on working me open a bit more before coming up for air. "I'm not *that* flexible, B, but I'm more than happy to feast on your perfect cunt all day."

I froze. "Excuse me?"

He slowly stood and crowded me against the wall, holding me in place with one hand on my waist while using the other to rub his now unleashed cock along my crack. "I said your *cunt* is perfect. Because that's what your hole is when you're dressed like this for me. A hot, wet, tight little cunt."

Jesus. Fucking. Christ.

"I… I don't…" My brain had officially gone offline. Part of me *thought* it wanted to argue—to assert how manly I was—but mostly, that part needed to shut the fuck up and sit the fuck down.

"You can always safe out, Baltasar." Zion's tone turned gentle as he replaced his cock with his finger—sliding in first one, then two. "If you truly don't want to be my pretty princess."

"Oh, my gawwwdddd…" I groaned, fucking myself on his fingers, loving the feel of the scratchy material bunching up between us. "Fuck… I want…"

I want…

"What do you want, beautiful?" His voice was low and sultry again as he withdrew his fingers and began to slowly—so slowly—stuff me full of ridged lizard dick.

"I want…" The stretch of Zion inside me—the bite of soreness left over from earlier that registered as pure pleasure now—was making me delirious. Making me *want.* "I want you to fuck my pretty princess cunt with your fat cock. *Please…*"

Just call me Isabella FrouFrou.

"So fucking good," he growled as his knot bumped up against my tender hole. "Such a good little princess with such a tight little cunt. All for me. All mine."

"Yes," I gasped as he moved—fucking me achingly slow and deep. "All yours."

I meant it, too. Not only was Zion Salah the only one I would let call me his pretty princess, but he was the only one. Period. Full stop. I was so fucking gone for this man, I was already forgetting everyone I'd been with in the past.

Because no one else mattered to me before.

Not like this.

"I can't believe I get to have you," he continued, reaching around to caress me from my balls to my cock. "That you *want* to be with me and Daisy, like a family. That as soon as this bullshit is over, I'll get to hold you every night... knowing only I get to touch you... to bury myself inside your cunt and breed you whenever I want."

His hips snapped against me as he increased his pace, the tutu fluttering erratically as he stroked my cock in time with his thrusts. "Fuck, beautiful... I can't believe you're finally mine."

It wasn't clear if Zion was even talking to *me* anymore. I still chanted *yes, yes, yes* as he owned my pretty princess cunt, and my pretty princess cock, and told me I belonged to him.

While telling me I'm pretty.

"I love you," I whispered, turning my head so he could see how much I meant it. "I'm yours, Z."

Always.

"B..." he groaned before crashing his lips to mine, holding me tightly against him as he shattered.

The feel of his hot cum marking my insides sent me over the edge. Whimpering into his mouth, I unloaded all over Zion's hand, the wall, and the ridiculous tutu. Riding out the heady loop of sensations prolonging my orgasm until my knees went weak.

We eventually untangled ourselves, and Zion reluctantly helped me remove the tutu so we could use it to clean up. When I tried to take it from him—assuming I should throw it in with my dirty clothes for washing—he cackled and held it out of reach.

"If I can't sleep with *you* in my bed, this is the next best thing." He casually shrugged, as if that wasn't the most disgustingly hot thing I'd ever heard.

"Such a fucking animal," I teased.

But I absolutely mean it as a compliment.

"Goddamn right," Zion replied, giving me a quick kiss after we'd mostly straightened ourselves out again.

As straight as we'll ever be.

"So, does this mean I'm cleared for practice again?" I joked as I peered into the main hallway to check if the coast was clear.

"Nope. I have other plans for us tomorrow." He smirked. "Super secret spy in the city plans—on the hunt for leverage against my parents."

I laughed, already knowing I was game, whatever it was. I also couldn't wait until this bullshit was over—until we could just live our lives and openly be together, free from deals made by clan leaders hungry for power. Thinking for ourselves, for once.

The sooner, the better.

CHAPTER 40
ZION

On the drive into Sunrise City the next day, I finished filling in Baltasar on everything I knew.

"Why was Preek going to a perfumery, of all places?" he asked, his brow furrowing in an adorably distracting way. "That seems suspicious."

I beamed with pride in his direction before returning my attention to the road. "Exactly my thoughts. And he definitely reacted to it when I brought it up." I sighed, more annoyed with myself than anything. "What I should have done was interrogate the little shit when I had the chance—about that and the unapproved flight he took."

But now he's disappeared.

And I'm trusting a spaceman to find him for me.

Baltasar reached across the console and gave my thigh a comforting squeeze that did more to affect my heart than my cock. "Don't beat yourself up over it, Z. It's not like you could've known something like this would happen."

"But I should have expected it!" I barked, although all he did was tighten his grip. "I was raised to assume *everyone* was working against me—that even my own siblings could be a threat to my birthright. The issue is that *I* got complacent the last several years. I went soft."

My mate was quiet for a moment before he thoughtfully spoke. "My parents raised us to know our place in the pecking order. Wolfy was the heir—and we were all taught to fear him—but we also knew both Vi or the twins could easily rule the clan if something happened to him. Xanny was supposedly a dud, but he proved himself in other ways. And, well..." He looked out the window, hiding his face. "I wasn't even worth considering."

"B..." I began, debating pulling over so I could drag him into my lap for a cuddle and comfort fuck.

He held up a hand. "Even though I was already less than impressive, my parents still controlled what I could do with my powers. They forced me... to control myself."

"Tell me what they did," I gritted out.

I just know I'm going to lose my shit over this

Baltasar reached up so he could remove one of my hands from the wheel and hold it in my lap, although whether the touch was for me or him, I couldn't be sure. "Xanny invented these bindings that could hold supes, mostly for my father's work in his lair, but my parents would occasionally use them on me. They'd tie me up and provoke me, just to see what would happen. They wanted to teach me to not half-shift just because someone was pissing me off—to only fully Hulk out when it was necessary."

I wish I could've killed them first.

Using some of my breathing techniques, I forced myself to calm down before carefully replying, "Well, now I know why you don't like being restrained. And as angry as I am for how your parents treated you—tortured you—I'm even more pissed off that they hid how powerful half-shifting is."

He snapped his gaze to me. "What do you mean?"

I fucking knew it.

"Half-shifting is a way to have the best of both worlds," I explained, burying my rage so I could educate. "You're at full power with strength and stamina without losing speed due to bulk."

I didn't dare say anything more—assuming he needed time to process—but I held on tight to his now shaking hand, for both our sakes. It wasn't until I pulled into a parking spot near Xolo Parfumerie that he finally blew out a breath of his own.

"Why didn't you half-shift during the Games then?" he asked. "I probably never would have sacked you if you had."

A smirk twisted my lips. "Maybe our new alien friend was right. Maybe I *liked* you catching me. It gave me an excuse to roll around in the mud with you, if nothing else."

He rolled his eyes, but then raised our clasped hands to brush his lips over my knuckles. "I'm going to miss playing against you, Z. Star Hopper might give me a challenge, but it won't be the same."

Well, now's as good a time as any to tell him.

"You won't be playing against Star Hopper—at least, not how you think." My smile grew as his eyes widened. "Your coach is booting Nitro Dart off the line. You're the new starting long-shot."

"What?!" he choked out. "I-I'm not a *cum-shot,* dude. That's the most important position on the team."

Oh, beautiful.

"It is," I calmly replied, releasing his hand and exiting the car. After he hustled to join me on the sidewalk, I continued. "And it's exactly why *you* should play it. Stop selling yourself short, B. Just because your parents wanted to keep you small doesn't mean that's where you belong."

He simply cleared his throat before gazing up at the building and rapidly blinking. "So this is the perfume place you saw Preek go into?"

I nodded, more than happy to give him the out. "Yeah. He was inside for about twenty minutes, but unlike with his other stops, he didn't buy anything. I came back the day Butch and Smoldering Siren visited the house—to question the employees—but it was closed."

Baltasar nodded. "Well, it's open now. So, let's fucking do this."

Works for me.

"May I help you?" A sharply dressed normie snooty enough to make my mother weep approached us the instant we stepped into the crisp, air-conditioned retail space. I don't think he had an issue with *us,* per se, but he was eyeing my 'In My Defense, I Was Unsupervised' graphic tee with palpable disdain.

Another gift from my mate.

I glanced at the love of my life. He was looking around the maze of glass display cases with his nose wrinkled and his signature confused expression firmly in place.

Okay, I'll take the lead, then.

"Yes, you may, little guy." I grinned as the normie bristled, but he was a good foot shorter than me, so he couldn't get upset over facts. "I'm looking for a new cologne. Something extra special. I'm getting married soon and—"

"Who the fuck are you getting married to?" Baltasar asked, his eyes flashing sexy reptilian as he scowled at me.

This man must be protected at all costs.

"You, B," I softly replied, trying my damnedest not to smile. "I just hadn't gotten around to asking you yet."

"This is... weirdly cute," the normie mumbled, although he sounded annoyed by the fact. Before he could say more, a buzzer rang and his gaze snapped to the back room. "Ah, please excuse me for a moment. I have a delivery I need to attend to."

Probably a delivery of fresh attitude.

"Do you *smell* that?" Baltasar loudly whispered as soon as we were alone.

"What? Perfume? Cologne?" I laughed. "You'll have to be more specific than that."

He huffed. "It just smells like... it smells *familiar.*"

Nothing smelled unusual to *me,* but before I could reply, my attention was drawn to the sound of voices arguing in the back. While I'd never been an active hero, I'd always been taught that our purpose was to protect helpless normies from nefarious situations.

From villains, *of course...*

Gesturing for the sweetest of all villains to follow me, I led Baltasar in the direction the normie had disappeared. Along the way, I half-shifted to access my enhanced lizard hearing.

"What do you *mean,* you don't have my order ready?"

I froze in the doorway as the second voice became clearer—so clear my entire world slowed to a halt.

Is that... my father?

"I'm sorry, Mr. Kent," the normie sniveled—confirming my suspicions with the use of Major Obscurity's civilian name. "Your publicity director told me you no longer needed the shipments—"

"WHY WOULD YOU TAKE ORDERS FROM ANYONE OTHER THAN ME?!"

I jumped backward, grabbing Baltasar's arm for support. Never in my thirty-one years had I heard my father raise his voice like that—not even when my brother Isaiah and I burned down the guest house during one of our ragers.

Holy. Shit.

"Is that…?" Baltasar asked, and I nodded before motioning for him to follow me. As far as I knew, he also hadn't seen much action on the battlefield—since his Deathball career took precedence as well. But every supe was bred for warfare, so I trusted he could hold his own.

We moved as one, slinking further into the back room where this unexpected altercation was going down. Peering around the corner, I saw my father with his hand wrapped around the normie's neck, lifting the poor man off the ground completely.

"Do you have any idea what you've done?" Major Obscurity ranted. "How delicate the situation is at this point in time? If I cannot guarantee continued doses, decades of hard work could have all been for nothing."

What the fuck is he talking about?!

"Mr. Preek said…" The normie's voice was faint as he struggled to speak. My father growled, but loosened his grip to give him air. "He said he'd been to the lab and spoken to—"

"The lab?!" My father dropped the much smaller man into a crumpled heap. "How the *hell* does he know about the lab?"

"I don't know!" The normie wheezed, massaging his bruised throat and having the balls to glare up at my father from where he lay. "But that's who *I* work for, not *you*, so—*AACK!*"

Wrong answer, little guy.

Unsurprisingly, my father's boot was now on the normie's cheek, grinding his face into the cement floor of the back room, squishing him like a bug. "Well, you can tell your *boss* I'll be out to the lab to see him. Tonight. So he should clear the tarmac for my arrival." With that, The Major swept out the back door, leaving the carnage behind to work itself out.

And we wonder why normies are afraid of us…

"We should help him." Baltasar moved to enter the room, but I grabbed his arm.

"No," I whispered, eyeing the normie to make sure he was at least still breathing. "It's better if he thinks we were just random customers who got sick of waiting and left."

My mate obediently followed me back through the shop and out the front door, even though I could tell leaving the victim behind didn't sit well with him. But we had bigger problems.

And a plane to catch.

I waited until we were in my car before I spoke again. "We need to hitch a ride to this lab, B."

Baltasar nodded. "We do. Because what I smelled in that shop…" He leaned across the console and inhaled deeply before meeting my gaze. "It reminded me of *you*."

CHAPTER 41
ZION

My mind wouldn't settle.

A million different scenarios played themselves out in my head, but nothing was adding up. Obviously, we now knew the lab and perfumery were connected—and my parents had a hand in both—but that was where it stopped making sense. I'd never known them to be involved in either industry, so it was safe to assume this wasn't a business arrangement.

It's personal.

I hadn't smelled anything unusual inside Xolo, but Baltasar insisted he did, and I trusted my mate to recognize my scent —just as I would for him.

But why did it smell like me?

"I don't think you want to know."

I most certainly fucking do.

As soon as we got back to the house, I cornered Dahlia, but she swore up and down she hadn't known Preek canceled any of our parents' deliveries. His undocumented plane ride had supposedly been for intel gathering only, and he'd reported back that it was a dead end.

So Preek was playing her as well.

My sister also claimed not to know what these deliveries were for—only that they came in every six weeks or so—but she was convinced they had something to do with me.

Yeah, we figured out that part on our own, thanks.

Realizing my sister wasn't much of a detective only solidified my decision to take matters into my own hands and sneak onto the plane tonight. I did have a brief moment of panic as the day went on, and asked Baltasar to stay behind in case something happened to me.

Since he's the only one I trust to take care of Daisy.

Unsurprisingly, he refused.

"Like hell I'm staying here, Z," he hissed as we lingered in the service hallway outside the kitchen door. "What if shit hits the fan? We have an *inventus* bond now. That means we're twice as badass—*together.*"

I frowned. The last thing I wanted to do was piss on his inventus parade, but I'd felt no evidence of increased powers. That might have been because our basic abilities were so similar, but even the scales he'd sprouted had disappeared.

Too bad, because they were sexy as fuck.

Besides wanting to breed my mate constantly—which was nothing new, to be fair—the biggest difference was how acutely I could sense Baltasar's moods.

And Jesus, he has a lot going on in that head of his…

Even without my mate's jumbled emotions adding to my anxiety, I would have been on edge about everything we did —and didn't—know about the lab.

350

Before we entered the kitchen, I took a few calming breaths to recenter myself, not wanting Daisy to suspect anything.

Of course, my daughter missed nothing. "What were you two gossiping about out there?" she asked the instant we swung open the door—narrowing her eyes in accusation.

Spy mode activated.

"Grown up stuff," I instinctively replied, which only made her glare harder.

"Well, I've decided I want Bluntycups to read me my new *Isabella FrouFrou* book tonight," she sniffed. "In full costume."

Baltasar paled, and I barked a laugh before coming to his rescue. "That won't be possible, sweetie. Blunty spilled some… *milk* on the dad tutu, so we need to wash it before he wears it again."

Because he will *be wearing it again.*

Daisy wrinkled her nose. "Only psychopaths drink milk."

It was my turn to narrow my eyes. "How do you even know that word?"

She shrugged and flipped her hair with maximum sass. "It was in some documentary I was watching about supes."

Note to self: Check the parental controls on all devices.

"Um… I don't think I can read you a story tonight, little queen." Baltasar glanced at his watch as he sat down and began shoveling stir fry into his mouth. "Your dad and I have a… thing we need to go to…"

Daisy's suspicious gaze briefly slid to me before a change I knew well washed over her deceptively sweet face.

Oh, no…

BRACE YOURSELF, B!

"B-but..." Daisy's lower lip trembled as she turned to Baltasar—her big brown eyes filling up with fat tears. *"You're my dad now, too, Blunty."*

"Oh, my godddd," Baltasar gasped, and it was all I could do not to laugh at how close to crying *he* looked. "I'm sorry, D. I-I'll make it up to you, okay? We could go shopping this weekend. How does that sound?"

"Deal." She smirked, returning her attention to her dinner—all traces of alligator tears magically evaporated.

Lizard Queen, indeed.

Baltasar looked so confused, I reached across the small table to give his massive biceps a comforting squeeze. "You got hoodwinked, B. Never trust the tears."

His mouth dropped open, but the man knew he'd been beaten by a force more powerful than himself.

And lived to fight another day.

We ate quickly—with the usual comfortable banter I'd grown to appreciate—before walking Daisy to her room for a quick bedtime routine.

She waved us off. "Go do your top secret *thing* or whatever," she huffed. "I'm old enough to put myself to bed, anyway."

My heart panged at that announcement, but we didn't have time to argue. I'd tracked down our pilot earlier and casually asked him when they were heading out, under the guise of needing to catch my father beforehand. So I knew we only had about fifteen minutes to sneak onto the plane before the attendant started her preflight routine.

Not that I can't charm her if she discovers us.

My concerns were unfounded, as Pops was apparently in such a hurry, he skipped the flight attendant altogether. That allowed Balty and me to hide out in the crew area with no risk of being caught.

"Do you think Preek knows how to fly a plane?" Baltasar whispered as we leveled off at 40 thousand feet.

I would have thought this question came out of nowhere if I didn't now have a front-row seat to the general vibe of his scattered thoughts.

It's like riding a rollercoaster.

Or... bumper cars.

"I don't know, beautiful," I hummed, determined to treat everything he said like it mattered—because it did. "Why do you ask?"

He chewed on his lower lip, and I marveled as the static suddenly became clear. "You said your pilot had the night off when Preek took the plane. It would have been a trek for someone on the outside to sneak onto the property and meet up with him. You know, since your haunted murder mansion on the hill is kind of remote. No offense."

My lips twitched. "None taken. One of the main reasons I wanted to play Deathball—besides my parents pushing me to compete—was to get the hell away from the estate. If it was up to me, I'd live in the city, or at least in a more modern house."

Baltasar smiled, looking so hopeful, I already knew where the conversation was going. "You'd like my family's house. And there's plenty of room for both you and Daisy to live there..."

Oh, beautiful.

"You miss your siblings, huh?" I softly asked, assuming *that's* why he kept bringing it up.

And I want to figure out a solution to keep him happy.

He shrugged, trying to play it off. "Yeah, but I also know they'd have to pry me away from you with a crowbar at this point. Maybe I'm just selfishly trying to sell you on the idea so I can have it all."

I chuckled. Big City *was* nice, and my beast loved nothing more than swimming in the ocean. However, Baltasar still wasn't understanding how clan heirs confronted each other. At best, it was a power-flexing, dick-measuring contest. At worst, it was a fight to the death—or until one was so beaten down, the other took over their clan.

And I can't see either Wolfgang or me simply letting the other win.

But the 'one big, happy family' negotiations would have to wait. "So you actually think *Preek* has a pilot's license? The little dude never struck me as that much of a badass."

Baltasar licked his lips nervously. "You know how I was always going out to bars and clubs in Big City? It wasn't because I loved partying. Well, I do love it, but I also like just hanging out at home… watching movies and stuff…"

He smiled shyly at me through his eyelashes, and I had never in all my life wanted to cuddle-fuck someone so badly.

Perhaps sensing my mood, he cleared his throat and continued. "Anyway, the reason I was out so much was because I was sent to gather drunken intel from powerful supes and normie politicians. But I picked up some weird gossip along the way, so I started collecting what I could on… lessers, too…"

Why would he bother with lesser supes?

My mate must have noticed the question in my eyes as he clarified. "They *hate* us, Z. Most of them do, anyway. There's been chatter about an underground rebellion being organized —full of lesser supes with all sorts of useful skills… like pilot licenses. So far, no major incidents have been reported, but it's brewing. We act as if the big divide was always between heroes and villains, but it's actually between those of us with real powers and those with barely enough juice to light a match."

So they do have an angle, after all.

And Preek was an inside man.

"Well, fuck." I dragged a hand down my face, realizing we needed to do an audit of the house staff immediately. "I'm glad I have you to tell me what's what, B. Lord knows, I act like I'm invincible."

Like a true clan heir.

He smiled again, looking like a big, beefy heart-eyes emoji. "I've got your back now, Z. I'm in this until the end."

I opened my mouth to reply—or maybe to tackle him and get in a quickie before we landed—when a familiar voice piped in.

"I've got your back, too! Where are we going, anyway?"

Baltasar's eyes widened in horror—matching my expression perfectly—and we both turned to confront our little stowaway.

Daisy.

CHAPTER 42
ZION

"Daisy Michaela Salah!" I hissed, full-naming her so she knew exactly how much trouble she was in. "On what planet do you think following us is okay?"

She shrugged, as unbothered as ever. "I didn't *follow* you. I eavesdropped on your plans and then hid myself on the plane before you guys got here."

I can feel my gray hairs multiplying.

Baltasar glanced at me before taking over. "I'm impressed with your spy skills, little queen, but you should probably stay here while we investigate."

She cocked her head, her expression concerningly impassive. "Would it make you feel better if I did?"

He nodded just as the pilot announced we were already beginning our descent. This meant our destination was barely outside of Sunrise City. I had to assume taking the plane was more about my father shaving off a few hours of travel time and avoiding traffic.

Along with covering his tracks.

Once again, I internally scolded myself for being so detached from my family's business all these years. I'd believed my parents would be the ones hurt by my withdrawal, but the only one I'd negatively affected was myself. In our world, knowledge was power.

And I willingly gave mine away.

Discovering lesser supes saw us as the enemy—that some were possibly plotting against us—was the harsh wake up call I needed. While they couldn't take us in battle, many worked for us and were privy to the inner workings of powerful households. An NDA wouldn't mean shit if the one breaking it intended to slip away before they were caught.

I need to talk to Wolfgang.

But first things first.

"Daisy, go hide wherever…" I trailed off as I turned to find she'd already disappeared.

All that disaster preparedness training clearly worked.

Baltasar softly chuckled as we concealed ourselves again for landing. "Well, I guess we have backup now."

I growled, although it was more playful than angry. "Oh, I see how it is. You're the *fun* dad while I'm the one enforcing all the rules like a wet blanket."

He kissed me, slowly and thoroughly, and I was fine with temporarily letting him take the lead. Nothing compared to having hot, hard muscles pressed against me, and Baltasar's put all others to shame.

Of course, I could only give up control for so long. Knowing he went weak for my ridged lizard tongue, I forced it down his throat, loving how he gagged around it while simultaneously melting in my arms. Like the good little mate he was.

All fucking mine.

"Jesus, Z," he gasped when I finally let him breathe again. "I really don't want to go in there with a..." He lowered his voice, furtively searching for our tiny spy, before dropping his gaze to his crotch. "You know..."

Yeah, I do.

I shrugged as the plane landed and came to a stop—wherever we were. "I just wanted to prep you for what you'll be choking on later."

You know...

He *definitely* did, as his pretty amber eyes darkened with desire. Our flirting was cut short by the sound of the airlock door being opened, followed by my father's murmured parting words to the pilot as he exited the plane.

The instant we heard the pilot shut himself in the cockpit again, we both crept out of the crew compartment and hustled down the aisle. Luckily, the door had been left open with the airstair extended, implying my father didn't intend to stay long.

Looks like we need to make this quick.

As soon as we hit the tarmac, I shifted into full lizard mode for the armor my scales provided. I waited for Baltasar to shift as well, but he was busy eyeing my supe form hungrily.

Finally dragging his gaze away, he gave me a sheepish look. "I... haven't been able to make my scales appear again. Maybe we need to practice together?"

I can definitely get some lizard inside you again.

Swallowing down my filthy thoughts, I told him to stay behind me and took off running toward a large industrial building. A glance over my shoulder revealed my old rival chasing me—just like old times—half-shifted and easily keeping up with my pace.

Such a good little student.

There were no guards stationed outside. Paired with the fact my father hadn't brought backup, this implied the relationship here was symbiotic, with equal power on both sides. Besides being helpful intel to know, it made infiltrating the building uneventful.

"Jesus. It smells like *you* times infinity in here." Baltasar stifled a cough before blowing out a hard breath through his nose. "Fuck... I don't want to get hard while I'm on a mission..."

The scent was heavy enough this time that I picked up on it. My brow furrowed as I took a deep inhale, trying to place what it reminded me of. "It smells like..."

Oh, shit.

"Like your death pond," Baltasar grimly confirmed.

We both just stared at each other as I partially forced my beast back under my skin. If whatever they were cooking up here smelled like my pond, it was safe to assume *that's* where the mysterious shipments had been ending up.

For decades, apparently.

Have my parents been dosing *me all this time?!*

My father's angry shouts abruptly broke the silence, but then the sound of a door slamming shut cut him off. Canting my chin, I led the way down the sterile hallway, although even with my lizard hearing, I couldn't pick up any voices.

I soon figured out why. We peered around a corner to find Major Obscurity—in full supe gear—ranting to a boardroom full of suits and scientists. Behind what was probably sound-proof glass.

All the better for keeping shady discussions under wraps.

Baltasar already had his phone out, zooming in to capture the faces of everyone we could see—like the Suarez spy he apparently was.

No wonder he and Daisy make such a good team.

There was one man with his back to us, but his size alone pegged him as either a powerful supe or a goddamn body-builder. Mystery man was obviously in charge, as my father was now furiously addressing him alone. For a moment, I absently wondered what I'd do if he suddenly attacked my flesh and blood.

Since I no longer know where my loyalties lie there.

But I know who has my back here.

"I bet there's an office around here with records we could dig through," I whispered to my mate.

My *inventus.*

He pocketed his phone and fell in step as I again led the way —deeper into the facility. We followed the sound of whirring machinery until we arrived at an enormous warehouse space.

A bottling plant.

It appeared to be fully automated, but I suspected there was at least *some* human involvement. Lifting my gaze, I spotted what looked like an overseer's office high above, fitted with a wall of thick glass to watch operations below.

Bingo.

Baltasar followed my gaze before leaning closer to shout over the noise. "I'll meet you up there. I want to grab a few of these bottles as evidence."

I nodded and headed toward the office, hoping there wouldn't be any normies along the way to incapacitate or kill. While my beast was roaring for revenge, I knew this was just a job for most people involved. I didn't want to get my hands any dirtier than necessary.

Because I want to keep the blame squarely where it's deserved.

There was no one in the office—probably because whoever normally occupied it was currently having their ass handed to them by Major Obscurity. I knew from experience my father's tirades didn't last long, so set to work opening drawers and file cabinets, looking for evidence. Weirdly, there wasn't a laptop in sight, but I assumed it had joined the party down the hall.

Or this is the sort of operation without a digital paper trail.

Unfortunately, I wasn't finding much in the way of a *regular* paper trail, either—at least, nothing out of the ordinary. Everything was by-the-book standard records. Invoices, purchase orders, and certificates from the Department of Human Health and Services.

How ironic.

Sidling closer to the window, I was relieved to see Baltasar heading my way with bottled evidence in hand.

We make a great team, too.

By the time he arrived, I had my ear pressed up against the fireproof safe I'd discovered—using my lizard hearing like a stethoscope. Proving once again just how equipped he actually was for high stakes situations, my mate immediately made a beeline for the windows to keep watch.

I hissed in triumph as the mechanisms clicked and the safe swung open. My enthusiasm quickly faded as I found a ridiculously large stack of manilla folders waiting for me inside.

If I wanted to deal with paperwork, I'd have taken over the clan already.

"This is going to take years to document," I grumbled, flipping through the first folder to see if anything caught my eye.

To my annoyance, it contained nothing but scribbled formulas. I cared less about how they did whatever the fuck they were doing here than why, so quickly moved on to the next folder.

"Yes, by the way," Baltasar murmured, drawing my attention back to him. He turned away from the window to meet my gaze with that same unwavering intensity he used to give me on the Deathball field. "Whenever you get around to asking me, I'm gonna say yes."

This fucking man.

"Good to know, Suarez," I replied, battling to keep my voice steady. "Because I wasn't sure if you liked me the way I like you."

He scoffed. "I doubt you've felt unsure a day in your life. Your confidence is one of the many things I've always admired about you."

Immediately dropping my gaze to the mountain of folders in my lap, I rapidly blinked to get rid of the weird blurriness that had appeared for no apparent reason.

I must have something in my eye.

"Oh, no," Baltasar gasped, and the father in me immediately recognized the distinct brand of terror.

No.

Tossing the stack aside, I raced to the windows, staring down in horror to find *Daisy* wandering around the machinery.

"B…" I grabbed his arm. "Just take the folders and get her the hell out of there. I'll make sure there's nothing else hidden up here and meet you both on the plane."

My *inventus* looked like he wanted to argue, but something in my expression must have convinced him otherwise. He snapped his mouth shut and obediently headed for the evidence instead.

After shoving the folders into a bag we'd brought with us, he gave me a hard look. "If you fucking die on me, I'll kill you, Salah."

This. Fucking. Man.

I laughed, so smitten it was ridiculous. "I promise, I won't die. Now get our girl to safety."

It wasn't ideal to take the folders with us—since it would blow our cover the instant someone looked in the safe—but there was no way to document everything in time.

It's time to blow this whole thing wide open, anyway.

I waited until Baltasar reached Daisy before I tore myself away from the window—intent on giving the room one last sweep before joining them.

That's when the door slammed shut and the alarm went off.

CHAPTER 43
BALTASAR

I was about to scold Daisy when an ear-splitting alarm blared through the warehouse, accompanied by blinding, flashing strobes.

No.

My little queen yelped and covered her ears, but I'd already scooped her up and started running to Zion—needing to reach him before security arrived.

I stopped in my tracks as I realized the stairs leading up to the office had retracted, and the door far above was now sealed shut like a bank vault, trapping him inside.

Nonononono....

Backing away, I looked up. Zion was in full lizard form, throwing himself against the floor-to-ceiling window, rattling the pane. When he noticed me dumbly watching, he stopped and roared something intelligible while gesturing for me to get the hell out of here.

Please, no.

I frantically shook my head—unwilling to believe this was happening—but then he pointed at the little girl in my arms. He may as well have punched me in the heart.

Don't make me do this, Z.

I can't…

The heavy vibration of approaching boots and the echo of angry voices shouting commands ramped up my anxiety. This combined with Zion banging on the glass while silently screaming at me to *run, run, run…* until my head and heart both felt like they were going to explode.

I can't leave my inventus!

I can't, I can't, I can't—

"Blunty," Daisy's little voice was in my ear, sure and strong. "We have to go. I know what to do."

Thank fuck one of us does.

My gaze landed on an emergency exit sign at the far end of the room, just as a dozen armed *scientists* arrived behind us.

And immediately opened fire.

"THERE'S A GODDAMN KID HERE!" I roared, crouching and twisting my body so the bullets would hit me instead of Daisy.

To my shock, absolutely no one stopped shooting. So I half-shifted, held onto my sobbing girl like a Deathball, and ran for the exit like the long-shot Zion had been training me to be. Shielding Daisy from the shattering glass, I dodged between machines—hissing as a well-aimed bullet grazed my shoulder blade.

MOTHERFUCKER!!!

Normie weapons couldn't kill supes, but it still hurt like a bitch to get hit. I was more concerned with protecting the fragile half-normie in my arms. Tucking her tightly against my chest, I cleared the last few yards before using my good shoulder to barrel through the exit door.

It took every ounce of willpower to slam the door shut behind us and leave Zion on the other side. The shooting continued —along with the sounds of shattering glass—and I choked on anguish, imagining the worst.

He's like a fish in a barrel in that office!

Briefly setting down my precious cargo, I hauled a dumpster in front of the exit to slow down our pursuers. The gunfire was *still* going, and I suddenly realized they weren't aiming to kill.

They're destroying the evidence.

Snatching Daisy again, I headed for the towering chain-link fence surrounding the facility, spying the lights of the highway beyond. I was preparing to climb one-handed when a semi-circle of heat suddenly burned its way through the metal, creating the perfect opening for me to pass through.

Well, that was convenient.

"You certainly know how to make an entrance. Or an exit..." A familiar voice had me spinning to find Ziggy Andromeda strolling out from the shadows.

I froze, seeing the backup I needed, but gripped with indecision. If Daisy wasn't here, I would have already raced back inside—would never have left Zion behind in the first place. But no way in hell was I handing my girl over to someone who could whisk her away to another planet while I played hero.

"Zion's still in there!" I yelled, wild-eyed and desperate. "You have to... please, just get him out of there. Do your star hopping whatever thing—fucking *please!*"

At this moment, I had no shame and gave zero fucks. If Ziggy needed me to get on my knees and properly beg, I would. Anything to save the love of my life.

Fuck... he's the love of my life.

The alien's eyes widened before his gaze snapped to the *now smoking* warehouse Zion was still trapped inside.

"Very well." Ziggy nodded once. "I should be able to get in there. Just let me situate—"

His words were lost as the entire bottling plant exploded in a fiery inferno that felt like it ripped straight through my soul.

And my bond.

"NOOOO!!!" I howled, dropping Daisy and running full-speed toward the burning building.

I barely made it a few feet before I was tackled to the ground so hard my breath was punched out of me.

Jesus, he should play grabber...

"Are you fucking crazy?!" Ziggy shouted in my ear—his voice somehow cutting through my blind panic. "You don't look fireproof to me, so why on Earth would you try to burn yourself alive?"

"My mate... my *inventus* is in there!" I sobbed. "Please, I need... I-I can't lose him!"

Not when I finally found him.

"Like a stellar collision..." Ziggy whispered reverently, helping me to my feet as Daisy elbowed past him to reach me.

"Pull yourself together, Blunty," she sternly scolded, even as tears were running down her sweet little face. "We need to get to the city—to the club where my mom used to work. Can you do that?"

I...

"You need to *go*. Now." Ziggy gazed overhead as the Salah family plane took off—unsurprisingly leaving us behind to fend for ourselves. "I assume emergency personnel will arrive soon, so this is my only chance to get in there for you."

When I didn't budge, he leveled me with a hard look, and I gasped as what looked like *galaxies* shimmered in his eyes. "I will retrieve your *Lacertus* mate."

"Are *you* fireproof?" I asked, still too shaken to move or make sense of what he was offering.

"Something like that." Ziggy grinned—his teeth so perfect, I assumed they were part of the elaborate skinsuit I was suspecting he wore.

What are *you under there?*

"C'mon, Blunty!" Daisy barked, and I immediately clamored to my feet, rallying for *her*. "Daddy will know where to find us."

I sniffled and picked her up again, not having the heart to tell her Zion probably hadn't survived.

Not having the heart to tell myself.

With a meaningful nod at the mysteriously helpful alien, I turned toward the highway and took off.

I focused on the feel of Daisy in my arms, the whooshing sounds of the cars to my left, and the burn of my muscles as my legs swallowed the distance to Sunrise City. Anything to escape the reality of what I'd left behind.

What I'll never have again.

It was nearly midnight when we reached Lycra and Lace—the hot pink neon sign flickering above us like a beacon of heartache.

Axel the bouncer was nowhere to be seen, but as I headed for the entrance, Daisy groggily lifted her head and squinted at our surroundings.

"That way," she rasped, pointing down a sketchy side street I hadn't noticed the last time I was here.

With Zion.

I shuddered to think of her navigating this situation on her own. Pulling my girl more tightly against me, I dutifully followed her directions—thankful at least one of us knew what to do.

I've lost him. I've lost him, I've lost…

"Found it!" she crowed, pointing at a brownstone that showed no signs of life.

"Are you… sure?" I asked, wary of what waited for us inside. "We could just go to the club. I'm sure your mom's old friends would be more than happy—"

"No," Daisy cut me off with a confidence she only could have gotten from Zion. "This is where we need to be."

Aye, aye, Capitana.

I followed Daisy's instructions for retrieving the hidden key and getting us inside. To my surprise, it wasn't an abandoned building or a drug den, but a modern apartment. The walls were a light gray, bright and welcoming, with a hardwood floor so polished it reminded me of the surface of Zion's pond. It was decorated with comfy furnishings that warmed the space, even though no one was here.

Despite being empty, the apartment was obviously being regularly maintained. Everything smelled freshly cleaned—not at all like the earthy scent I now associated with *home*.

The same scent as whatever they were bottling up in that fucking factory.

I placed the bag of evidence on the kitchen island—too wrecked to even consider looking at it now. Food and sleep were the two most important things for us at the moment. Everything else would have to wait.

Including my broken heart.

In the morning, I'd call Wolfy to fill him in on everything that had happened. Then he could fly out here and rain down hell on Zion's parents before bringing Daisy and me back to the Suarez family compound.

The only home I have left.

"Whose house is this?" I asked as I poked around the oddly well-stocked fridge.

"My mom's," she answered, sliding onto the bench seat at the built-in corner table. "Dad bought it for her when Gran and Pop-Pop refused to let her live at the big house."

My blood *boiled,* but I focused on completing a few sets of the breathing technique Zion had taught me while I poured us some cereal and milk.

I'm in no mood to go gourmet.

"Does it make you… sad?" I asked as I joined her at the table. "Being here, I mean."

The last thing I wanted to do was trigger Daisy's grief—or address the fresh loss looming over us—but I didn't want to ignore the topic completely.

She deserves that much, at least.

My girl crunched on her cereal for a few minutes, looking so exhausted I didn't know if she'd find the energy to answer.

"Yes and no," she finally replied. *"Yes,* because I miss my mom and being surrounded by her things makes me sad. And *no,* because being here feels like I'm surrounded by her. Not her stuff—just *her.* But I feel like that all the time."

I stopped chewing, shivering as a chill danced along my spine. "You feel her around you? Like a… *ghost?"*

Creepy.

Daisy laughed, although it ended with a yawn. "I'm not *haunted,* Blunty. Gawd, you're too easy."

Her reply reminded me so much of something Zion would say, I had to push aside my bowl and rest my forehead on the table.

Why'd you have to die on me, asshole?

My chest was so tight, I could barely breathe. I wondered if it would forever feel like a physical part of me had been amputated—like a phantom limb that *ached and ached.*

Please, come back to me.

Daisy's arms were suddenly wrapped around me as she hugged me from behind. "Thank you for saving me again, Blunty. I'm so glad I have you."

I turned my head so I could look at her peering around my shoulder, hating how life kept beating her down. "Always. And I'm glad I have you, too, little queen."

We have each other.

She straightened and let out a loud yawn. "I need to go to bed before I fall asleep standing up. Do you want me to show you where my mom's bedroom is?"

A sick feeling settled in my stomach. "Um, no thanks. I'm good. Do *you* need help with bedtime? I know I'm a mess right now, but I promise, I'll take good care of you from now on."

As your only dad.

She squeezed me in another hug, planting a messy kiss on my cheek. "I know you will, Blunty. But it's okay to be sad, too."

With that heartbreaking advice, she shuffled off and padded up the stairs. I rose and looked around the too-quiet kitchen—wishing Cook was here to bang around and yell at me—before gathering our dishes to leave in the sink overnight.

Everything can be dealt with tomorrow.

Having absolutely no interest in sleeping in Mikki's old bedroom—not without Zion—I splashed some cold water on my face, dried my tears, and passed out on the couch.

Let me just forget about everything until tomorrow.

CHAPTER 44
ZION

Stars.

All I could see was millions of stars—with one glowing brighter and bluer than the rest—and the air so cold, my breath froze to ice in my lungs.

The journey took only seconds... or eons. Time held no meaning while floating through fathomless space. Assuming this was my reality now, I admired the sparkling amethysts and mauves surrounding me. The inky darkness felt like a weighted blanket—and I settled into the quiet that resonated deep in my tired bones.

Beautiful.

"It is, isn't it? Even I agree... and this is my home."

Home.

A kaleidoscope flash of rainbow light was the only warning I got before I suddenly found myself alone.

So alone.

I was lying on an uncomfortably hard, damp surface that smelled like rotting garbage, so I lifted my head to get my bearings.

Is that…?

I didn't know what I expected to see in death, but it wasn't a row of brownstones that uncannily matched Mikki's old street. I'd helped her settle into a place like this years ago—once we realized things would never work between us.

They probably never would have, anyway.

Because it was always him.

Picking myself up off the asphalt, I cautiously approached the replica of Mikki's house and climbed the stairs. Trying the knob, I found it locked.

That's a weirdly realistic detail…

Retrieving the key from the same hiding place where I kept it in life, I quietly entered the sacred space before closing the door behind me.

And then almost tripped over a pair of my daughter's sneakers.

That's… even weirder.

In the real world, I paid a discreet service to keep the place clean and stocked, in case of emergencies. But this dream version felt *different*—more alive than usual.

Slowly creeping along the hallway, I glanced into the kitchen, spotting dirty bowls left in the sink, illuminated from the harsh glow of the range hood light.

And weirder still.

The smell of freshly baked cookies teased my nostrils, and I almost groaned at the memories it invoked. A quick glance around the countertops showed no sign of snickerdoodles, so I turned and moved further down the hall.

A shaft of light from the living room was cutting across the hardwood floor ahead of me. Padding closer, I peered around the doorframe, and my breath lodged in my throat at what I saw.

An angel.

Baltasar Suarez was sprawled out on the worn couch, fully dressed and snoring peacefully. He looked just as delicious as I remembered him—all gorgeous golden skin, messy hair, and hard muscles—only he was also streaked with dirt.

Which only makes him hotter.

Wondering if this fantasy—or afterlife—would be kind enough to let me touch my mate one last time, I snuck closer and kneeled at his side. Reaching out a shaking hand, I lightly trailed the back of my knuckles over his cheek, sharply inhaling as a jolt of electricity shot down my arm.

Fuck… it feels so real…

Baltasar's pretty amber eyes fluttered open, and I almost wept with how perfectly he scowled at me.

"What's this shit?" he grumbled, his voice raspy from sleep. "You gonna *haunt* me now? Nope. No fucking thank you. I'm closing my eyes and when I open them again, it better be morning, because I have too much to do tomorrow to be tired. So kindly fuck off ghost-Zion. I need my goddamn beauty sleep—"

Unable to resist, I leaned down and pressed my lips to his—swallowing his adorably angry words. I didn't care if it would immediately end this fever dream, because a flustered, annoyed Baltasar was my favorite Baltasar.

And I don't want to remember him any other way.

"Fuuuuck..." he groaned against my mouth. "You feel so fucking real..."

So do you...

The contented noises my mate was making as our tongues tangled had me climbing onto the couch to cage him in beneath me. His familiar scent instantly awakened my beast, and I rutted against him—finding him just as hard as me.

Huh...

"Tell me you're real, Z," he whispered, desperately gripping my biceps. "Because if I have to wake up without you, I'm gonna fucking die." His nails were digging into me enough for it to *hurt,* but I relished the pain—coveted it.

Maybe this is *real...*

It was only then that I thought to look down at myself. I was stark naked and covered with cuts and bruises, all of which were already in various stages of advanced healing. Patches of filthy scales dotted my body—the edges of each melted into my skin, as if they'd been subjected to high temperatures.

Like what you'd find in a bottling plant explosion.

Oh, shit.

"I'm real," I croaked, tensing as if simply stating it aloud would make it all disappear. When nothing happened, I dared to add, "This is real, B."

It better be real.

Baltasar scrambled to sit, knocking me backward onto my heels. "How?" he gasped, running his hands over my chest and arms, down my abs and thighs, touching every inch of me. "How did you not explode into a million tiny pieces?"

Like millions of stars...

I shook my head, grasping at the hazy details. "The office I was in… I think it was reinforced. I was trying my hardest to break the glass—to get down to you and Daisy—and it wouldn't budge, even against my full strength."

My mate blew out a shaky breath before asking, almost inaudibly, "So, what caused the explosion?"

Something seemed *off* about his question, so I paused and looked him over. Zeroing in on how aggressively he chewed his plump bottom lip, I realized it was trembling. *He* was trembling.

Baltasar was in shock, and understandably so. If it had been *me* watching a building explode while he was still inside, I probably wouldn't have been able to take a single step. But he'd put on a brave face for Daisy—ran miles to get her to safety—even as he internally shattered.

I'm so sorry, beautiful.

Right now, he was still in survival mode—wanting to get the facts instead of facing his fears.

I took a deep breath, determined to tell him everything he needed to know. "The workers kept shooting after you left. They weren't aiming for *me*—since I don't think the bullets would have penetrated the glass, anyway. The goal was to first destroy the evidence. Who knows if they had plans for me afterward… because someone else had plans for them."

He sat up straighter, suddenly alert. "What do you mean?"

I briefly hesitated because of Baltasar's mental state, but knew he *needed* something external to focus on.

But he should still buckle up for this.

"That man we saw in the boardroom with my father…" I carefully continued. "The big one with his back to us? He showed up. Snapped his fingers and set the place ablaze."

Baltasar nodded, absorbing the intel. "Okay, so he's obviously a supe—"

"No," I interrupted. "He's something else." When he looked at me expectantly, I exhaled. "We made eye contact afterward, and he smirked like we shared a secret..."

I shuddered as I recalled his face. He was attractive enough, with strong features that were almost too perfect, but his *eyes* gave him away. They were empty. Not void of anything, but *depthless*—like the strange scenery on the trip I took to arrive here.

But that wasn't the worst part.

"Then he turned and left the warehouse..." I grabbed Baltasar's hand to steady him. "But sealed everyone else inside."

The look of horror on my mate's face solidified once and for all how not-villainous he was. "He..."

"Destroyed the evidence," I confirmed. "Along with everyone who might talk."

Except me.

I couldn't be sure if the mystery man meant to kill me, too, or if trapping me in there was just another part of his research, but the next thing I knew...

"Then I was in *space*." I chuckled self-consciously, running a hand over the back of my neck, knowing how crazy it sounded. "At least, it looked like space. I thought I was *dead*, B, and that this"—I gestured to him—"was heaven."

He blushed, furiously and adorably, before meeting my gaze. "I might know the answer to that. Star Hopper randomly showed up outside the lab and helped us escape. I asked him

—*begged* him—to get you out of there while I brought Daisy here." His anguished expression softened as he smiled at me. "I think you took a trip to the stars with an alien, Z."

"This is my home."

And then, he brought me to mine.

I huffed and shook my head. "Well, that explains some things… I am glad to know I'm not actually dead."

When Baltasar sharply inhaled—triggered by my words—I pulled him close and pressed a kiss to his traitorously trembling lips. "I hope you know I *would* haunt you, Suarez. This bond we have? It's not the kind of thing someone can break with a snap of their fingers."

Especially not creepy dudes with galaxy-eyes.

I had no idea if my father made it out of the lab alive, but I also didn't particularly care about him or my mom at the moment. They'd obviously seen me as their little science experiment, and I fully intended on taking them to task for their betrayal.

But first things first…

"I know you said you needed your beauty sleep," I purred, carding my hands through Baltasar's thick hair, smiling as his eyes fluttered closed. "But can I tempt you into taking a shower with me? I need water on my scales. I also need my mate."

On my dick.

He opened his eyes and smirked, effortlessly reading the subtext. "I need you too, you big lizard. And I'm glad you didn't die on me. I would've hated to have to kill you."

CHAPTER 45
ZION

Having Baltasar's hard, slippery muscles pressed against me in the tight confines of the walk-in shower felt like a gift.

Especially since I thought I'd never experience it again.

He moaned into my mouth—the sound so *helpless* it was all I could do not to shift into *Lacertus* form and impale him on my full-sized dick.

He did *say he wanted it…*

"I love how much bigger than me you are." His voice had that breathless quality that made me *feral.* "When this bullshit is all over, I want you to chase me through the woods again… hold me down while you absolutely fucking own my ass."

Anything you want, beautiful.

I was about to reply with that exact sentiment when a wayward thought made me freeze. Baltasar blinked up at me in confusion as I backed away, but this was a request that required discussion.

Because the last thing I want to do is hurt him.

"B..." I carefully began—hoping I wasn't about to come across as judgmental, but needing us to be on the same page. "You know you don't... *have* to stay smaller than me, right? I don't expect you to let me be in control all the time. I love it, don't get me wrong, but I don't want *you* to think—"

I don't want you to think your body isn't your own.

The confusion on Baltasar's pretty face had given way to understanding as I fumbled my words, and he stepped closer to cup my face in his hands.

"I know," he murmured, raising himself up on his toes to deliver a gentle kiss. "This is *nothing* like what my parents did to me. What we do together is my choice, and I know if I told you to stop, you would. You make me feel *safe*, Z. I trust you. You always take such good care of me."

Always.

For once, I didn't try to hide the goddamn tears rolling down my cheeks. I wanted this perfect man to see how much I trusted him, as well—how safe he made *me* feel.

"Fuck, I love you," I sighed, lowering my face to where his shoulder met his neck, so I could nuzzle the bite that visibly marked him as *mine*. "I love taking care of you... and would *really* love fucking you into the tile right now."

"Yes..." he gasped, already lifting a leg and attempting to climb me like a tree. "Please, fuck me into the tile."

With pleasure.

Spitting on my hand, I rubbed it over my throbbing cock before easily lifting his deliciously *smaller* body and wrapping his legs around my waist. I circled his hole with my wet fingers a few times—oh-so-slowly sliding them in and out— teasing my mate as I stretched him.

"Enough. I'm ready," Baltasar huffed, as bratty and impatient as ever. "I've been ready for that lizard dick since I woke up. Been ready my entire life."

Chuckling, I lined myself up and slid him down my length until he was fully seated. "Such big talk from such a tiny little thing," I purred, my smirk growing as he *shuddered* at my words. "Should we see how much of me you can take?"

His gaze was glassy but coherent. "Yes, please. Fill me the fuck up, Salah. I need to *feel* you."

I need to feel you, too.

It wasn't like I hadn't experimented with making certain parts of me... *bigger*. Any shapeshifter with a dick who tried to claim otherwise was probably lying. But I also didn't want to injure my mate, so I took my time expanding inside him, watching his face closely to ensure he was enjoying himself.

"Zion... I... oh, *fuck!*" Baltasar clawed at me, thrashing his head from side to side as he squirmed in my hold. "Fuck, fuck, fuck, I'm... I'm gonna come..."

He'd barely gotten the word out before his cock was pulsing, spraying cum all over both our chests. I groaned as he clenched around me—so impossibly tight, I could barely think.

The desire to breed him again was all-consuming, but we needed to *sleep* tonight—not be locked together until my knot subsided.

It doesn't mean I can't still fuck him into the tile.

I quickly shrunk to a reasonable size and clamped my mouth onto Baltasar's shoulder—appeasing my beast by sucking on the bite while I pounded into my mate. Chasing my release.

Mine, mine, mine.

With a primal growl, I soon followed Baltasar over the edge, emptying all I had inside him, completely spent and light-headed from his sweet, sugary scent.

All mine.

"Jesus," he croaked, his chest heaving as he blinked at me with a dazed expression. "I hope we didn't wake Daisy."

I laughed and carefully withdrew before setting him down and reaching for the washcloth. "Doubtful. That girl could sleep through an earthquake. Plus, I'm sure she was exhausted after everything that happened…"

After you saved her life.

When I couldn't.

Overcome by emotion, I focused on providing aftercare for a few minutes before trusting myself to speak again. "We should get some sleep too, B, but I need you to call Wolfgang first. Ask him to get on a plane and meet us at Lycra and Lace tomorrow afternoon, so I can explain everything to him in person. I'm…" I swallowed down my instincts and my pride. "I'm gonna need his help with confronting my parents."

Since they'll see him *as their equal.*

Unlike me.

Baltasar pressed his lips into a thin line as we stepped out of the shower, but he didn't argue. After drying off, I herded him into Mikki's bedroom and tossed him a pair of athletic shorts from the stash I kept there.

Then, I grimly watched as his curious gaze found the pristine shelf in the corner, set up like a shrine.

The giant urn makes it hard to miss.

"Is that… Mikki?" he hesitantly asked, and it took me a moment to realize he was referring to the framed photograph off to the side.

I joined him where he stood and gazed down at the face of the woman who'd left this world too soon. It was a candid shot of her and Daisy, eating ice cream from Swirlies in the park, and both laughing at whatever our daughter had just said.

It was taken soon after we found out about her diagnosis, but before the cancer took its toll. Mikki still had her gorgeous mane of thick, black hair, tied back in a casual ponytail that showed off her golden brown skin and sparkling amber eyes.

As always, the genuine *love* radiating from her smile strengthened me, while almost sending me to my knees.

Miss ya, Mik.

"She looked like she could've been a Suarez, huh?" I broke the awkward silence by addressing the elephant in the room, head on.

It's not like any of this is a secret anymore.

If it ever was…

When Baltasar glanced at me in alarm, I placed my hand on his shoulder and gave him a squeeze. "Don't worry. Mikki's *job* was to cater to fantasies like mine—to give men the chance to have the supe of their dreams. Apparently, she was also well aware that my obsession went deeper than the green Lycra of a certain infamous villain."

He blew out a slow breath and tentatively brushed a finger over the glass covering her smiling face. "I'm glad you met her, Z. Not just because she gave you Daisy—although I'm obviously thankful for that—but because she took care of you until I was ready."

Well, shit.

"Yeah, well, I wasn't able to return the favor," I choked out, no longer surprised at how willing I was to crack my heart wide open for this man.

Gesturing toward the urn, I decided to share one of my most painful regrets—unable to keep the venom from my voice. "Mikki didn't want to be cremated... But I haven't been able to give her the peace she deserves because my *parents* refuse to let me bury her on our land."

With an uncharacteristically angry growl, Baltasar turned and stalked back into the ensuite. He reappeared with his phone, and I sank onto the bed to watch as he called Wolfgang, fascinated by his sudden take-charge demeanor.

And here I thought he couldn't get any hotter.

As soon as his brother answered, Baltasar launched into a very abbreviated version of our situation. He wrapped it up with a request—bordering on a demand—for Wolfgang to fly out to meet with us and intervene. There was unnerving silence on the other end of the line, but my mate didn't backpedal. He simply held my gaze and calmly waited for his clan leader to respond.

Good boy.

Wolfgang finally replied, but his voice was too low for me to hear what he said. Luckily, his decision seemed to be in our favor, as Baltasar visibly relaxed, thanked him, and said his goodbyes.

"Okay, he'll help, but I-I can't promise he won't try to use this to his advantage." His worried gaze met mine, but he stood a little taller, as if realizing he was clearly siding with *me* by sharing this intel.

Good man.

I smirked—amused at how Baltasar *still* didn't understand how clans operated at the top. "Yeah, I figured he might scheme a bit. He's probably had a plan all along, hmm?" When Baltasar tensed, I laughed. "I can handle Wolfgang, B, as long as *you* trust me to do it my way. Can you do that for me, beautiful?"

He smiled tiredly, rapidly succumbing to exhaustion, but nodded. "Of course. I trust you with my life."

I smiled in return before opening my arms so he'd join me in bed. "Good, because you should."

Even if you're not gonna like what I have to do tomorrow.

CHAPTER 46
BALTASAR

Of course, I'd witnessed Wolfy in terrifying clan leader mode before, but *I* had never been on the receiving end of his death stare.

I think I'm gonna pass out.

Zion had just finished sharing everything that had gone down the past few weeks, ending with the lab and the evidence we had. Instead of waiting for a reply, he then *demanded* Wolfy force his parents to step down as clan leaders so he could take their place.

If I don't die from anxiety first.

The neon blue glow of Lycra and Lace's private room made my brother look even more menacing than usual as he coldly stared down my *inventus*. Zion barely budged under the weight of his scrutiny—and his boldness was doing all sorts of inconvenient things to me as I tried not to fidget.

Please don't let me get a boner in front of my brother during this very important negotiation.

My gaze drifted to where Simon sat by Wolfy's side, *his* expression unsurprisingly furious over Zion's sexy audacity.

Standing directly behind the seething **Mafia Queen** was Violentia. She was also glaring at my man, effortlessly playing her role as the Suarez family muscle—our enforcer.

The One With the Biggest Dick.

Vi was getting stared down by Dahlia, who Zion had called in as backup. I'd thought it was unnecessary, but now realized it put us on equal footing with our opponents.

Since I'm apparently on this *side of the battleground.*

"Did you bring this supposed evidence, Zion?" Wolfy calmly asked, his eyes never leaving my *inventus'* face. "I would need to check the authenticity of your claims before accusing Major Obscurity and Lady Tempest of such grave crimes on your behalf."

Zion remained silent for a moment before nodding. Recognizing her cue, Dahlia stepped forward. She placed the stack of file folders on the low table separating the clans before retreating to her bodyguard position.

"These are photocopies, of course," Zion lightly remarked. "The originals are being kept at an undisclosed location. Along with a few bottles of lizard juice that survived the lab's unfortunate destruction."

Wolfy made a sound that might have been considered a laugh —if it didn't kick my survival instincts into flight mode. "Of course."

This is so goddamn stressful!

Both Suarez clan leaders took their time looking over the evidence, but even with Wolfy's poker face, I could tell he was affected by what he saw.

Understandable.

Zion and I had spent our morning pouring over every piece of paper—finding each document more damning than the last. Apparently, he'd been born with the Lacertus gene—just like me and my siblings. Although, in his case, it seemed like it had been latent in previous generations.

Thanks to Doc's research, my family knew this gene was what formed *inventus* bonds, but Zion's parents hadn't focused on that. They'd only cared about bringing their firstborn's dormant traits roaring to the surface. To create an heir as threatening as the newly registered Hand of Death.

To ensure their clan would remain as powerful as mine.

The only reason the Salahs knew of our alien origins was because a newly married Lady Tempest did some digging. Early negotiation transcripts revealed she wanted to understand why powerful heroes obeyed normie politicians.

But then she veered off the path. Her investigation turned up the name Richard Cabrera—the late archeologist whose loose lips resulted in the contracts. Using civilian tricks, Jacqueline pretended to be an eager anthropology grad student and flirted her way into a tour of the Argentinian caves.

While there, she met an entrepreneur who claimed to be developing a serum that could enhance existing Lacertus DNA in powerful supes.

A man who was more than happy to accept funding from a super rich family with skin in the game—to build a lab and begin clinical trials.

A man she only ever knew as 'T.'

Wolfy suddenly cleared his throat, making me jump. "Excuse us for a moment. I'd like to discuss this with my family in private."

Okay, soooo…

For a moment, I didn't know if *I* was included in this private meeting. But when Wolfy and Simon rose and stalked from the room with Vi—who decisively slammed the door behind them—I got my answer.

Dahlia eyed the door warily. "How do you think this is gonna go?"

"Oh, Wolfy will want to unseat our parents either way." Zion chuckled dryly. "If only to stop another clan from becoming more powerful than his in ways he can't control."

"We should get one of the lizard juice bottles to Xander," I suggested, racking my brain to figure out how to keep the peace between our families. "So he can, you know, do scientific tests and shit."

I'm helping!

Zion pressed his tasty lips together, considering. "He'll probably want a DNA sample from me, too—"

"You are *not* giving another clan your DNA!" Dahlia hissed. *"We* have a scientist in the family, remember? Micah could—"

"I don't trust any of my siblings," Zion retorted, making Dahlia flinch. "And that includes *you* until proven otherwise."

OoooOOOooo…

"What the hell did *I* do?" she scoffed haughtily. "Besides graciously tell you about the lab—"

"You didn't tell me shit!" my *inventus* growled. "I had to randomly stumble upon you gossiping with *Preek* to even know something was going on. Funny how you had no trouble telling *him*, though."

His sister's brow furrowed. "I didn't... Preek was the one who told *me* about the lab."

Fuck.

Zion and I exchanged a look, and I had a feeling we'd both come to the same conclusion.

Preek took the job with the Salahs already knowing about the lab.

But how?

Dahlia cleared her throat. "Preek and I were talking about my engagement one day, and I just straight up *told* him I didn't want to marry Baltasar. No offense," she added with a dismissive wave of her hand, although she sounded unconcerned if I was offended or not.

"None taken," I scoffed.

The feeling was mutual.

"Anyway," she continued. "Preek claimed he'd overheard our parents talking about top secret tests at a lab and offered to help dig up dirt to use as leverage. I agreed because I thought I could use whatever we discovered to get myself out of the marriage contract. But the deeper we dug, the more it sounded like something that could take down our entire clan —starting with..."

Starting with Zion.

Her rich brown eyes met my *inventus'*, and I saw nothing but regret. "I-I couldn't let that happen, but I still wanted to figure out what was going on. I'm sorry for keeping things from you... I never *dreamed* a random lesser supe would—"

"It was stupid of you to trust an outsider, Dahlia," Zion growled. "You *know* we can only trust our own family—"

"Not this one," she sneered. "Isn't that what you just said? That you don't trust *any* of us?"

Zion stared back, coldly assessing her. "Not at the moment. But for once, I hope to be proven wrong."

Dahlia's eyes widened in surprise, but before she could reply, Wolfy alone reentered. I could hear Simon tearing him a new one before he shut the door again, muffling the racket.

Someone's in the doghouse.

"You. Out," he said to Dahlia in a tone that left no room for argument. "Zion and I need to talk."

Dahlia muttered something about 'clan heirs being bossy as fuck' but she obeyed—joining Vi and a still ranting Simon in the hall.

I leaped to my feet. "Um, so... do you want me to leave, too, or..."

This is awkward.

Wolfy gave me a passing glance before fixing his predatory gaze on my *inventus*. "I would prefer to speak to Zion alone, but I presume he won't let you out of his sight."

Zion chuckled and pulled me back down to sit—on his lap. "You've got that right. Baltasar here is my leverage."

Both my brother and I froze, and Wolfy narrowed his eyes. "What do you mean?"

Zion's hand wrapped around the back of my neck, holding me in place. "Let me guess, Wolfgang. You were coming back in here to tell me you'd gladly unseat my parents, but that *you'd* then be taking over my clan. Does that sound about right?"

He wouldn't!

Indignation worked its way up my throat, clawing to get out. Yes, Wolfy had his sights on the Salah clan since I arrived, but

I thought with the evidence we'd just shared—with Zion being my *inventus*—he'd leave us be.

Much to my dismay, Wolfy didn't deny it. He simply leaned back and gave Zion an assessing look. "And what of it, Salah? You've shown little to no interest in your own clan for *years*. You were so detached from the family business that you weren't even aware your parents were involved in this mysterious lab, much less using *you* as their little lab rat. You are unfit to lead."

HOW DARE HE?!

Anger was a living thing inside of me, scorching with the fires of swift retribution. I wanted to leap over the table separating us, grab Wolfy by the throat—death touch be damned—and *demand* he apologize to my mate.

"You have no *idea* what Zion has been through!" I snarled, but my *inventus* tightened his grip, wordlessly silencing me.

"How safe do you think *Simon* is right now, Wolfgang?" Zion casually replied, making Wolfy go dangerously still.

What?

My brother lifted his chin to better glare down at my *inventus*. I could *feel* his power building like a gathering storm—filling the small room until it was almost suffocating.

"Ultra Violent is with him," he replied impassively, although his tone held a warning.

Watch yourself.

"Atmosphera is a long-range fighter," Zion shot back, and I felt the visceral satisfaction in his words. "She could take out both Ultra Violent and your beloved *half*-normie before either got close enough to strike."

Shit.

At the mention of Simon's secret heritage, Wolfy's disappointed gaze briefly flickered to me before landing on Zion with pure hatred.

"If your sister so much as *breathes* on my *inventus*, yours is as good as dead, Zion."

Wait, WHAT?!

I tried to catch Wolfy's eye, but his focus was on the only supe in the room he considered a threat. Just as I tried to process that my own brother would *kill me* for petty revenge, I felt Zion's fingers move to wrap around my throat.

Claws extended.

"Maybe I'll just preemptively kill him myself, Wolfgang," the man I loved sneered at my murderous brother—handling me like I was nothing. "Then you wouldn't have any leverage at all."

WHAT THE ACTUAL FUCK IS HAPPENING?!

If Wolfy was The Stare of Death, Zion would have been dead, buried, and already returned to the earth. This tense standoff lasted a full minute—with both powerful supes glaring daggers. Meanwhile, I sweated profusely, questioning every life choice I'd ever made.

Am I really that expendable to both of them?

"Go ahead then." Wolfy shrugged, as if he *wasn't* telling a psychotic Godzilla to tear into his own flesh and blood.

"Fine," Zion replied, dragging his claws across my neck— drawing enough blood to make me flinch.

Don't…

"No, don't!"' Wolfy lurched forward, his expression turning anguished as he involuntarily reached for me.

Holy fuck.

My brother just showed weakness in front of a rival heir.

For me.

"*There* we go," Zion chuckled, relaxing his hold on me. "You know, when I ran into you and Simon in Villefranche, I was pleasantly surprised to discover you had any emotions at all. But more importantly, I realized Wolfgang Suarez falling in love gave me exactly the ammunition I needed—should I ever need it. Ammunition in the form of a sassy little *half*-normie."

Wolfy was still glaring at Zion through his villain monologue. Although, apparently, he was nowhere near as shocked as I was to discover the man I'd fallen in love with was as ruthless as him.

I'm really not cut out for this clan heir business.

Like a true villain, Zion wasn't done. "And then your sweet brother told me how much you actually care about your siblings. So while I would have no qualms about killing your *inventus*—even though I happen to like Simon on a good day —*you* would never let anything happen to your precious Baltasar. I will always have the upper hand here, Wolfgang. Never forget that."

Has he been using me this entire time?!

Just as I was about to have a full-fledged mental breakdown, I felt a wave of calm wash over me. It took me a moment to realize it was *Zion* soothing me through our bond—still caring for me, even as he pretended I was nothing more than leverage.

Tricky asshole.

He's definitely groveling after this.

"What about *Daisy?*" Wolfy raised an eyebrow, and my blood ran cold. "What about the ammunition I have on *your* half-normie?"

His steady amber gaze flickered to my face—most likely checking on my well-being—but as far as I was concerned, my brother just crossed a line.

Nobody threatens Daisy.

I impassively stared back and kept my damn mouth shut.

"I'd bet money you have no idea where my daughter is," Zion murmured, squeezing my neck in approval. "And by the time you figure it out, she'll be long gone with an entirely new identity."

I now realized *this* was why Zion left Daisy at the brownstone, in the care of Ginger and other ladies from the club. They might not know his true heritage—or his daughter's—but Mikki had been like family to them.

And they will gladly protect one of their own.

Even though I'd just been put through the emotional wringer, I did my best to focus on the zen Zion was pumping me full of, letting it soothe my lingering anxiety.

Wolfy leaned forward, resting his forearms on his knees as he studied my *inventus*. "What's your endgame here, Zion? Did you honestly believe that once your parents handed off the throne, you could then come for mine? Because I guarantee that wouldn't end well for you."

Please don't start a war, Z…

"No, Wolfgang," Zion sighed, releasing me so I could fully breathe again. "I simply want *my* throne—with Baltasar by my side—and for you and me to work together. Two equally formidable families, joined as one in power. That's it."

My brother cocked his head, visibly confused. "You're... not trying to take over my clan?"

Zion scoffed. "I know this might be a shock, but just because it's 'how the game is played' doesn't mean we *need* to continue playing."

Wolfy chuckled in a self-deprecating way I'd never heard from him before. "I actually couldn't agree more, Salah."

"Deal, then?" My *inventus* smiled.

"Yes. Deal." Wolfy nodded, a smirk curling his lips before he sobered. "However, I require everything in writing. I like to keep things legal."

'Legal' being loosely defined.

"Well, good thing I brought a contract with me, then." Zion lightly laughed, back to his friendly self as he produced a single sheet of paper and a pen and laid both on the table. "I'll give you a few minutes to send it off to your lawyer, of course."

"Of course," Wolfy huffed, already taking a photo to send to Randal.

Is it safe to pass out now?

"Still think I'm unfit to lead my clan?" Zion joked, although there was an edge to his question. A dare.

"Not at all," Wolfy chuckled. "To be honest, I simply wanted to see what you were made of." His gaze slid to me. "What *both* of you were made of."

"But I didn't do anything!" I protested, beyond annoyed at both alpha male idiots for using me as leverage in their dick measuring contest.

Hmph.

Wolfy quickly typed out an email on his phone before solemnly meeting my gaze again. "Don't underestimate yourself, Balty. You're just as important as anyone else in this family. In *both* families." He turned to Zion as a truly villainous grin stretched across his face. "Now, who's ready to conquer a kingdom?"

EPILOGUE

BALTASAR - THREE WEEKS LATER

"GOOOOAAAAAALLLLL!!!"

I re-enacted my game-winning point with a dramatic leap and slide across the living room of the Suarez family compound.

Never mind that I almost took out the tapas spread Betsy had laid out for us earlier. Or that absolutely no one except Zion wanted to see my sweet moves for the millionth time. I didn't even care. Weeks later, I was still on top of the world.

Two-time Supremacy Games Champion, right here!

It was hard to believe Zion had made a long-shot out of me. The gold medal hanging in our Sunrise City brownstone kitchen suggested it had been the right call, but it was still wild to think about. It was even wilder that I was now happily retired from Deathball and co-leading a clan of powerful *heroes.*

With my *inventus* by my side.

Unsurprisingly, Lady Tempest and Major Obscurity hadn't wanted to give up their thrones, but Wolfy had a way of convincing others to do his bidding.

The danger of dismemberment usually helps.

It was the threat to their *heroic* reputations that finally made them cooperate. We had enough evidence to bring Zion's parents to trial with the supe council in Geneva. But Wolfy offered to sweep everything under the rug if they handed off the reins to their son.

Initially, I was surprised by my brother's leniency. Then Zion explained how Wolfy just wanted to hoard the 'lizard juice' research for himself. Without the council confiscating the evidence.

I'll eventually get the hang of this clan leader business…

Maybe.

Probably not.

It was ironic that the Wolfy-Zion showdown Lady Tempest dreamed of had happened, but not with the outcome she'd hoped for. While I was thrilled that Zion had now taken over his clan, it still made my blood boil to think of what his parents had involved him in—without his consent.

Zion made a big show of forgiveness to his parents, which confused me. In my opinion, being stripped of political power was the least they deserved. Once again, my *inventus* patiently explained he'd rather keep them close, so he could kill them first if they stepped out of line again.

It's how the game is played.

Despite Dahlia's protests, Zion gave me permission to send one of the lizard juice bottles to Xander, so my brother could recreate it for production.

A necessary evil.

At this point, whatever natural powers Zion was originally destined to develop had been swallowed up by his now dominant *Lacertus* DNA. And without knowing how his body would react to withdrawals, we felt it was best for him to continue his doses.

At least, until we can find this mysterious 'T' and learn more.

This meant Zion's death pond was off-limits to everyone else, including me. Xander figured out that my sudden lizard-like appearance was from swimming in the polluted water—not from our inventus bond. Even though that pond held a lot of good memories, my man didn't want me to also end up dependent on the serum.

No matter how sexy he thought my scales were.

I didn't even question how I felt about Zion anymore—or what it meant for how I identified. We fit together perfectly for reasons that went well beyond him having a dick, anyway.

Although access to my favorite rocket pop is a pretty big perk.

It bummed me out that Zion's artificially altered DNA made it so we couldn't power-share like other *inventus* pairs. But our connection was solid just the same.

Thanks to *him* I no longer thought of myself as nothing but a dumb jock. I'd discovered how capable I actually was—how I could be counted on when it mattered—and that I didn't need to prove my worth to anyone.

I'm good enough, just the way I am.

I now understood I deserved the love of my birth family and my officially adopted daughter. And that I was worthy of the unwavering attention and undying devotion of one slightly possessive Godzilla.

Good thing, because the obsession is mutual.

It was Dahlia's idea to tell the press she'd agreed to play the role of my fake fiancé until I was comfortable announcing my relationship with her brother. SNZ ate it up—forbidden, super gay love story that it was—and even our most hardcore Deathball fans were rooting for Zion and me by the time I took the podium at the Games.

SupeSports convinced us to do a 'rivals to lovers' special that ended with us getting married on the field in full gear. It was kind of cheesy—and my supersuit felt like it shrunk again—but Butch offered for us to renew our vows in our own way during his destination wedding to Xander.

Wherever and whenever that will be.

In the meantime, my family decided to throw me a Big Gay Party—even if they tried to disguise it as Daisy's West Coast birthday soirée.

The rainbow "Congrats, UR Gay!" decor kind of gave it away.

This was a bonus celebration, since Z and I had already spoiled our girl with a no-expenses-spared party back on the East Coast. All eight of his siblings and their families joined in, as well as his parents. I was worried how Lady Tempest and The Major would behave, but they surprised me by dutifully playing their roles of Gran and Pop-Pop.

Genuinely, for once.

We even set aside part of the day for a proper burial of Mikki in the Salah cemetery plot on top of Murder Mountain. While a single event couldn't erase a decade of hurt, Zion's family obviously wanted to make amends for how they'd shunned Daisy—and her mother—over the years.

All because of her heritage.

When our heritage overall is even weirder.

Luckily, Butch hadn't acted like a total Boy Scout and gone running to Sylvano Ricci about Daisy's existence. She was still safely unregistered with the USN, and her two dads intended to keep it that way.

He'd also made up for scaring the crap out of her in *Blade Runner* mode by taking our little queen flying high above Big City, way past her bedtime. When they returned, she confidently announced she was *sure* she'd be able to fly someday.

The truth was, we weren't sure if she would ever have powers—especially as her *Lacertus* genes were as dormant as Zion's before he got juiced. But she fit right in with my family, anyway.

With Simon *especially.*

"What you want to do is stab *up* into the ribs, then twist." Our **Mafia Queen** was patiently instructing the Lizard Queen, using his jewel-encrusted dagger as a helpful prop. "The goal is to fracture bone whilst collapsing a lung."

Inspirational.

Daisy was eating it up faster than she'd devoured her goth unicorn cake, but I put my foot down when Simon tried to bestow the razor-sharp knife as a gift.

Not until she's twelve, dude!

We'd soon have more Suarez offspring to spoil. Butch and Xander's bestie, Kai, was officially carrying their baby boy as their surrogate. This also meant the poor normie—currently sandwiched between the soon-to-be dads on the couch—had no hope of escape from our family.

I couldn't help cautiously eyeing my brother and future brother-in-law. They were both watching Kai like a hawk while she obediently nibbled on the protein-packed nosh options I'd helped Betsy prepare just for her.

Thoughts and prayers, bestie.

Violentia had also been keeping a close eye on their dynamic all day, and I wondered if she was thinking about her own future. I'd been worried that settling down into domestic life would affect my fun-loving relationship with my older sister. My concerns were quickly erased. Even though Vi seemed about 15% less psychotic nowadays—at least when interacting with her own family—she was still always down for a joyride with me.

Usually in one of Xander's vehicles.

I guess we're all just growing up.

Only the twins were missing from the Big Gay Celebration. That was because Wolfy had sent them on a top secret assignment the rest of us weren't cool enough to know about.

Whatever, losers.

Simon had just suggested we all move outside—so Daisy could enjoy some target practice with various weapons—when the doorbell rang.

"We have a doorbell?" Xander blurted out, even as he—and every other supe in the room—had gone on high alert.

Well… most of them.

"Jesus, you villains are jumpy," Zion chuckled as he rose to stand. "I doubt an assassin would ring the doorbell."

That's just what an assassin would want you to think!

My *inventus* shook his head and disappeared to answer the door. I debated following him, but noticed Wolfy checking out his smart home app. He looked more intrigued than alarmed by what he saw, so I relaxed.

Kind of.

"Are you collecting former Deathball rivals, Balty?" he asked, his lips twisting in a smirk.

Huh?

To answer my unspoken question, Zion reappeared with Ziggy Andromeda, who was dragging along a much smaller figure wearing a black bag over their head.

Okay…

"Oh, a party!" Ziggy cheerfully remarked, casually taking in the scene as if he hadn't just arrived with a hostage. "What are we celebrating?"

"My birthday!" Daisy smiled widely at our visitor, probably remembering how he'd shown up outside the lab and helped us escape.

Although we still don't know what he was doing there in the first place.

"And that Balty finally realized he's super gay for Zion," Xander unhelpfully added. His attention quickly shifted to the futuristic contraption binding the hostage's wrists together. "Did you make those handcuffs yourself?"

Ziggy glanced at our resident inventor. "I don't create my weapons. I simply use the tools I'm given to deliver justice."

Calm down, alien Rambo.

Before Xanny could fire up twenty nerdy questions, Ziggy smiled at Daisy. "Happy birthday, little *Lacertus!* Perhaps I've brought you a present." He squinted at her. "That is, if you're considered old enough in this world to witness the results of a lengthy interrogation—"

"Nope," Zion and I answered as one, even as Xander leaned across Kai to whisper, "Did he say *'this world?'*" to *Blade Runner* Butch.

Wolfy threw a pointed look at Simon, who loudly sighed, but then dutifully covered Daisy's eyes.

Good enough.

Ziggy roughly forced the hostage to its knees before yanking off the hood. This drama revealed a face that was familiar, despite the intense bruising and missing eyeballs.

Preek.

"*Mon chou*," Simon crooned in Wolfy's direction, placing a hand over his heart dramatically. "Doesn't this remind you of when you taught REM a lesson for me back in Berlin?"

My brother hummed at the apparently fond memory before addressing Ziggy. "Has he said anything useful?"

The alien shrugged. "A bit. He mostly spouted vague threats about how 'his kind will emerge victorious.'"

Yeah, that tracks.

"It became so repetitive, I debated cutting out his tongue," Ziggy absently mused.

Gross.

"Cool," Daisy whispered, earning her a proud chuckle from Simon.

"So why bring him here to bleed everywhere?" Wolfy asked, eyeing his expensive flooring for signs of damage.

Ziggy glanced between Zion and me. "I wanted to give the Salahs the option of further interrogation. Otherwise, I am happy to dispose of him for you. It will only take a minute."

"Yeah, toss him to the curb with the rest of the trash," Zion replied dismissively. "He was always expendable."

Preek croaked out something like a laugh—the first noise the snarky publicity director had made since arriving on our doorstep.

"Spoken like a true classist asshole," he spat. Then he turned his sightless gaze toward Zion. "No wonder it was so easy to convince your idiot sister to dig up dirt on her own family, while helping to cover my tracks. You *purebred* supes think you're invincible—respected and feared by everyone in your sphere. But all you've accomplished is giving your *lessers* countless reasons to want to see you kneel. And thanks to your parents' unethical experiments, pretty soon we'll all be monsters. Just. Like. You. Starting right in your precious villain's backyard."

Holy fuck.

My gaze met Zion's, and I could tell we'd come to the same conclusion.

Preek didn't cancel the last Salah shipment from the lab...

"Yes, that was the only truly useful thing he had to share," Ziggy confirmed. "Apparently, a large shipment of *Lacertus* serum was sent here shortly before the lab was destroyed."

...he redirected it to Big City.

I wanted to find the missing serum and continue investigating the rebellion, but all I could focus on at the moment was Preek's ignorant assessment of my mate.

The only monster *here is about to die.*

"Trash him," I growled, ready to never see the lesser supe's mangled face ever again.

Good riddance.

Ziggy nodded and disappeared from sight—along with Preek —only to reappear a second later.

Empty-handed.

"Done." He decisively brushed off his hands before flashing a charming grin around the room. "Your traitor is now meeting his painful end in space. It will take a few minutes, but he'll first experience boiling bodily fluids and severe asphyxiation as his internal organs rapidly expand, one by one."

"Awesome," Daisy breathed, her now uncovered eyes fixed on Ziggy with open admiration.

A true villain.

Wolfy pinched the bridge of his nose. "Very well. So now we need to figure out who in Big City received this shipment— since there was no record of it in the evidence from the lab."

The Suarez clan is on the case!

Ziggy cocked his head, visibly confused. "I would assume the man in charge of creating the serum would be your next logical stop. Especially as his primary residence is in Big City."

Excuse me?

That there was barely any information on the lab's owner in the mountain of evidence we rescued had been the most frustrating part of this wild goose chase. Neither Major Obscurity nor Lady Tempest knew T's full name—which was standard supe business. And Zion was having trouble remembering exactly what he looked like, even after making direct eye contact the night of the lab explosion.

As if his skinsuit is meant to be forgettable…

I zeroed in on Ziggy Andromeda, wondering yet again what he was made of. "Obviously, *you* know more than we do, Star Hopper, so start talking."

He sighed, seeming more exasperated by our lower intelligence than anything. "It doesn't surprise me you would lack the instincts to recognize a well-disguised predator in your midst." His eyes snapped to Simon. "Even if you have a half-breed among you who *should* be able to sniff him out."

Simon bristled as Wolfy growled, but Ziggy wasn't done. Clearly having a death wish, he continued addressing our **Mafia Queen** directly. "Does the name Theo Coatl mean anything to you?"

Wolfy sharply inhaled and immediately fumbled his phone out of his pocket. Simon threw his *inventus* a look that chilled the room by 40 degrees before haughtily addressing the alien. "Not to *me*. Should it?"

"Fuck, fuck, fuck," Wolfy muttered as he frantically texted someone. He was so uncharacteristically flustered, he was losing his cool in front of an outsider.

Which means it must be bad.

Ziggy was barely paying any attention to our on-paper clan leader as he unwisely approached Simon. "You should. Like recognizes like. And you're like me. Well... half of you is, at least."

Mic drop.

Wolfy's phone dinged in reply. He read the text, sighed in relief, and stood—calmly placing himself between his dumbstruck *inventus* and the alien. "So if you, Theo Coatl, and..."—he cleared his throat—"aren't descended from *Lacertus*, what are you?"

Ziggy steadily held Wolfy's gaze from two harrowing inches away. "Something worse."

Ruh-roh.

Then our friendly neighborhood alien beamed, as if I hadn't almost pissed myself in fear. "But it sounds like we have similar goals, so... let's combine forces, shall we?"

That would be preferred to death-by-space-travel, yes.

Wolfy glanced at his phone again, looking like the weight of the world rested on his broad shoulders. "Well... I already have a man assigned to Theo Coatl. *Two* men, actually, and they're in the family, so can be trusted implicitly. And Zion and I have already discussed how Baltasar's been gathering intel on a lesser supe uprising for years..."

He paused to give me a warm smile, lighting me up, before returning his focus to Ziggy. "But let's go draft up a contract in my office before we discuss strategy. Simon...?"

He said his *inventus'* name with extreme caution, as if he were addressing a cobra emerging from a basket.

Good call, big bro.

Simon uncoiled himself from the chair, rising to his full height of five-foot-nothing to coolly observe his *inventus*. "Oh? Am I to be included in your schemes now, Wolfgang? *Tres merveilleux!* I've been deemed worthy of such an honor. *C'est des conneries... casse-toi...*"

Our **Mafia Queen** then stomped off in the direction of Wolfy's office, muttering in agitated French and leaving our leader to close his eyes and sigh.

Ziggy barked a laugh. "Oh, Simon's definitely one of ours—without a doubt. How about I give you some pointers once we're done ensuring no one kills each other, hmm?"

Then he clapped Wolfy on the back good-naturedly.

And we all froze.

But then, nothing happened.

Well. Fuck.

Wolfy warily eased himself away from Ziggy's touch before gesturing in the direction Simon had disappeared. "Let's... get that contract signed, shall we? Zion?" He turned to my *inventus.* "Would you like to be involved in the negotiations?"

It might have been our *inventus* bond. Or that my professional —and personal—career had been spent learning Zion's tells. But I knew, without a doubt, he absolutely did not want to be involved.

What a lame way to spend your evening.

"Actually," I interrupted—something I never would have *dared* do a month ago. "I was hoping to take Zion out in Big City tonight. On a date."

The titty bars await!

Zion winked at me as another smile softened Wolfy's intimidating face. "Very well." My brother shrugged before gesturing for Ziggy to follow him down the hall. "Go enjoy yourselves. We'll babysit the little villain for you."

Just like family.

"Can we stay up late watching movies?" Daisy excitedly asked a smirking Vi and the soon-to-be parents on the couch. "And eat the rest of the cake and ice cream? Can I sleep in my *Isabella FrouFrou* tutu?"

Butch looked torn, but everyone else nodded enthusiastically. "Yes, yes, and yesssss..." Xander replied gleefully, grabbing Daisy's hand and leading her toward our home theater room.

She'll probably be half-feral on sugar by the time we get back…

I wasn't *that* worried about it. Even though Daisy wasn't related to my family by blood, she was important to *me*. And one of the most surprising things I'd learned during this whole adventure was just how important I was in a family of much more impressive supes.

Blood is thicker than murder.

But murder doesn't hurt.

BONUS: THE RABBLE GROUP CHAT STRIKES AGAIN

The Mouthy One: *I have an announcement to make.*

The One with the Biggest Dick: *Oh? Have you and second-place himbo FINALLY decided on a wedding venue? Because unlike you boys and your monkey suits, I need to actually plan my outfit.*

The Mafia Queen: *Have we met, Violentia? I shall be dressed in something far more elaborate than a simple tux, thank you very much.*

Clan Daddy: *Should I not wear a tux?*

The Mafia Queen: *You, Sir, are required to. In fact, you should be wearing one when I get home later.*

Butt Pirate: *Stop sexting in the group chat.*

The Mafia Queen: *Hush yourself, Baby Hulk, or I shall change your name to* **The Gayest One***.*

Butt Pirate: *I really don't think I'm the gayest one in this chat, dude.*

The Mafia Queen: *Certainly not the most fabulous. How about* **Only Gay for Lizard Dick***?*

Lizard Dick: *Why the fuck do I even need to be in this chat?*

The Token Hero: *Don't fight it, Zion. They'll never let you leave.*

> **The Token Hero** *has left the chat.*
> **The Mouthy One** *added* **The Token Hero** *to the chat.*

The Token Hero: *See.*

The Mouthy One: *Sweetheart, not even death could take you away from me.*

The Token Hero: *[A million heart eye emojis]*

The One With the Biggest Dick: *You're all gross. What's this super important announcement, Xanny? Just spit it out already.*

The Mouthy One: *In the interest of saving time, I will maturely ignore that opening.*

The Mouthy One: *I have decided…*

The Mouthy One: *To open a strip club.*

The Token Hero: *OMG XAN WHY CAN NOTHING BETWEEN US STAY PRIVATE?!*

The Mouthy One: *Because you're cute when you blush.*

The Mouthy One: *Anyway, when we all flew out to watch Balty play in the Games, Butch and I went to Lycra and Lace. I needed to see this Captain Masculine act for myself.*

The Mouthy One: *It was oddly hot considering I don't *personally* do pussy, but it also gave me an idea.*

The Mouthy One: *So I chatted with the owner and offered to buy the rights to open a franchise in Big City.*

The Mouthy One: *With a catch…*

The One With the Biggest Dick: *The suspense is killing me.*

The Mouthy One: *It will be an all male revue (including male identifying, obviously) with everyone dressed in the sluttiest little supe gear. You know... like what old-school lady supes wear for some ridiculous reason.*

The Mafia Queen: *Okay, but I support this. Will there be a Hand of Death on the roster? I already have a slutty design in progress for Wolfy that could work for the stage.*

Clan Daddy: *This is the first I've heard of this.*

The Mafia Queen: *It was to be an anniversary gift. To me. Surprise!*

The Mouthy One: *ANYWAY... So during my research at the Sunrise City location, I discovered something interesting about Balty and his Lizard Dick.*

Butt Pirate: *DON'T YOU FUCKING DARE!*

The Mouthy One: *Apparently, Zion's favorite dancer... the mother of his child, in fact...*

Butt Pirate: *I'M GONNA POUND YOU INTO THE GROUND, XANNY!!!*

The Mouthy One: *...performed as none other than BLUNT FORCE! Methinks someone had a crush on our Baby Hulk for a while, hmm?*

Lizard Dick: *Heh. You got me.*

Butt Pirate: *Why are you encouraging them, Z?!*

Lizard Dick: *Because you're also cute when you blush.*

The One With the Biggest Dick: *[A million puking emojis]*

Clan Daddy: *Tell me something I didn't already know, Xanny.*

The Mafia Queen: *Excuse me? Is this yet ANOTHER thing you felt compelled to hide from me?*

Clan Daddy: *Perhaps. Maybe I knew full well Zion had feelings for Balty, and suspected Baby Hulk felt the same. Maybe I decided to set up some forced proximity through his engagement with Dahlia.*

Butt Pirate: *What.*

Lizard Dick: *What?*

The Mafia Queen: *WHAT?!*

The Mouthy One: *[Popcorn emoji]*

Clan Daddy: *Maybe I just wanted to see what would happen. Including whether I would finally earn that spanking you constantly threaten me with Simon, but never deliver.*

The Mafia Queen: *THIS FAMILY IS FULL OF UNRULY BRATS!!!*

The Mafia Queen: *I'll be home in thirty minutes, mon chou.*

The Mafia Queen: *If you're not blindfolded, naked as the day you were born, and ass up when I get there, so help me.*

Clan Daddy: *Yes, Boss.*

Clan Daddy *has turned their alerts to silent.*

The One With the Biggest Dick: *Looks like I'm getting a hotel room for the night. [Another puke emoji]*

Lizard Dick: *This chat is wild.*

The Token Hero: *Welcome to the family, Zion.*

———

Want more of Balty being "I'm baby" for lizard dick?

Sign up for my newsletter for the BONUS epilogue: **Idiots in Love**, and preorder the twins' tale: **Enter the Multi-Verse** (Ignore the Amazon date! I always move them up, promise.)

VILLAINOUS THINGS PLAYLIST

Please enjoy the Spotify playlist that inspired the Villainous Things series (and let me know if you have a song to add):

BALTY & ZION PRINTS AVAILABLE

LINK TO ORDER PRINTS ON THE BOOKS BY C. PAGE

And more!

BOOKS BY C. ROCHELLE

Looking for signed paperbacks, N/SFW art prints, bookplates & other goodies? My store can be found at **C-Rochelle.com/shop** (and **Patreon** members get discounts on art prints and signed books, plus extra swag and personalized inscriptions in their books!)

VILLAINOUS THINGS - SUPERHERO/VILLAIN MM ROMANCE (SLOWLY COMING TO AUDIBLE):

Not All Himbos Wear Capes (*sign up for the newsletter to get the Only Good Boys Get to Top Their Xaddys bonus epilogue*)

Gentlemen Prefer Villains (*sign up for the newsletter to get the Yes Sir, Sorry Sir bonus epilogue*)

Putting Out for a Hero (*sign up for the newsletter to get the Idiots in Love bonus epilogue*)

Enter the Multi-Vers (*sign up for the newsletter to get the Among the Stars bonus epilogue*)

Rabble: End Game (*a just for funsies reunion book, set at Butch and Xander's wedding, and featuring POVs from everyone - including Vi and her lady love. Be sure to **sub to my newsletter** to know when the preorder goes live!*)

Want More Villainous Tales?

Join Patreon (MVPs of DP+) for existing & upcoming bonus content, and **follow the evil author everywhere** to stay in-the-know on various spin-offs!

MONSTROUSLY MYTHIC SERIES (ALSO ON AUDIBLE):

The 12 Hunks of Herculeia (Herculeia Duet, Book 1)

Herculeia the Hero (Herculeia Duet, Book 2) (*sign up for the newsletter for the bonus epilogue: Three Heads Are Better Than One*)

Herculeia: Complete Duet + Bonus Content (*includes Calm Down Monster-Fucker, Three Heads Are Better Than One, & the Thanksgiving*

Special: Get Stuffed, plus UNcensored art)

More Monstrously Mythic Tales:

Valhalla is Full of Hunks (Iola's story)

THE YAGA'S RIDERS TRILOGY (ALSO ON AUDIBLE):

Rise of the Witch

A Witch Out of Time

Call of the Ride

The Yaga's Riders: Complete Trilogy + Bonus Content *(The Asa Baby Christmas Special & the Too Peopley Valentine's Day Special)*

More Yaga's Riders Tales:

A Song of Saints and Swans *(Anthia spin-off novella, which includes From the Depths & the Halloween Special: It's Just a Bunch of Va Ju-Ju Voodoo)*

WINGS OF DARKNESS + LIGHT TRILOGY:

Shadows Spark

Shadows Smolder

Shadows Scorch

Wings of Darkness + Light: The Complete Trilogy + Bonus Content *(Oversized Cupids V-Day Special, The Second Coming Easter Special, & the Sexy Little Devil Halloween Specials Pt. 1 & Pt. 2)*

More from the Wings Universe:

Death by Vanilla (Gage origin story novella)

CURRENT/UPCOMING ANTHOLOGIES:

Snow, Lights, & Monster Nights charity anthology *(featuring The Yule Log: A Valhalla is Full of Hunks bonus tale)*

For 2024: Something gay (featuring normies from the Villainous universe!) and something creepy (with original characters) - *stay tuned for more info!*

ABOUT THE AUTHOR

C. Rochelle here! I'm a naughty but sweet, introverted, Aquarius weirdo who believes a sharp sense of humor is the sexiest trait, loves shaking my booty to Prince, and have never met a cheese I didn't like. Oh, and I write spicy paranormal/monster/sci-fi love-is-love romance with epic plots and dark, naughty humor.

Want More?

- **Join my Clubhouse of Smut on Patreon**
- **Subscribe to my newsletter at C-Rochelle.com**
- **Join my Little Sinners Facebook group**
- **Stalk me in all the places on Linktree**

AUTHOR'S NOTE & ACKNOWLEDGMENTS

This was simultaneously the easiest and hardest book for me to write. Easy, because I adore this universe and characters almost as much as you super smut lovers do, but hard, because of the themes of grief.

The character of Mikki is based on an actual person—the mother of one of my oldest friends (with her permission, of course). She was the type of mom who made EVERYONE feel like one of her kids, and for someone who rarely felt like they fit in anywhere, that was a gift. Mikki was a badass and a warrior—successfully kicking cancer to the curb, twice. The third time, however, was too much for her to take on, so now she's watching over all her kids (Amie, Katie, and the rest of us) from wherever badasses go when they pass.

And, back in April, I lost my dad after a twenty-year battle with Parkinson's disease. I've shared a bit about him on social media (and more on Patreon)—and don't want to make this book any longer than it is—but, in short, he was an amazing dude. He's also the person who first introduced me to super-heroes and villains, starting with the Dark Knight (aka Batman... who could be both a hero or a villain on any given day). Looking back, I probably should have dedicated this series to him in the first place, but it feels appropriate to include him in this book in particular. Major Obscurity's advice that, "sometimes, in life, you have to eat shit" was a Daddio classic in my house, and I hope it makes you laugh when life sucks the most.

I'm currently running a fundraiser on Instagram for the Michael J. Fox Foundation—in my dad's memory. If you feel so inclined, please donate. If that fundraiser has ended, any donations to the foundation would be appreciated.

And I'm also typing this out with my longtime writing buddy at my feet—Grim-cat—knowing I have to say goodbye to him in a couple of days. So yeah… it's been a lot.

Despite the layers of grief weighing heavy on my black heart, I am incredibly thankful for all of YOU. Some of you took a chance on an "unknown" author in MM. Others encouraged this (fairly known/feared) PNR/monster Why Choose author to explore MM relationships outside of polyamorous groups. Either way, you've made the Villainous Things series my most successful to date. Thank you.

Thank you to my alpha readers: Author Ariel Dawn, my head cheerleading crew from Patreon—Billie, Katie, Kayla, and Kristina—and my long-suffering comma-checker, Lindsay Hamilton. It's thanks to them you got that bonus rabble group chat.

To ALL my Weird-Ho's+ in my Clubhouse of Smut on Patreon—thank you for continuing to cheer me on through the advanced chapters, N/SFW art, cover designs, and all the Baby Hulk/Lizard King treats, etc. that I share. We definitely have a good time in there.

An extra smutty shout-out to my Va Ju-Ju Voodoo Queens: Adrienne, Brooke, Ciara, Elizabeth, Emily, Fawn, Jamie, Jasmine, Kaitlyn, Kayla, Kaylah, Kelly, Kristina, Kyla, Lauren, Liz, Natasha, Shawn, Shawna, Stephanie, Taylor, and Wraithy. Thank you for supporting (and continuing to support) my author journey in this way!

As always, the creepiest love to my author friends—whether monster fudgers, polyam peddlers, or the ones who make the men kiss. As someone who despises group chats (or peopling, in general…), I always look forward to our controlled (kind of) pockets of chaos. Thank you for being true blues!

And as always, extra butt pats and sloppy kisses to the newest victim of my organizational shit show—Alexandra Sherrod—and my ARC and Street Team! I appreciate every bit o' hype you loud, proud Weird-Ho's can spare for me and my dirty little books.

Love is freakin' love, y'all!

XXX
-C

GLOSSARY

While many people have gone over this book to find typos and other mistakes, we are only human. **If you spot an error, please do NOT report it to Amazon.**

I *want* **to hear from you if there's an issue, so I can fix it.** Send me an email at **crochelle.author@gmail.com** or **use the form** found pinned in my FB group or in my link in bio on TT & IG.

GLOSSARY NOTE: Because our favorite Mafia Queen makes some cameos, I have included this short glossary for Simon's infamous French swearing.

SLANG NOTE: There is always a bit of slang peppered into my writing. When in doubt, use Google, or contact me using the methods above if you truly believe it's a typo.

Capitana *(Spanish):* Captain (feminine).
Casse-toi *(French):* Fuck off.
C'est des/conneries *(French):* This is/bullshit.
Délicieux *(French):* Delicious.

Inventus *(Latin):* Find / discover. Perfect passive participle of invenio and the word used to describe supe soulmates.

Lacertus *(Latin):* Strength, muscles, vigor, force. Upper arm muscle. In this case, it's derived from *lacerta* ("lizard").

Mon chou *(French):* A term of endearment that is used to refer to someone you love (lit. My cabbage, but Simon chooses to interpret it as **choux à la crème** - a sweet little murder baby cream puff)

Supay *(Incan, etc. mythology):* In the Quechua, Aymara, and Inca mythologies, Supay was both the god of death and ruler of the Ukhu Pacha, the Incan underworld, as well as a race of demons.

Très merveilleux *(French):* Wonderful.

Printed in Great Britain
by Amazon